Power of L

☆ ☆

SINCE 1

HEARTS

Girl Got Game

③

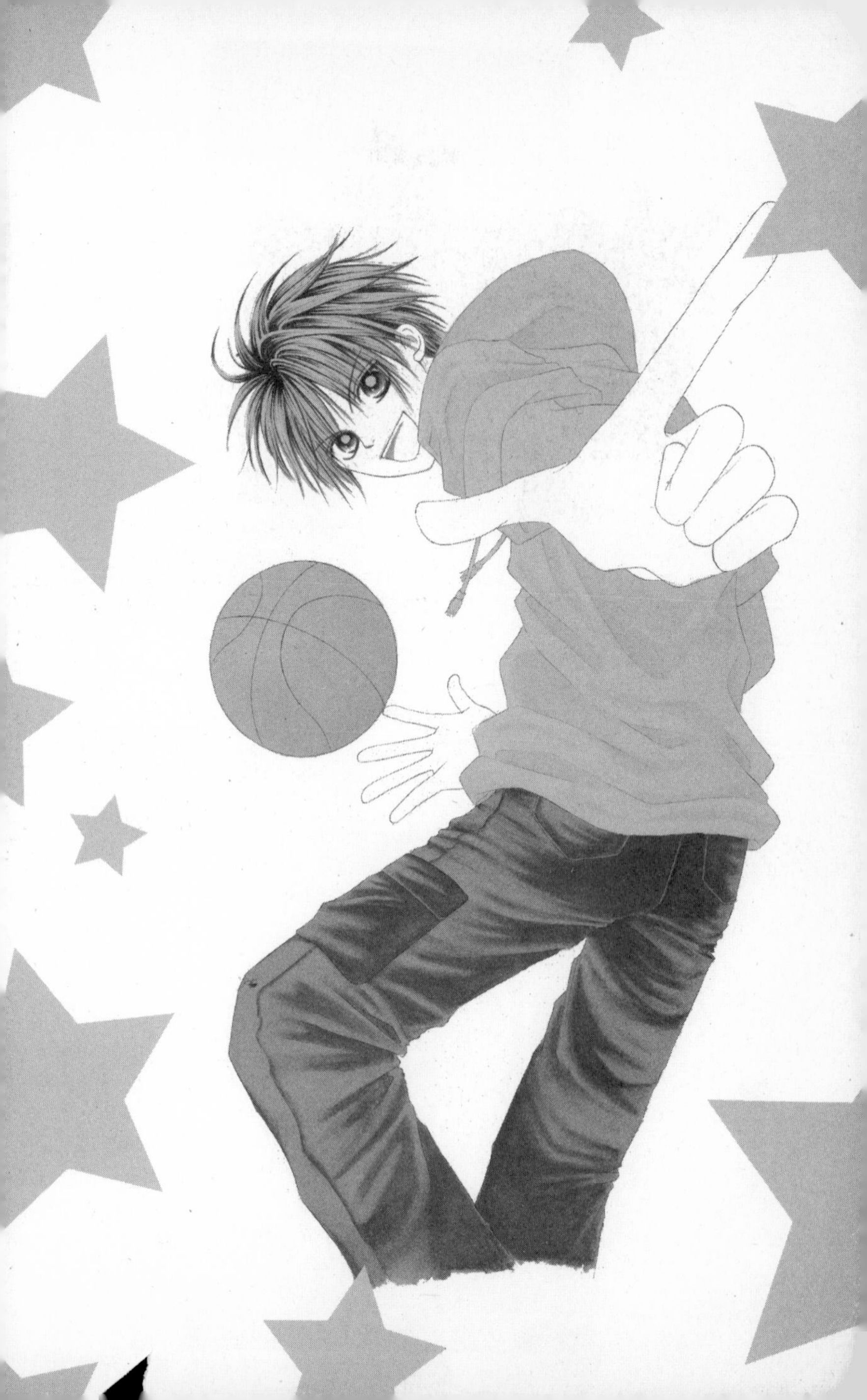

Girl Got Game

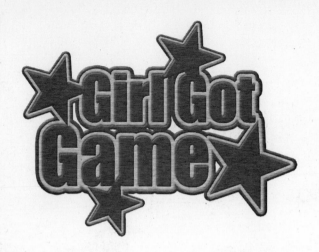

Translator - Aya Matsunaga
English Adaptation - Kelly Sue DeConnick
Copy Editors - Aaron Sparrow, Troy Lewter
Retouch and Lettering - Haruko Furukawa
Cover Artist - Christian Lownds
Graphic Designers - Steven Redd & James Lee

Editor - Rob Tokar
Digital Imaging Manager - Chris Buford
Pre-Press Manager - Antonio DePietro
Production Managers - Jennifer Miller, Mutsumi Miyazaki
Art Director - Matt Alford
Managing Editor - Jill Freshney
VP of Production - Ron Klamert
President & C.O.O. - John Parker
Publisher & C.E.O. - Stuart Levy

E-mail: info@TOKYOPOP.com
Come visit us online at www.TOKYOPOP.com

A  Manga

TOKYOPOP Inc.
5900 Wilshire Blvd. Suite 2000
Los Angeles, CA 90036

Girl Got Game Vol. 3

Girl Got Game volume 3 (originally published as "Power!!")
© 2000 Shizuru Seino. All rights reserved.
First published in Japan in 2000 by Kodansha Ltd., Tokyo.
English publication rights arranged through Kodansha Ltd.

English text copyright ©2004 TOKYOPOP Inc.

ISBN: 1-59182-698-5

First TOKYOPOP printing: May 2004

10 9 8 7 6 5 4 3 2 1

Printed in the USA

by Shizuru Seino
Volume 3

Los Angeles • Tokyo • London

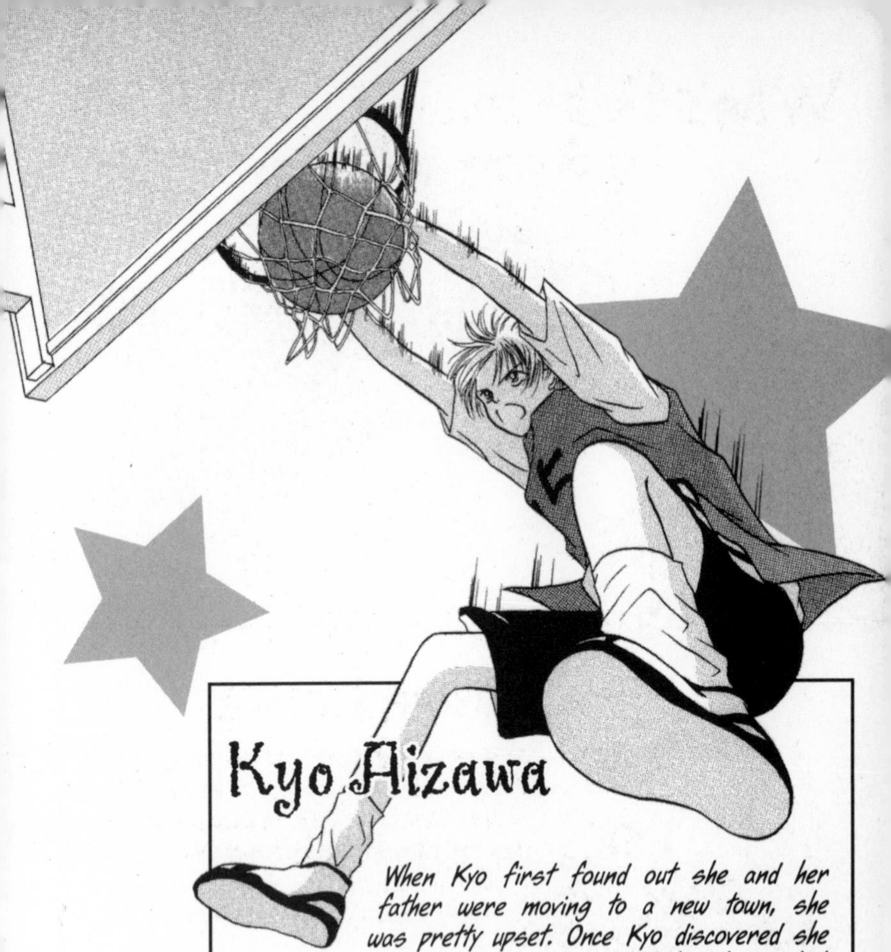

Kyo Aizawa

When Kyo first found out she and her father were moving to a new town, she was pretty upset. Once Kyo discovered she would be attending Seisyu High School--which is renowned for its ultra-cute girls' uniforms--her frown turned upside-down. However, when the package containing her uniform arrived, she was horrified to discover that her father enrolled her as a boy so she could play on Seisyu's top-ranked boys' basketball team and fulfill his unrealized dream of playing for the National Basketball Association.

As a result, Kyo had to cut her hair, dress as a boy, and move into the boys' dormitory. To make matters worse, she's forced to room with the boy whom she learned to loathe at try-outs: Chiharu Eniwa. After several ups and downs, Kyo found that she and Chiharu may actually be able to live in peace together...and that she may be falling for Chiharu in a big way.

Who's Who in... ★Girl Got Game

Chiharu Eniwa

Kyo's teammate on the court and roommate in the dorms, Chiharu has a well-deserved reputation as a hard-nosed tough guy. Chiharu was at his most abrasive during his first meeting with Kyo, but his taunts and jibes drove Kyo to really show her best moves at tryouts.

Though a private person, Chiharu has opened up to Kyo about some of the problems that have plagued him. Kyo has made several attempts to aid Chiharu who has shown his appreciation by taking care of Kyo in return.

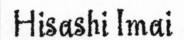

Hisashi Imai

The ever-friendly captain of the Seisyu High School boys' basketball team, Imai lives in room 310.

Coach

The coach of the Seisyu High School boys' basketball team comes complete with the wild mood swings and irritability that are essential to anyone working with teen athletes.

Mr. Aizawa

Kyo's father was once a great basketball player who aspired to play for the NBA. Unfortunately, a torn achilles tendon ended his career before it even started. Despite his disappointment, he passed his love of the game--and his moves--to Kyo.

HI, I'M AYAHA. I'M THE HOUSE MOM!

Ayaha

"House Mom" of the Seisyu High School boys' dormitory, Ayaha was a great basketball player when she was a student. Unfortunately, a knee injury ended her playing career prematurely.

Akari Tojo

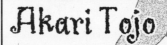

Manager of the Seisyu High School boys' basketball team.

Shinji Hamaya

A fellow freshman on the Seisyu High School boys' basketball team.

Girl Got Game

The Story So Far

Some people will do anything to realize their dreams...even if it means disguising a girl as a boy so she can play on a famous boys' basketball team. If you don't believe it, just imagine how Kyo Aizawa feels--her dad's the one who cooked up this crazy scheme! Kyo's father was once a great basketball player who aspired to play for the NBA. Unfortunately, an injury ended his career before it even started.

Despite his disappointment, he passed his love of the game--and his moves--to his daughter.

Kyo wants to *date* a boy, not *become* one, and she was not happy about her father's kooky plan...until she met Chiharu Eniwa, the boy who is her teammate on the court...and her roommate in the dorms!

As luck would have it, Kyo and Chiharu got on each other's nerves right from the start, but Kyo's attempts to get past Chiharu's gruff, sullen exterior eventually made the two of them friends.

Recently, on a day in which there was no Phys. Ed or practice scheduled, Kyo didn't bother to strap her breasts down as she normally would. Unfortunately, Chiharu just happened to trip over something and fall hands-first onto Kyo's chest! Kyo made several frantic attempts to seem more masculine--including trying to out-perv the other boys in the dorm--while Chiharu tried to figure out what it was that he felt...and why he kept blushing around Kyo.

In order to get some perspective...and some peace...Chiharu took Kyo off campus for some one-on-one practice outdoors. In the process, Chiharu's thoughtful kindness also swept Kyo off her feet...and she wondered if she might be falling for him in a big way.

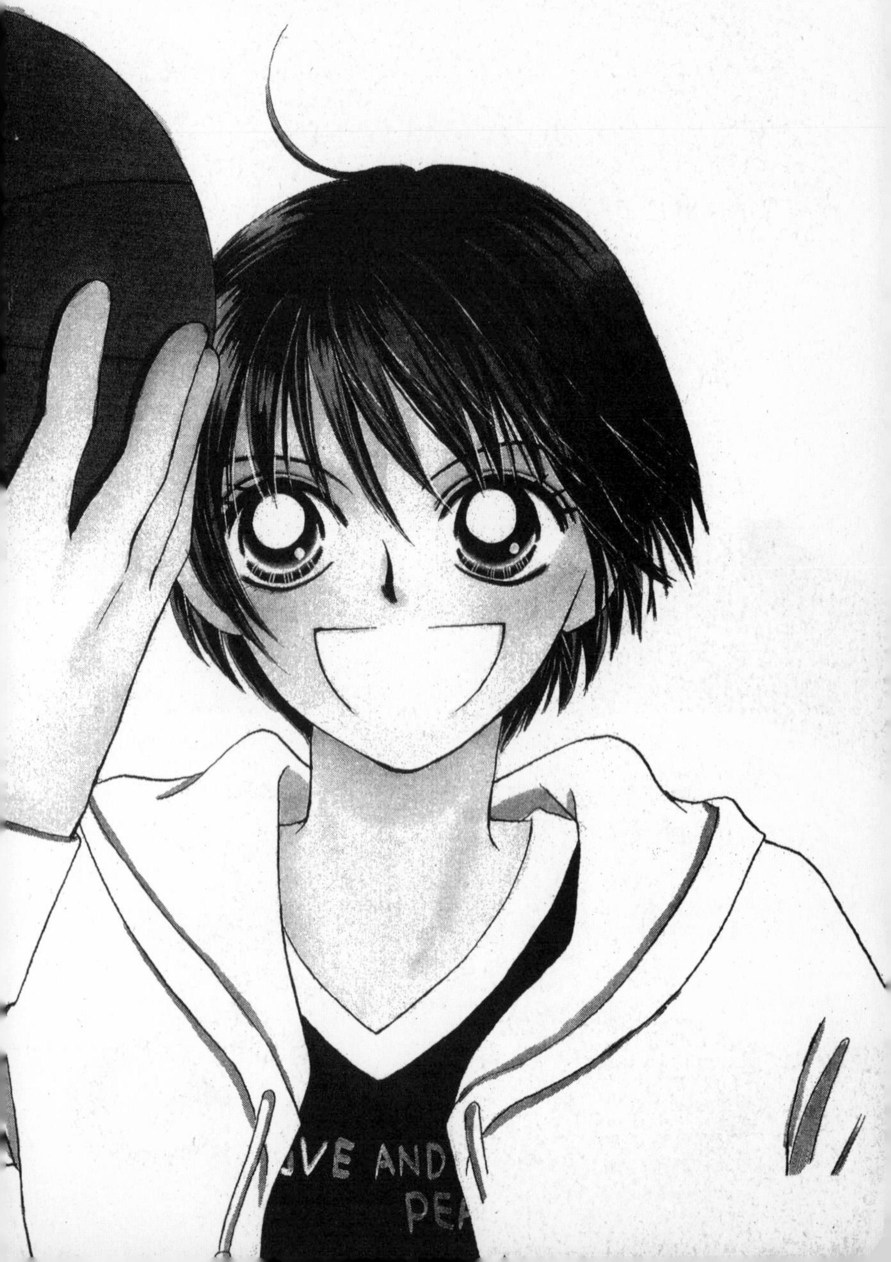

UVE AND
PEA

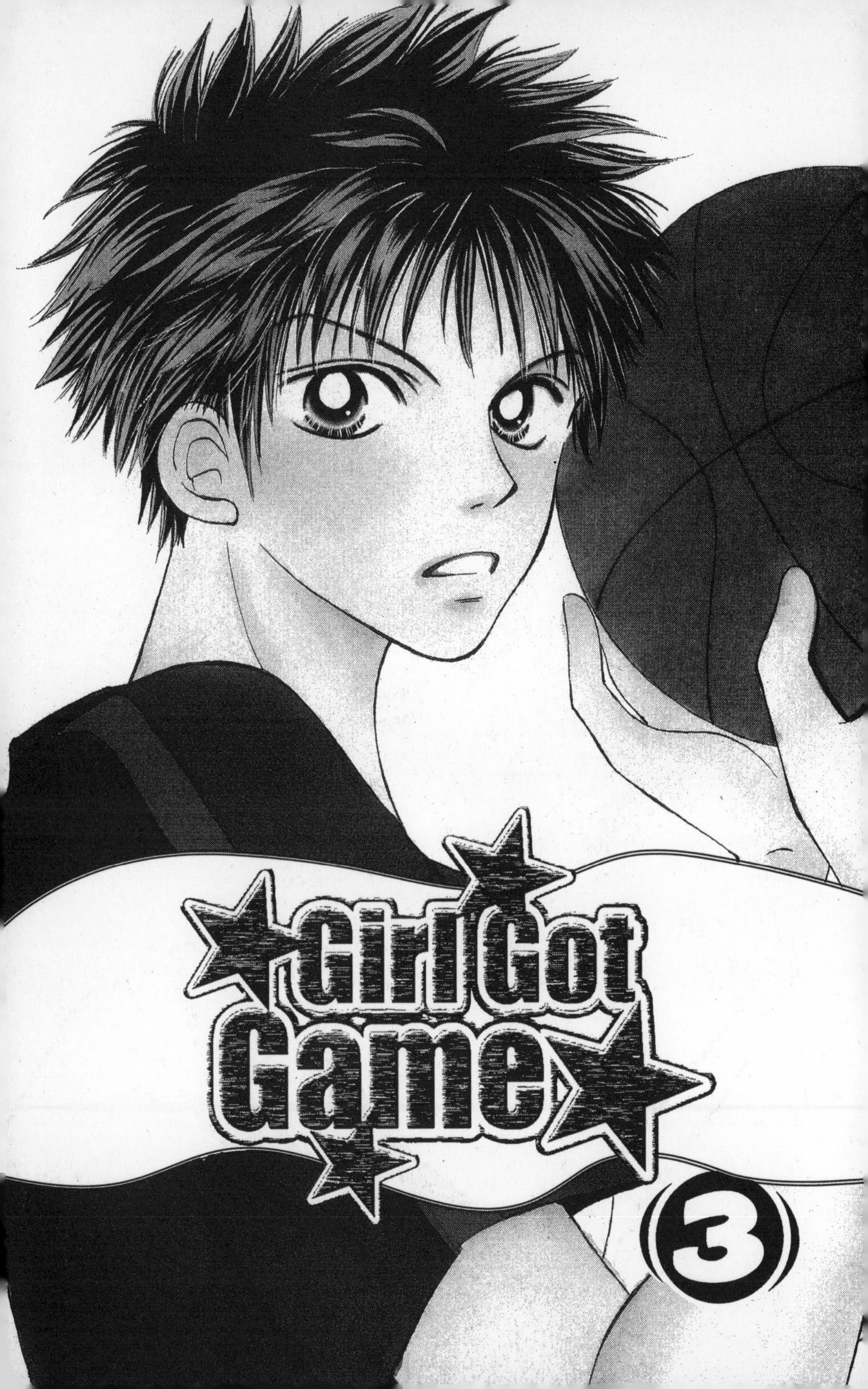
Girl Got Game
3

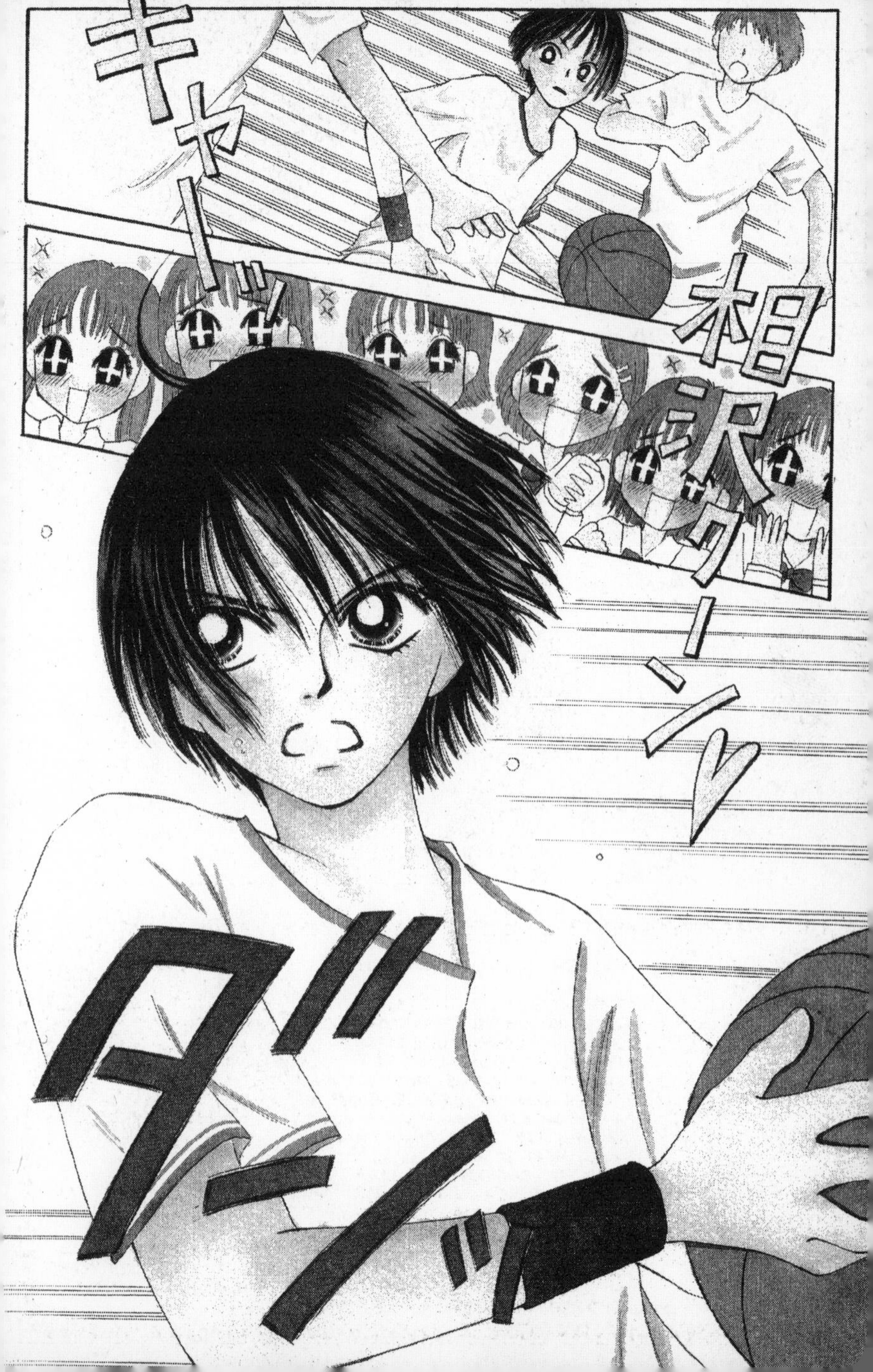
キャーーッ!
相沢クーーン♥
ダン

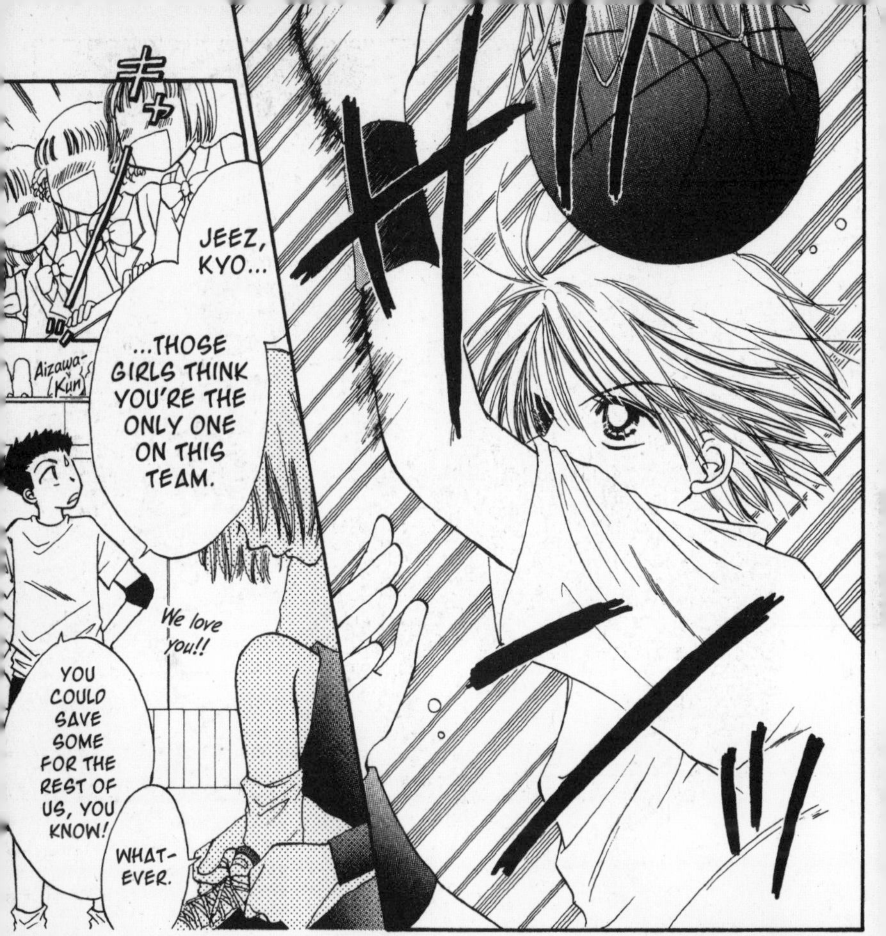
JEEZ, KYO...
...THOSE GIRLS THINK YOU'RE THE ONLY ONE ON THIS TEAM.
Aizawa-Kun
We love you!!
YOU COULD SAVE SOME FOR THE REST OF US, YOU KNOW!
WHAT-EVER.

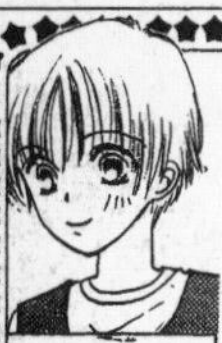

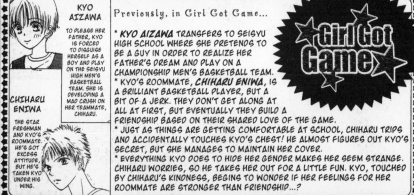

KYO AIZAWA

TO PLEASE HER FATHER, KYO IS FORCED TO DISGUISE HERSELF AS A BOY AND PLAY ON THE SEISYU HIGH MEN'S BASKETBALL TEAM. SHE IS DEVELOPING A MAD CRUSH ON HER TEAMMATE, CHIHARU.

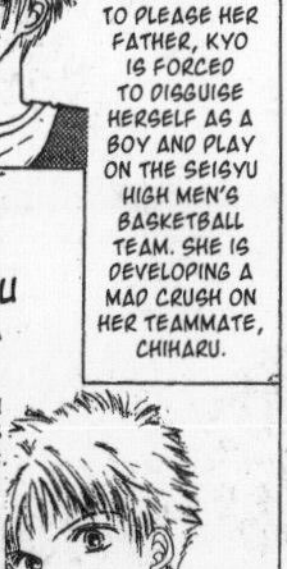

CHIHARU ENIWA

THE STAR FRESHMAN AND KYO'S ROOMMATE. HE'S GOT EXCESS ATTITUDE, BUT HE'S TAKEN KYO UNDER HIS WING.

Previously, in Girl Got Game...

Girl Got Game

* ***KYO AIZAWA*** TRANSFERS TO SEISYU HIGH SCHOOL WHERE SHE PRETENDS TO BE A GUY IN ORDER TO REALIZE HER FATHER'S DREAM AND PLAY ON A CHAMPIONSHIP MEN'S BASKETBALL TEAM.
* KYO'S ROOMMATE, ***CHIHARU ENIWA***, IS A BRILLIANT BASKETBALL PLAYER, BUT A BIT OF A JERK. THEY DON'T GET ALONG AT ALL AT FIRST, BUT EVENTUALLY THEY BUILD A FRIENDSHIP BASED ON THEIR SHARED LOVE OF THE GAME.
* JUST AS THINGS ARE GETTING COMFORTABLE AT SCHOOL, CHIHARU TRIPS AND ACCIDENTALLY TOUCHES KYO'S CHEST! HE ALMOST FIGURES OUT KYO'S SECRET, BUT SHE MANAGES TO MAINTAIN HER COVER.
* EVERYTHING KYO DOES TO HIDE HER GENDER MAKES HER SEEM STRANGE. CHIHARU WORRIES, SO HE TAKES HER OUT FOR A LITTLE FUN. KYO, TOUCHED BY CHIHARU'S KINDNESS, BEGINS TO WONDER IF HER FEELINGS FOR HER ROOMMATE ARE STRONGER THAN FRIENDSHIP...?

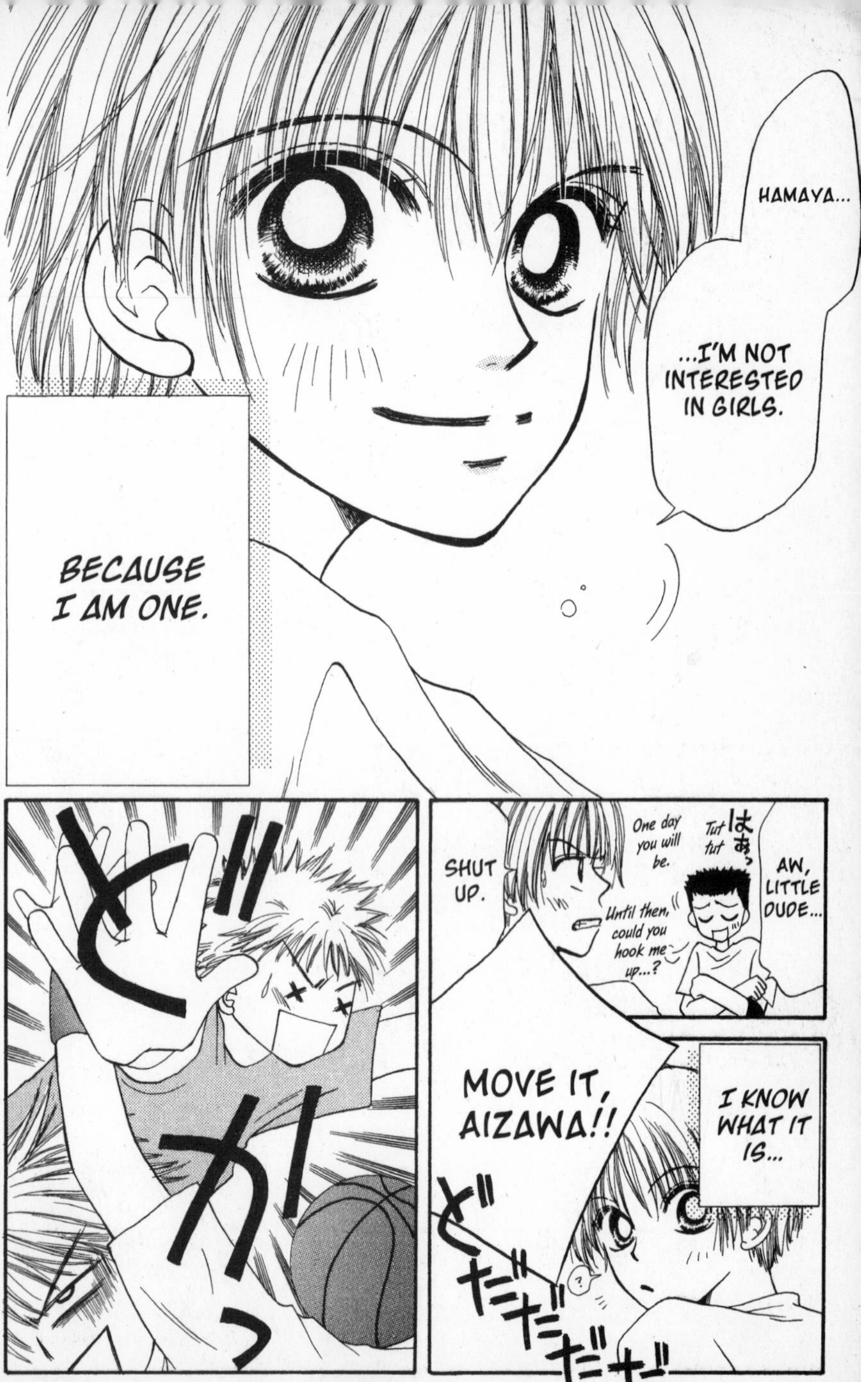
HAMAYA...
...I'M NOT INTERESTED IN GIRLS.
BECAUSE I AM ONE.
AW, LITTLE DUDE...
はぁっ
Tut tut
One day you will be.
Until then, could you hook me up...?
SHUT UP.
I KNOW WHAT IT IS...
MOVE IT, AIZAWA!!
どだだだだ
どかっ

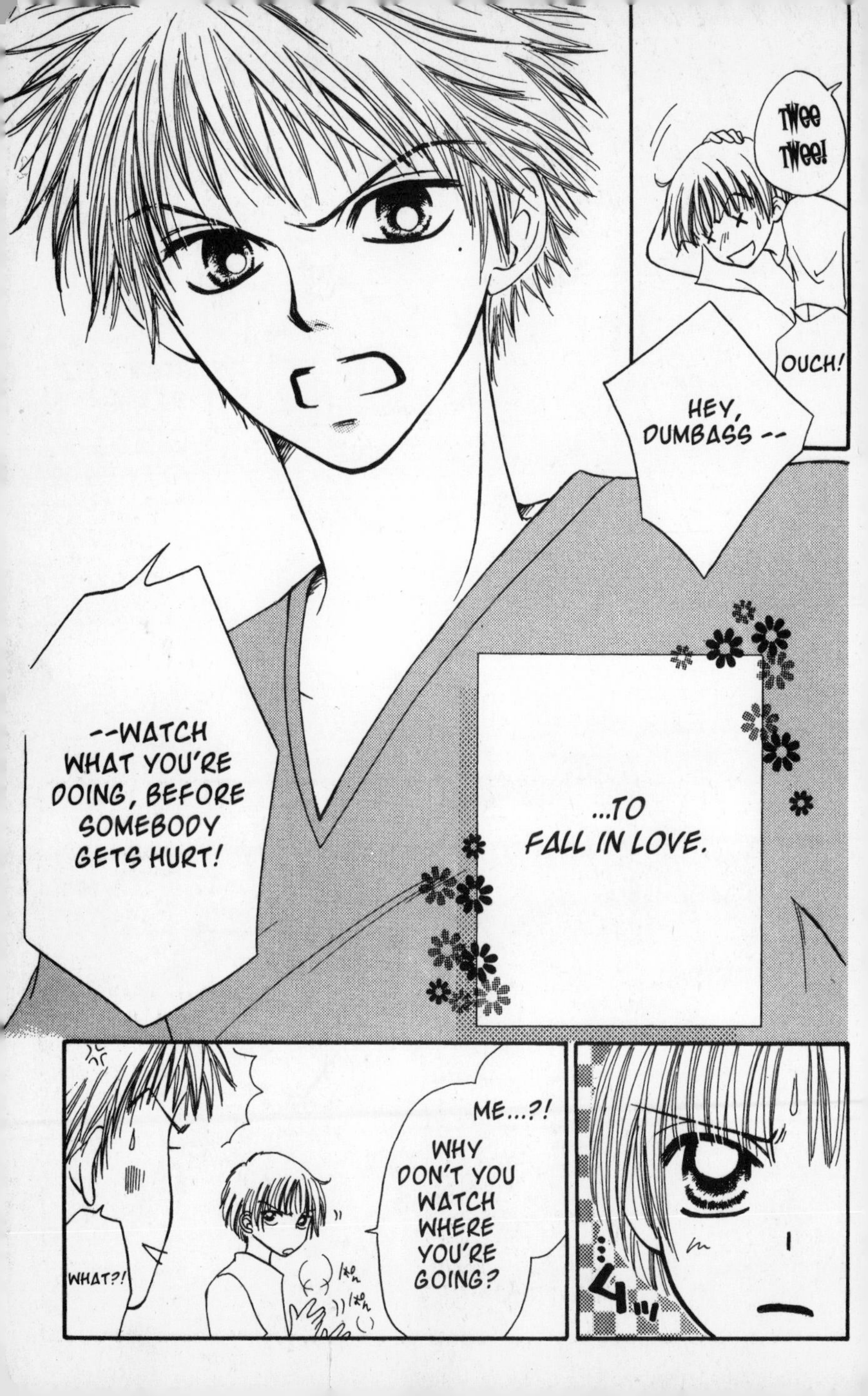
TWEE TWEE!
OUCH!
HEY, DUMBASS --
...TO FALL IN LOVE.
--WATCH WHAT YOU'RE DOING, BEFORE SOMEBODY GETS HURT!
ME...?!
WHY DON'T YOU WATCH WHERE YOU'RE GOING?
WHAT?!

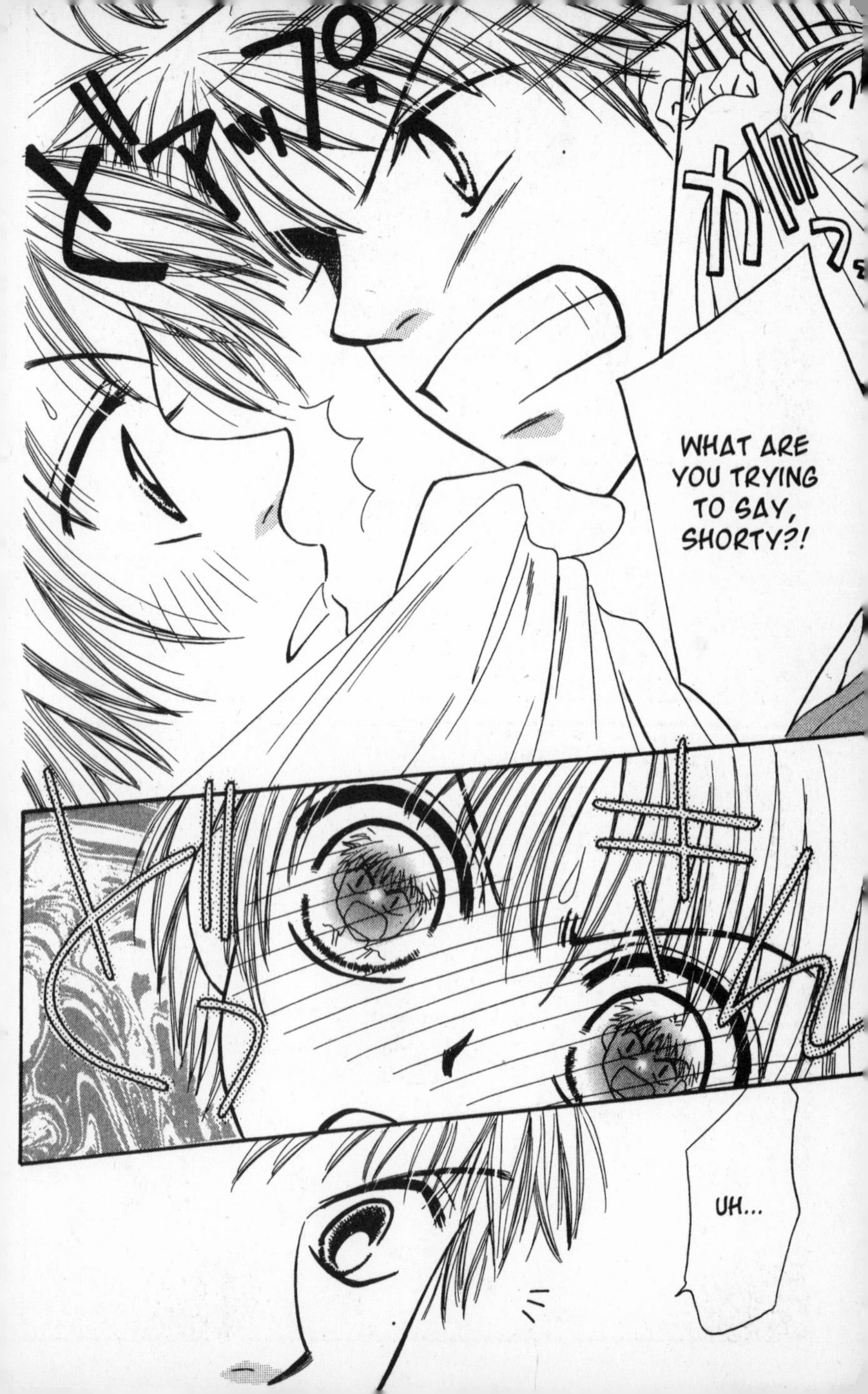
WHAT ARE YOU TRYING TO SAY, SHORTY?!
UH...

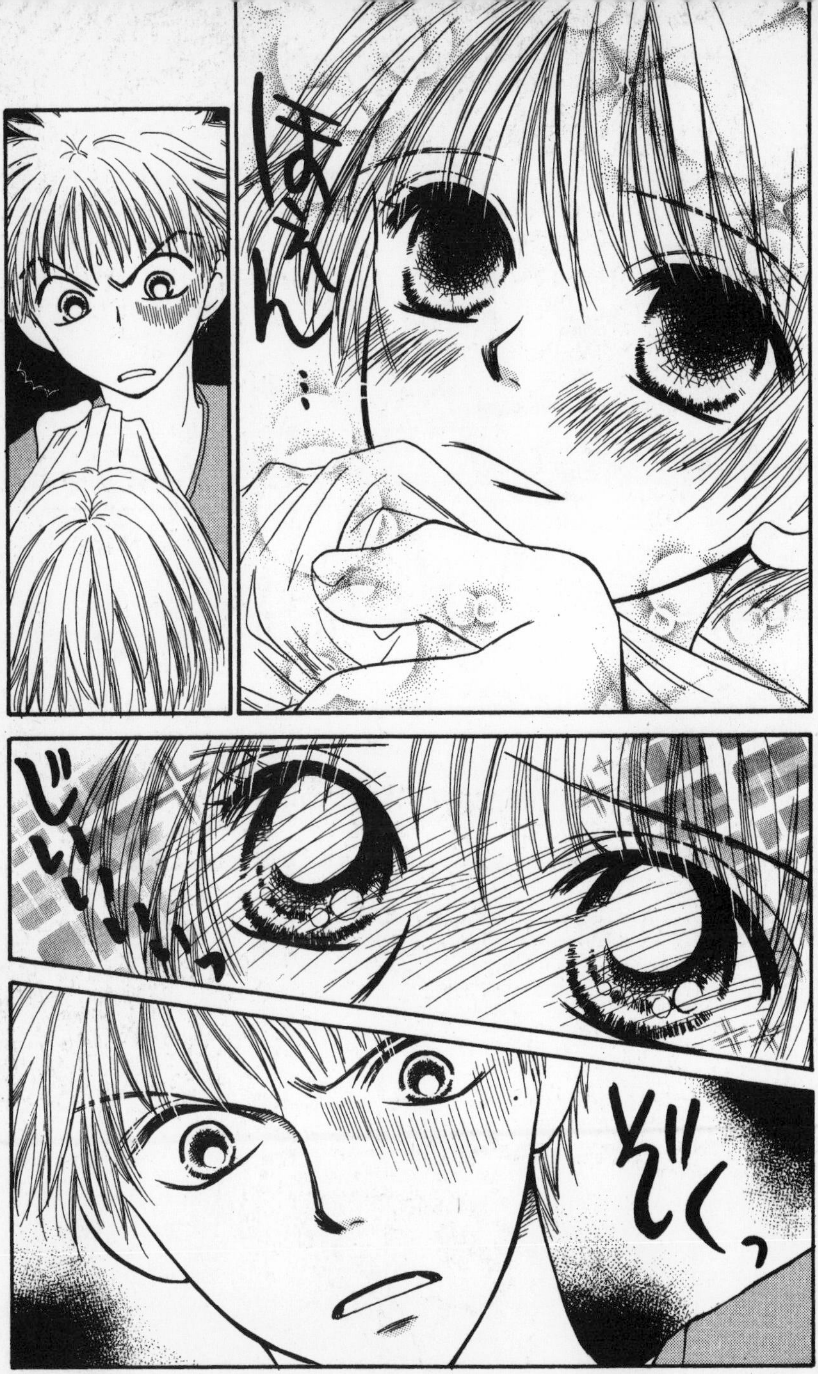
ほえん…
じいい……っ
ぞくっ

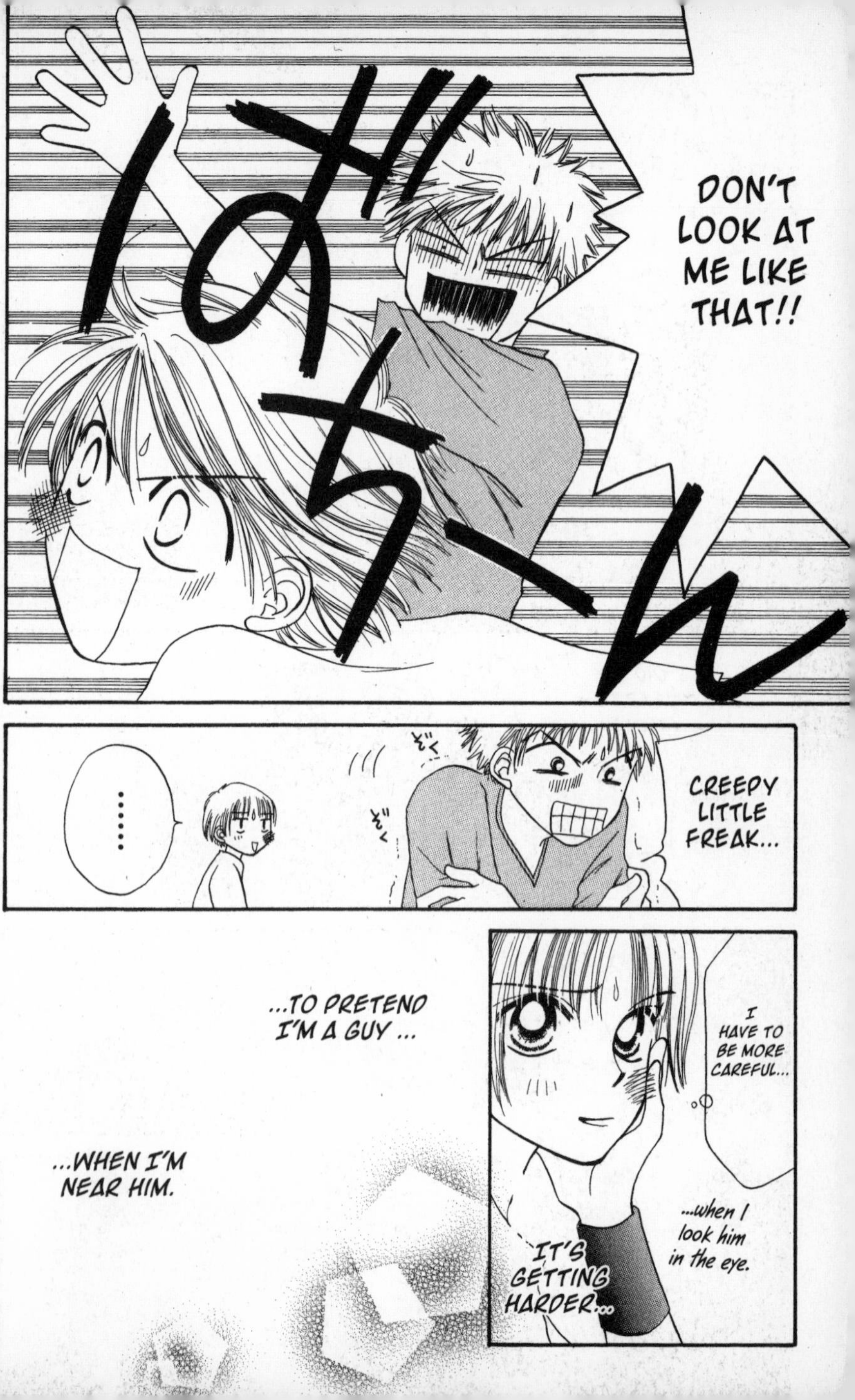
ばちーん
DON'T LOOK AT ME LIKE THAT!!
CREEPY LITTLE FREAK...
ぞく
ぞく
......
I HAVE TO BE MORE CAREFUL...
...when I look him in the eye.
IT'S GETTING HARDER...
...TO PRETEND I'M A GUY ...
...WHEN I'M NEAR HIM.

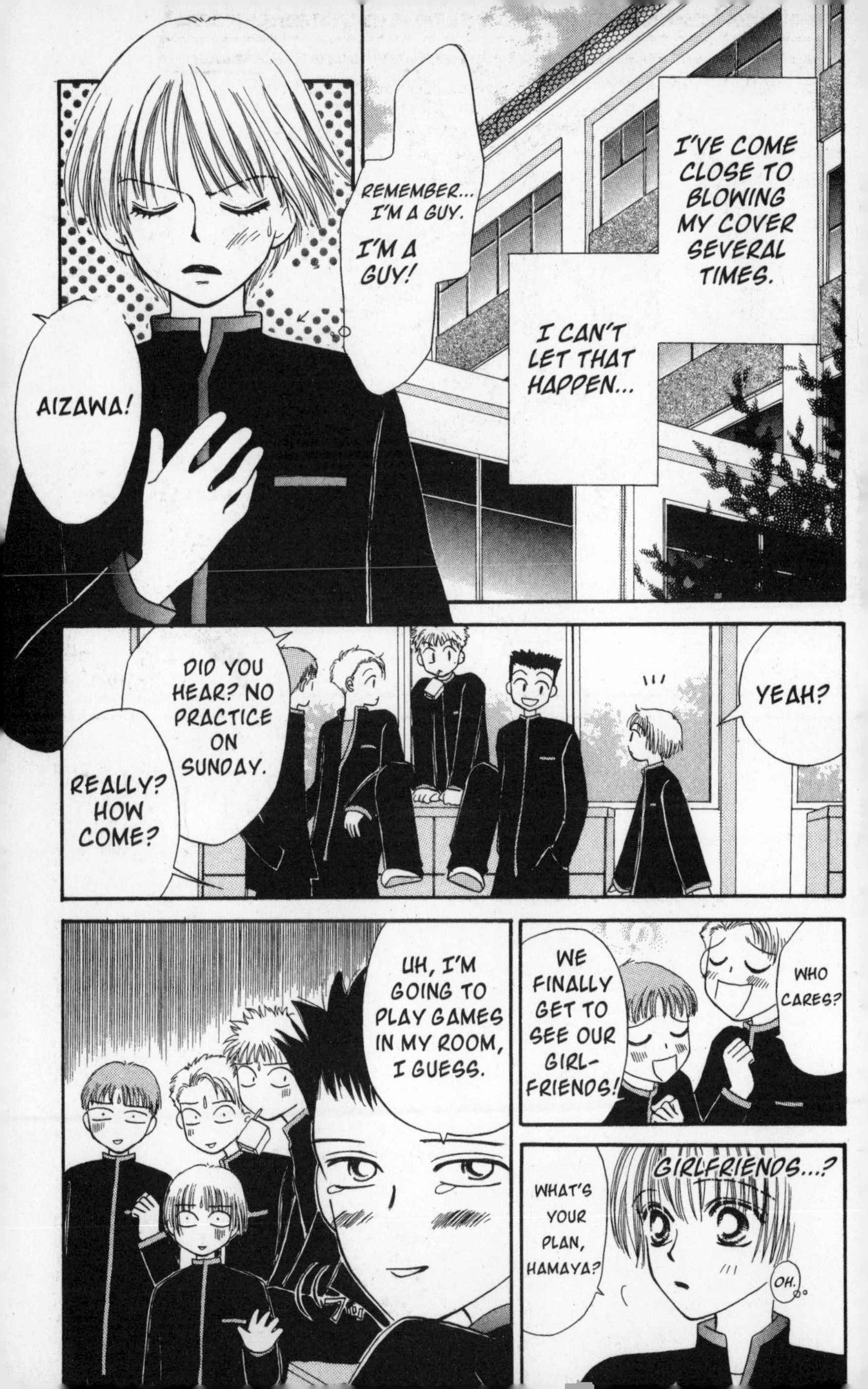
I'VE COME CLOSE TO BLOWING MY COVER SEVERAL TIMES.
I CAN'T LET THAT HAPPEN...
REMEMBER... I'M A GUY.
I'M A GUY!
AIZAWA!
YEAH?
DID YOU HEAR? NO PRACTICE ON SUNDAY.
REALLY? HOW COME?
WHO CARES?
WE FINALLY GET TO SEE OUR GIRL-FRIENDS!
GIRLFRIENDS...?
OH.
WHAT'S YOUR PLAN, HAMAYA?
UH, I'M GOING TO PLAY GAMES IN MY ROOM, I GUESS.

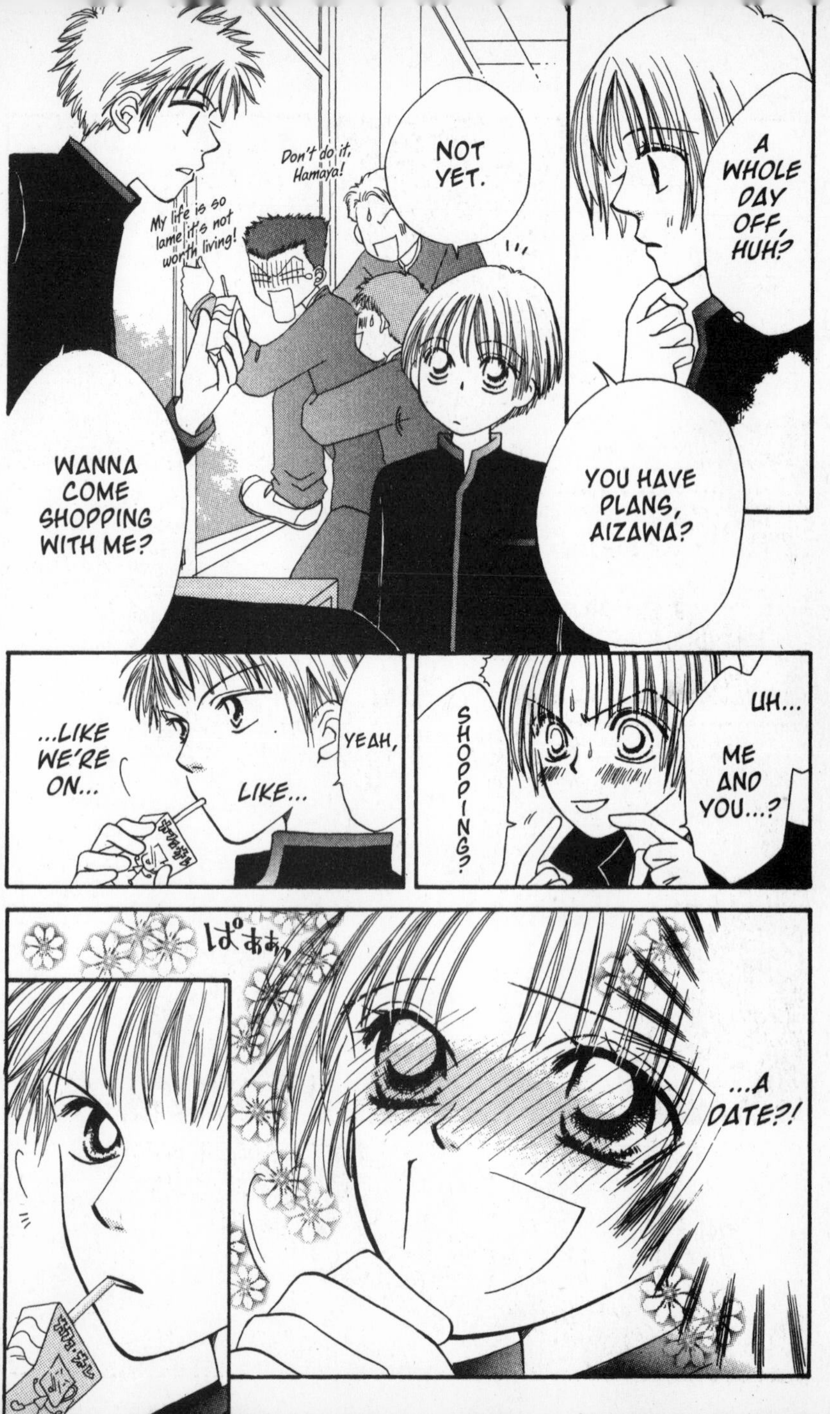
A WHOLE DAY OFF, HUH?
YOU HAVE PLANS, AIZAWA?
NOT YET.
Don't do it, Hamaya!
My life is so lame it's not worth living!
WANNA COME SHOPPING WITH ME?
UH...
ME AND YOU...?
SHOPPING?
YEAH,
LIKE...
...LIKE WE'RE ON...
ぱあぁっ
...A DATE?!

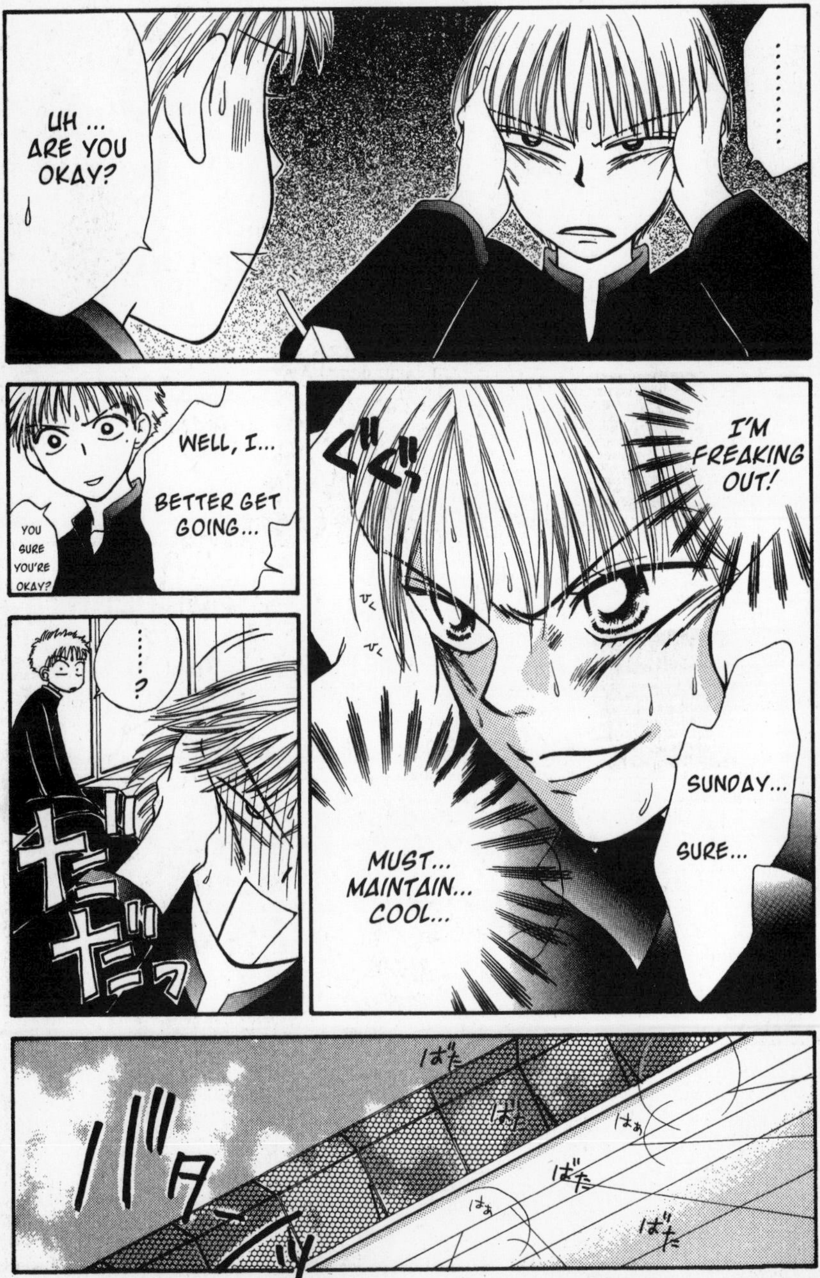

......
UH ... ARE YOU OKAY?
ぐぐっ
I'M FREAKING OUT!
びく
びく
SUNDAY...
SURE...
MUST... MAINTAIN... COOL...
WELL, I...
BETTER GET GOING...
YOU SURE YOU'RE OKAY?
......?
ばた
ばた
はぁ
ばた
はぁ
ばた
バターンッ

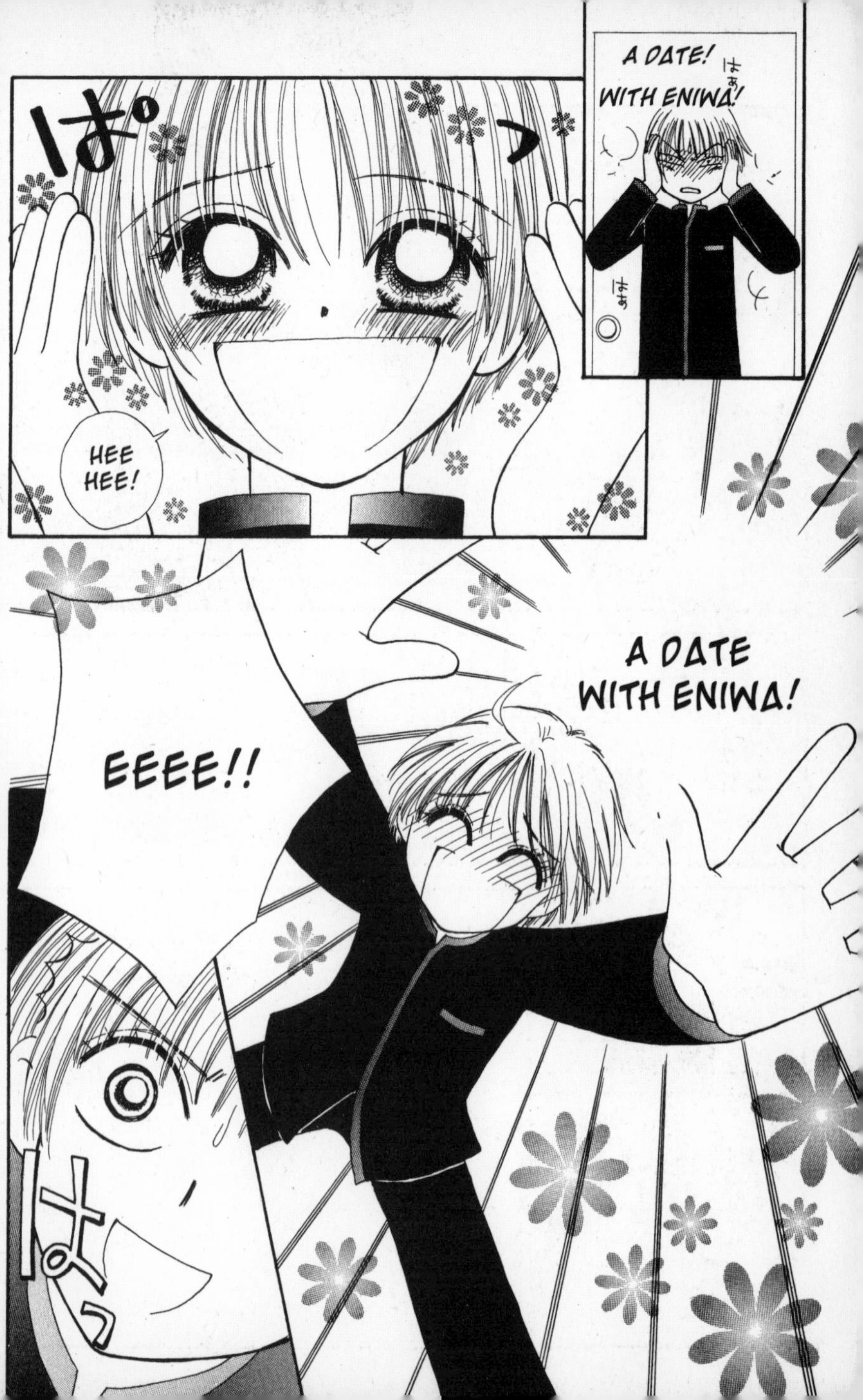
A DATE!
WITH ENIWA!
はあ
はあ
ぱっ
HEE HEE!
A DATE WITH ENIWA!
EEEE!!
はっ

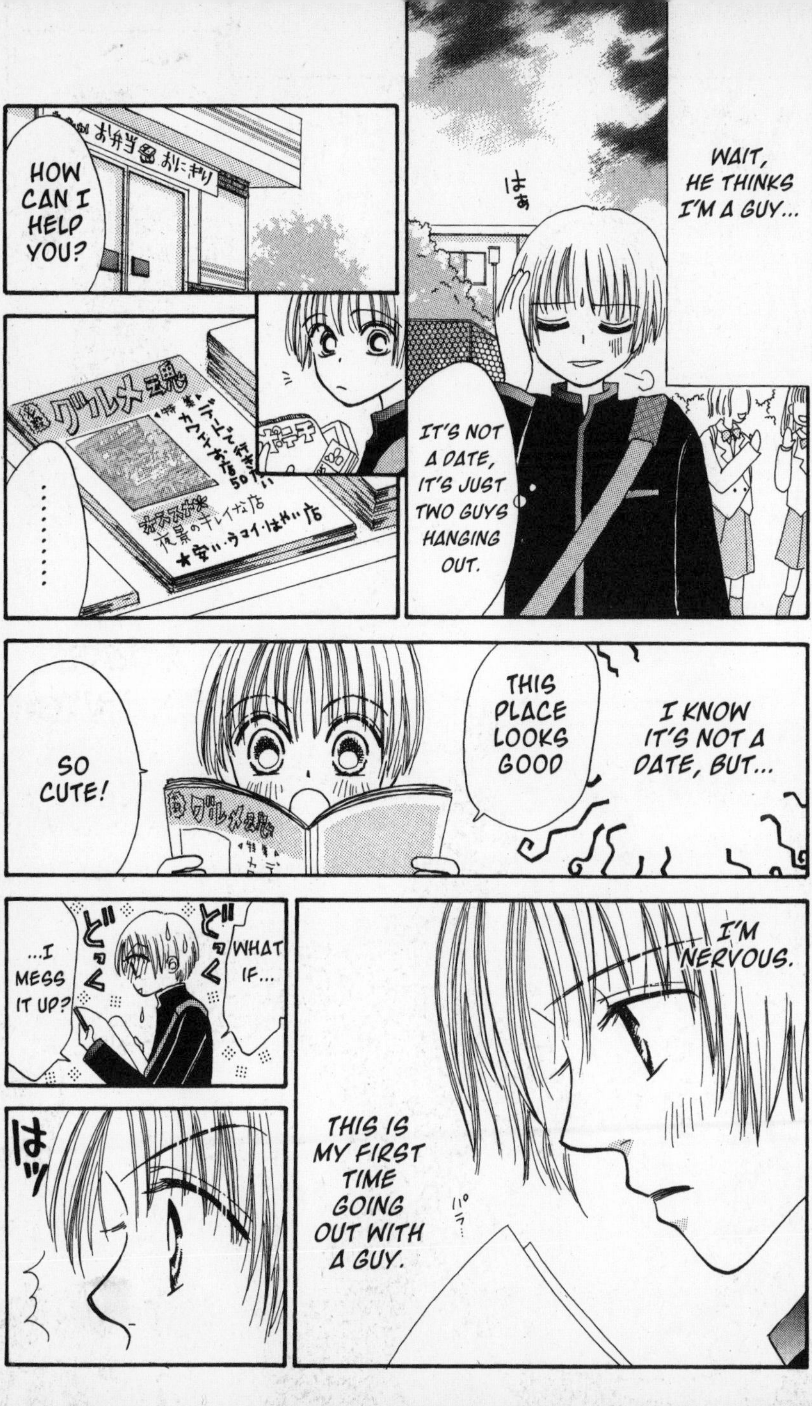
WAIT, HE THINKS I'M A GUY...
はぁ
IT'S NOT A DATE, IT'S JUST TWO GUYS HANGING OUT.
お弁当 おにぎり
HOW CAN I HELP YOU?
ポテチ
グルメ魂
特集 デートで行きたいカワイイお店50
オススメ 夜景のキレイな店
安い・ウマイ・はやい店
......
I KNOW IT'S NOT A DATE, BUT...
THIS PLACE LOOKS GOOD
SO CUTE!
I'M NERVOUS.
THIS IS MY FIRST TIME GOING OUT WITH A GUY.
パラ...
WHAT IF...
どくっ
どくっ
...I MESS IT UP?
はッ

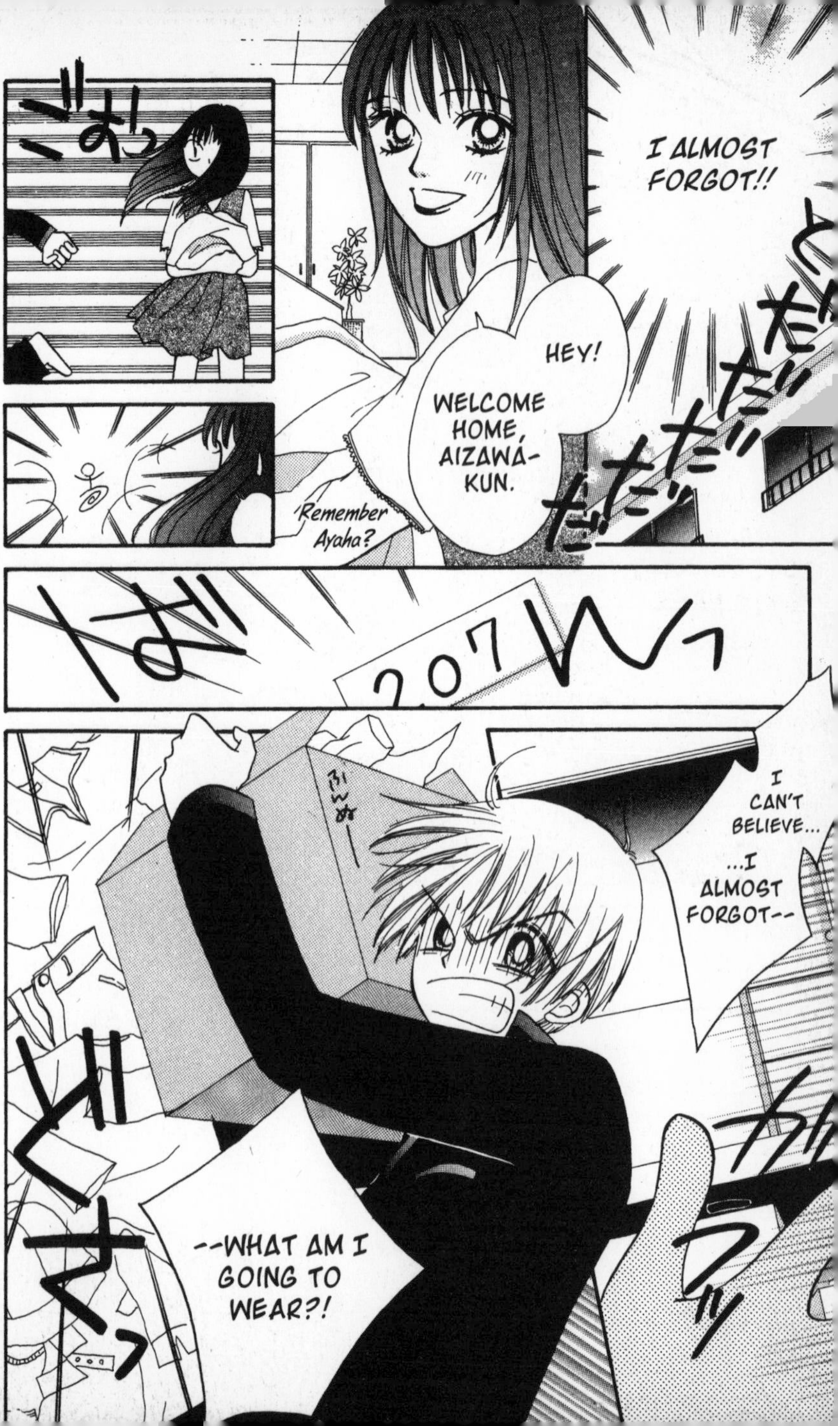
I ALMOST FORGOT!!
HEY!
WELCOME HOME, AIZAWA-KUN.
Remember Ayaha?
207
I CAN'T BELIEVE...
...I ALMOST FORGOT--
--WHAT AM I GOING TO WEAR?!

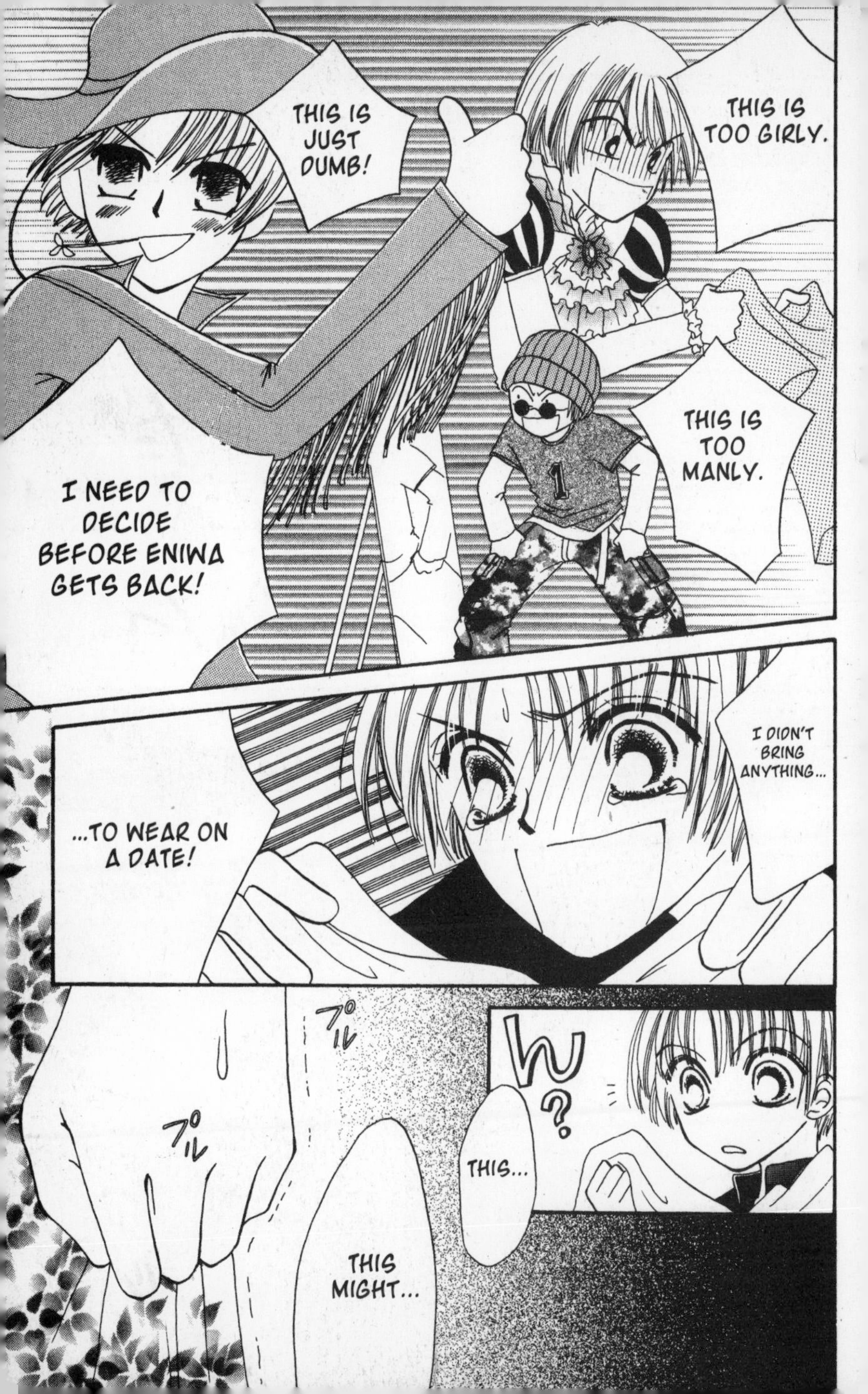
THIS IS TOO GIRLY.
THIS IS TOO MANLY.
THIS IS JUST DUMB!
I NEED TO DECIDE BEFORE ENIWA GETS BACK!
I DIDN'T BRING ANYTHING...
...TO WEAR ON A DATE!
W?
THIS...
プル
プル
THIS MIGHT...

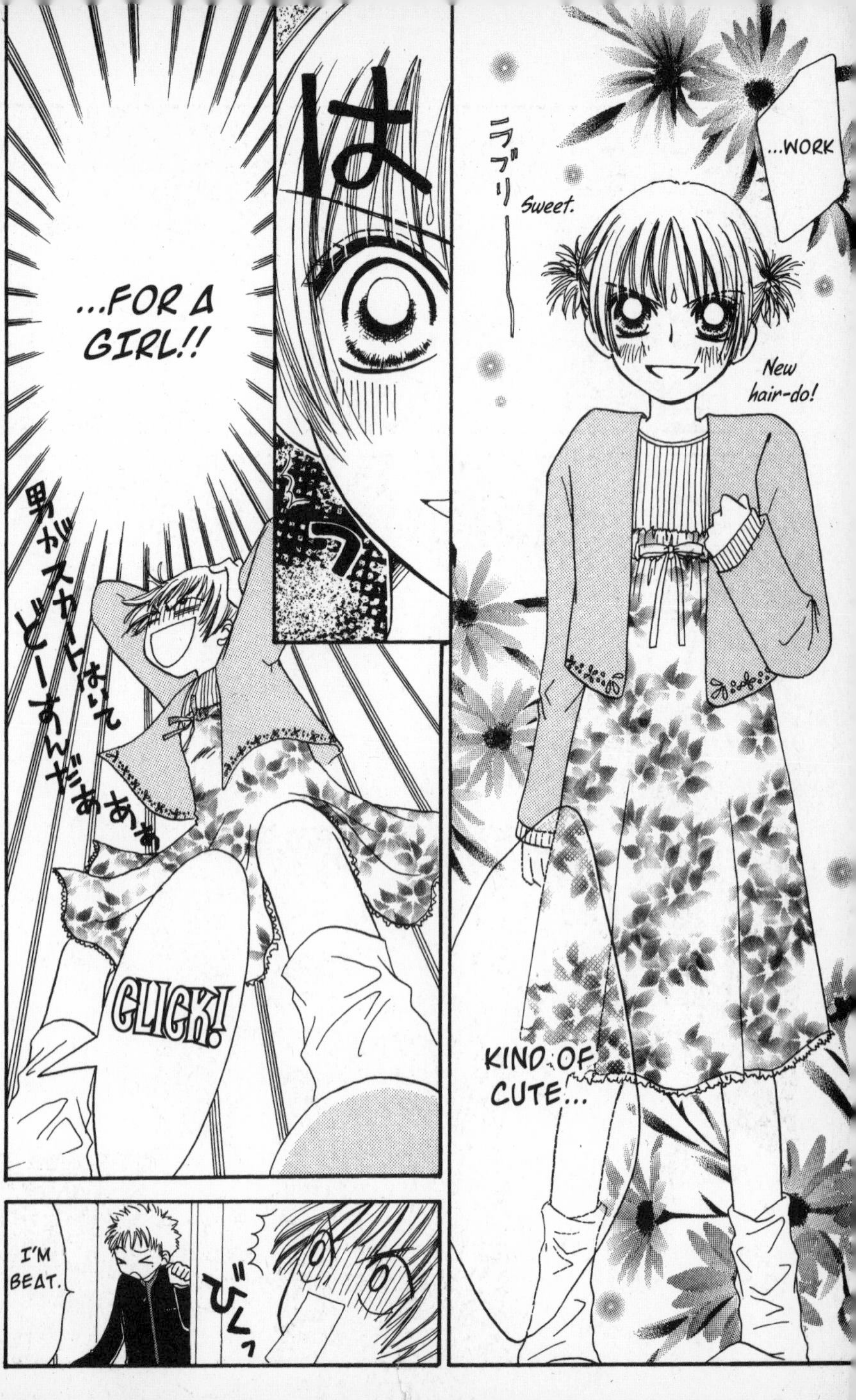
...WORK
ラブリー
Sweet.
New hair-do!
KIND OF CUTE...
は
...FOR A GIRL!!
男がスカートはいてどーすんだぁぁぁ
CLICK!
びくっ
I'M BEAT.

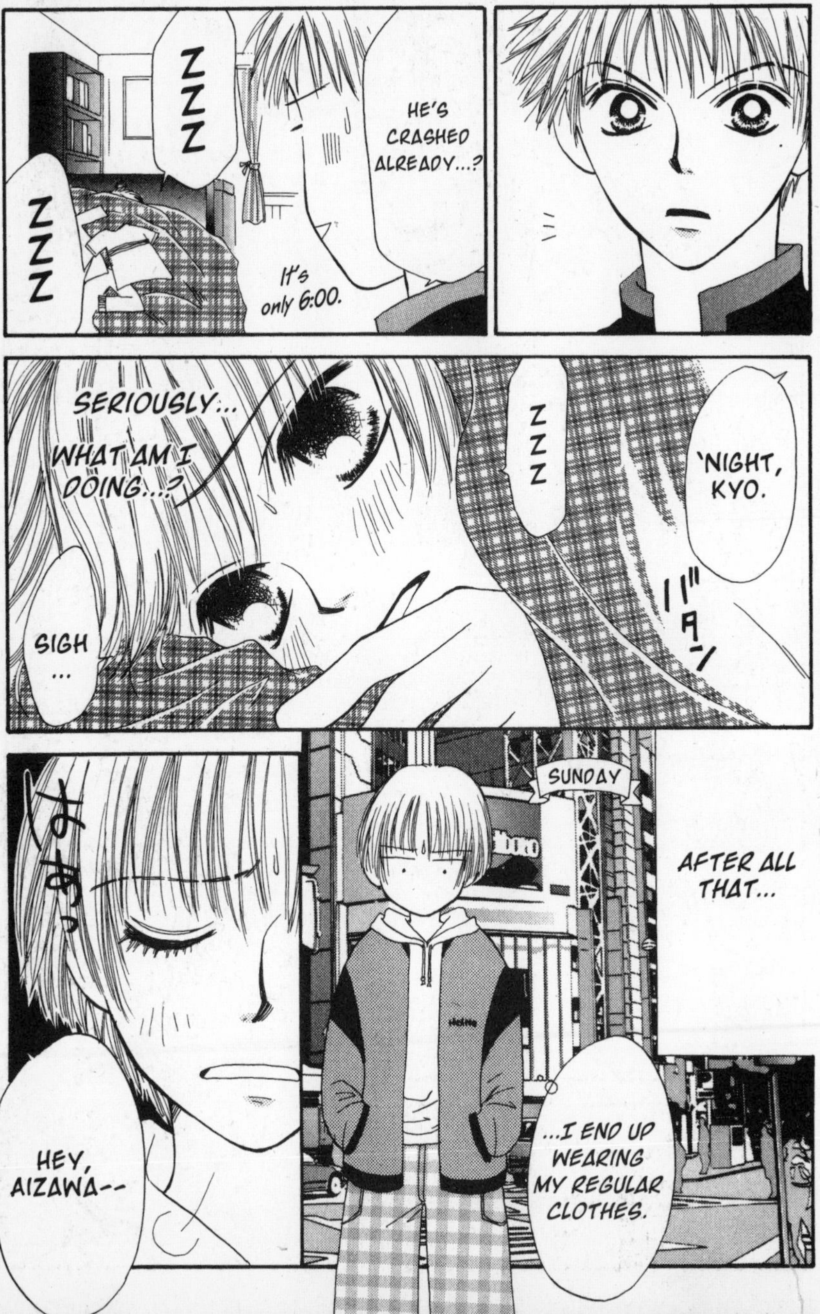
HE'S CRASHED ALREADY...?
ZZZ
ZZZ
It's only 6:00.
'NIGHT, KYO.
ZZZ
バタン
SERIOUSLY...
WHAT AM I DOING...?
SIGH...
SUNDAY
AFTER ALL THAT...
...I END UP WEARING MY REGULAR CLOTHES.
はあっ
HEY, AIZAWA--

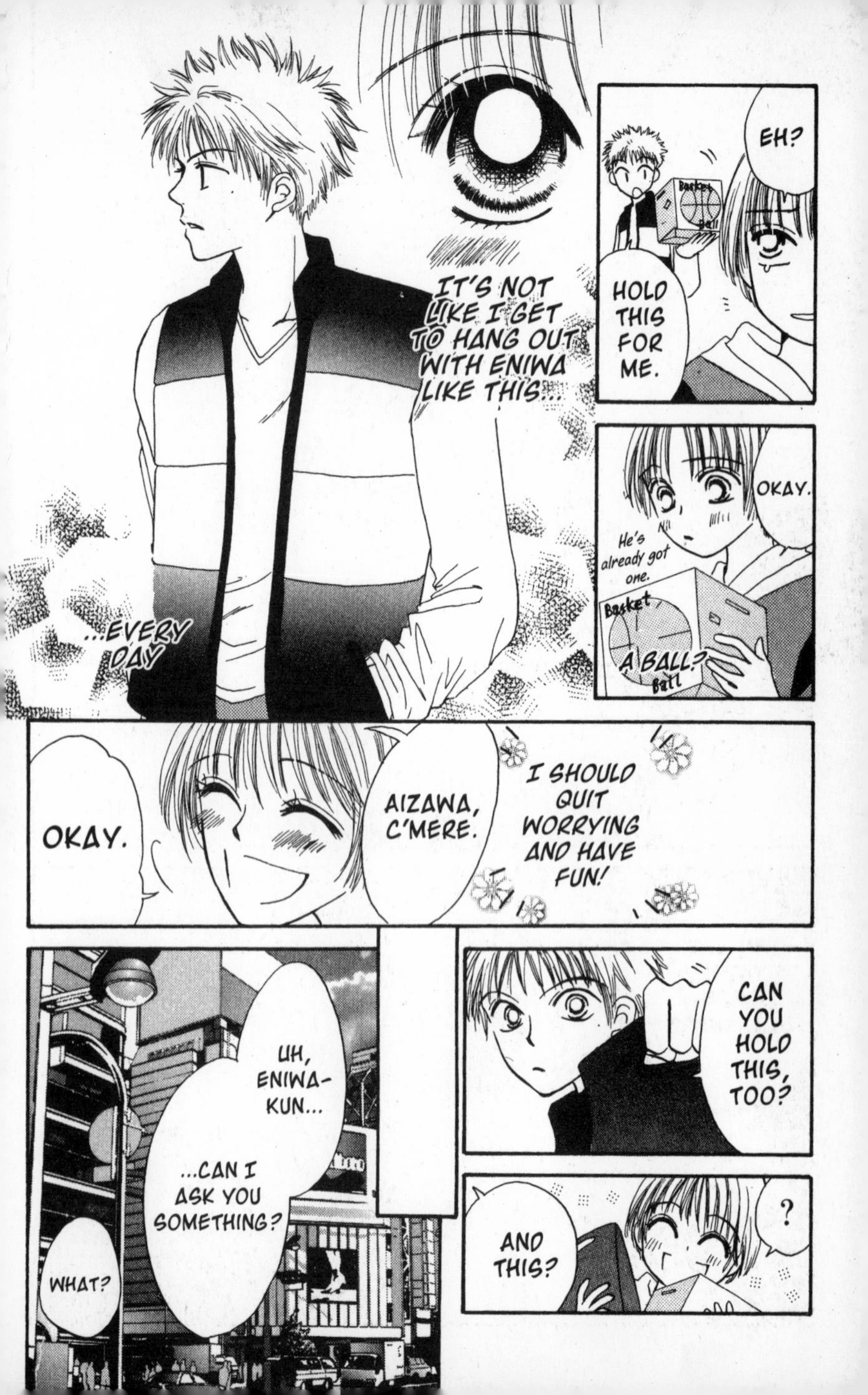
EH?
HOLD THIS FOR ME.
OKAY.
He's already got one.
Basket
A BALL?
Ball
IT'S NOT LIKE I GET TO HANG OUT WITH ENIWA LIKE THIS...
...EVERY DAY
I SHOULD QUIT WORRYING AND HAVE FUN!
AIZAWA, C'MERE.
OKAY.
CAN YOU HOLD THIS, TOO?
?
AND THIS?
UH, ENIWA-KUN...
...CAN I ASK YOU SOMETHING?
WHAT?

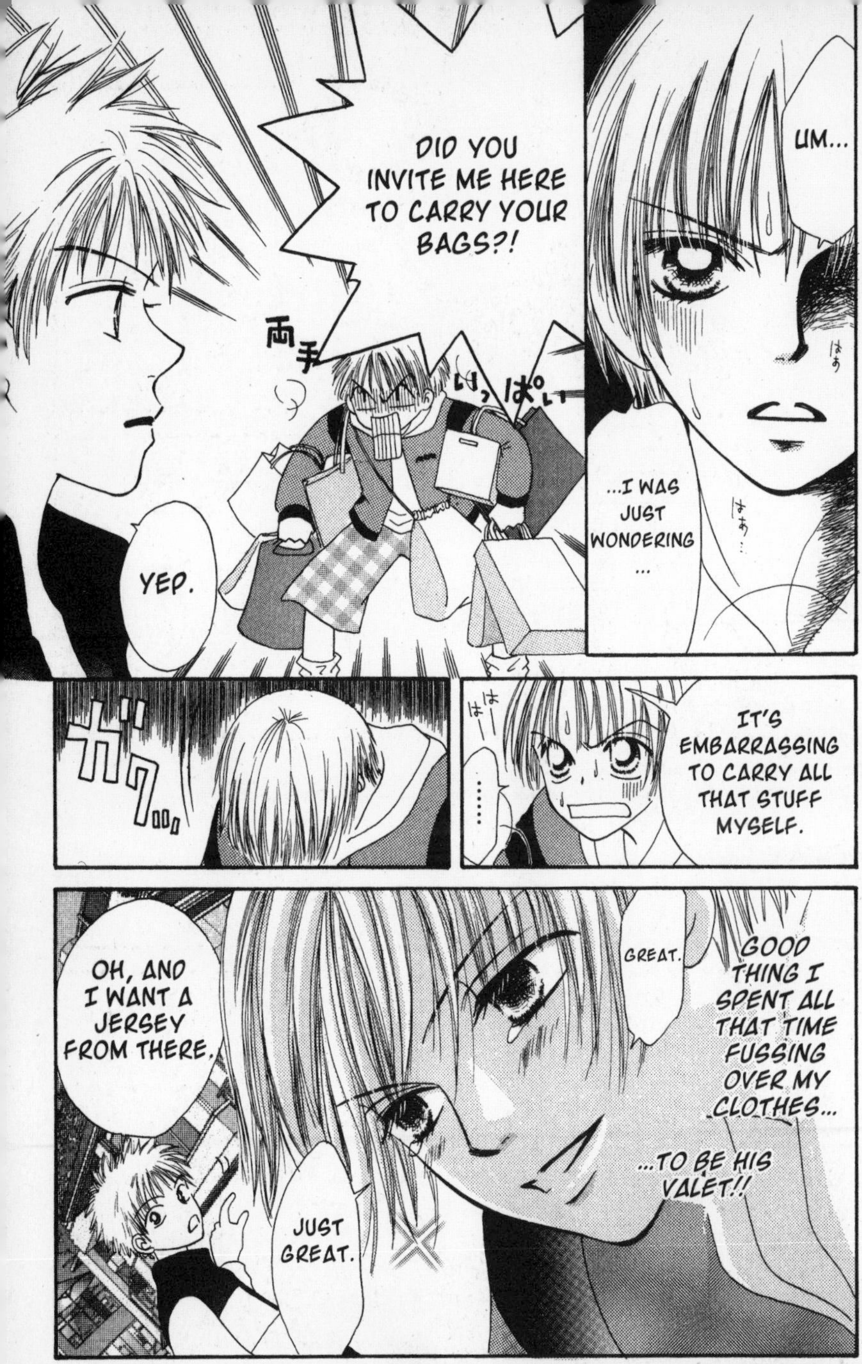
UM...
はぁ
...I WAS JUST WONDERING ...
はぁ…
DID YOU INVITE ME HERE TO CARRY YOUR BAGS?!
両手いっぱい
YEP.
はーはー
IT'S EMBARRASSING TO CARRY ALL THAT STUFF MYSELF.
......
ガク...
GREAT.
GOOD THING I SPENT ALL THAT TIME FUSSING OVER MY CLOTHES...
...TO BE HIS VALET!!
OH, AND I WANT A JERSEY FROM THERE.
JUST GREAT.

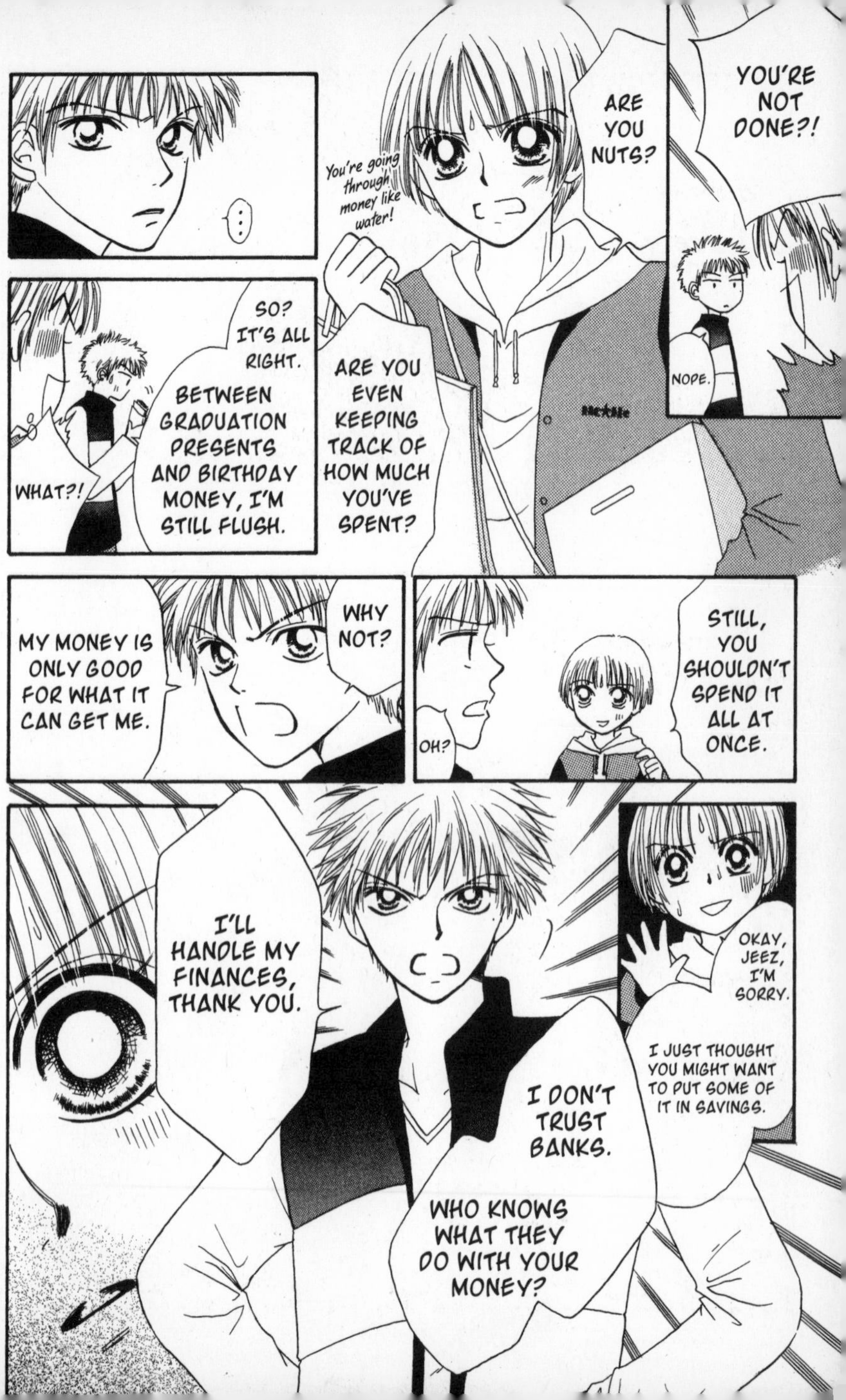
YOU'RE NOT DONE?!
NOPE.
ARE YOU NUTS?
You're going through money like water!
ARE YOU EVEN KEEPING TRACK OF HOW MUCH YOU'VE SPENT?
...
SO? IT'S ALL RIGHT.
BETWEEN GRADUATION PRESENTS AND BIRTHDAY MONEY, I'M STILL FLUSH.
WHAT?!
STILL, YOU SHOULDN'T SPEND IT ALL AT ONCE.
OH?
WHY NOT?
MY MONEY IS ONLY GOOD FOR WHAT IT CAN GET ME.
OKAY, JEEZ, I'M SORRY.
I JUST THOUGHT YOU MIGHT WANT TO PUT SOME OF IT IN SAVINGS.
I'LL HANDLE MY FINANCES, THANK YOU.
I DON'T TRUST BANKS.
WHO KNOWS WHAT THEY DO WITH YOUR MONEY?

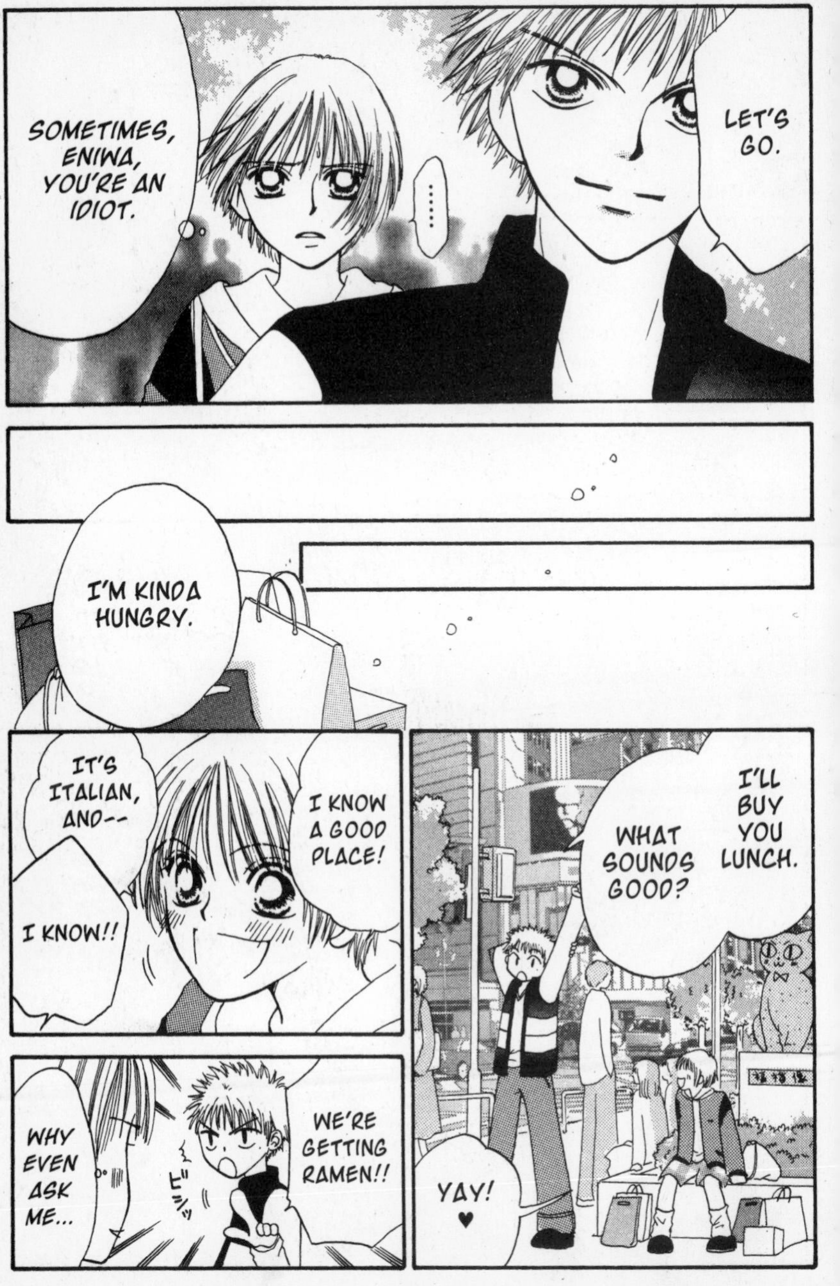
LET'S GO.
......
SOMETIMES, ENIWA, YOU'RE AN IDIOT.
I'M KINDA HUNGRY.
I'LL BUY YOU LUNCH.
WHAT SOUNDS GOOD?
YAY! ♥
I KNOW A GOOD PLACE!
IT'S ITALIAN, AND--
I KNOW!!
WE'RE GETTING RAMEN!!
ビシッ
WHY EVEN ASK ME...

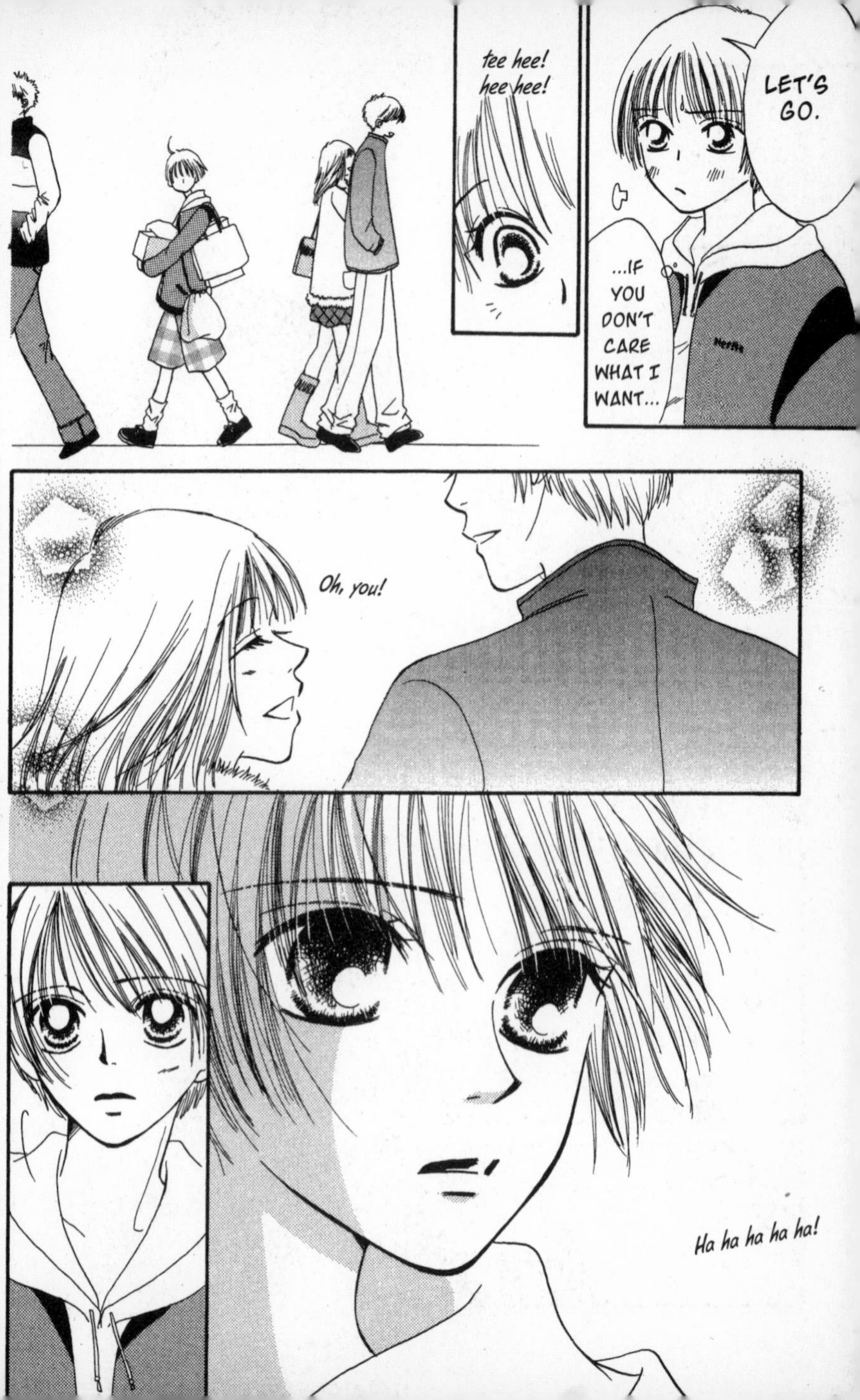
LET'S GO.
...IF YOU DON'T CARE WHAT I WANT...
tee hee! hee hee!
Oh, you!
Ha ha ha ha ha!

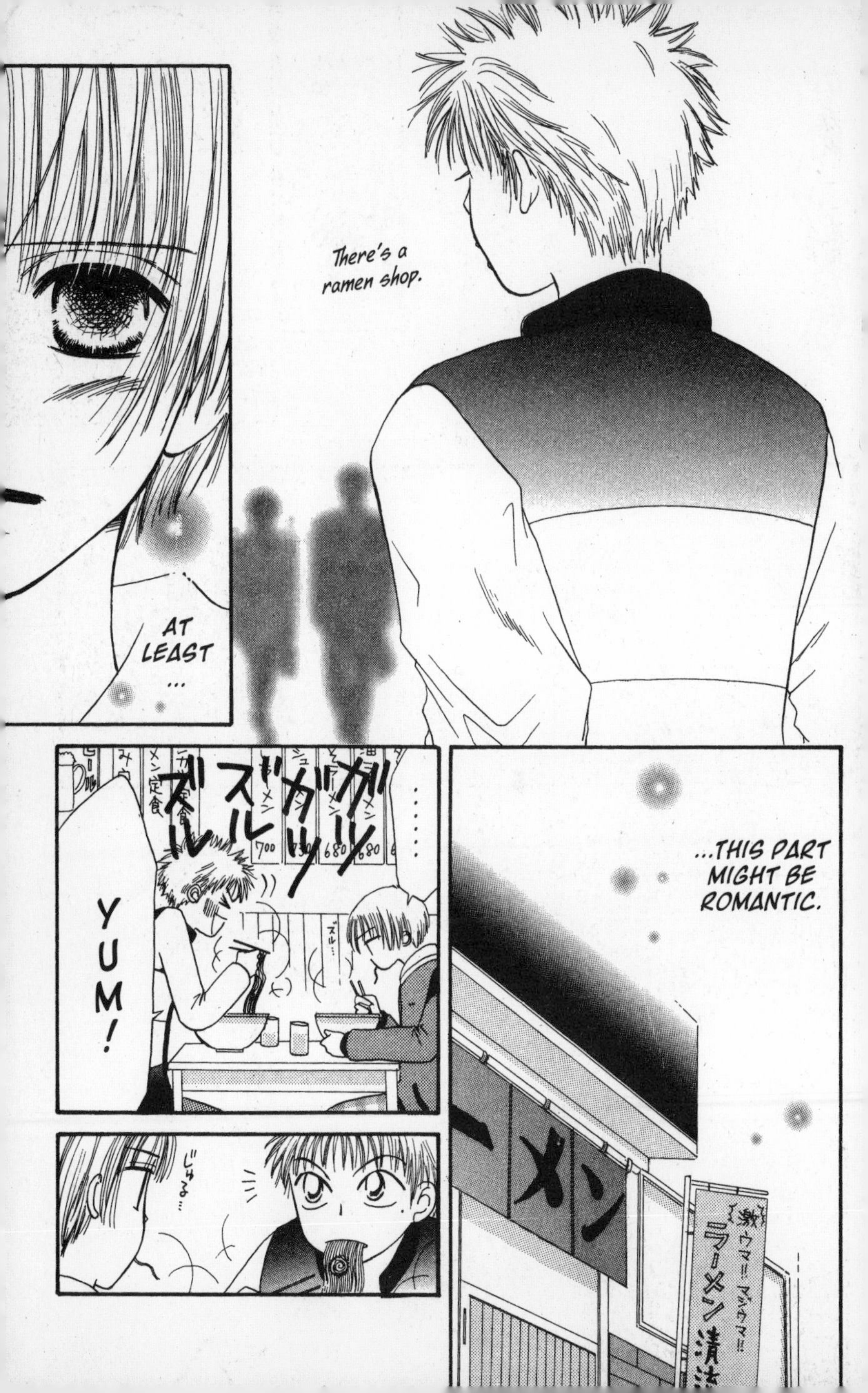
There's a ramen shop.
AT LEAST ...
...THIS PART MIGHT BE ROMANTIC.
ラーメン
ウマ!! マジウマ!!
ラーメン
YUM!

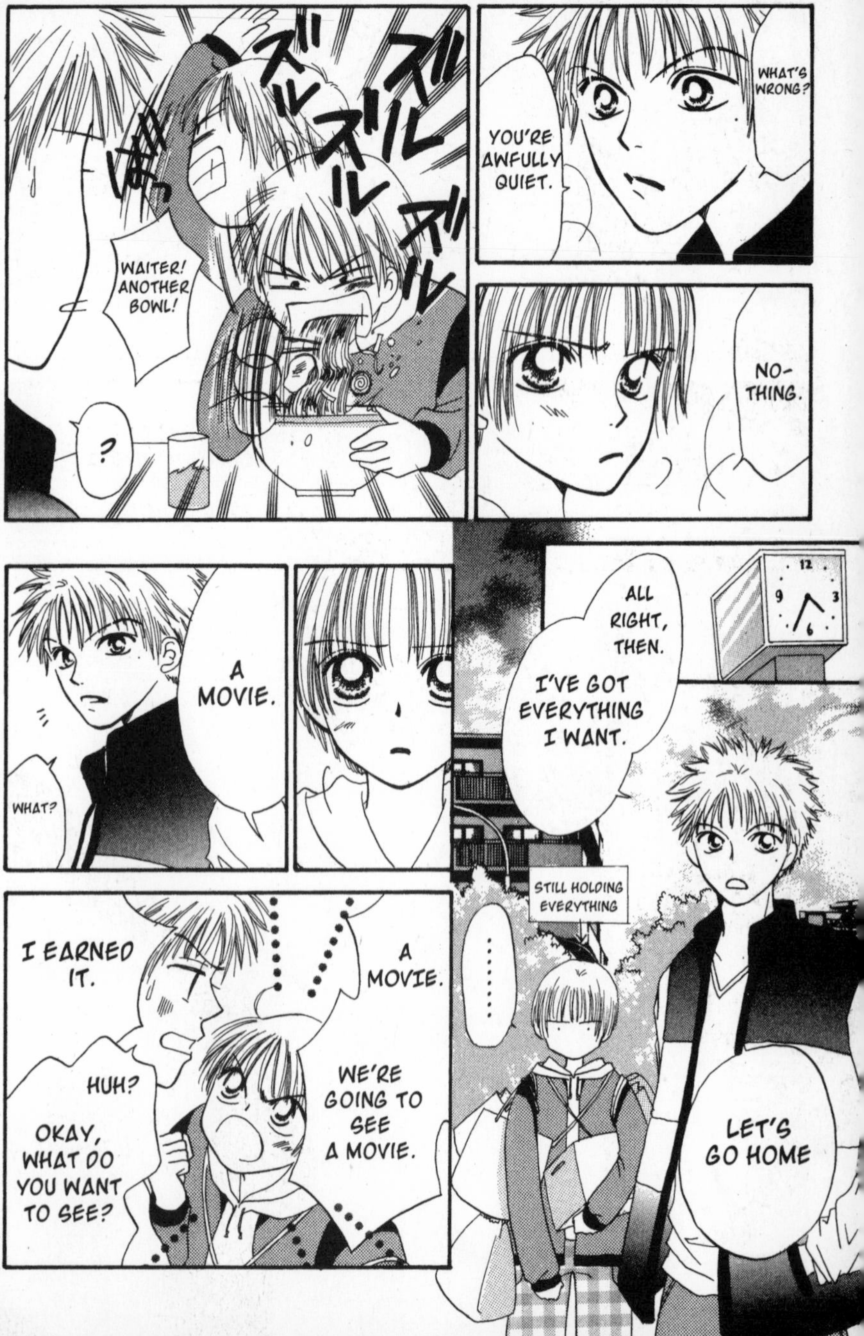
WHAT'S WRONG?
YOU'RE AWFULLY QUIET.
NO-THING.
ズル ズル ズル ズル
WAITER! ANOTHER BOWL!
?
ALL RIGHT, THEN.
I'VE GOT EVERYTHING I WANT.
STILL HOLDING EVERYTHING
......
LET'S GO HOME
A MOVIE.
WHAT?
A MOVIE.
WE'RE GOING TO SEE A MOVIE.
......
I EARNED IT.
HUH?
OKAY, WHAT DO YOU WANT TO SEE?

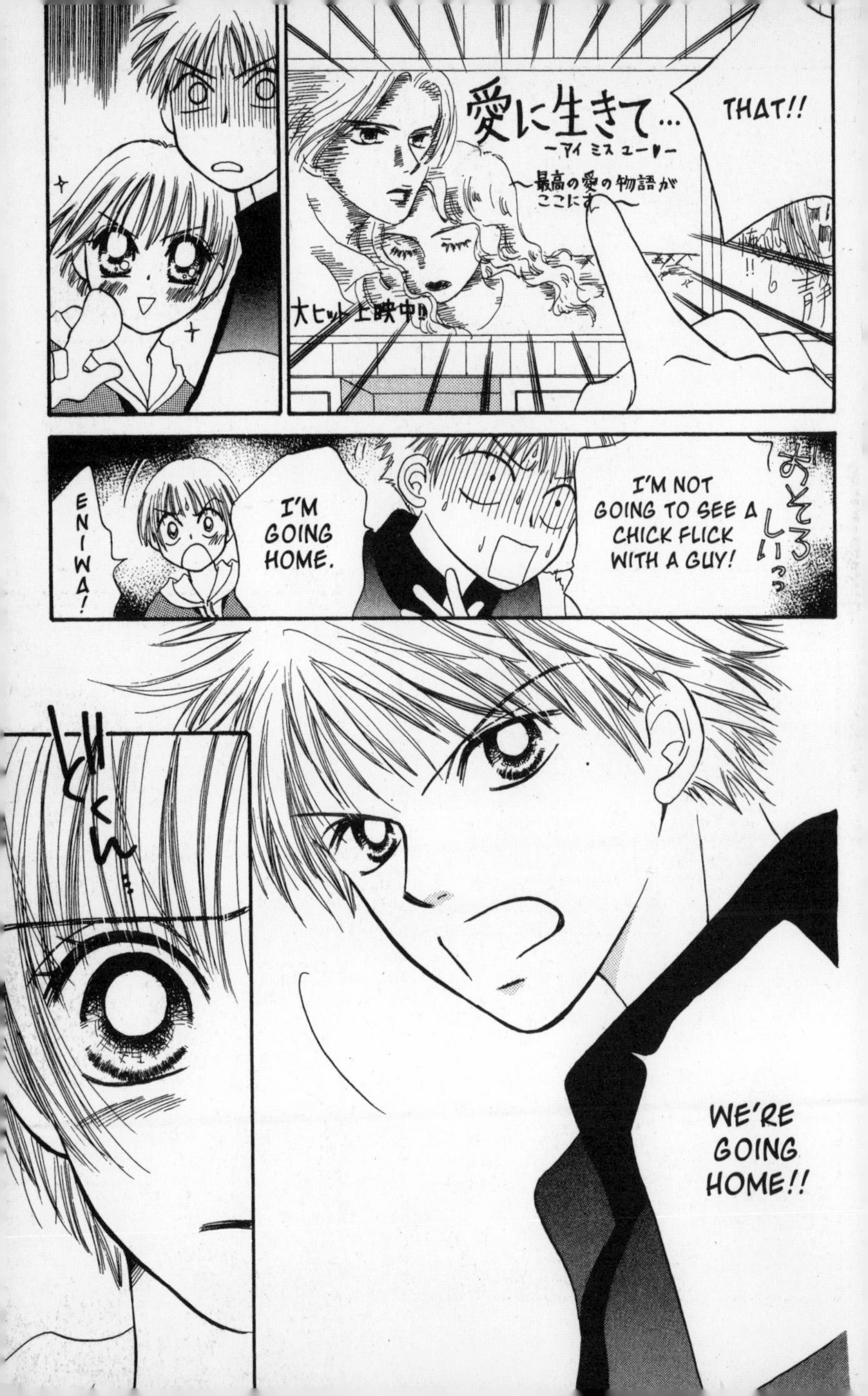
THAT!!
愛に生きて…
ーアイ ミス ユー♥ー
～最高の愛の物語がここに！～
大ヒット上映中!!
おそろしいっ
I'M NOT GOING TO SEE A CHICK FLICK WITH A GUY!
I'M GOING HOME.
ENIWA!
WE'RE GOING HOME!!
どくん!!

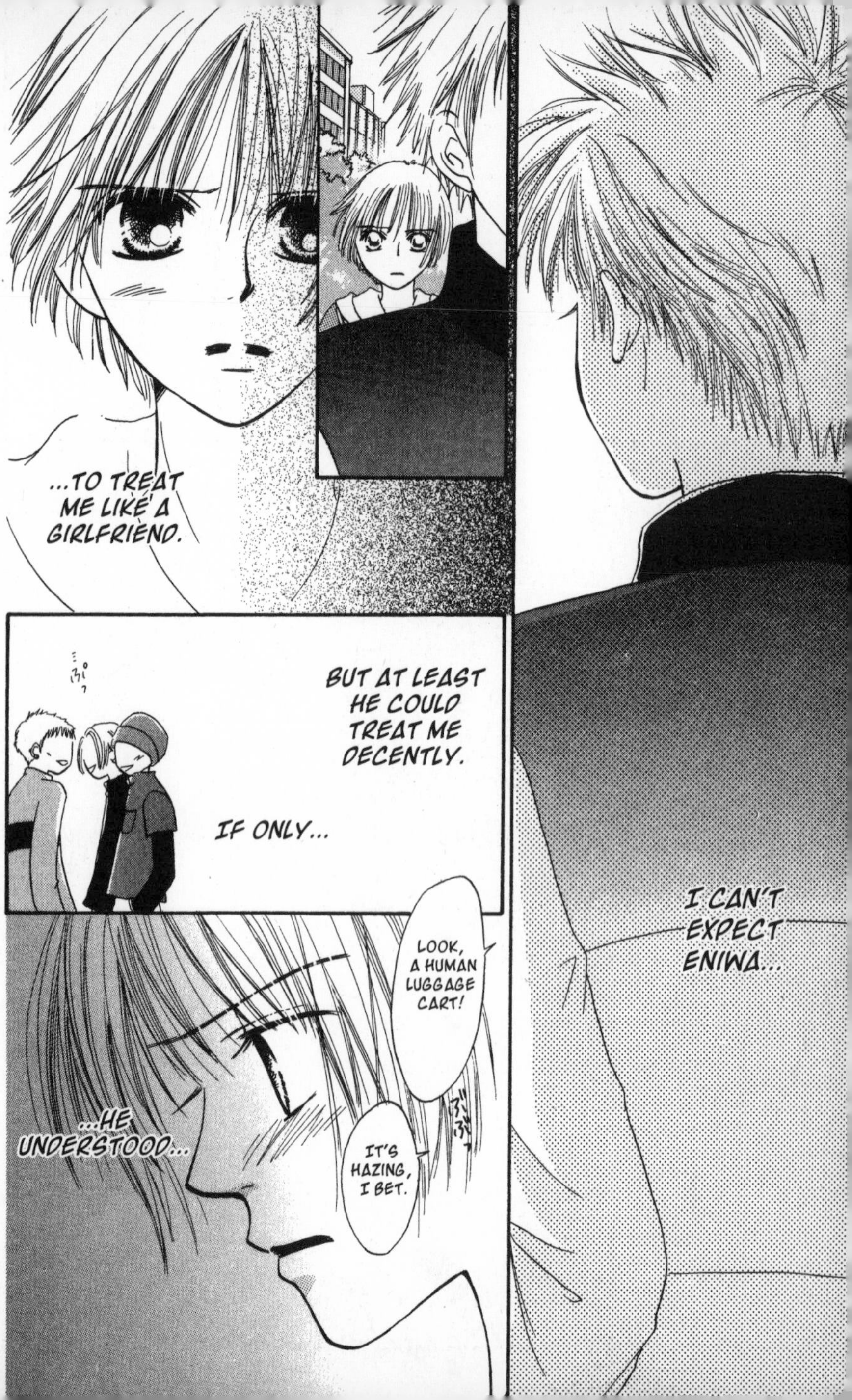
I CAN'T EXPECT ENIWA...
...TO TREAT ME LIKE A GIRLFRIEND.
BUT AT LEAST HE COULD TREAT ME DECENTLY.
IF ONLY...
LOOK, A HUMAN LUGGAGE CART!
IT'S HAZING, I BET.
...HE UNDERSTOOD...

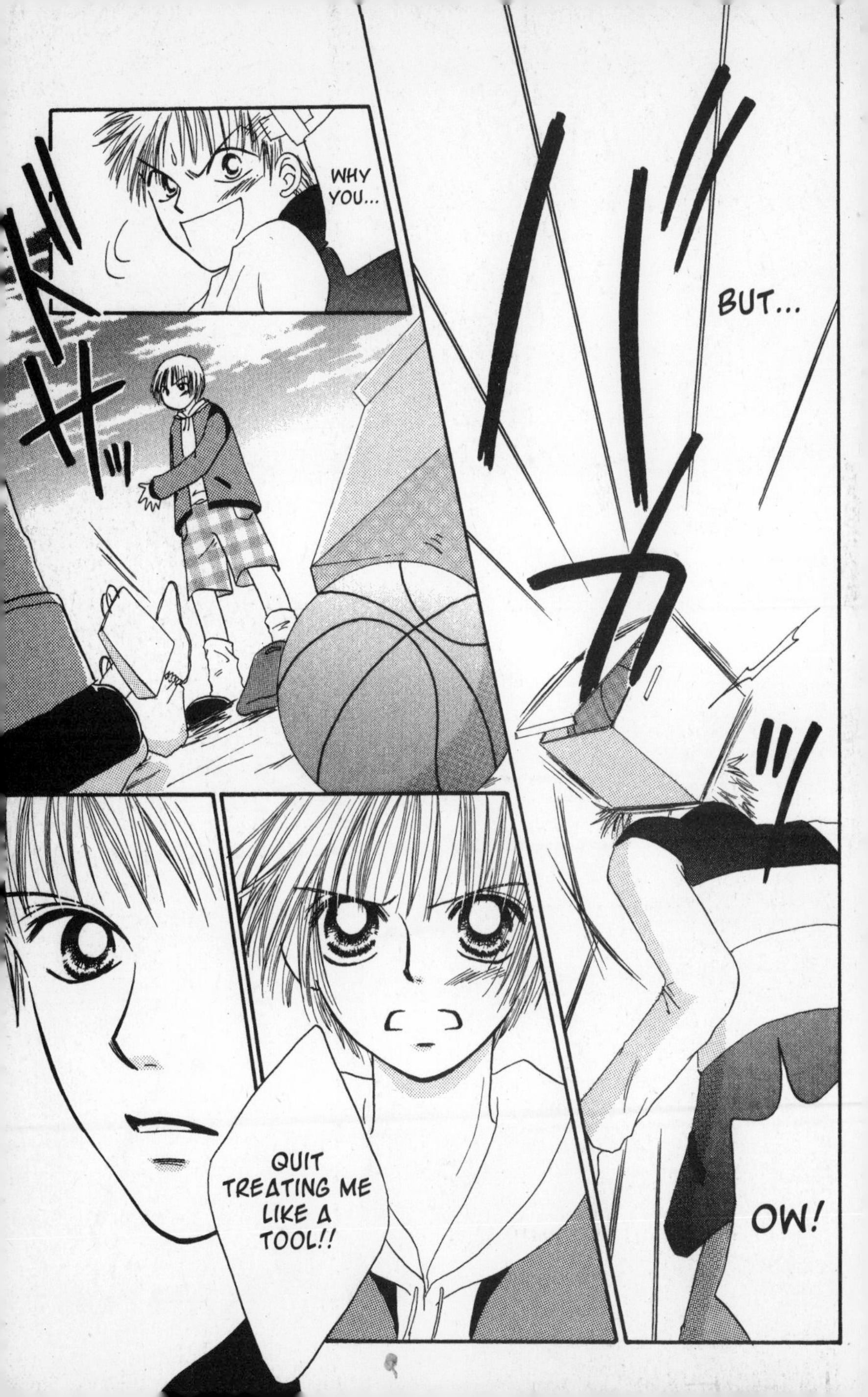
BUT...
OW!
WHY YOU...
QUIT TREATING ME LIKE A TOOL!!

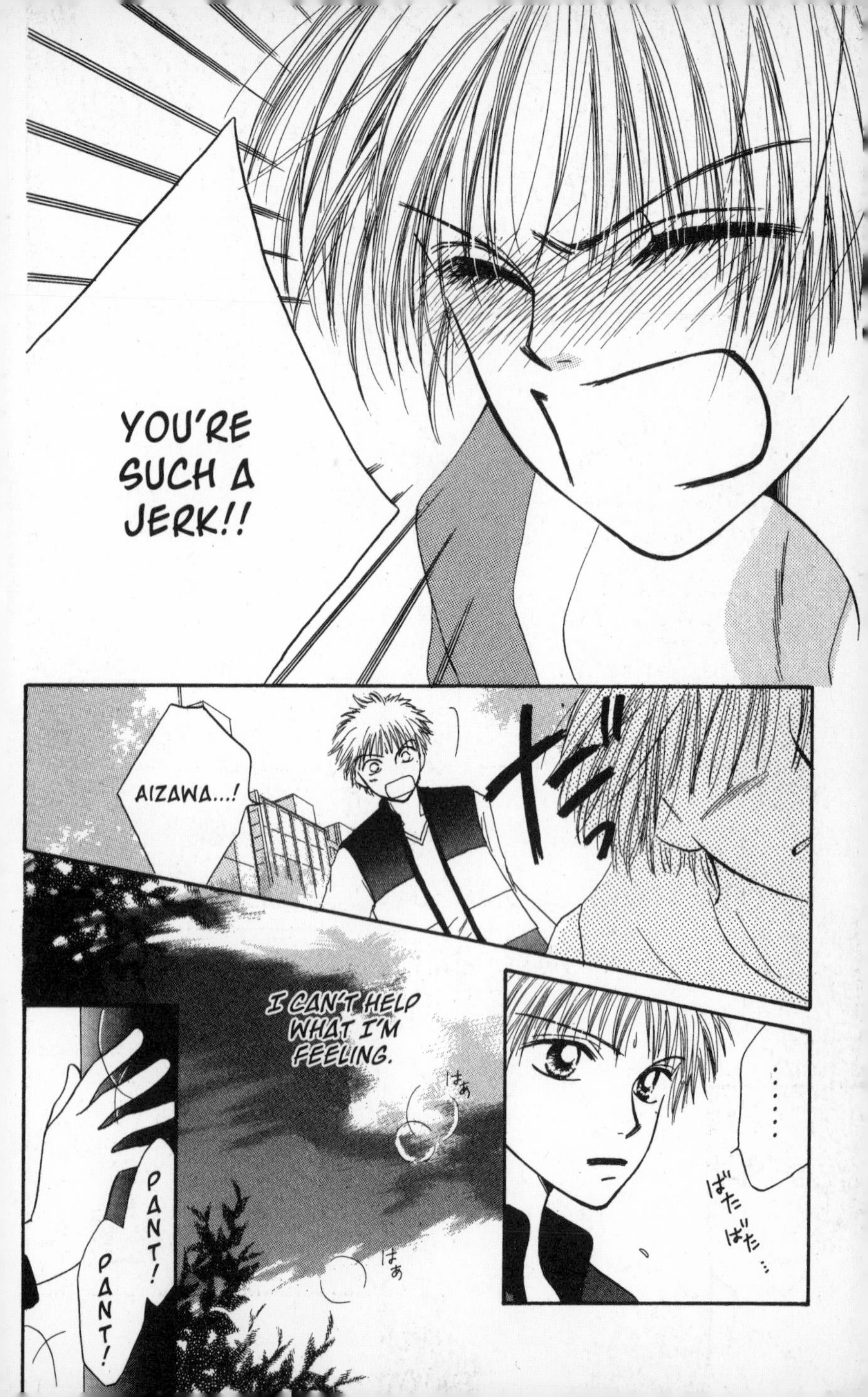
YOU'RE SUCH A JERK!!
AIZAWA...!
I CAN'T HELP WHAT I'M FEELING.
はぁ
はぁ
......
ばたばた...
PANT! PANT!
PANT! PANT!

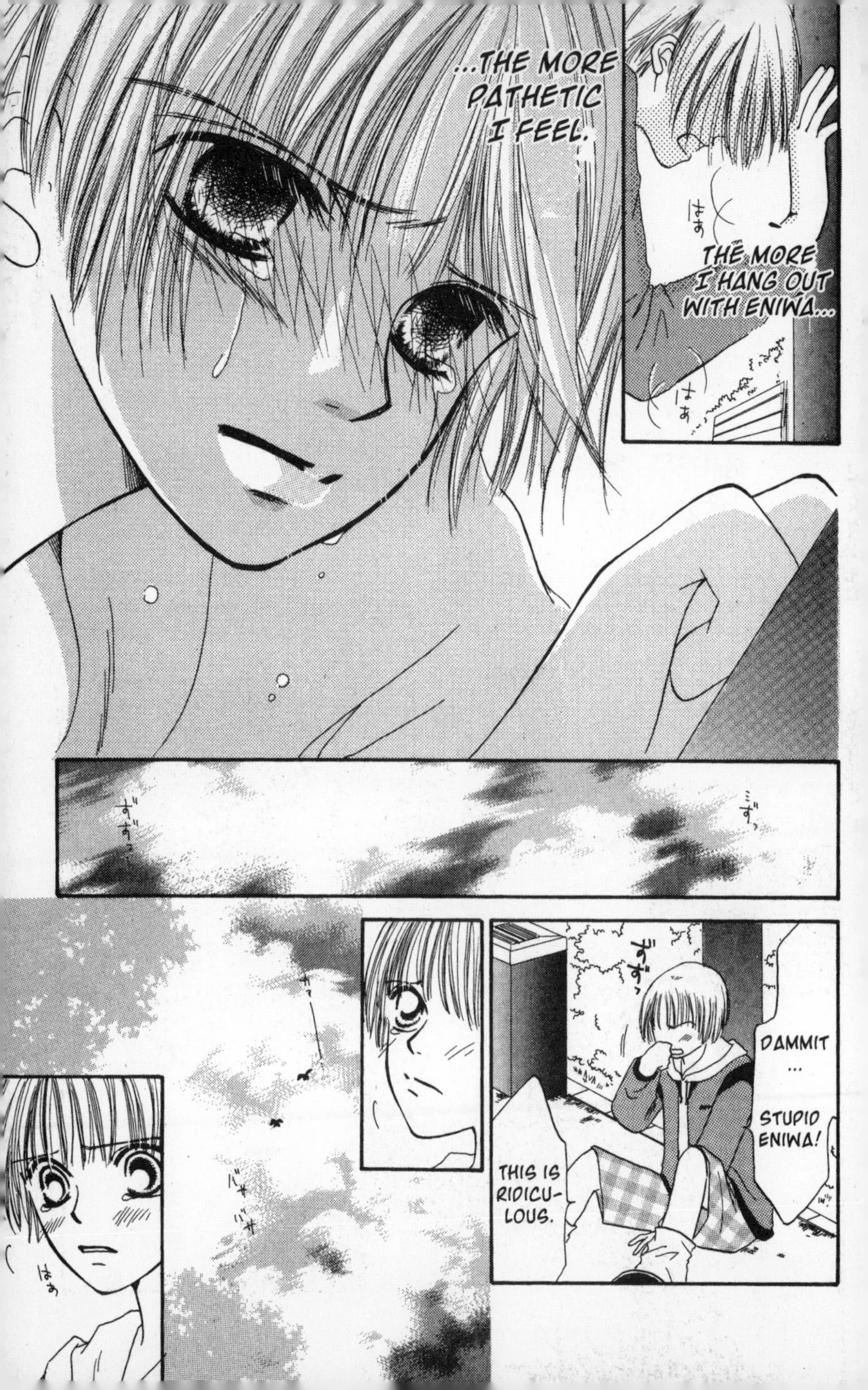
THE MORE I HANG OUT WITH ENIWA...
...THE MORE PATHETIC I FEEL.
DAMMIT ...
STUPID ENIWA!
THIS IS RIDICU-LOUS.

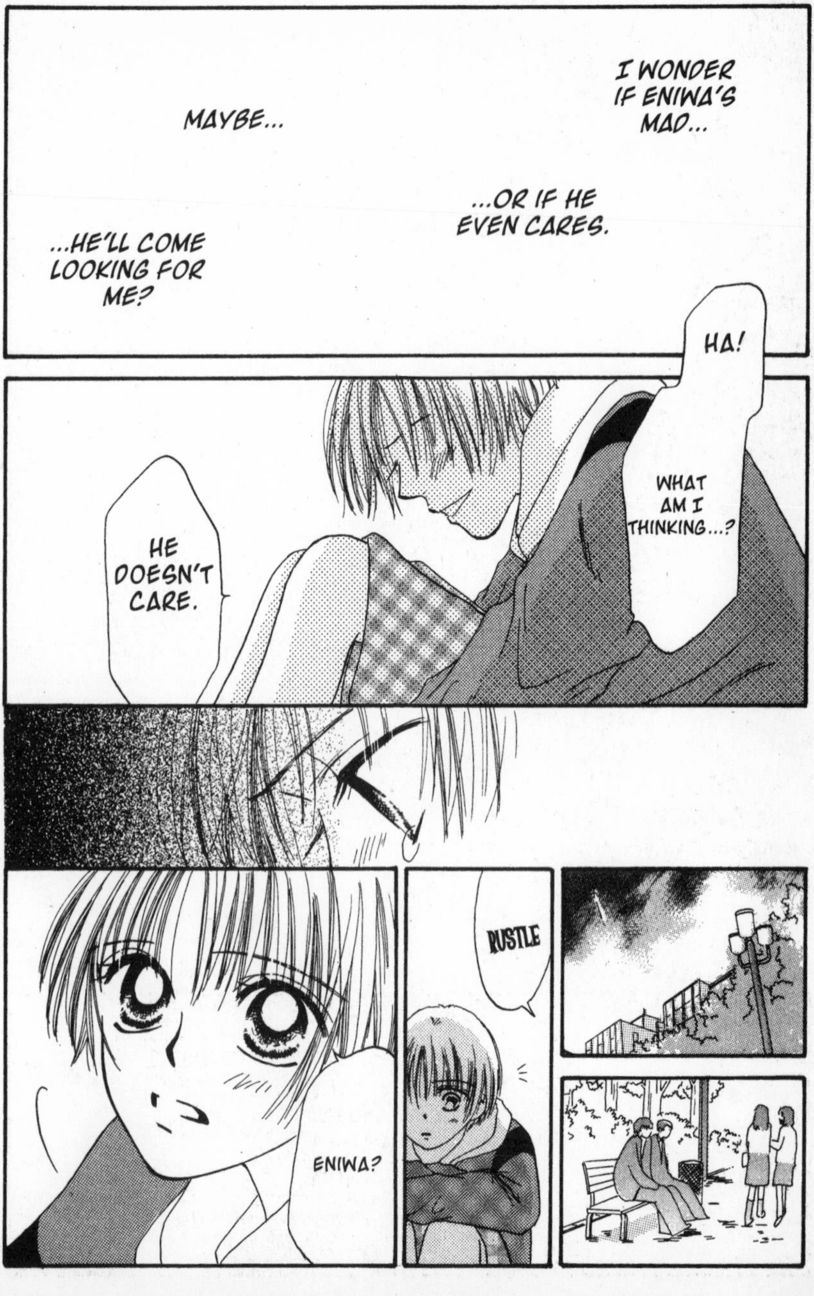
I WONDER IF ENIWA'S MAD...
...OR IF HE EVEN CARES.
MAYBE...
...HE'LL COME LOOKING FOR ME?
HA!
WHAT AM I THINKING...?
HE DOESN'T CARE.
RUSTLE
ENIWA?

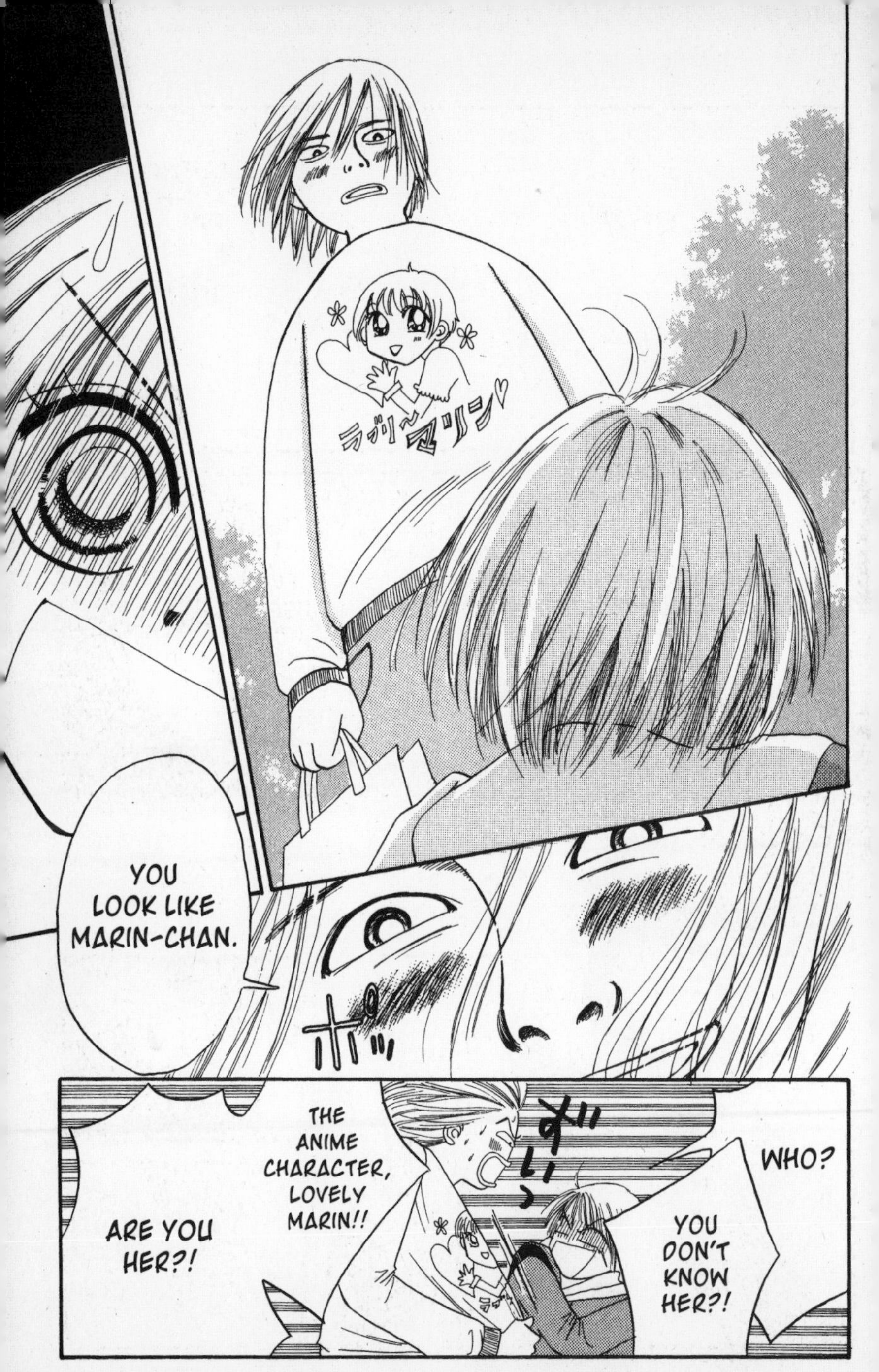
ラブリ〜マリン♡
YOU LOOK LIKE MARIN-CHAN.
WHO?
YOU DON'T KNOW HER?!
THE ANIME CHARACTER, LOVELY MARIN!!
ARE YOU HER?!

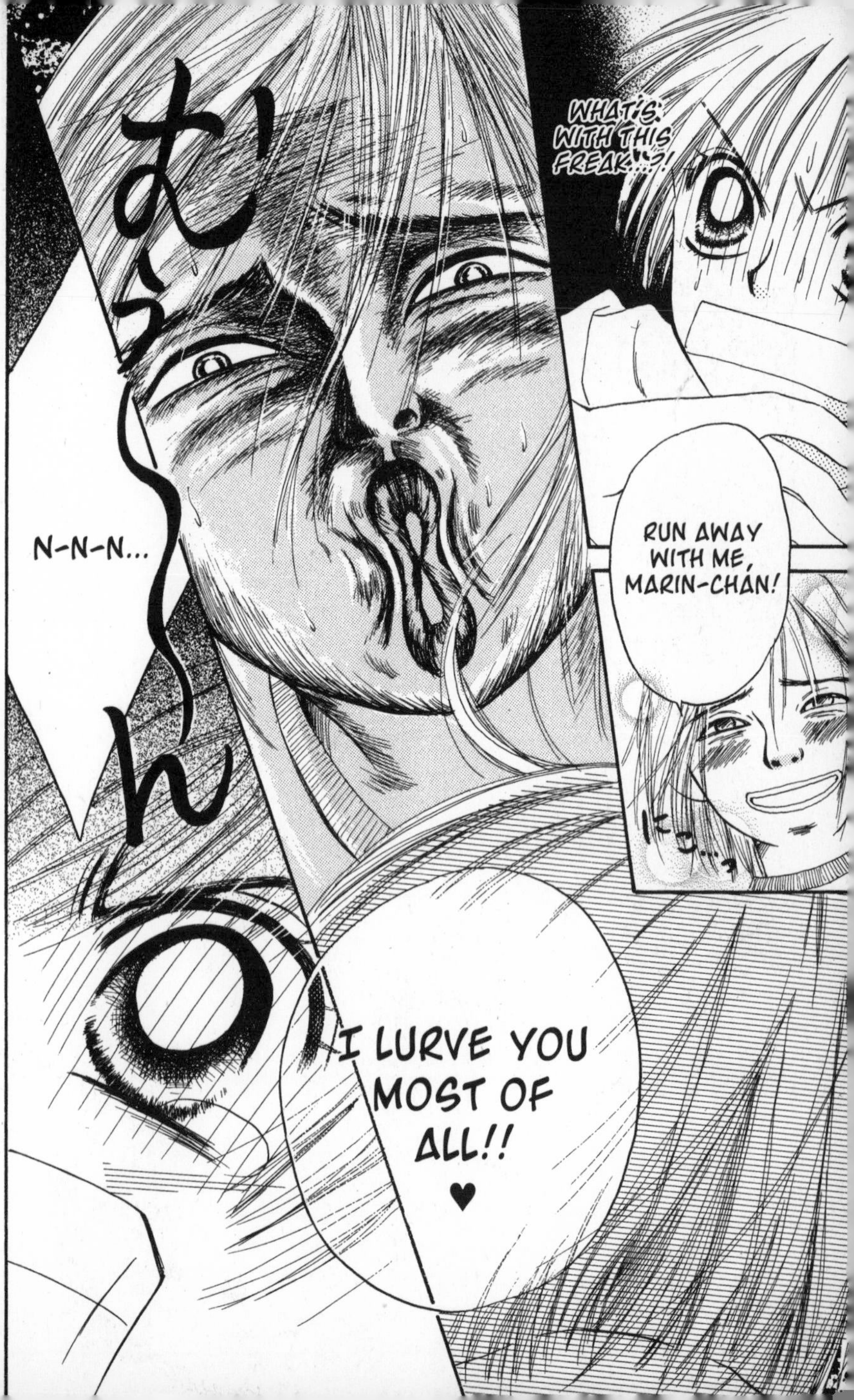
WHAT'S WITH THIS FREAK...?!
RUN AWAY WITH ME, MARIN-CHÁN!
N-N-N...
I LURVE YOU MOST OF ALL!! ♥

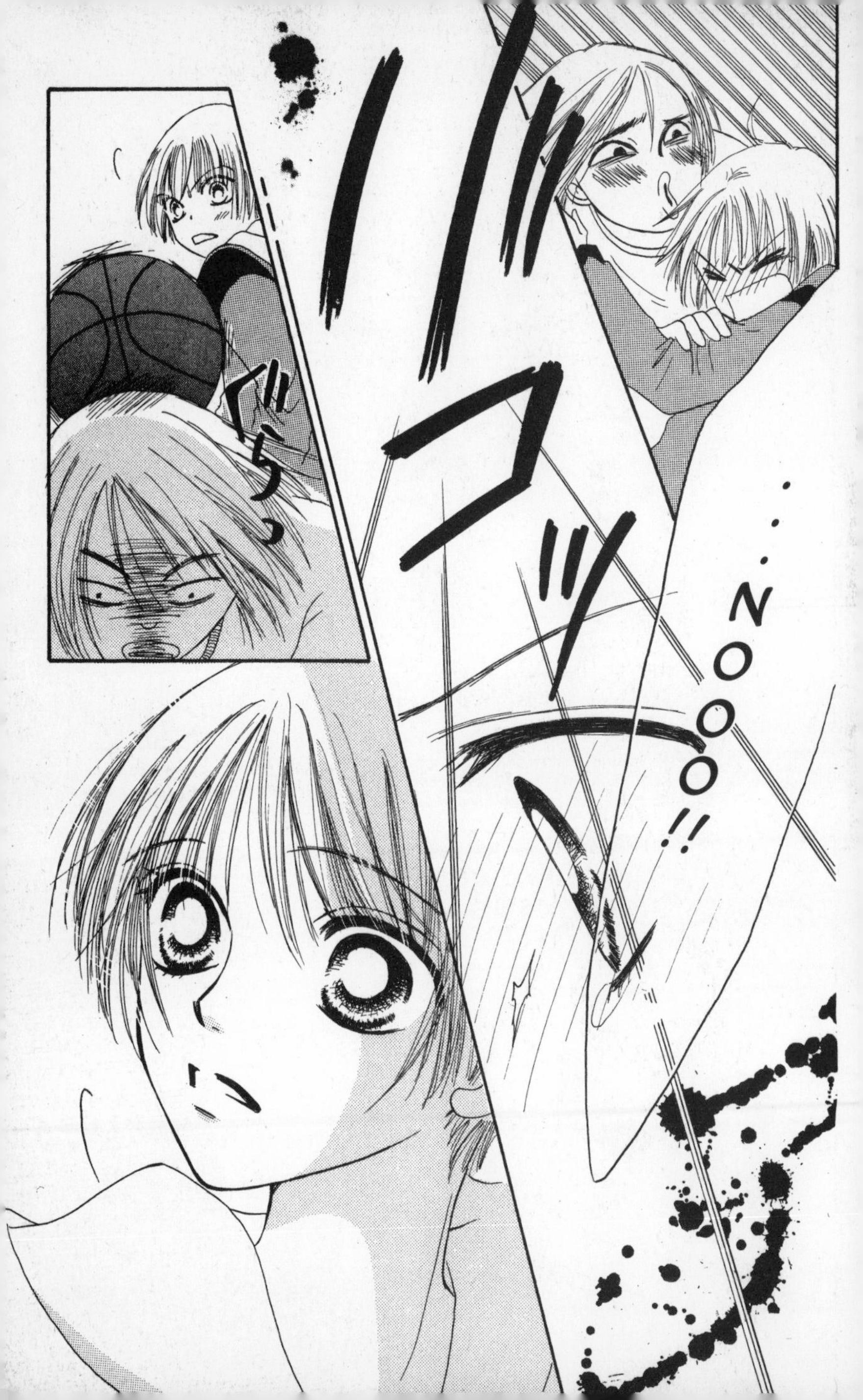
...NOOOO!!
ゴッ
ぐらっ

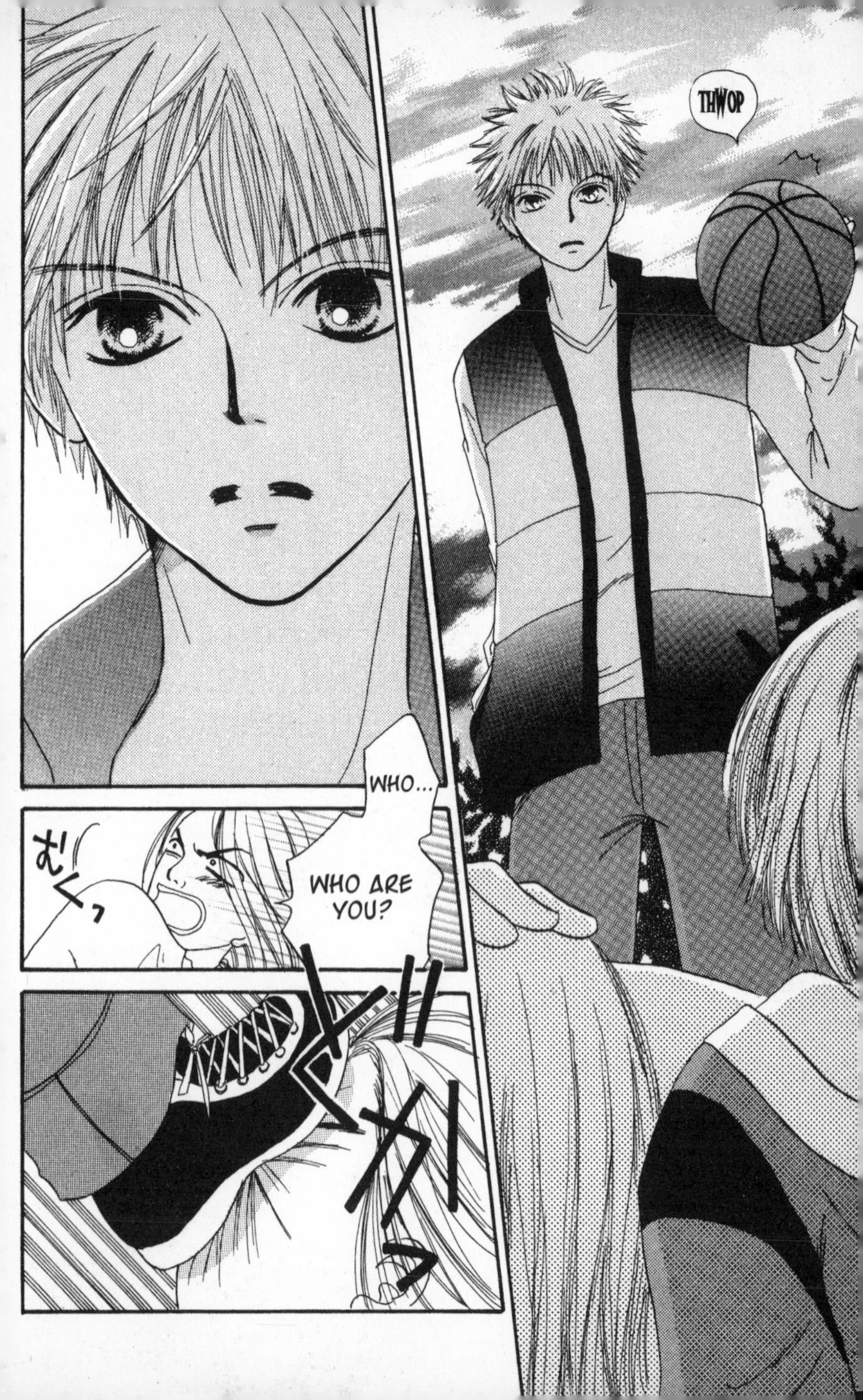
THWOP
WHO...
WHO ARE YOU?
むくっ

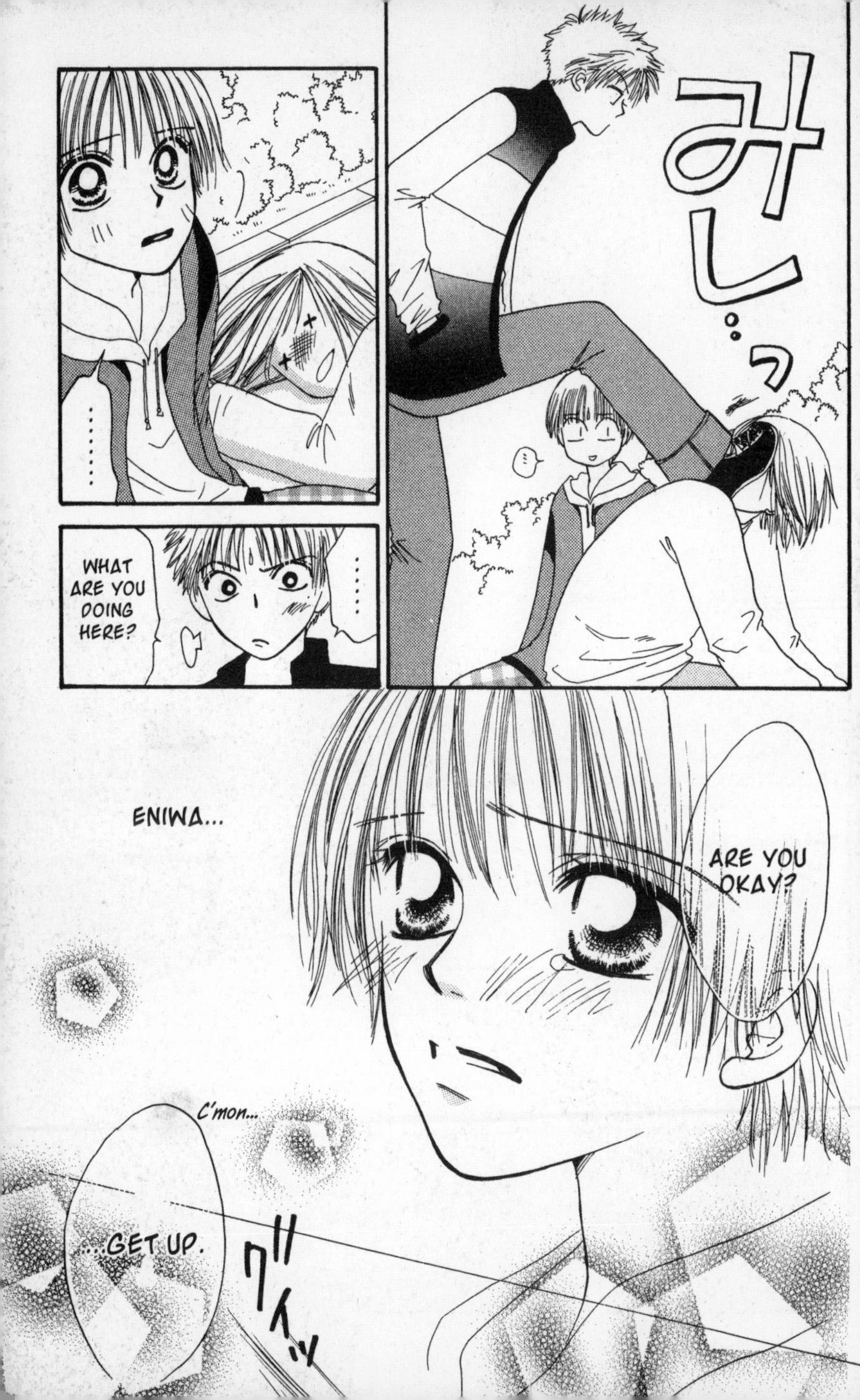
みしっ
......
......
WHAT ARE YOU DOING HERE?
ARE YOU OKAY?
ENIWA...
C'mon...
...GET UP.
グイッ

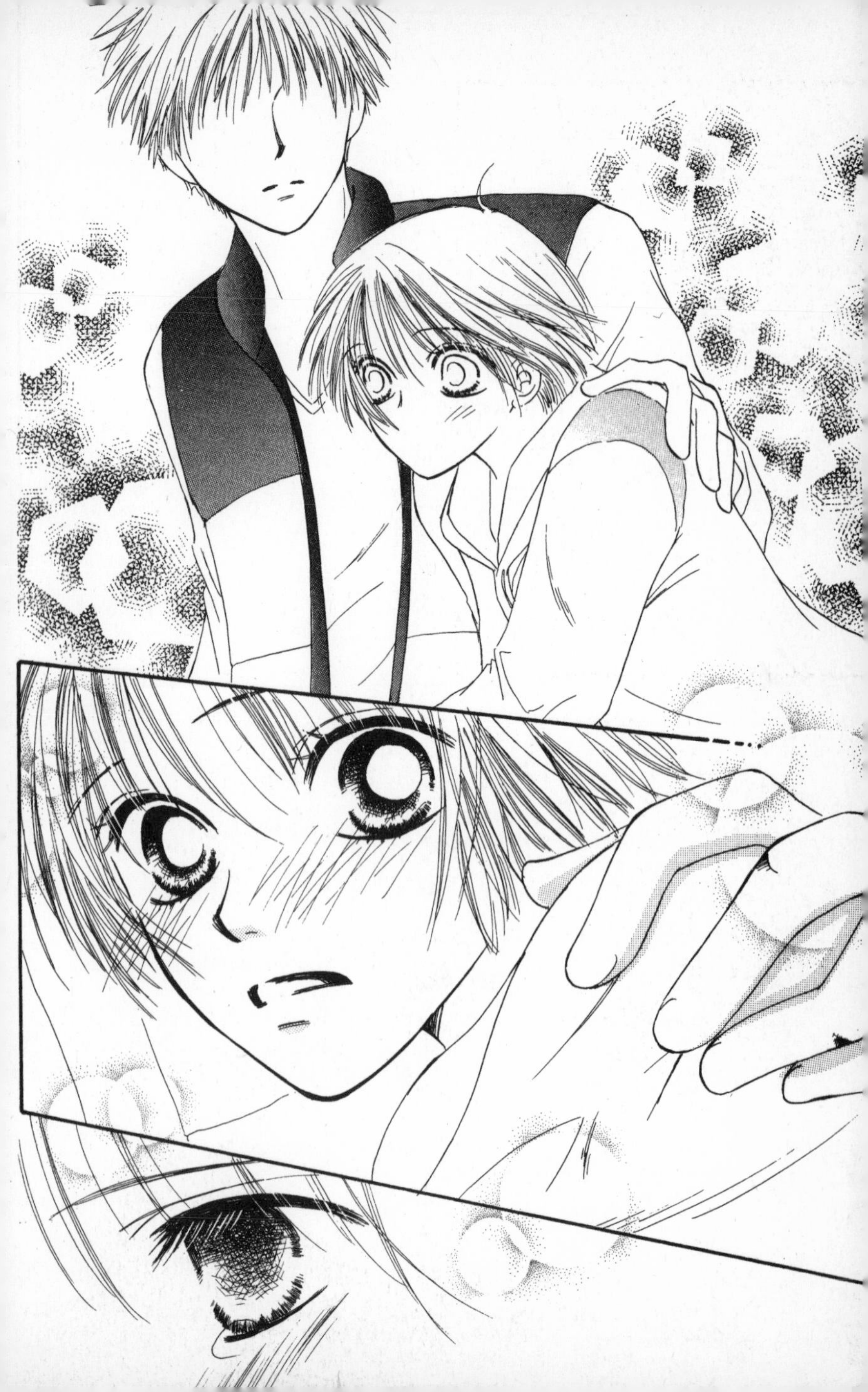

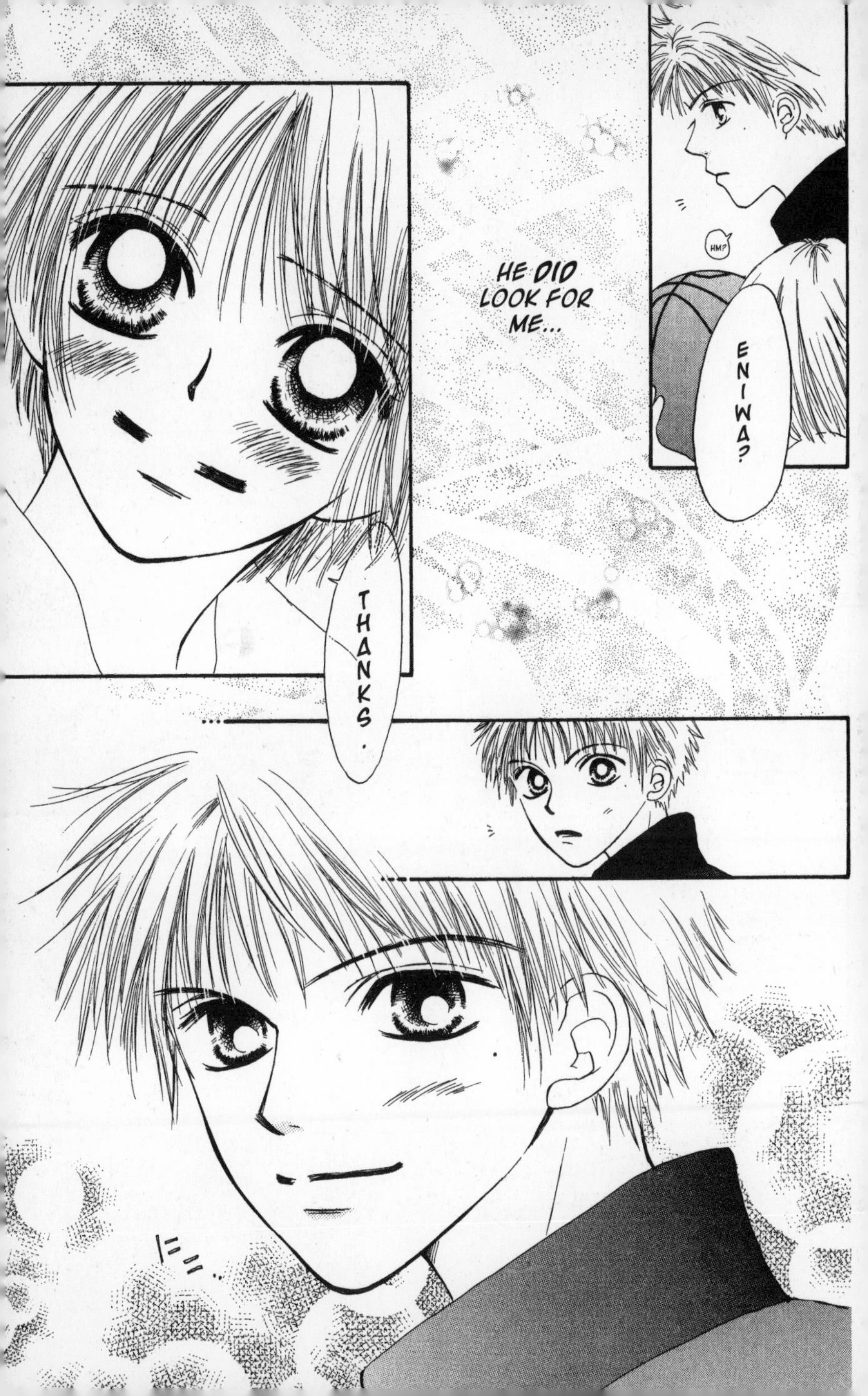
HM?
ENIWA?
HE DID LOOK FOR ME...
THANKS.

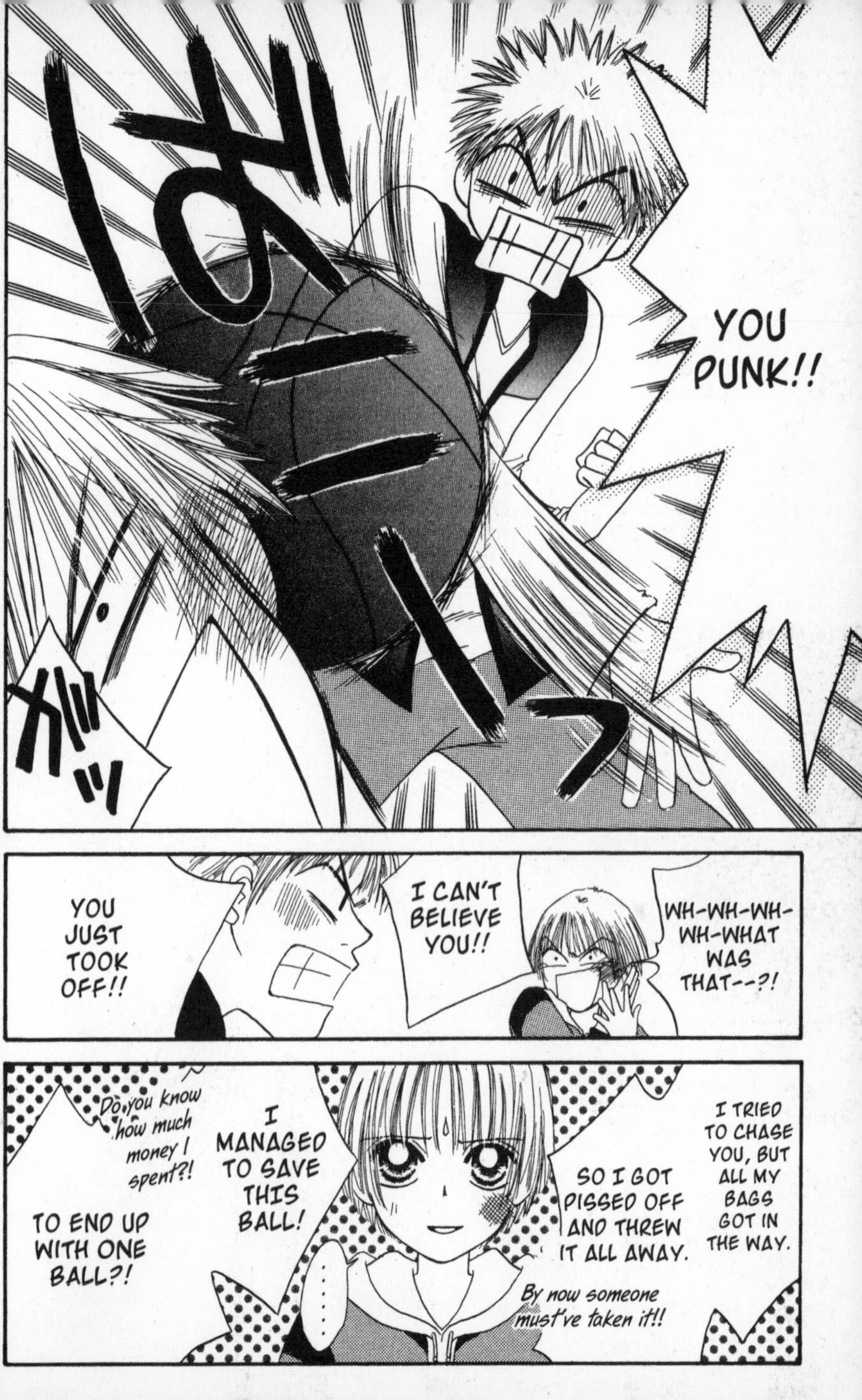
YOU PUNK!!
WH-WH-WH-WH-WHAT WAS THAT--?!
I CAN'T BELIEVE YOU!!
YOU JUST TOOK OFF!!
I TRIED TO CHASE YOU, BUT ALL MY BAGS GOT IN THE WAY.
SO I GOT PISSED OFF AND THREW IT ALL AWAY.
By now someone must've taken it!!
I MANAGED TO SAVE THIS BALL!
......
Do you know how much money I spent?!
TO END UP WITH ONE BALL?!

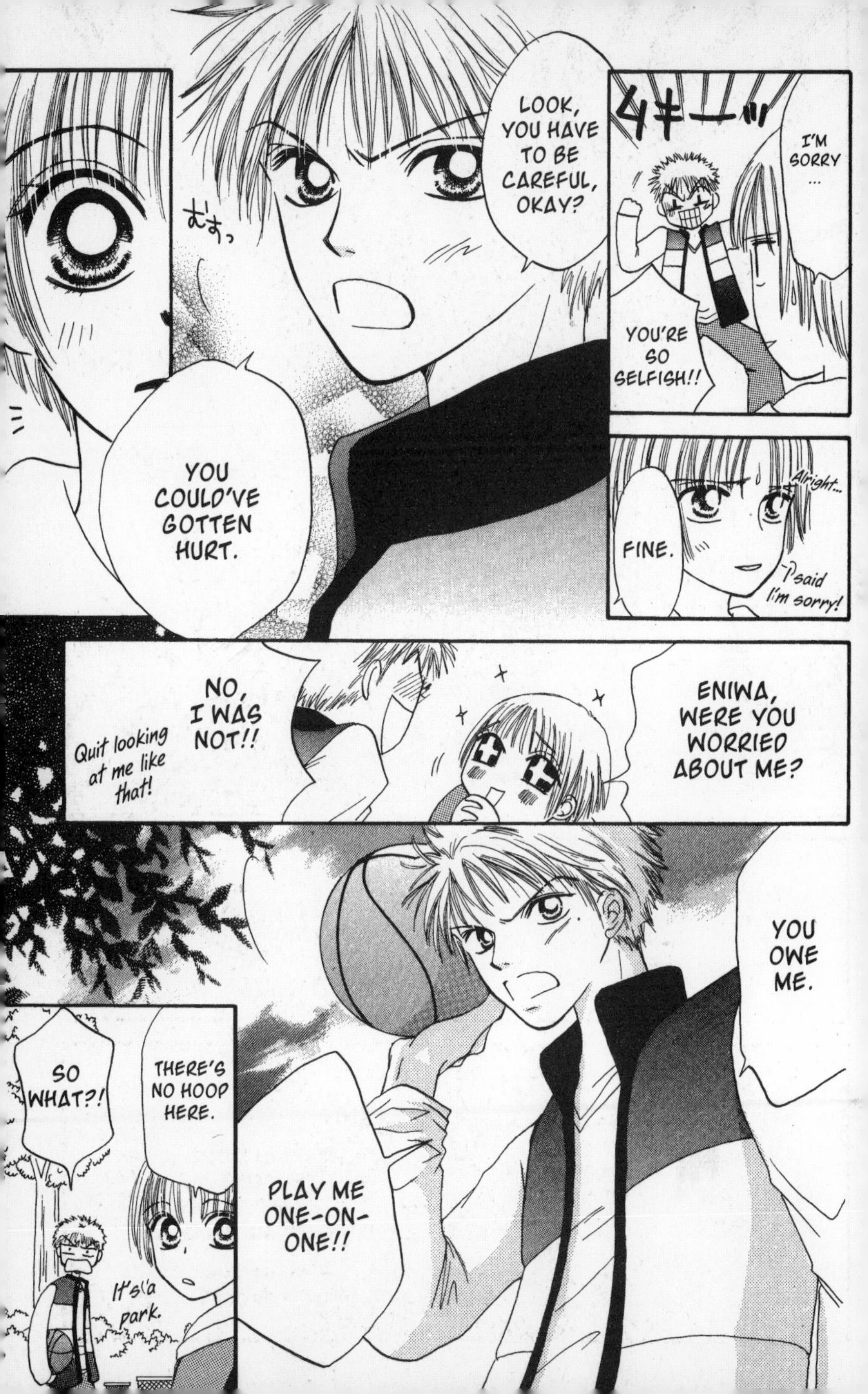
LOOK, YOU HAVE TO BE CAREFUL, OKAY?
むすっ
YOU COULD'VE GOTTEN HURT.
ムキーッ
I'M SORRY ...
YOU'RE SO SELFISH!!
Alright...
FINE.
I said I'm sorry!
ENIWA, WERE YOU WORRIED ABOUT ME?
NO, I WAS NOT!!
Quit looking at me like that!
YOU OWE ME.
PLAY ME ONE-ON-ONE!!
THERE'S NO HOOP HERE.
SO WHAT?!
It's a park.

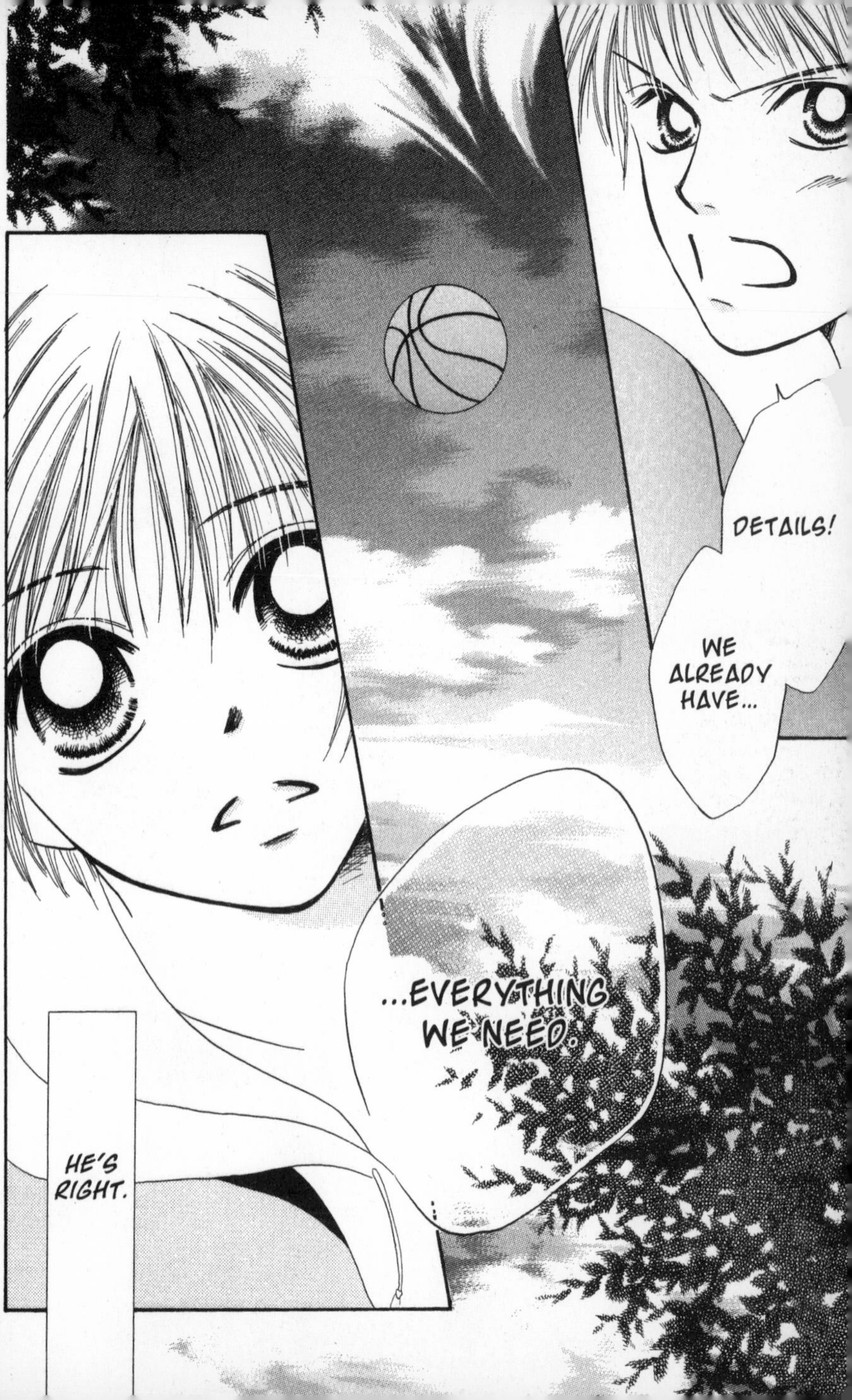
DETAILS!
WE ALREADY HAVE...
...EVERYTHING WE NEED.
HE'S RIGHT.

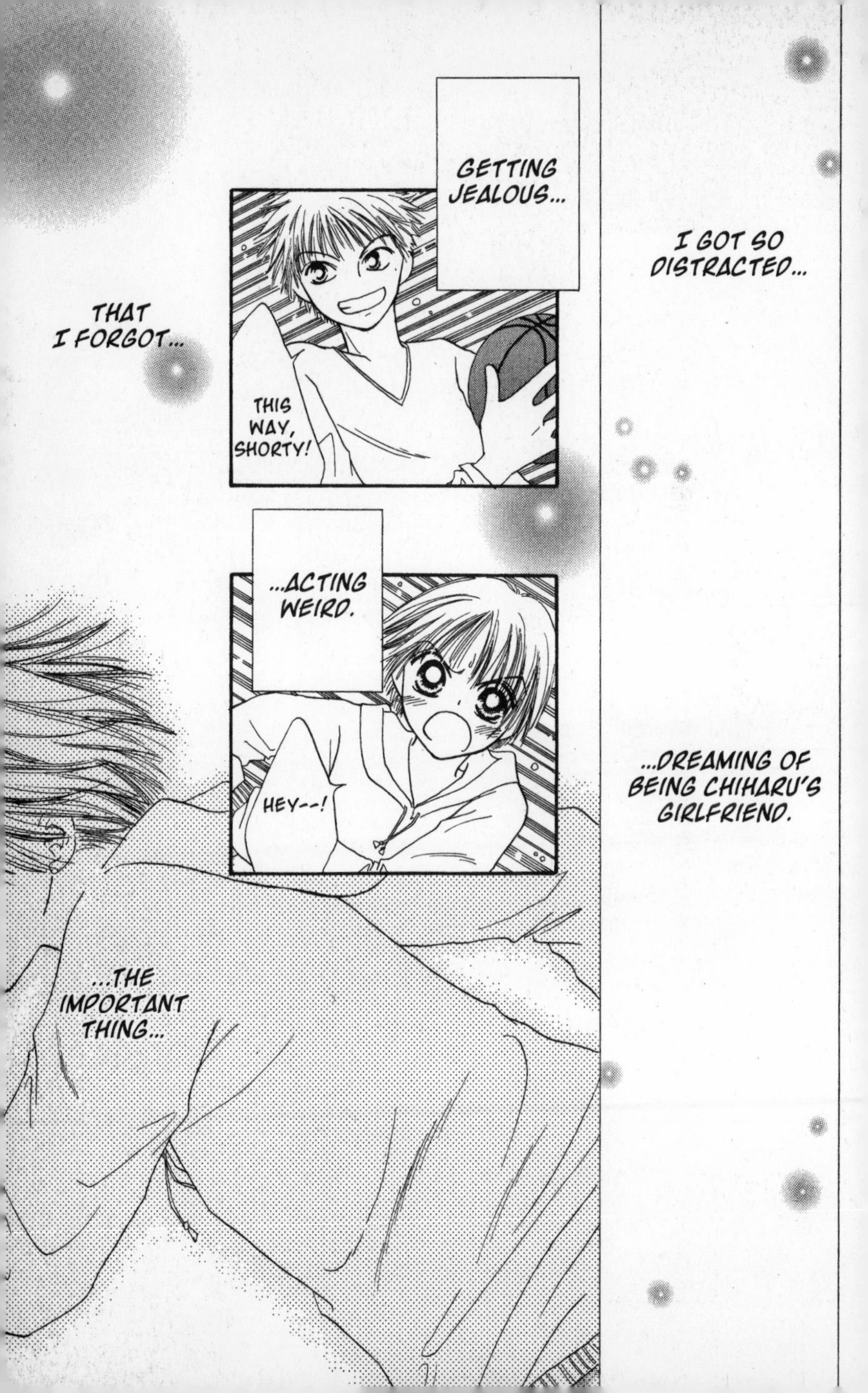
I GOT SO DISTRACTED...
...DREAMING OF BEING CHIHARU'S GIRLFRIEND.
GETTING JEALOUS...
THIS WAY, SHORTY!
THAT I FORGOT...
...ACTING WEIRD.
HEY--!
...THE IMPORTANT THING...

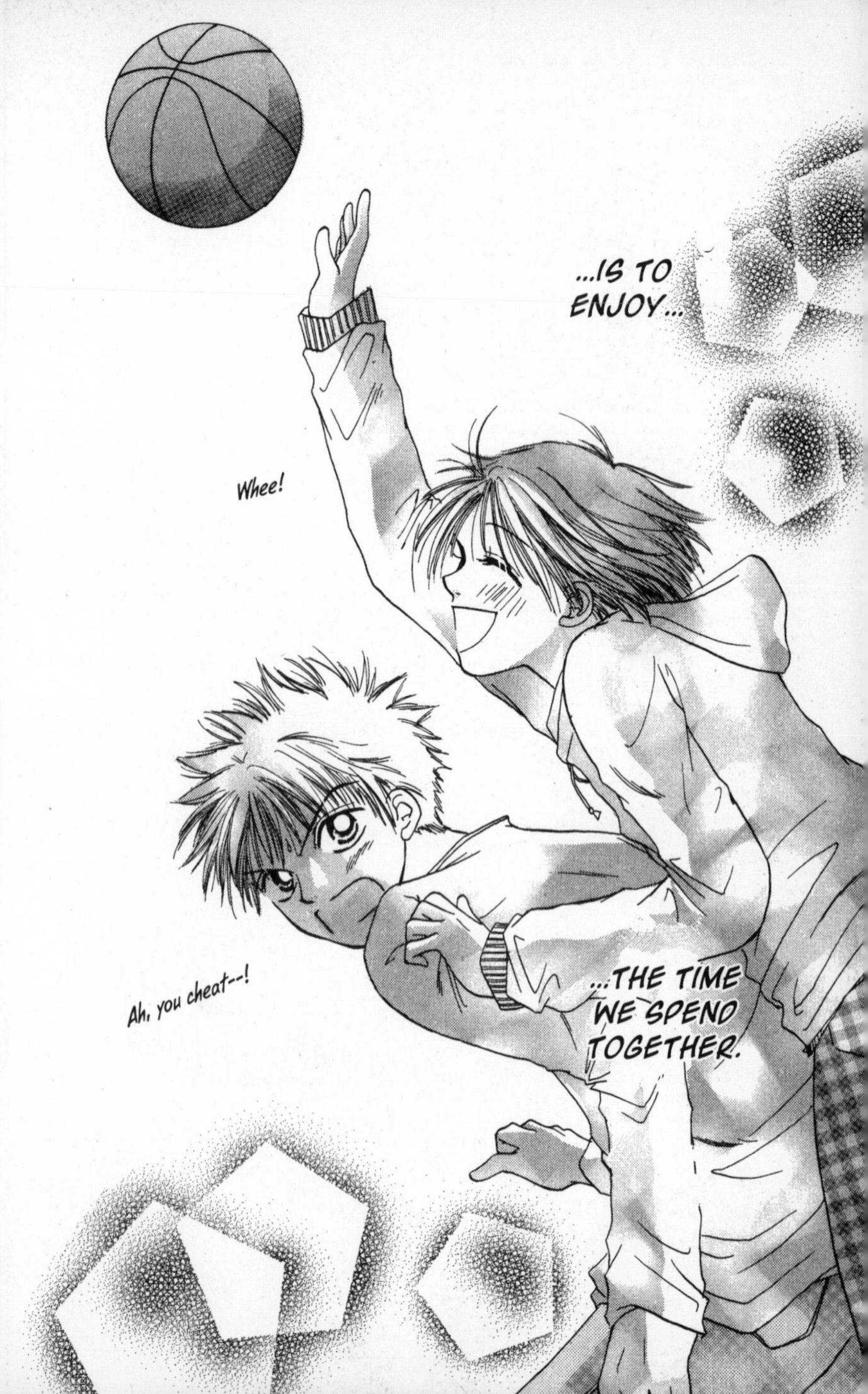
...IS TO ENJOY...
Whee!
...THE TIME WE SPEND TOGETHER.
Ah, you cheat--!

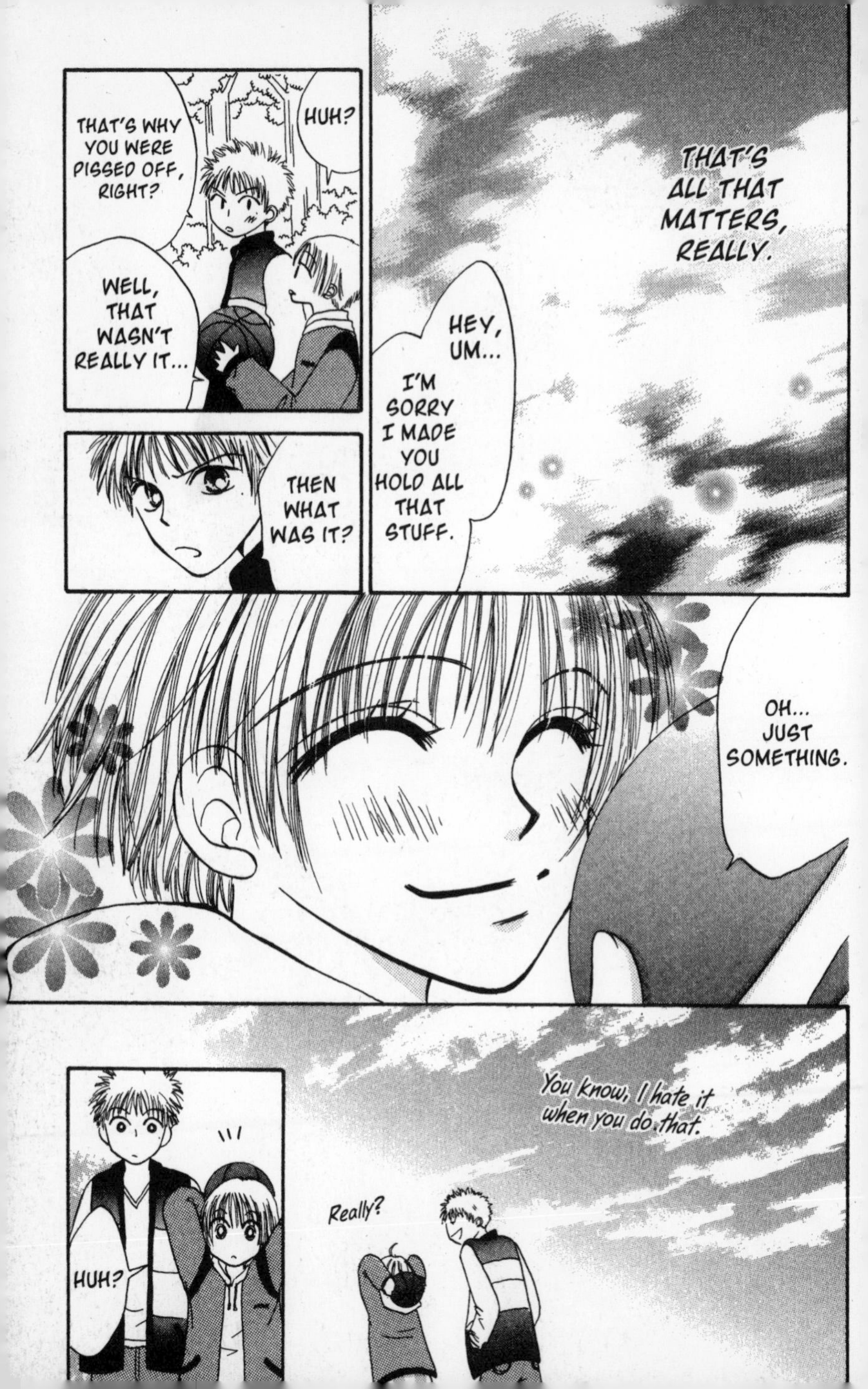
THAT'S ALL THAT MATTERS, REALLY.
HEY, UM...
I'M SORRY I MADE YOU HOLD ALL THAT STUFF.
HUH?
THAT'S WHY YOU WERE PISSED OFF, RIGHT?
WELL, THAT WASN'T REALLY IT...
THEN WHAT WAS IT?
OH... JUST SOMETHING.
You know, I hate it when you do that.
Really?
HUH?

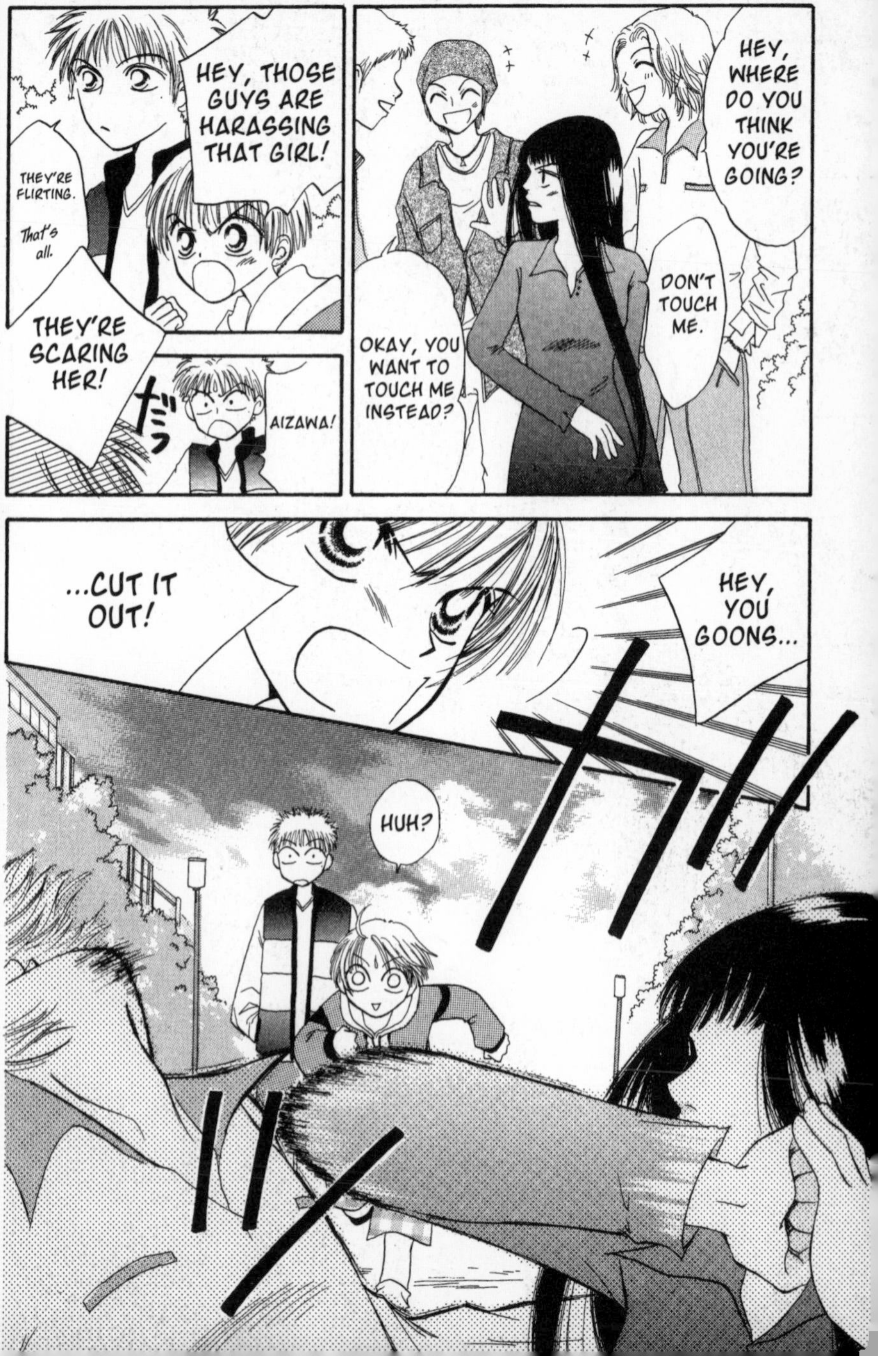
HEY, WHERE DO YOU THINK YOU'RE GOING?
DON'T TOUCH ME.
OKAY, YOU WANT TO TOUCH ME INSTEAD?
HEY, THOSE GUYS ARE HARASSING THAT GIRL!
THEY'RE FLIRTING.
That's all.
THEY'RE SCARING HER!
AIZAWA!
HEY, YOU GOONS...
...CUT IT OUT!
HUH?

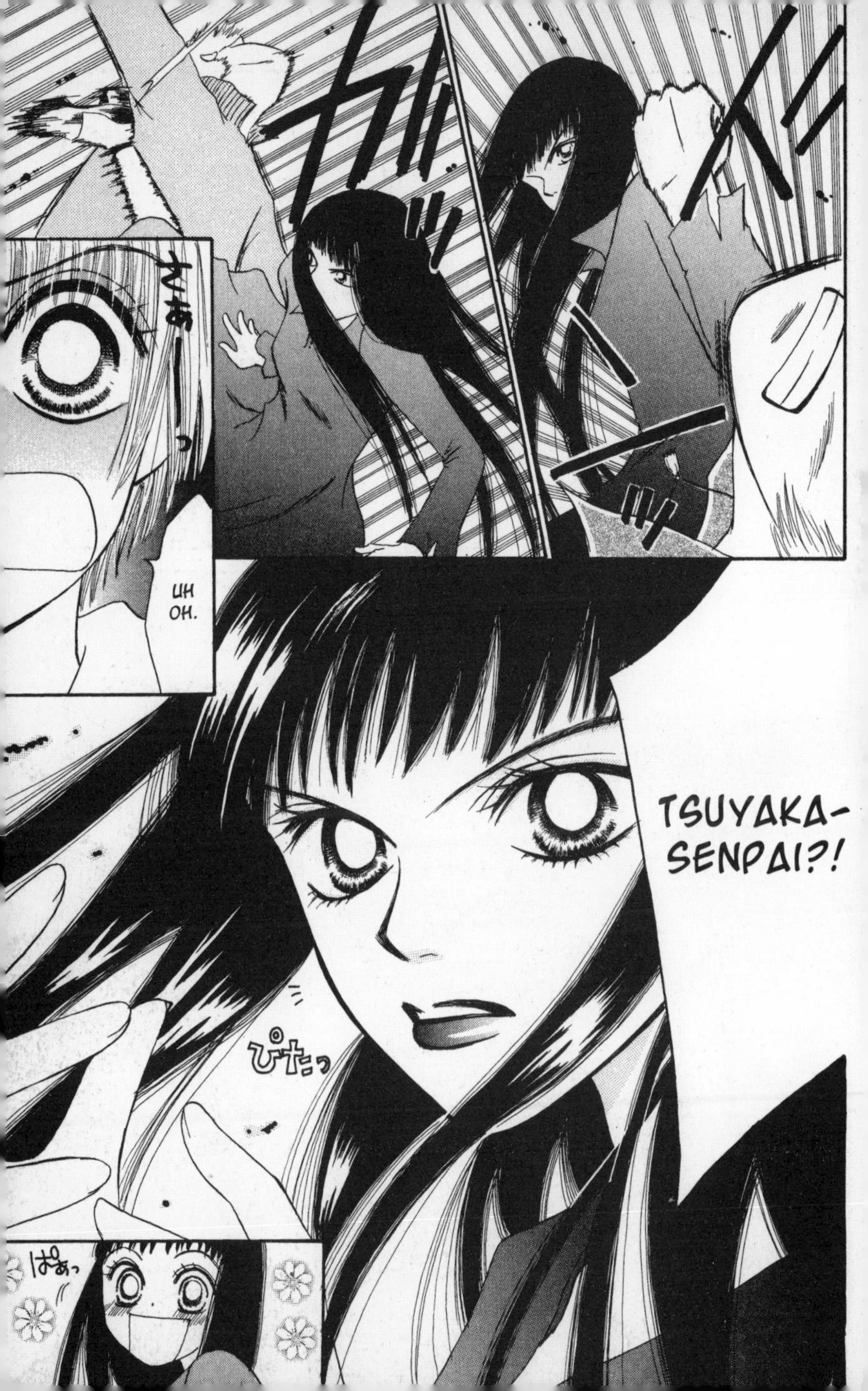
さぁーーっ
UH OH.
TSUYAKA-SENPAI?!
ぴたっ
ぱあっ

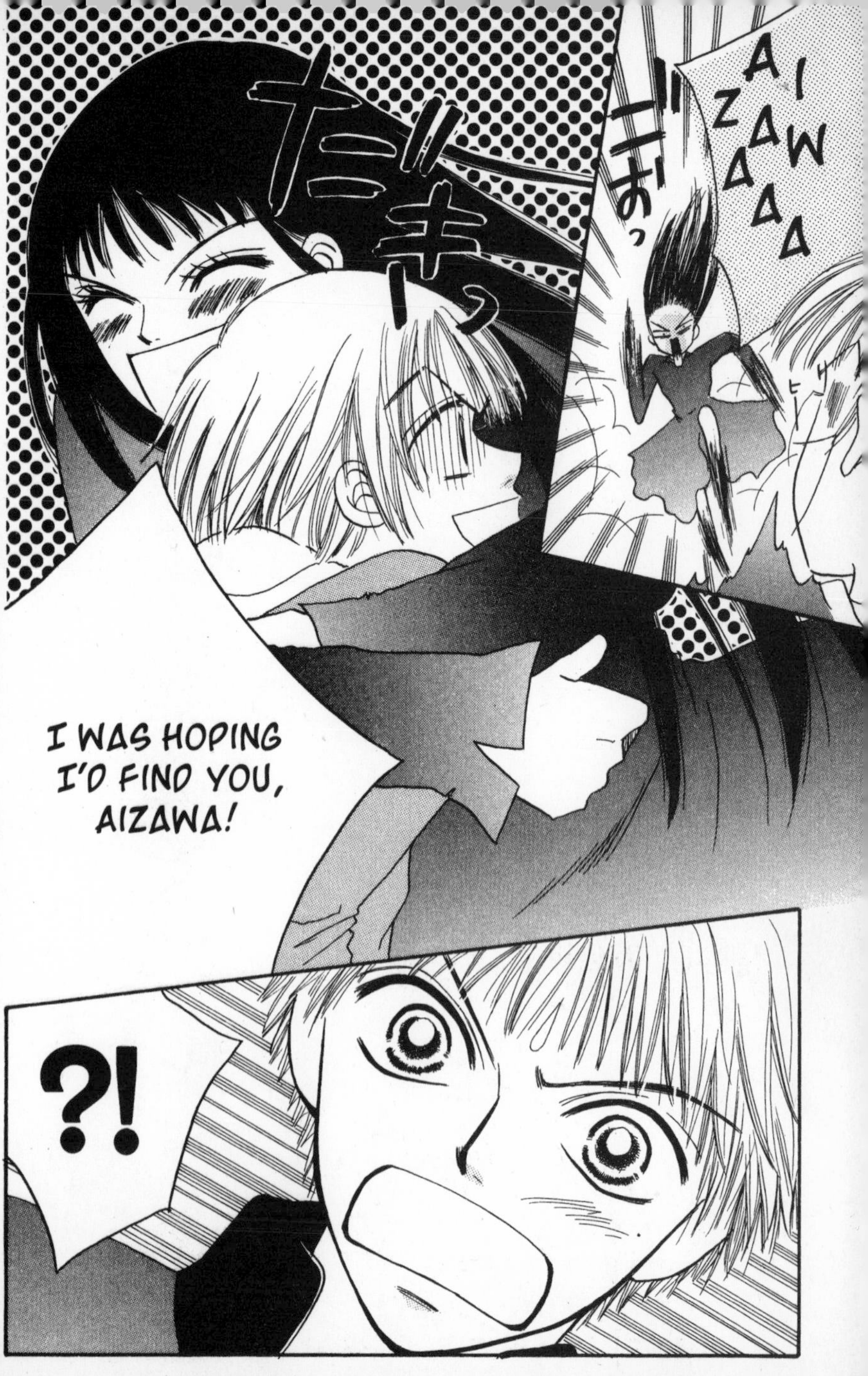
AIZAWAAAAA
ごおっ
だきっ
I WAS HOPING I'D FIND YOU, AIZAWA!
?!

ぱわー゜

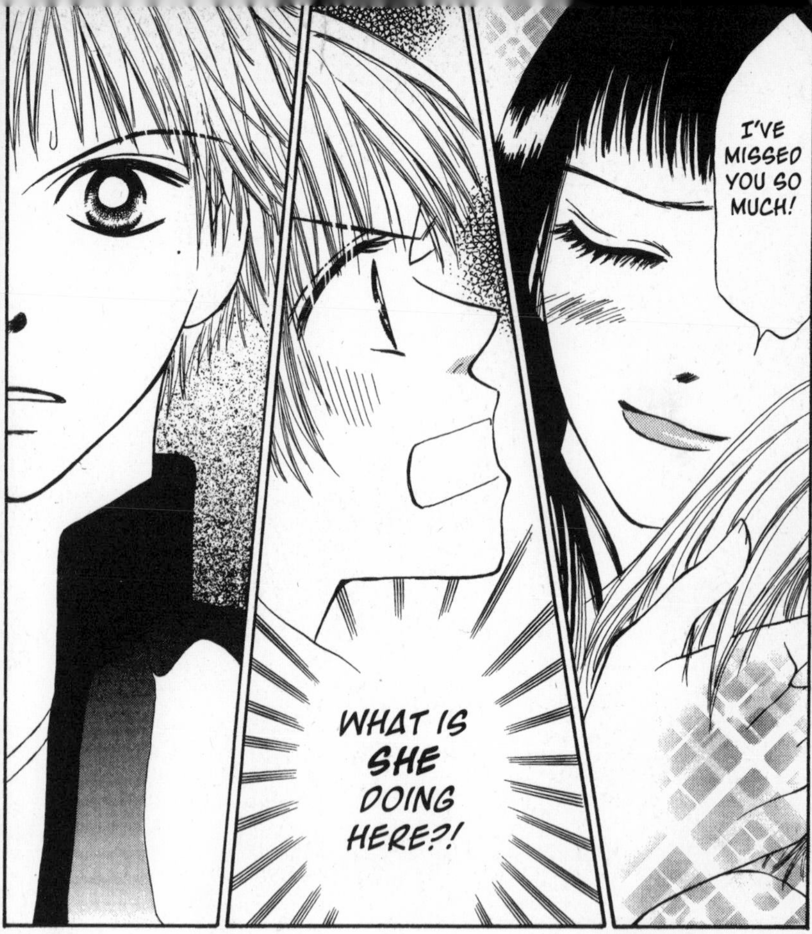
I'VE MISSED YOU SO MUCH!
WHAT IS SHE DOING HERE?!

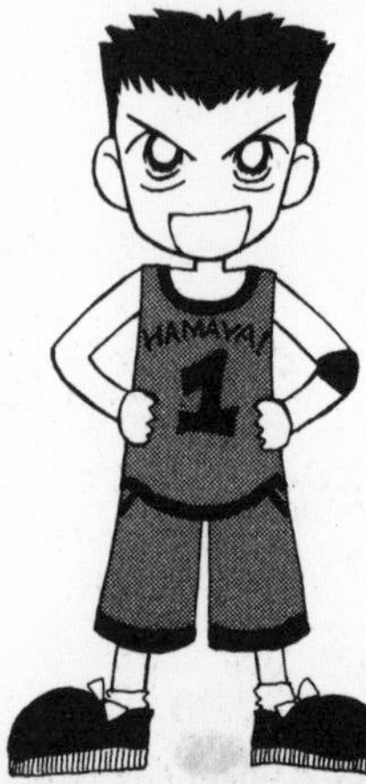

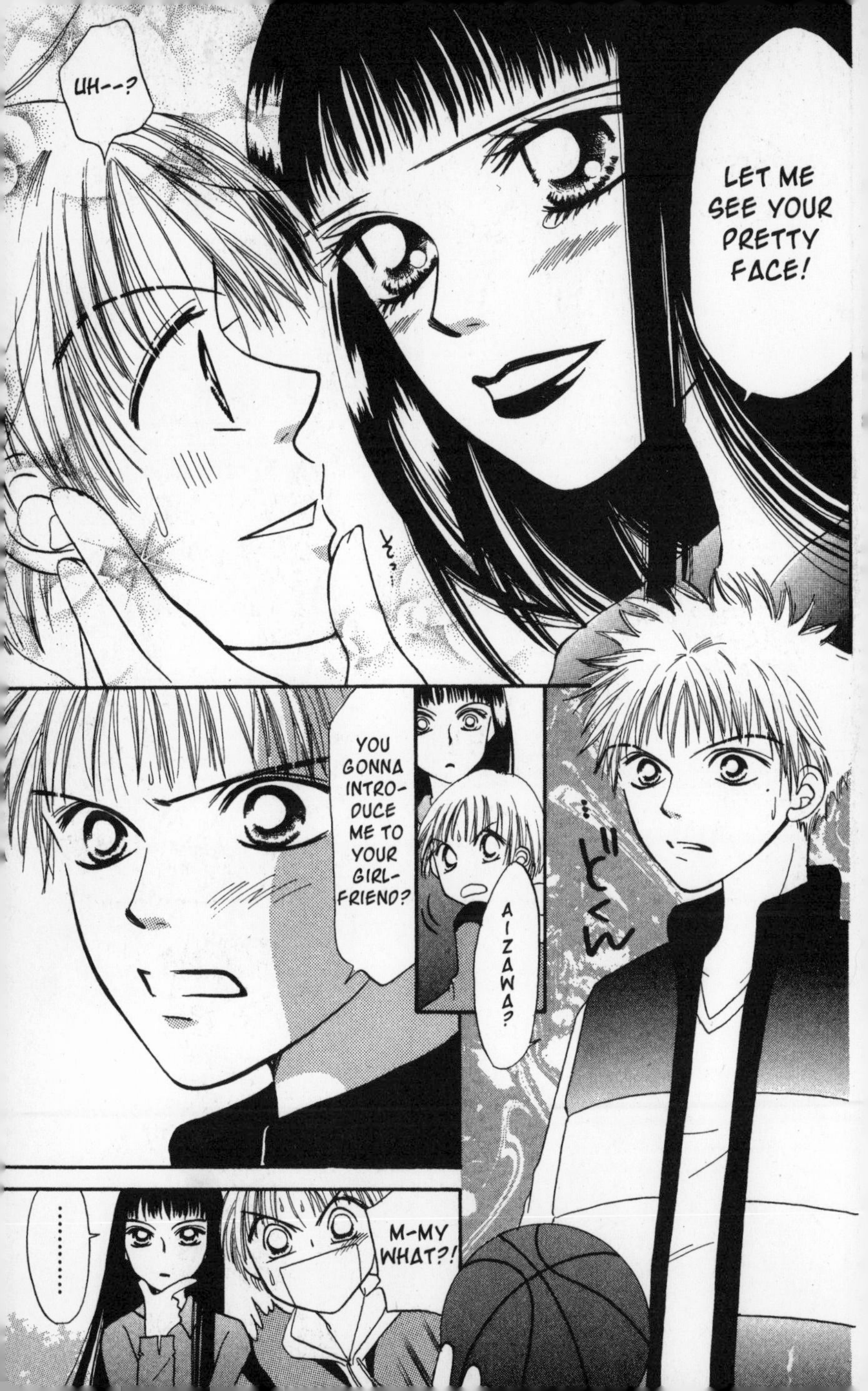
LET ME SEE YOUR PRETTY FACE!
UH--?
...
AIZAWA?
YOU GONNA INTRO-DUCE ME TO YOUR GIRL-FRIEND?
M-MY WHAT?!
......

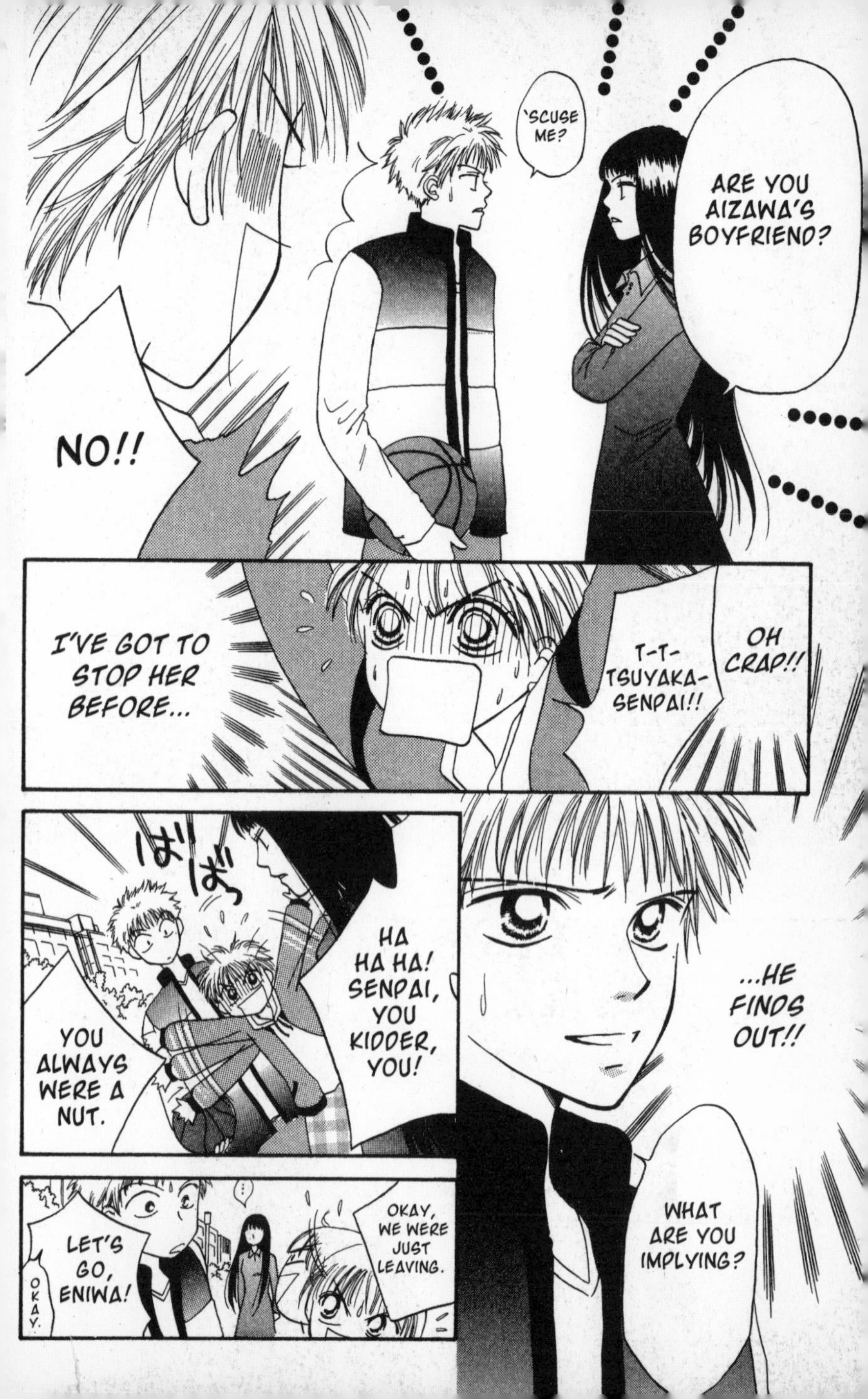
ARE YOU AIZAWA'S BOYFRIEND?
`SCUSE ME?
NO!!
OH CRAP!!
T-T-TSUYAKA-SENPAI!!
I'VE GOT TO STOP HER BEFORE...
...HE FINDS OUT!!
WHAT ARE YOU IMPLYING?
ばばっ
HA HA HA! SENPAI, YOU KIDDER, YOU!
YOU ALWAYS WERE A NUT.
OKAY, WE WERE JUST LEAVING.
...
LET'S GO, ENIWA!
OKAY.

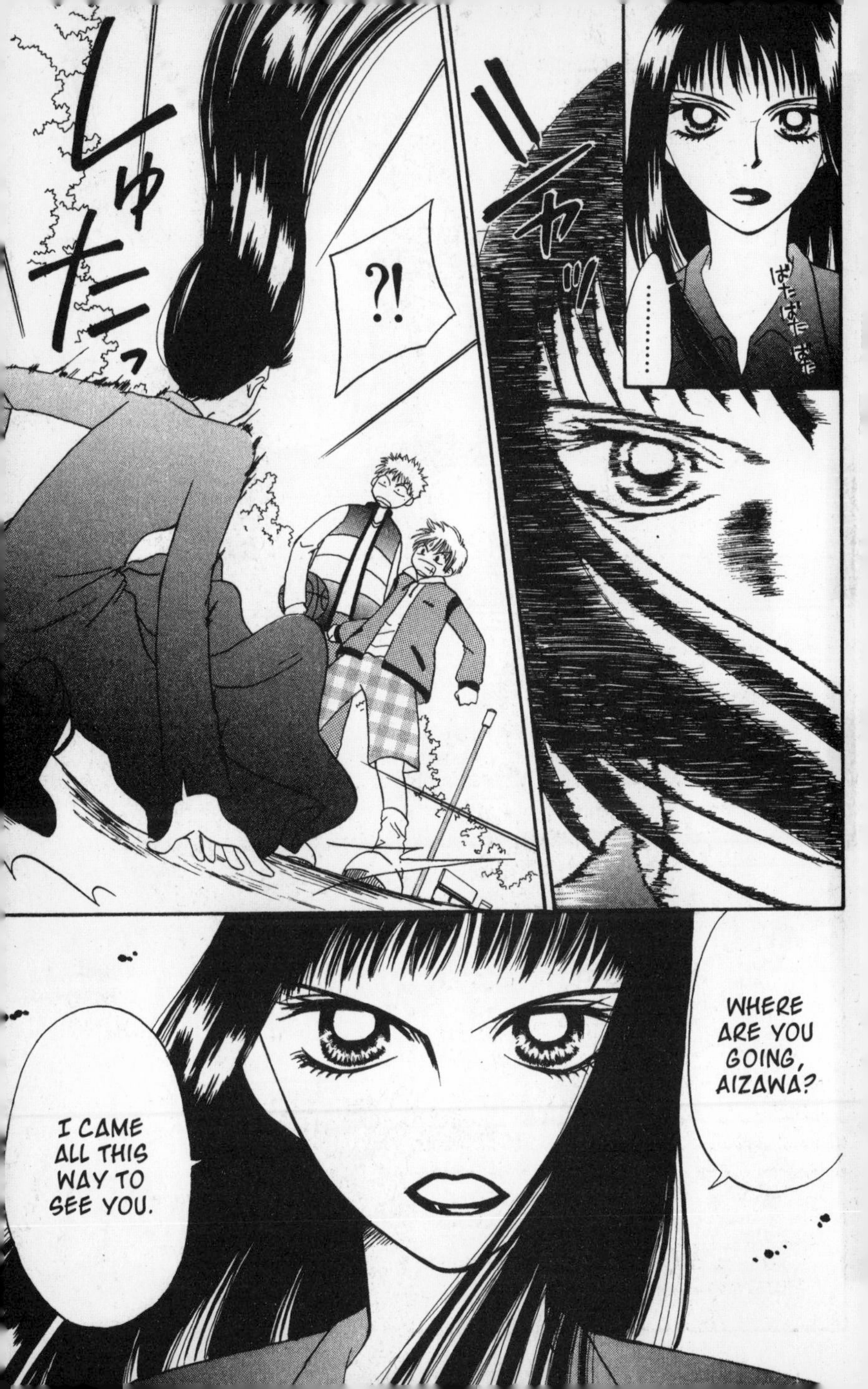
......
ぱたぱた ぱた
?!
しゅたーっ
WHERE ARE YOU GOING, AIZAWA?
I CAME ALL THIS WAY TO SEE YOU.

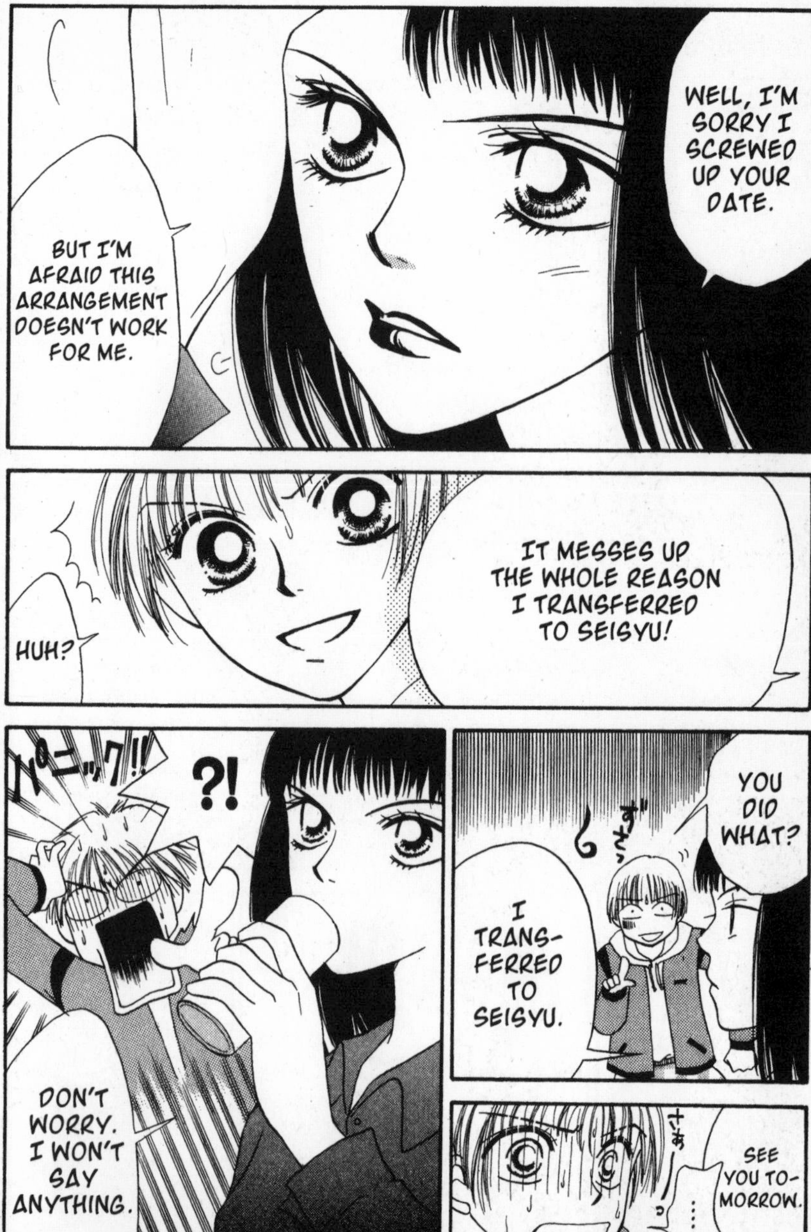
WELL, I'M SORRY I SCREWED UP YOUR DATE.
BUT I'M AFRAID THIS ARRANGEMENT DOESN'T WORK FOR ME.
IT MESSES UP THE WHOLE REASON I TRANSFERRED TO SEISYU!
HUH?
YOU DID WHAT?
I TRANS-FERRED TO SEISYU.
SEE YOU TO-MORROW.
……
パニック!!
?!
DON'T WORRY. I WON'T SAY ANYTHING.

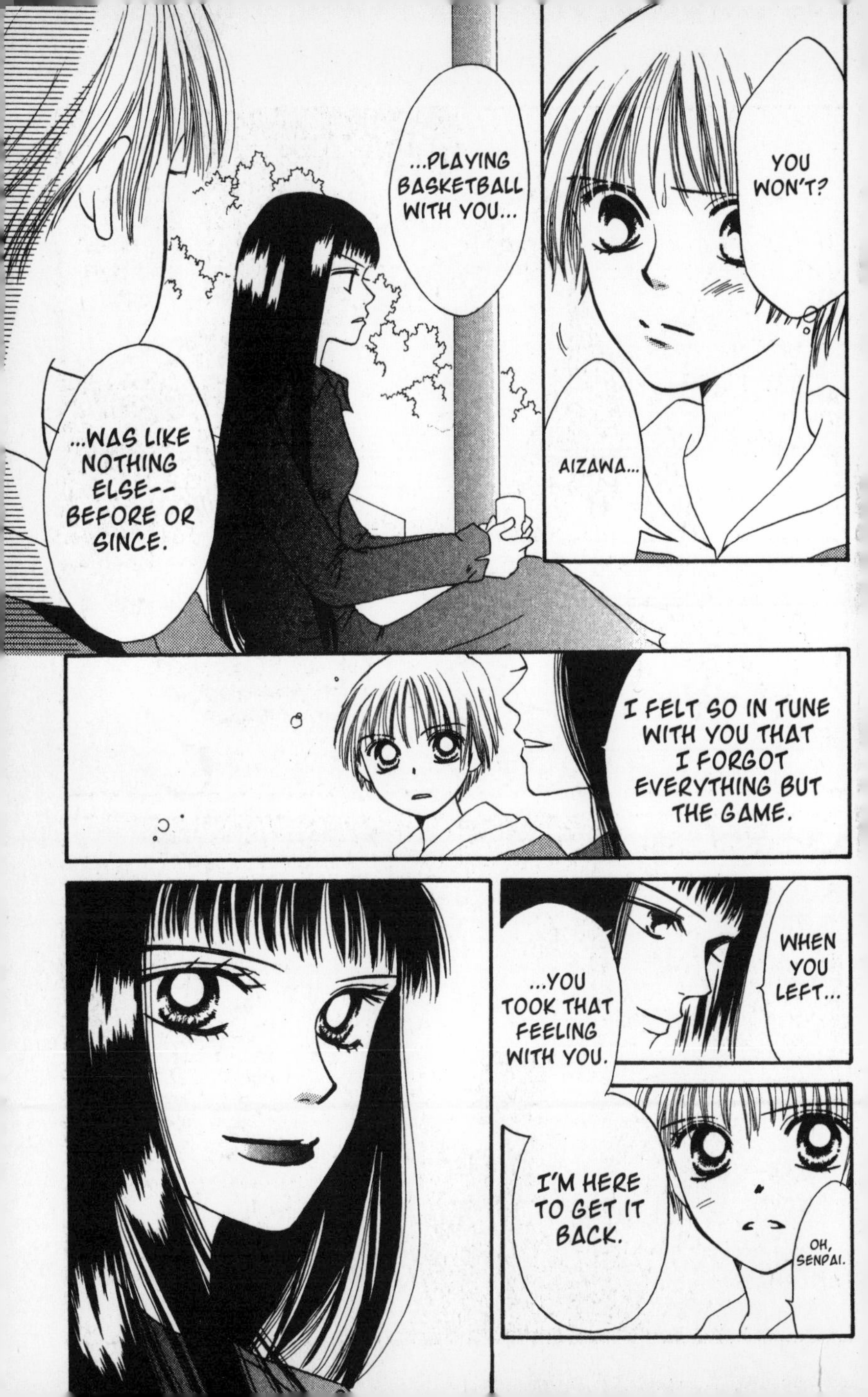
YOU WON'T?
AIZAWA...
...PLAYING BASKETBALL WITH YOU...
...WAS LIKE NOTHING ELSE-- BEFORE OR SINCE.
I FELT SO IN TUNE WITH YOU THAT I FORGOT EVERYTHING BUT THE GAME.
WHEN YOU LEFT...
...YOU TOOK THAT FEELING WITH YOU.
I'M HERE TO GET IT BACK.
OH, SENPAI.

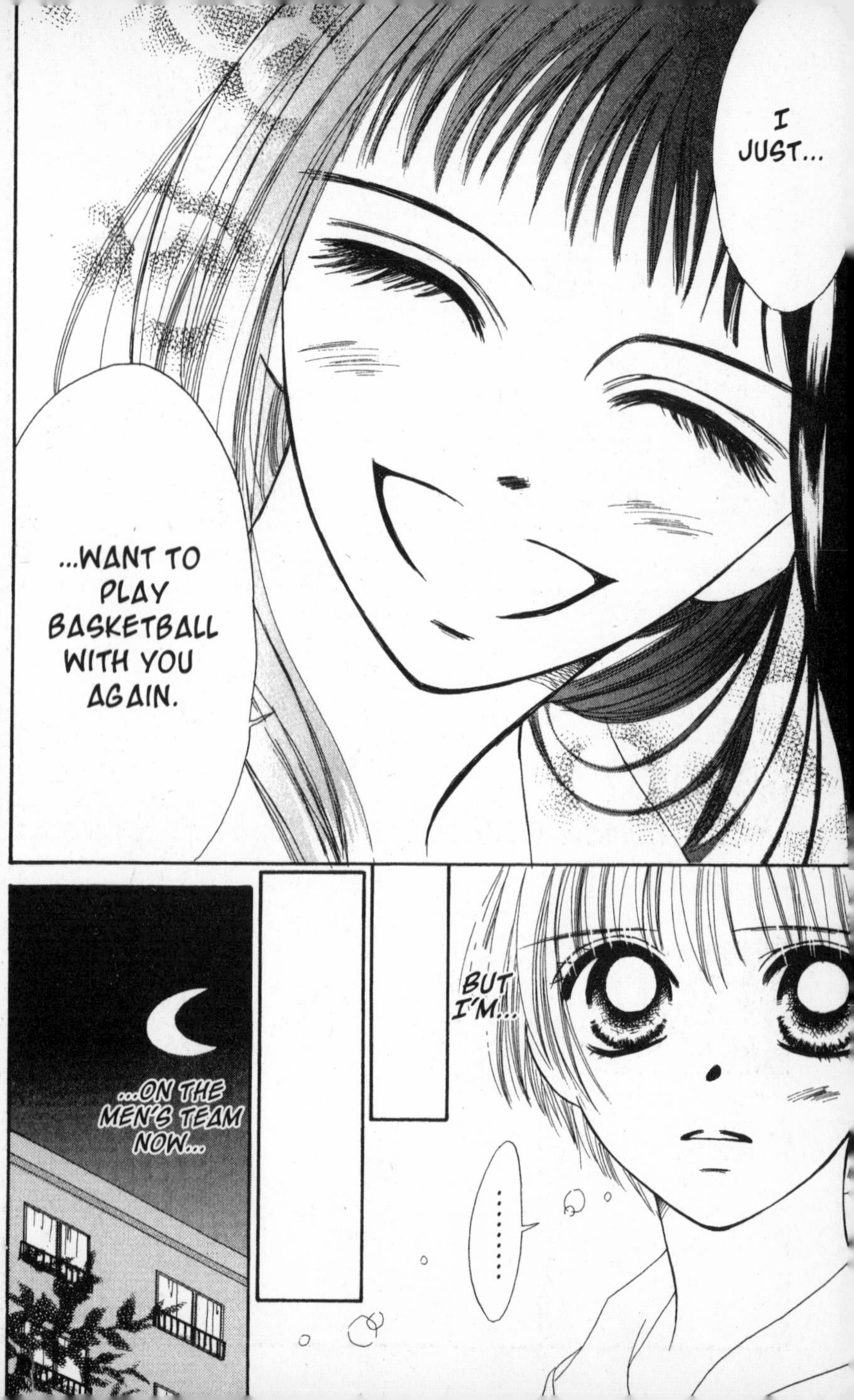
I JUST...
...WANT TO PLAY BASKETBALL WITH YOU AGAIN.
BUT I'M...
......
...ON THE MEN'S TEAM NOW...

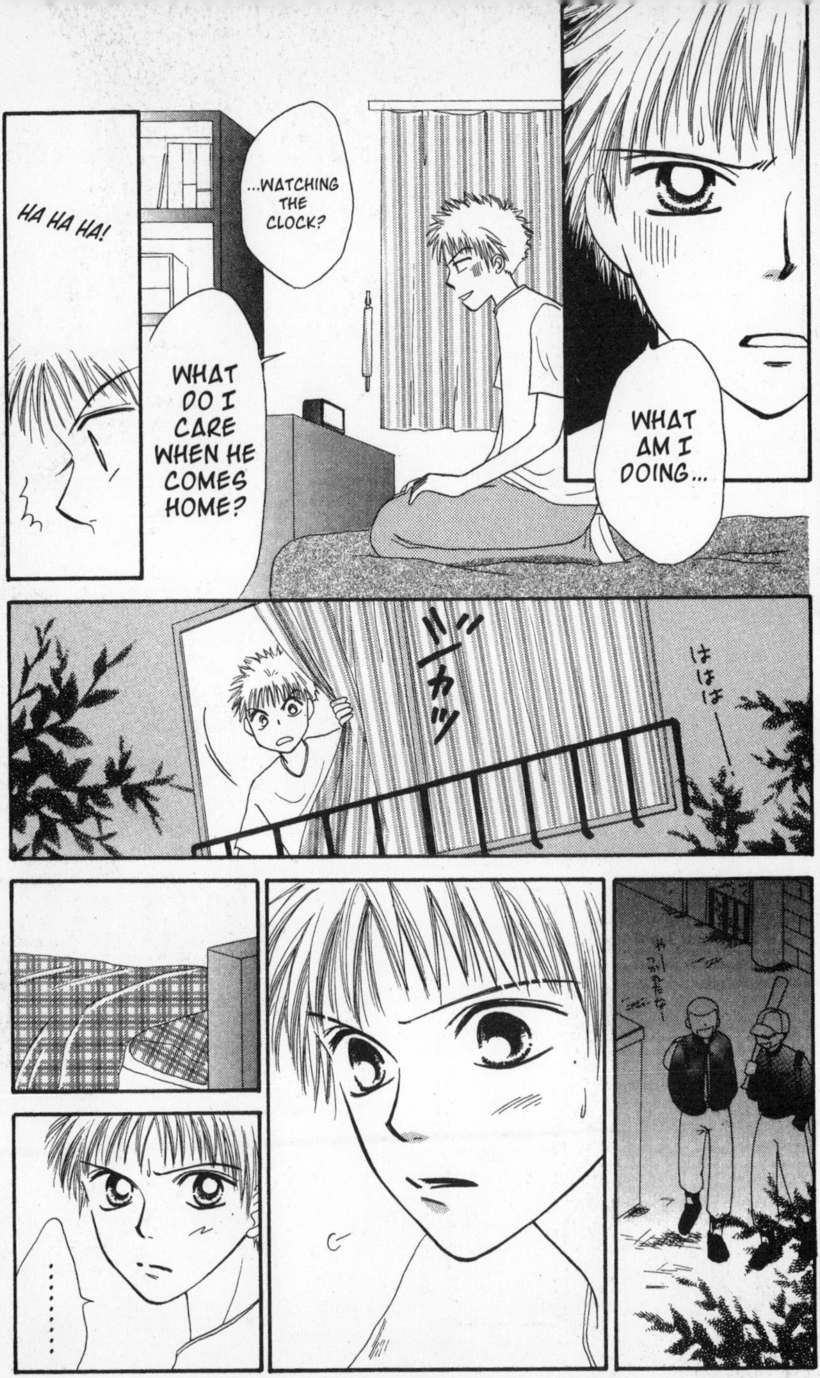
WHAT AM I DOING...
...WATCHING THE CLOCK?
WHAT DO I CARE WHEN HE COMES HOME?
HA HA HA!
ははは―
......

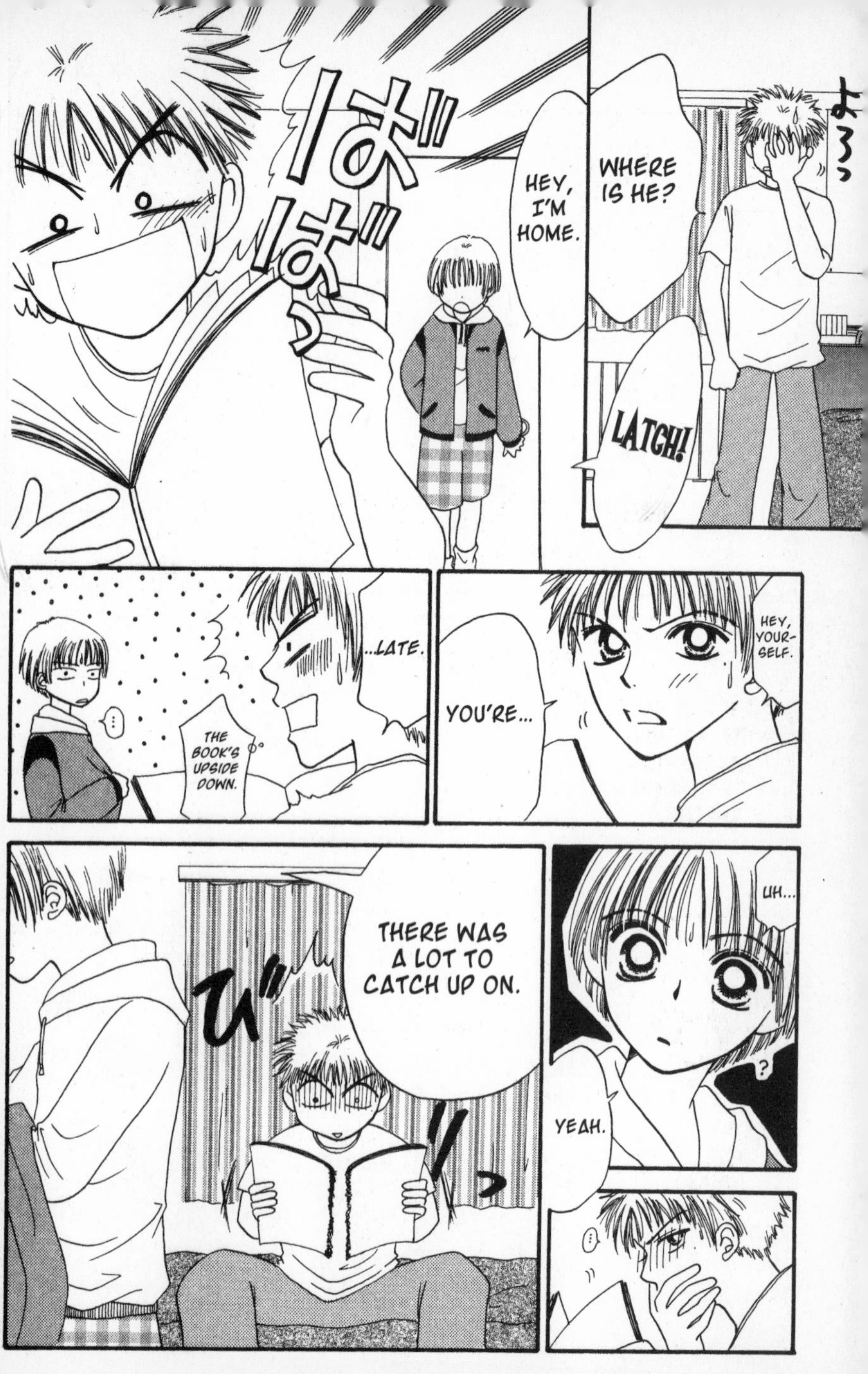
よろっ
WHERE IS HE?
LATCH!
HEY, I'M HOME.
ばばっ
HEY, YOURSELF.
YOU'RE...
...LATE.
...
THE BOOK'S UPSIDE DOWN.
UH...
?
YEAH.
...
THERE WAS A LOT TO CATCH UP ON.
び
!!っ

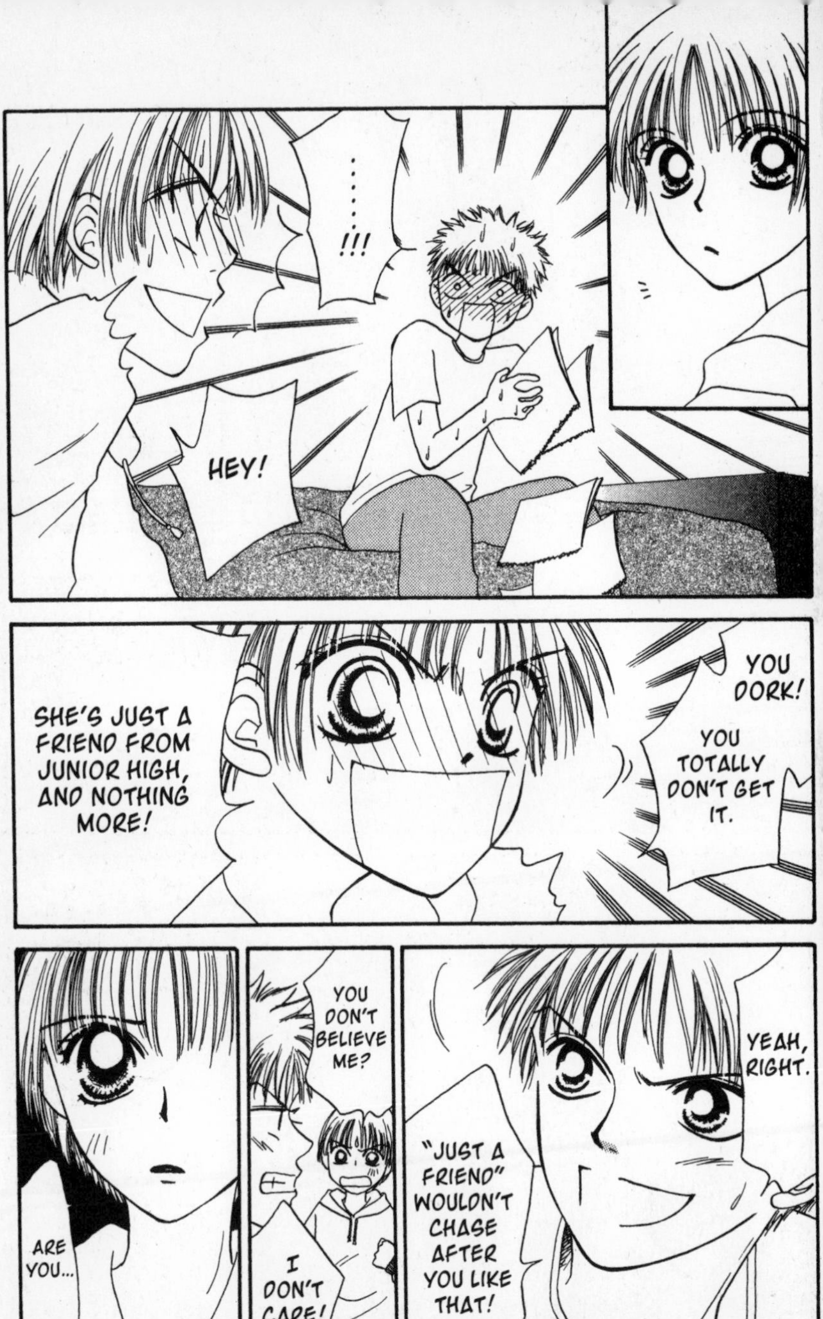
......!!!
HEY!
YOU DORK!
YOU TOTALLY DON'T GET IT.
SHE'S JUST A FRIEND FROM JUNIOR HIGH, AND NOTHING MORE!
YEAH, RIGHT.
"JUST A FRIEND" WOULDN'T CHASE AFTER YOU LIKE THAT!
YOU DON'T BELIEVE ME?
I DON'T CARE!
ARE YOU...

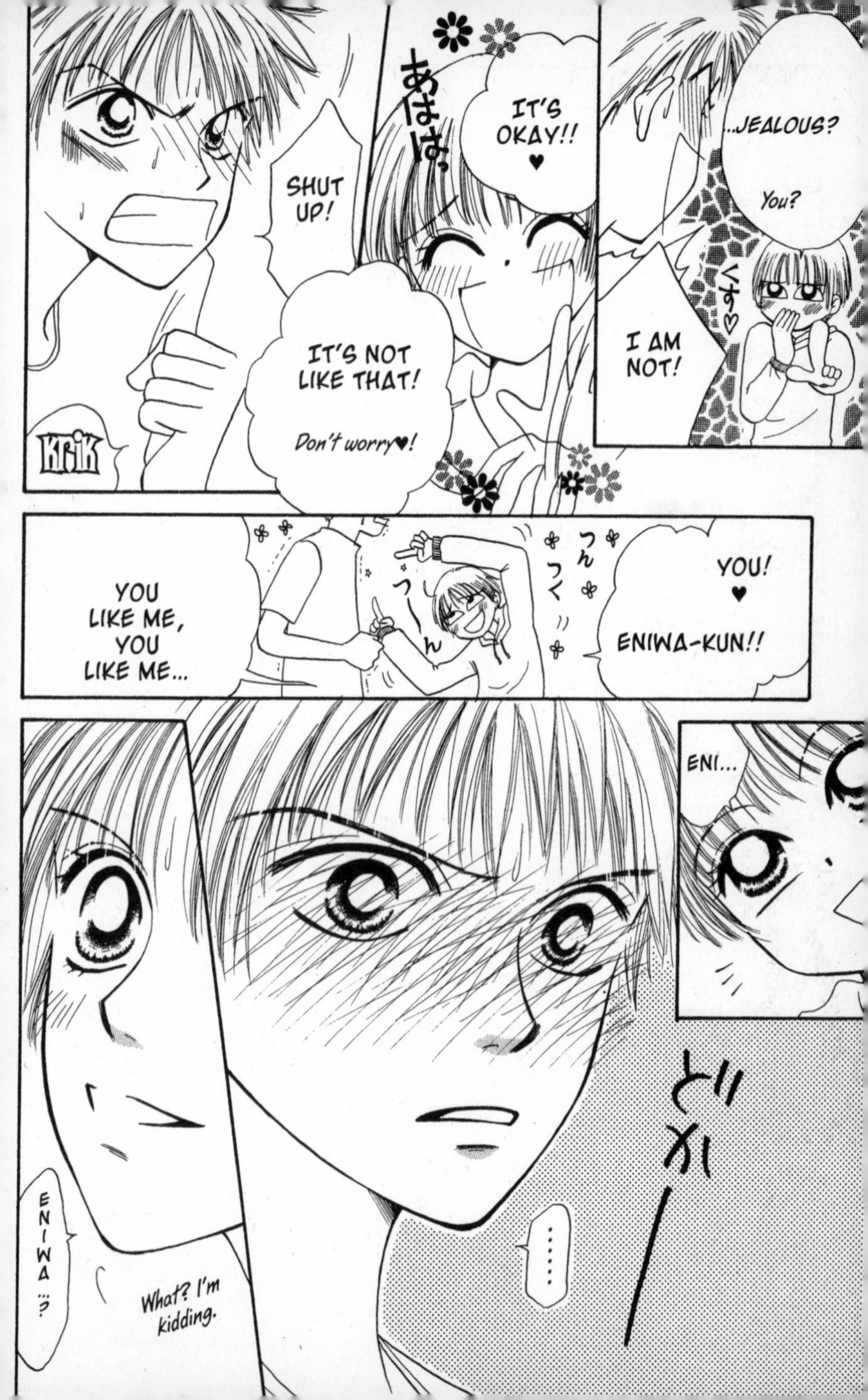

...JEALOUS?
You?
くす♡
I AM NOT!
あはは
IT'S OKAY!! ♥
IT'S NOT LIKE THAT!
Don't worry♥!
SHUT UP!
KRIK
YOU! ♥
ENIWA-KUN!!
つんつく
つーん
YOU LIKE ME, YOU LIKE ME...
ENI...
どれー
......
ENIWA...?
What? I'm kidding.

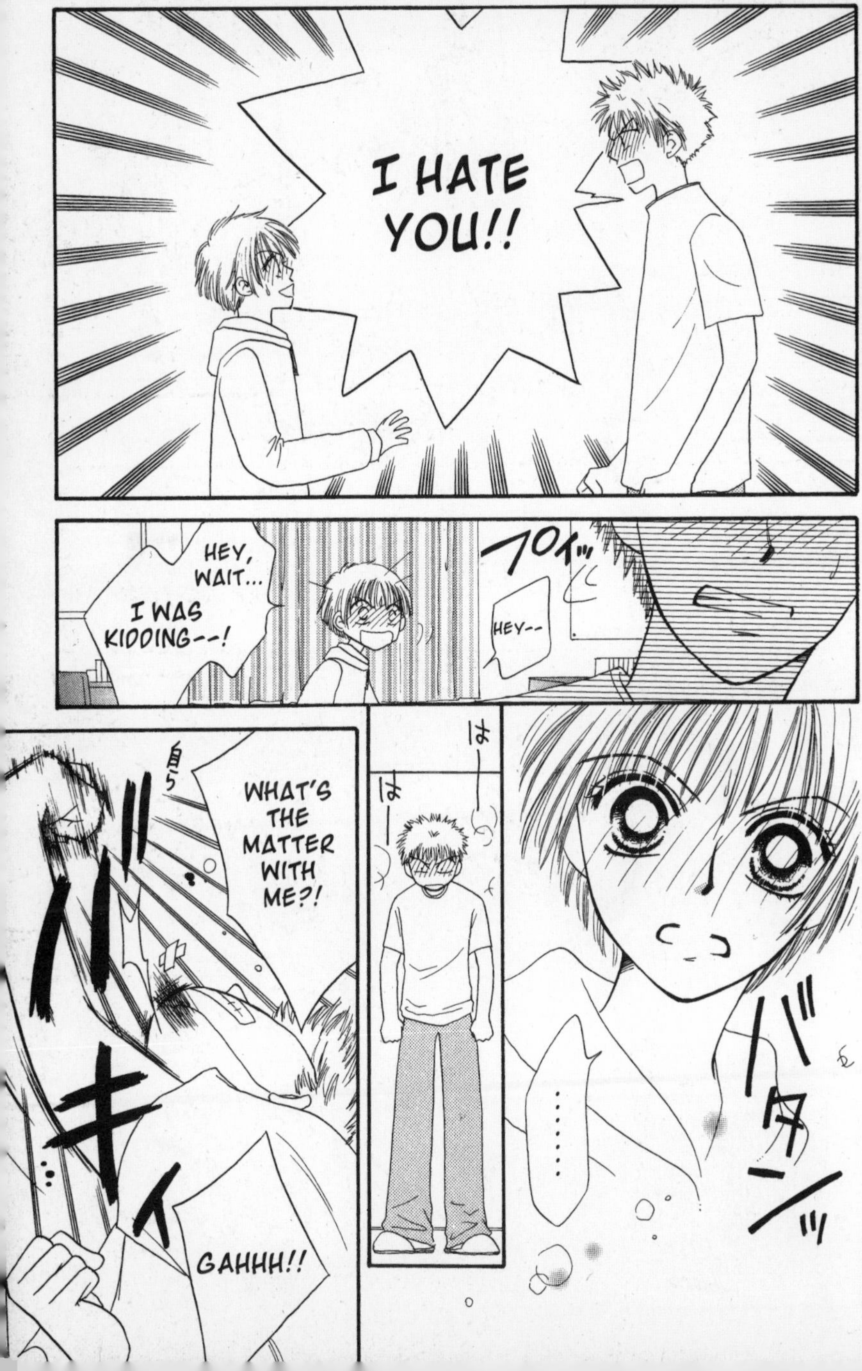
I HATE YOU!!
フイッ
HEY--
HEY, WAIT...
I WAS KIDDING--!
バタンッ
......
はー
はー
WHAT'S THE MATTER WITH ME?!
GAHHH!!

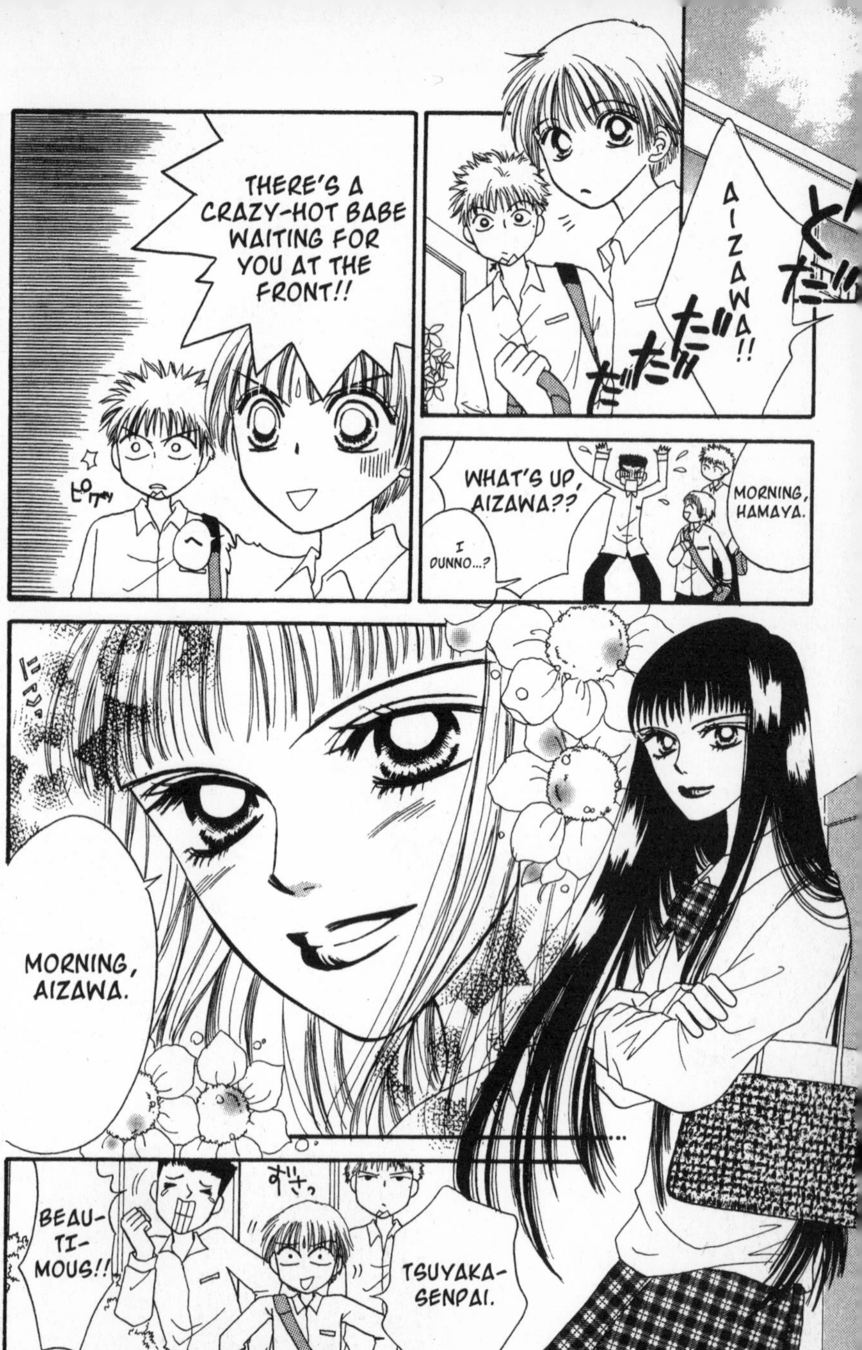
AIZAWA!!
MORNING, HAMAYA.
WHAT'S UP, AIZAWA??
I DUNNO...?
THERE'S A CRAZY-HOT BABE WAITING FOR YOU AT THE FRONT!!
ピクッ
にこっ
MORNING, AIZAWA.
...
TSUYAKA-SENPAI.
すさっ
BEAUTI-MOUS!!

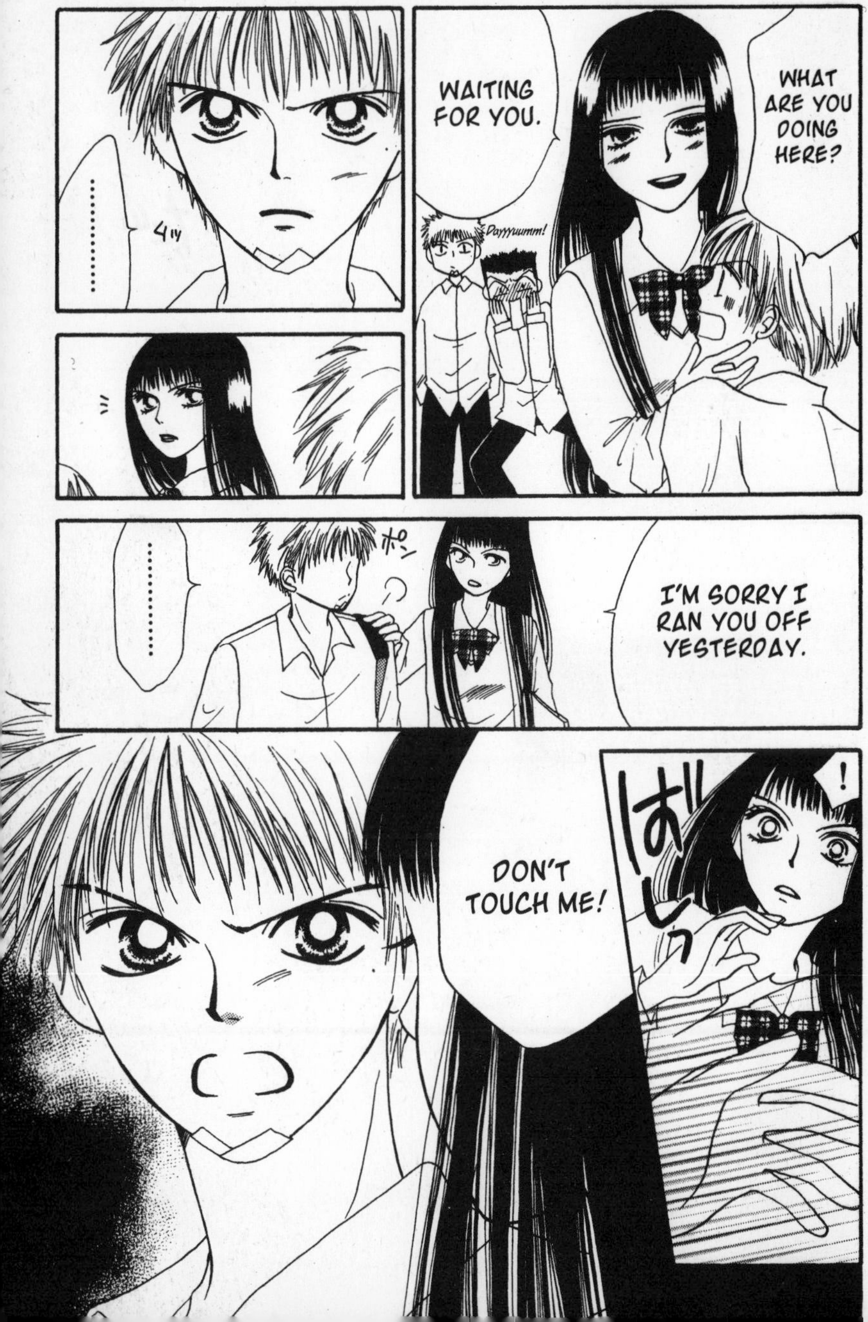
WHAT ARE YOU DOING HERE?
WAITING FOR YOU.
Dayyyuumm!
……
ムッ
I'M SORRY I RAN YOU OFF YESTERDAY.
ポン
……
!
ばしっ
DON'T TOUCH ME!

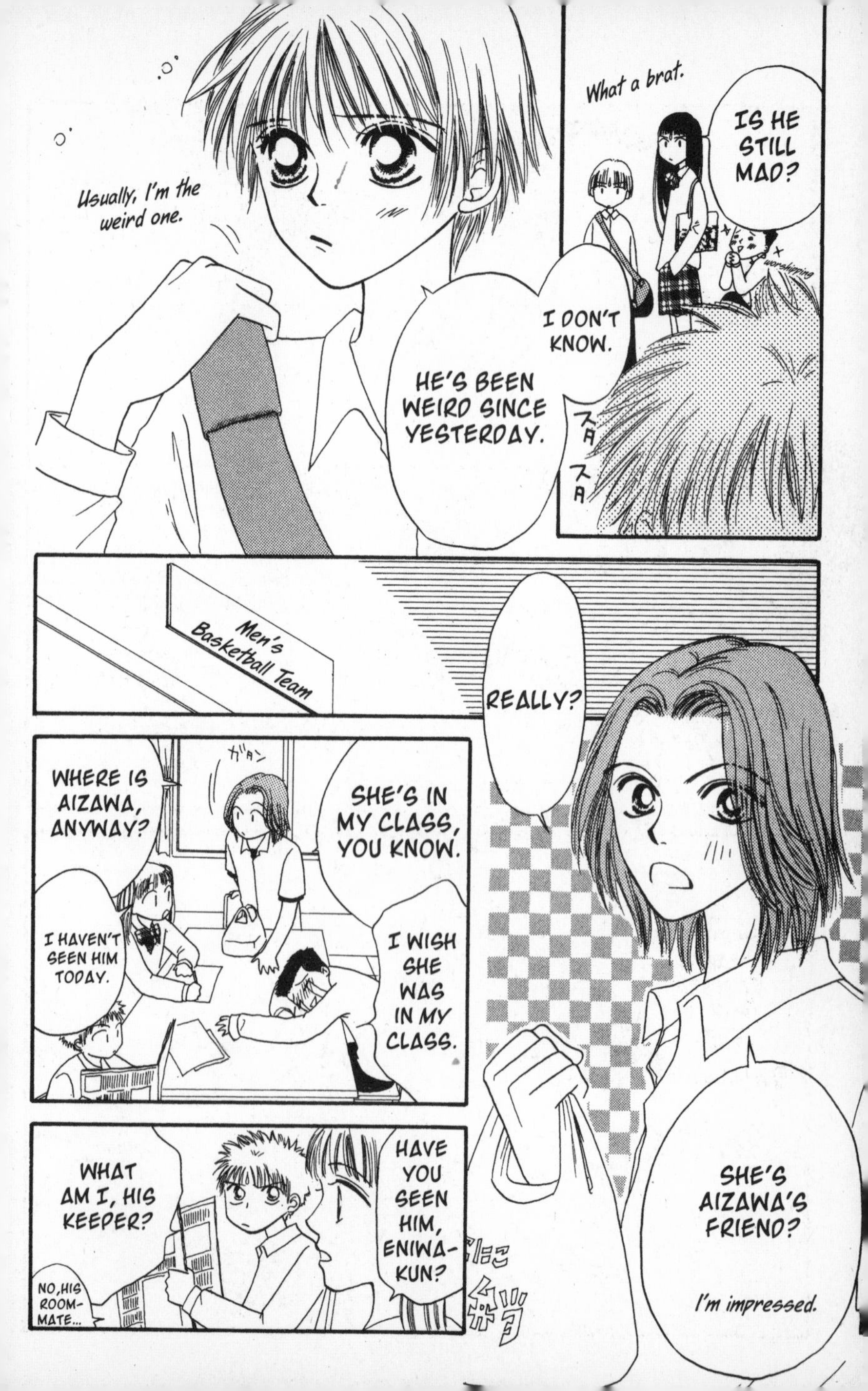
What a brat.
IS HE STILL MAD?
worshipping
I DON'T KNOW.
HE'S BEEN WEIRD SINCE YESTERDAY.
Usually, I'm the weird one.
REALLY?
SHE'S AIZAWA'S FRIEND?
I'm impressed.
Men's Basketball Team
SHE'S IN MY CLASS, YOU KNOW.
I WISH SHE WAS IN MY CLASS.
WHERE IS AIZAWA, ANYWAY?
I HAVEN'T SEEN HIM TODAY.
HAVE YOU SEEN HIM, ENIWA-KUN?
WHAT AM I, HIS KEEPER?
NO, HIS ROOM-MATE...

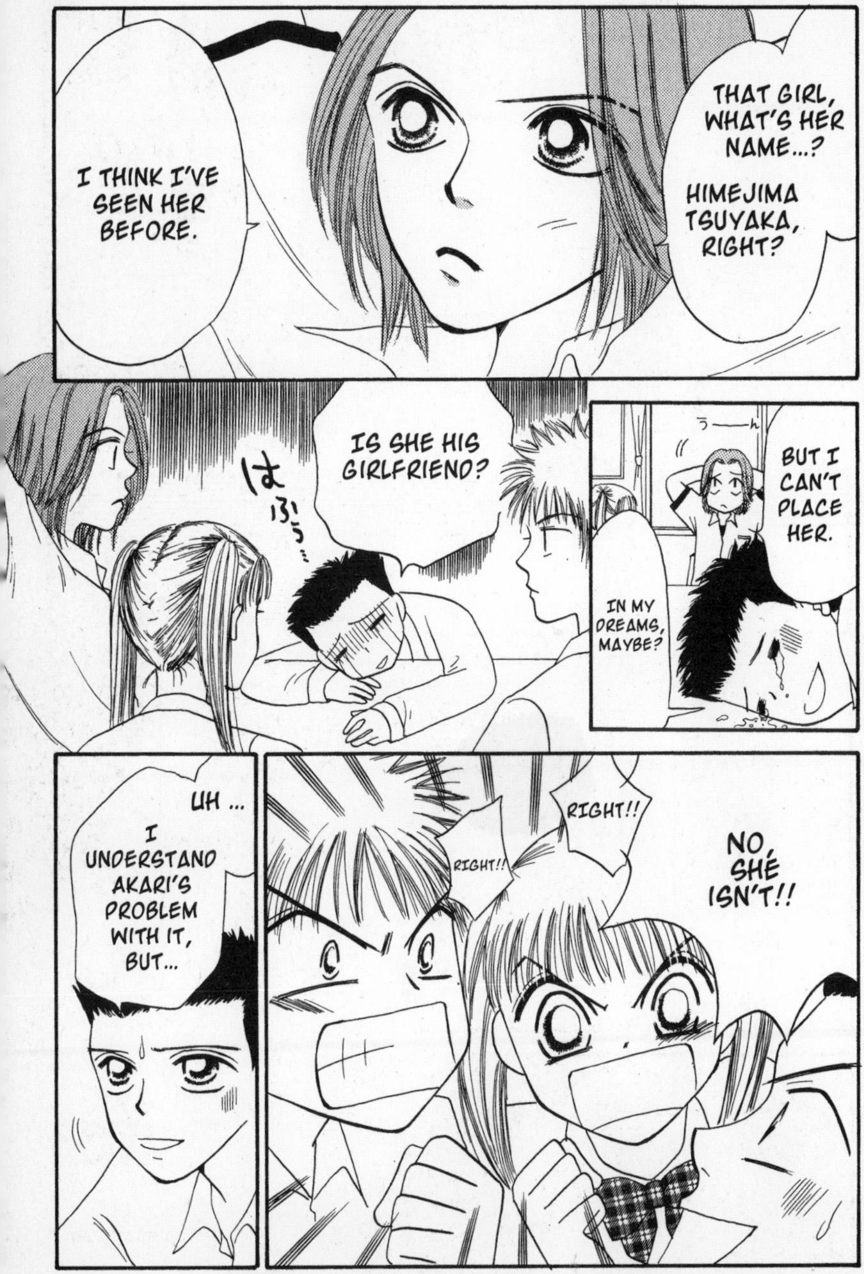
THAT GIRL, WHAT'S HER NAME...?
HIMEJIMA TSUYAKA, RIGHT?
I THINK I'VE SEEN HER BEFORE.
う——ん
BUT I CAN'T PLACE HER.
IN MY DREAMS, MAYBE?
IS SHE HIS GIRLFRIEND?
はふぅ…
NO, SHE ISN'T!!
RIGHT!!
RIGHT!!
UH ...
I UNDERSTAND AKARI'S PROBLEM WITH IT, BUT...

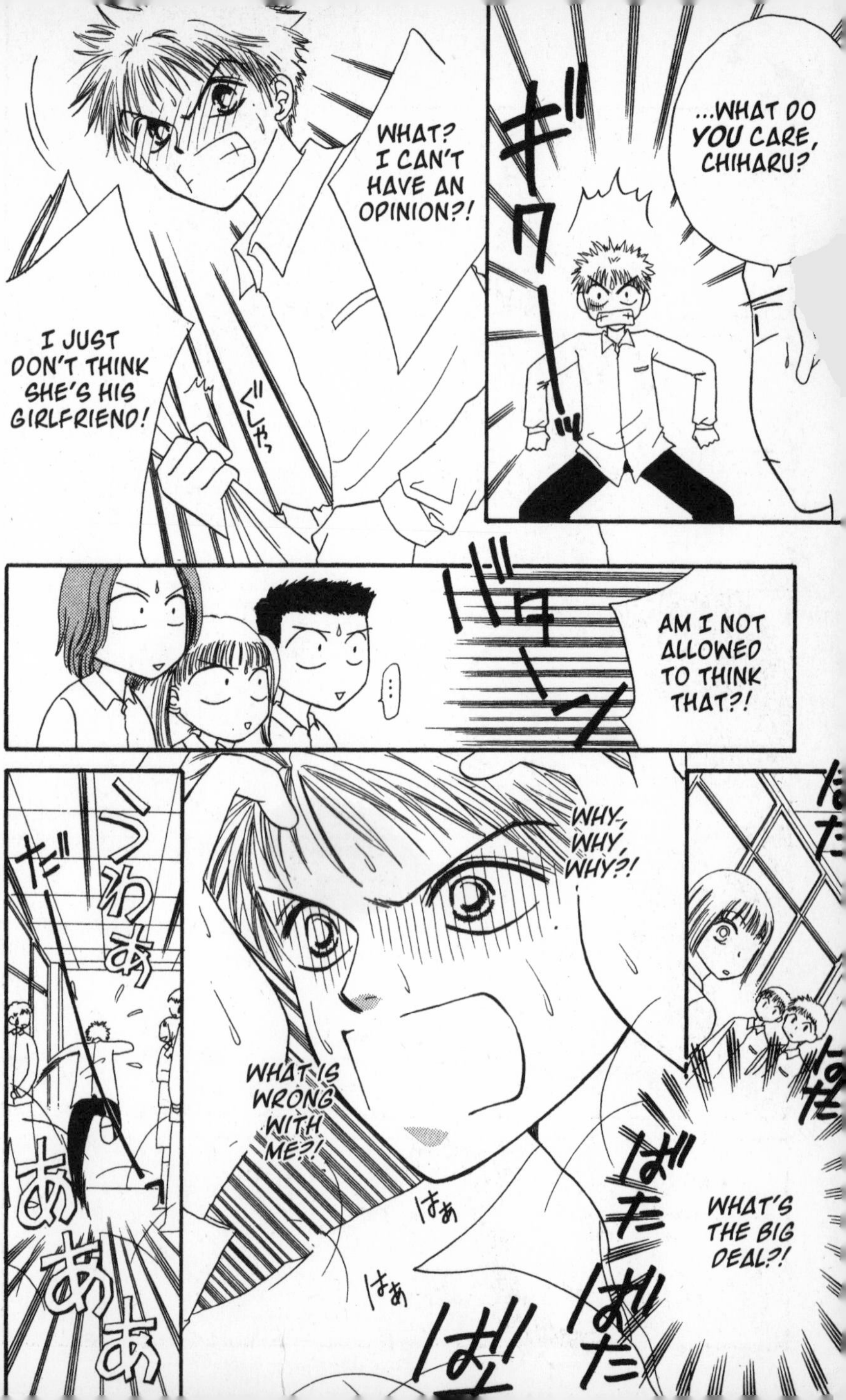
...WHAT DO YOU CARE, CHIHARU?
ギクーッ
WHAT? I CAN'T HAVE AN OPINION?!
I JUST DON'T THINK SHE'S HIS GIRLFRIEND!
ぐしゃっ
AM I NOT ALLOWED TO THINK THAT?!
バターン
...
WHY, WHY, WHY?!
WHAT IS WRONG WITH ME?!
WHAT'S THE BIG DEAL?!
はぁ
はぁ
うわあ
だ
あああ

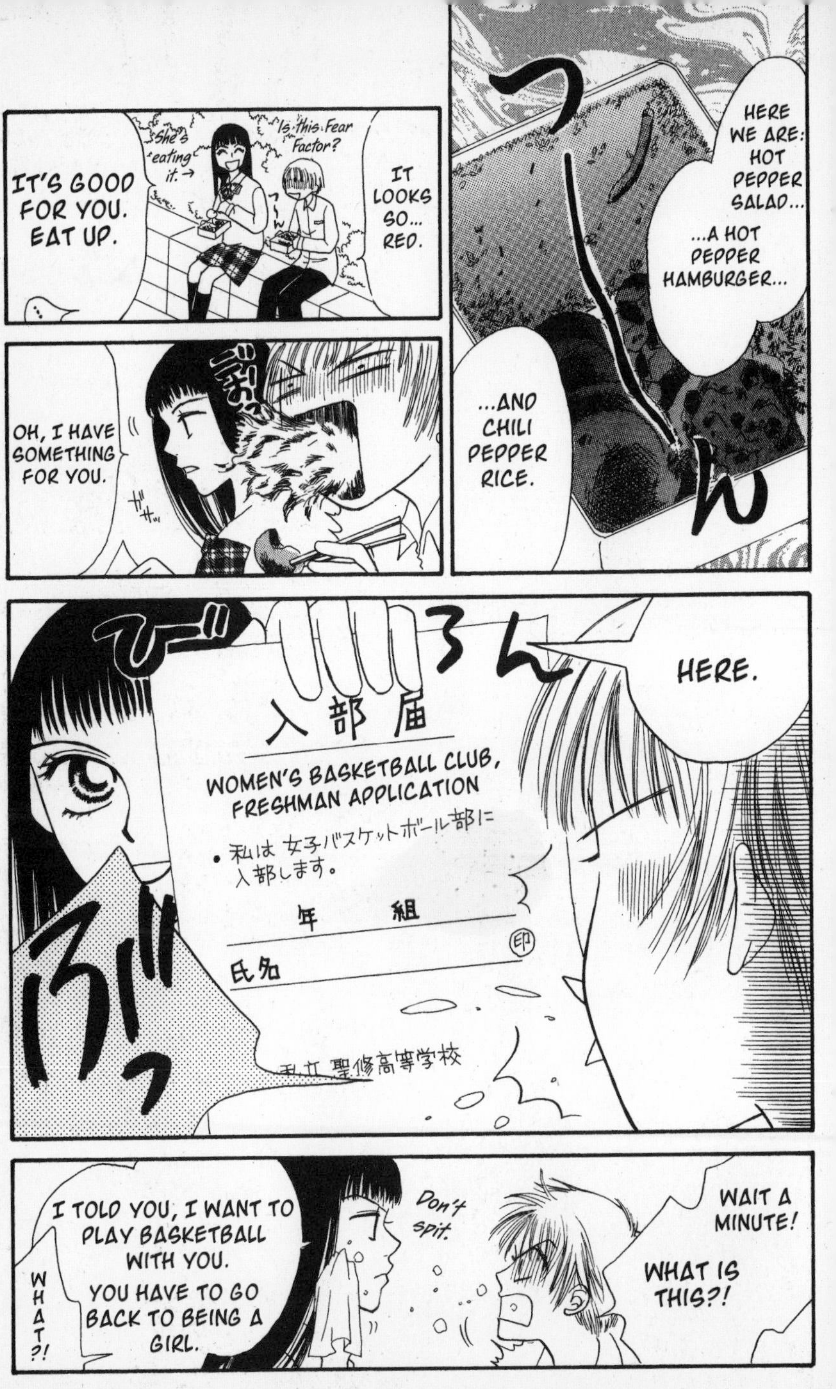
HERE WE ARE: HOT PEPPER SALAD...
...A HOT PEPPER HAMBURGER...
...AND CHILI PEPPER RICE.
IT LOOKS SO... RED.
Is this Fear Factor?
She's eating it. →
IT'S GOOD FOR YOU. EAT UP.
...
OH, I HAVE SOMETHING FOR YOU.
HERE.
入部届
WOMEN'S BASKETBALL CLUB, FRESHMAN APPLICATION
・私は 女子バスケットボール部に 入部します。
年 組
印
氏名
私立 聖修高等学校
WAIT A MINUTE!
WHAT IS THIS?!
Don't spit.
I TOLD YOU, I WANT TO PLAY BASKETBALL WITH YOU.
YOU HAVE TO GO BACK TO BEING A GIRL.
WHAT?!

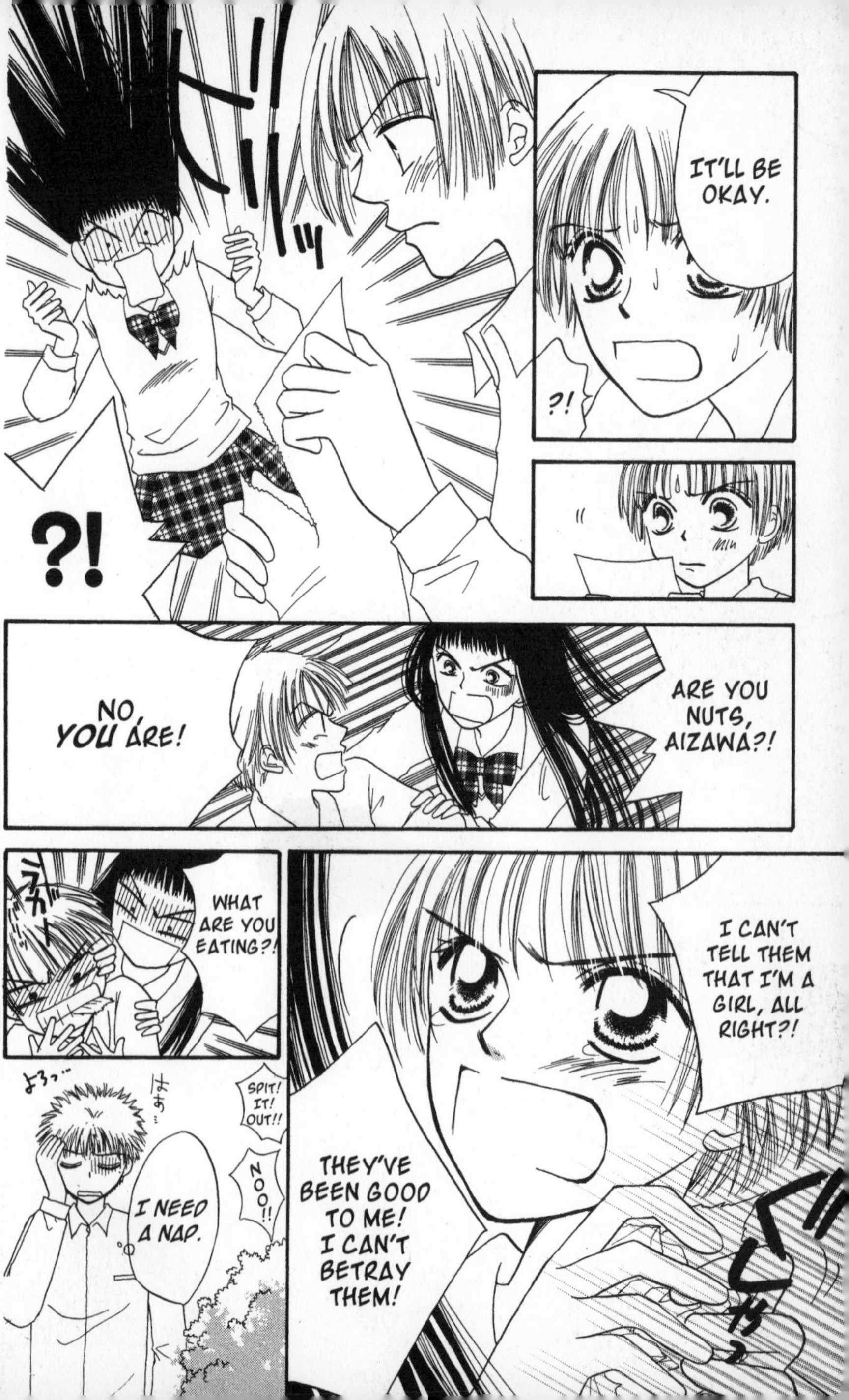
IT'LL BE OKAY.
?!
?!
ARE YOU NUTS, AIZAWA?!
NO, YOU ARE!
I CAN'T TELL THEM THAT I'M A GIRL, ALL RIGHT?!
THEY'VE BEEN GOOD TO ME! I CAN'T BETRAY THEM!
WHAT ARE YOU EATING?!
SPIT! IT! OUT!!
NOOO!!
I NEED A NAP.

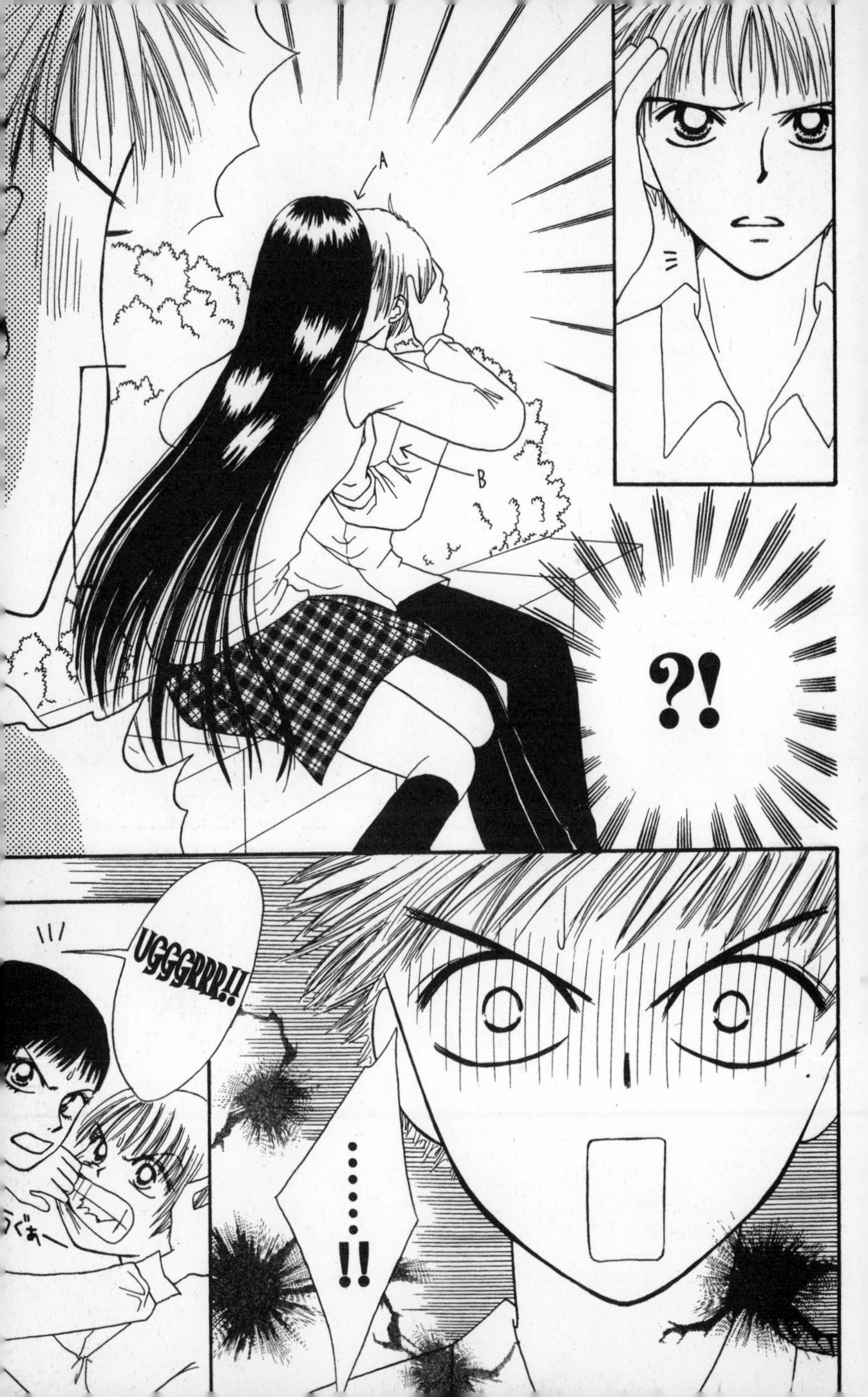
A
B
?!
……!!
UGGGRRR!!
うぐぁ〜

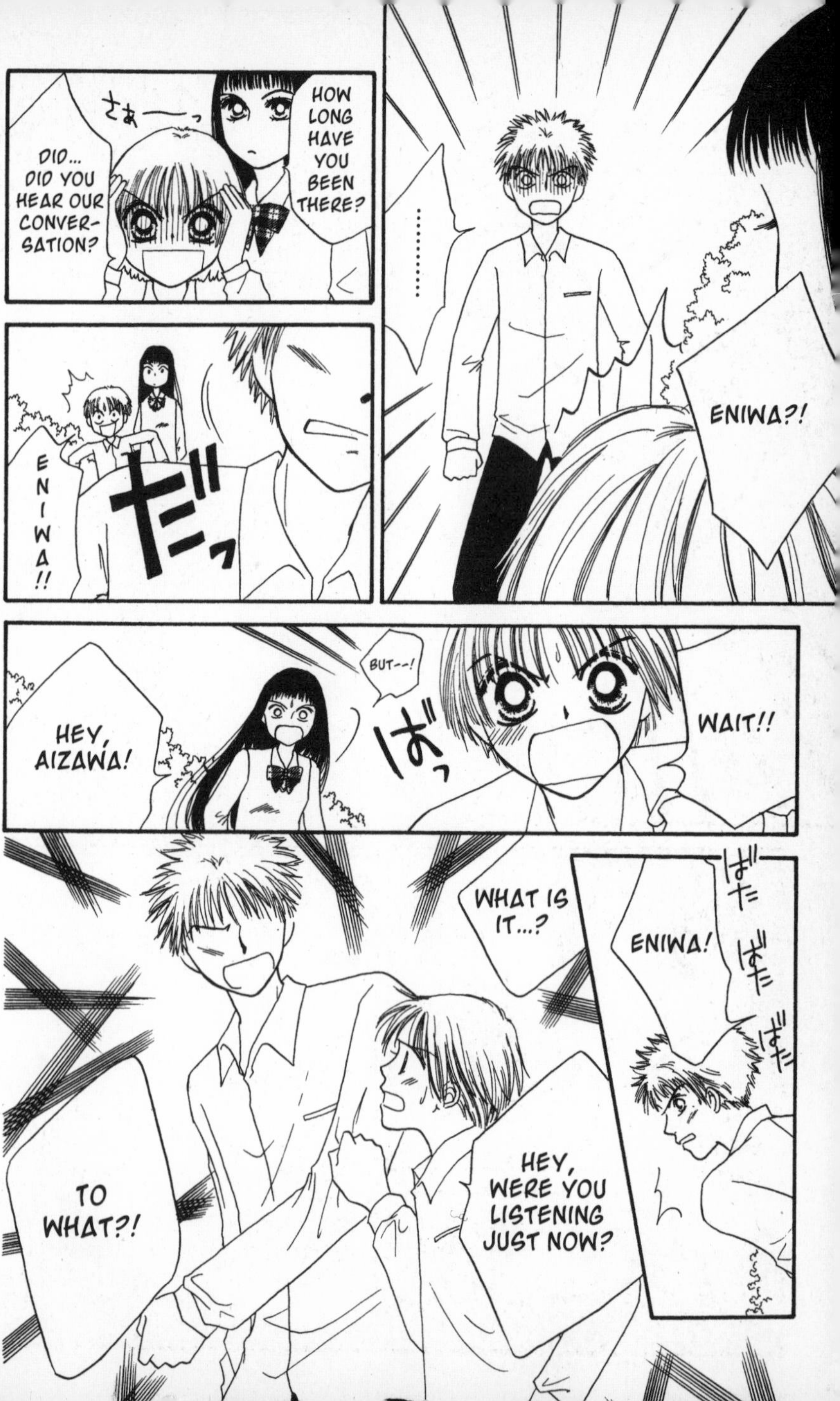
......
ENIWA?!
HOW LONG HAVE YOU BEEN THERE?
さぁーっ
DID... DID YOU HEAR OUR CONVERSATION?
だっ
ENIWA!!
WAIT!!
ばっ
BUT--!
HEY, AIZAWA!
ばた ばた ばた
ENIWA!
WHAT IS IT...?
HEY, WERE YOU LISTENING JUST NOW?
TO WHAT?!

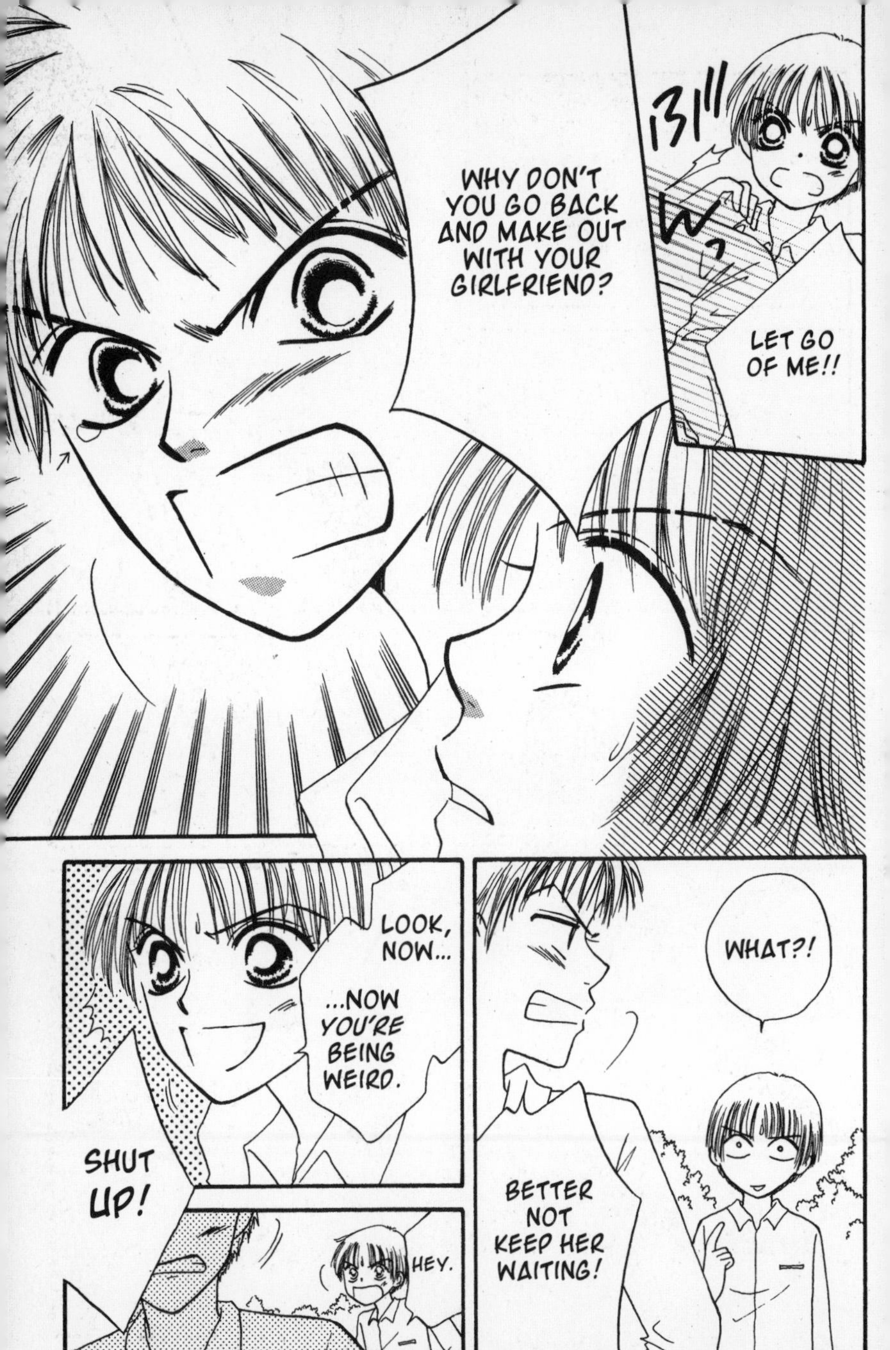
LET GO OF ME!!
WHY DON'T YOU GO BACK AND MAKE OUT WITH YOUR GIRLFRIEND?
WHAT?!
BETTER NOT KEEP HER WAITING!
LOOK, NOW...
...NOW YOU'RE BEING WEIRD.
SHUT UP!
HEY.

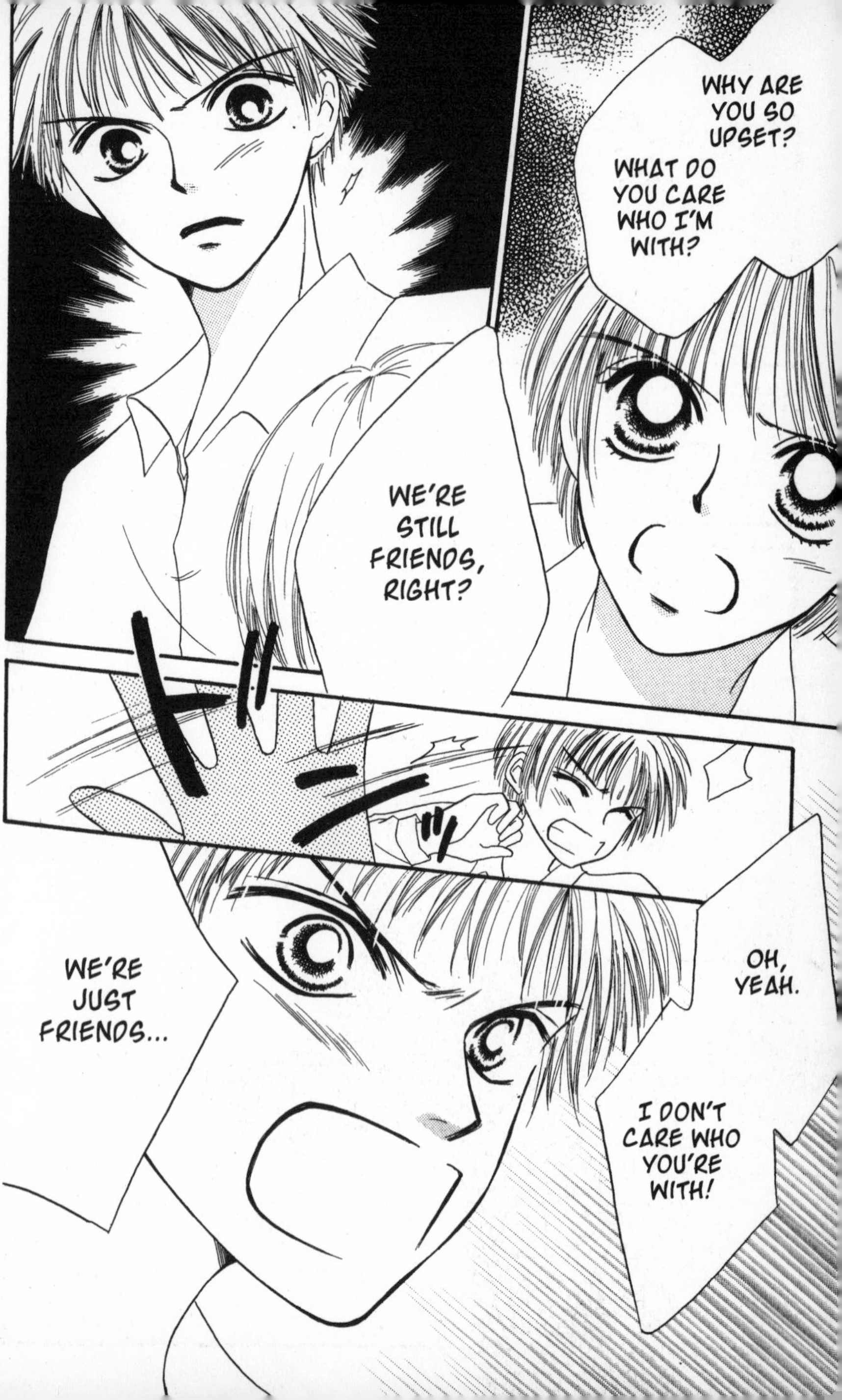
WHY ARE YOU SO UPSET?
WHAT DO YOU CARE WHO I'M WITH?
WE'RE STILL FRIENDS, RIGHT?
OH, YEAH.
I DON'T CARE WHO YOU'RE WITH!
WE'RE JUST FRIENDS...

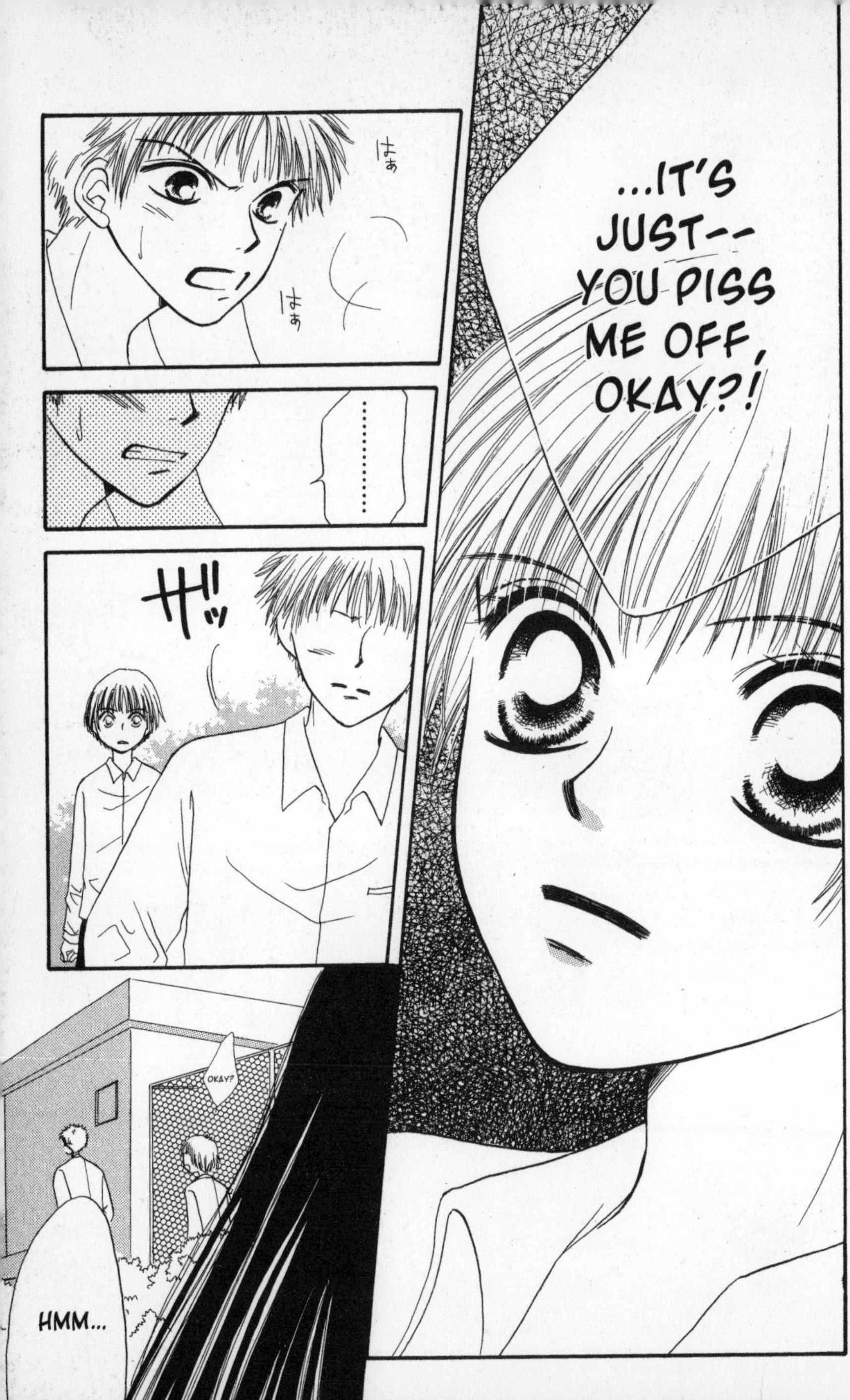
...IT'S JUST-- YOU PISS ME OFF, OKAY?!
はぁ
はぁ
......
ザッ
OKAY?
HMM...

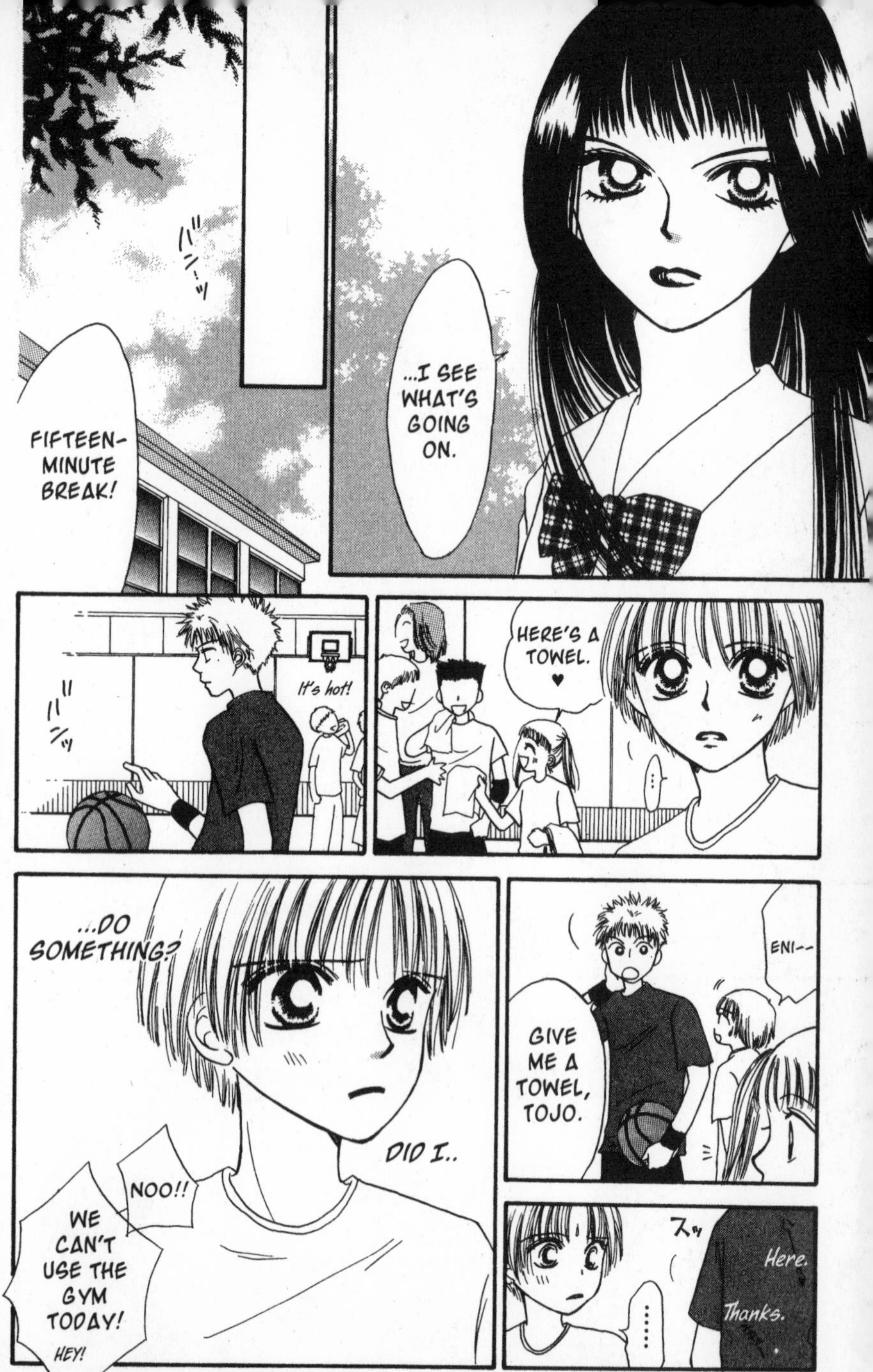
...I SEE WHAT'S GOING ON.
バシーッ
FIFTEEN-MINUTE BREAK!
HERE'S A TOWEL. ♥
...
It's hot!
バシッ
ENI--
GIVE ME A TOWEL, TOJO.
スッ
Here.
Thanks.
......
DID I..
...DO SOMETHING?
NOO!!
WE CAN'T USE THE GYM TODAY!
HEY!

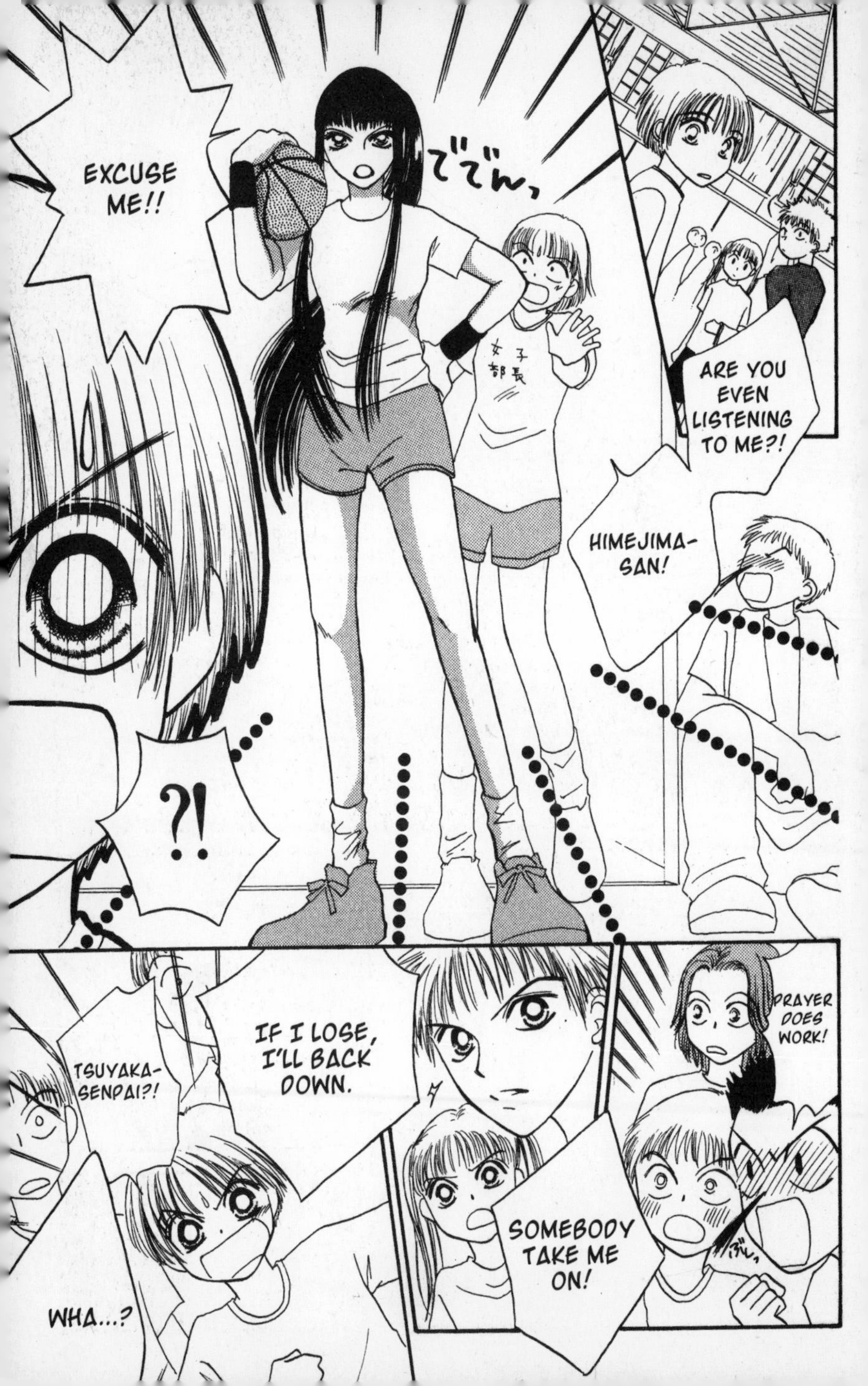
ARE YOU EVEN LISTENING TO ME?!
HIMEJIMA-SAN!
EXCUSE ME!!
ででんっ
女子部長
?!
PRAYER DOES WORK!
SOMEBODY TAKE ME ON!
IF I LOSE, I'LL BACK DOWN.
TSUYAKA-SENPAI?!
WHA...?

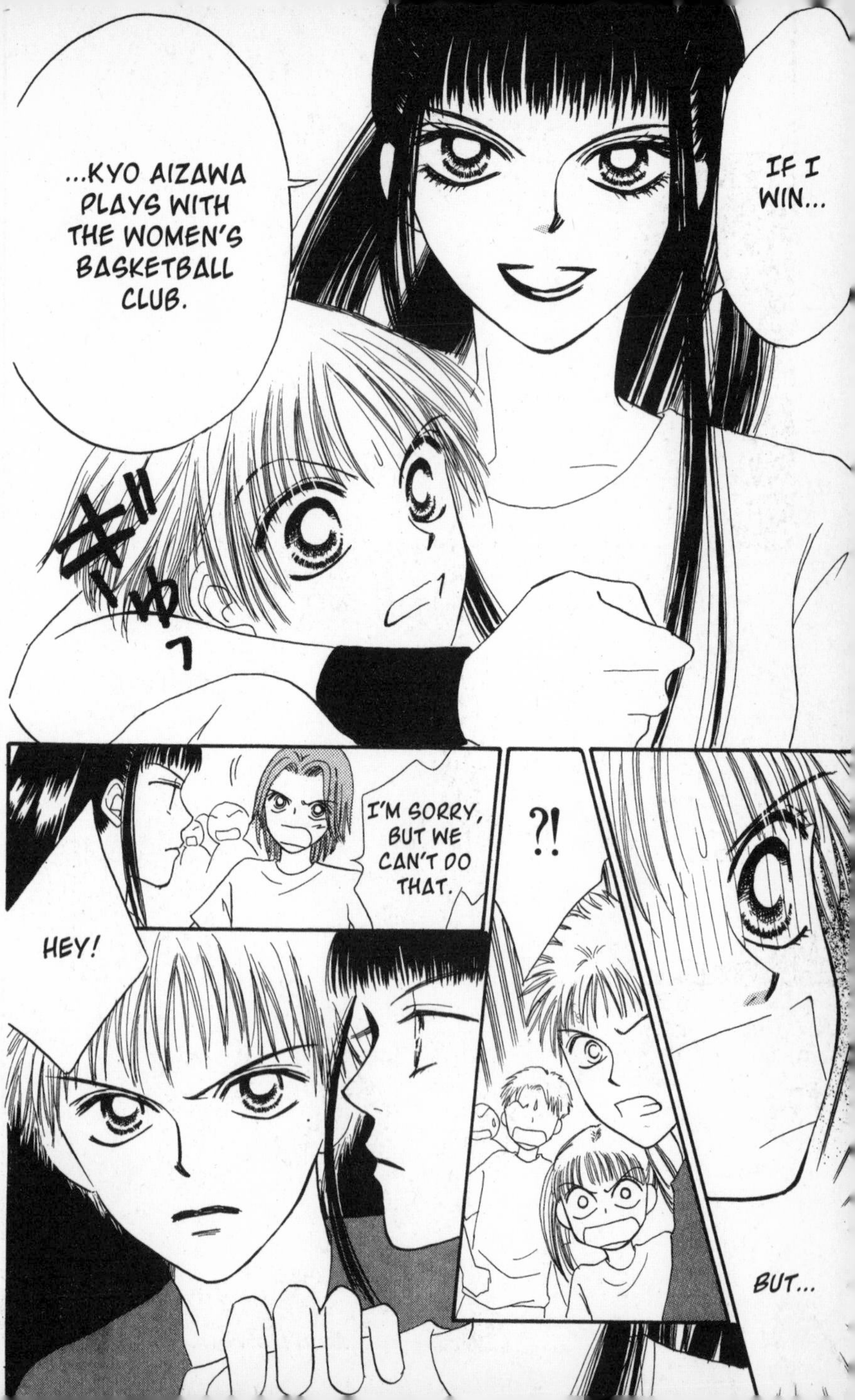
IF I WIN...
...KYO AIZAWA PLAYS WITH THE WOMEN'S BASKETBALL CLUB.
BUT...
?!
I'M SORRY, BUT WE CAN'T DO THAT.
HEY!

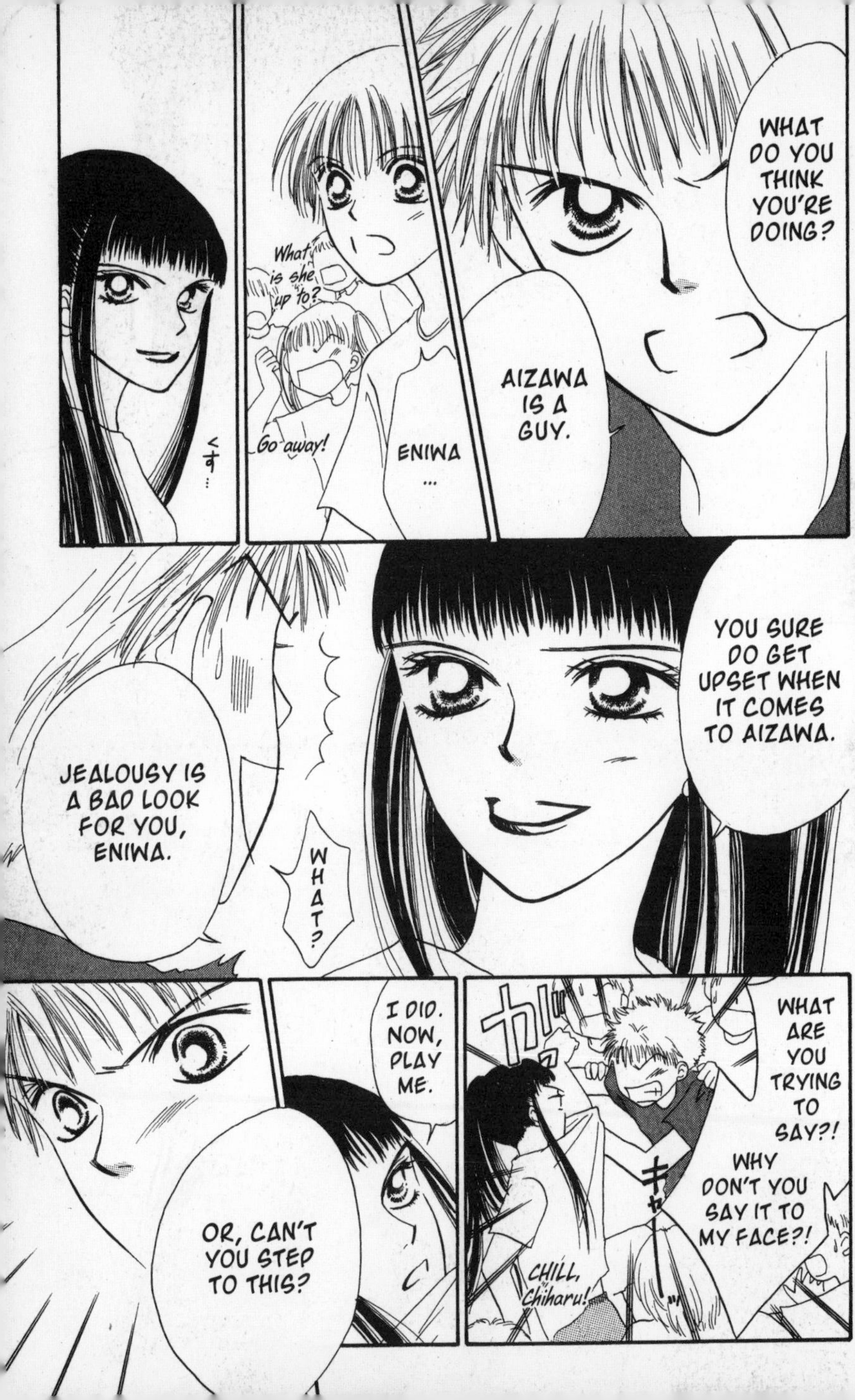
WHAT DO YOU THINK YOU'RE DOING?
AIZAWA IS A GUY.
ENIWA ...
What is she up to?
Go away!
くす…
YOU SURE DO GET UPSET WHEN IT COMES TO AIZAWA.
WHAT?
JEALOUSY IS A BAD LOOK FOR YOU, ENIWA.
WHAT ARE YOU TRYING TO SAY?!
WHY DON'T YOU SAY IT TO MY FACE?!
カッ
キャー
CHILL, Chiharu!
I DID. NOW, PLAY ME.
OR, CAN'T YOU STEP TO THIS?

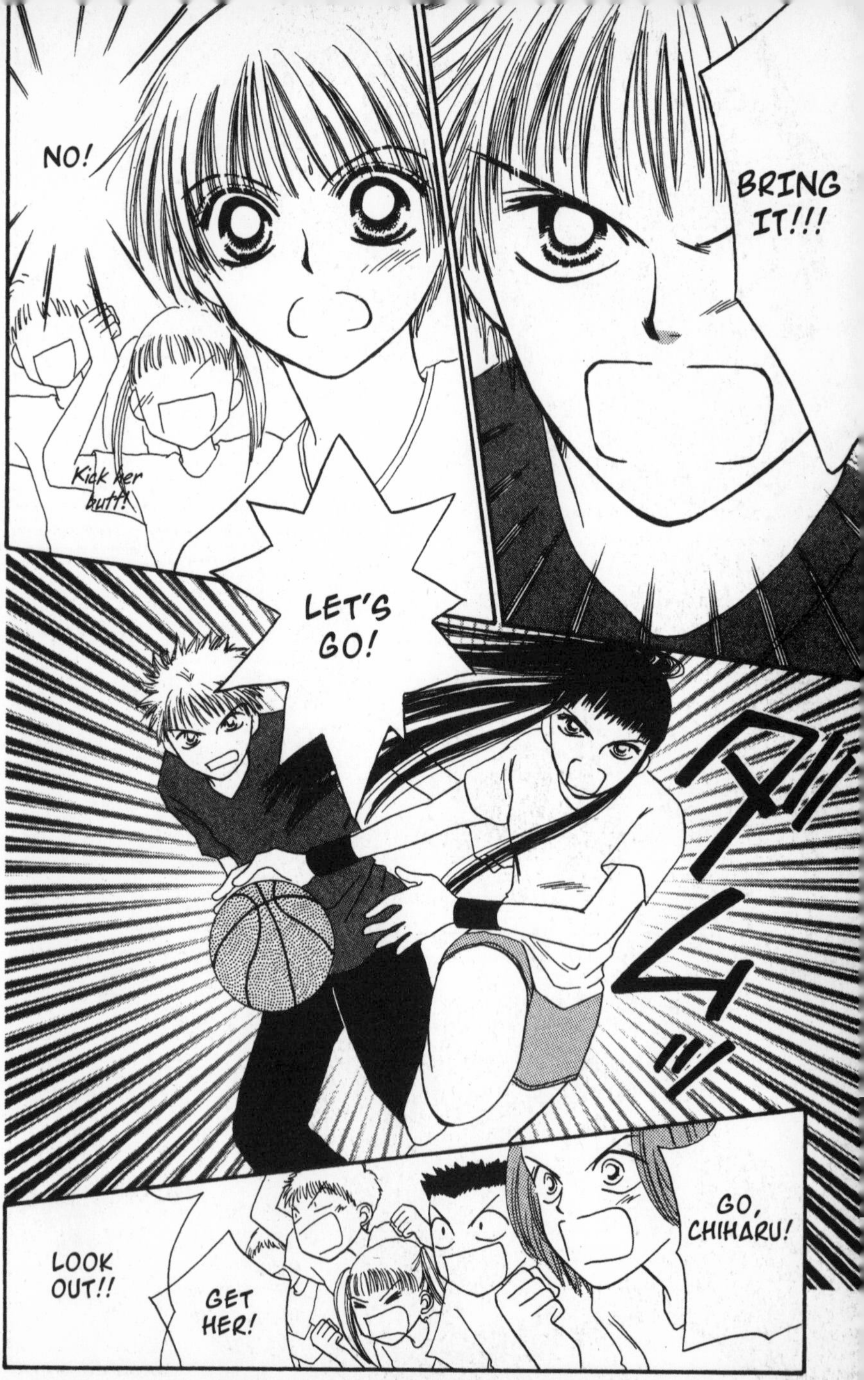
BRING IT!!!
NO!
Kick her butt!
LET'S GO!
ダムッ
GO, CHIHARU!
GET HER!
LOOK OUT!!

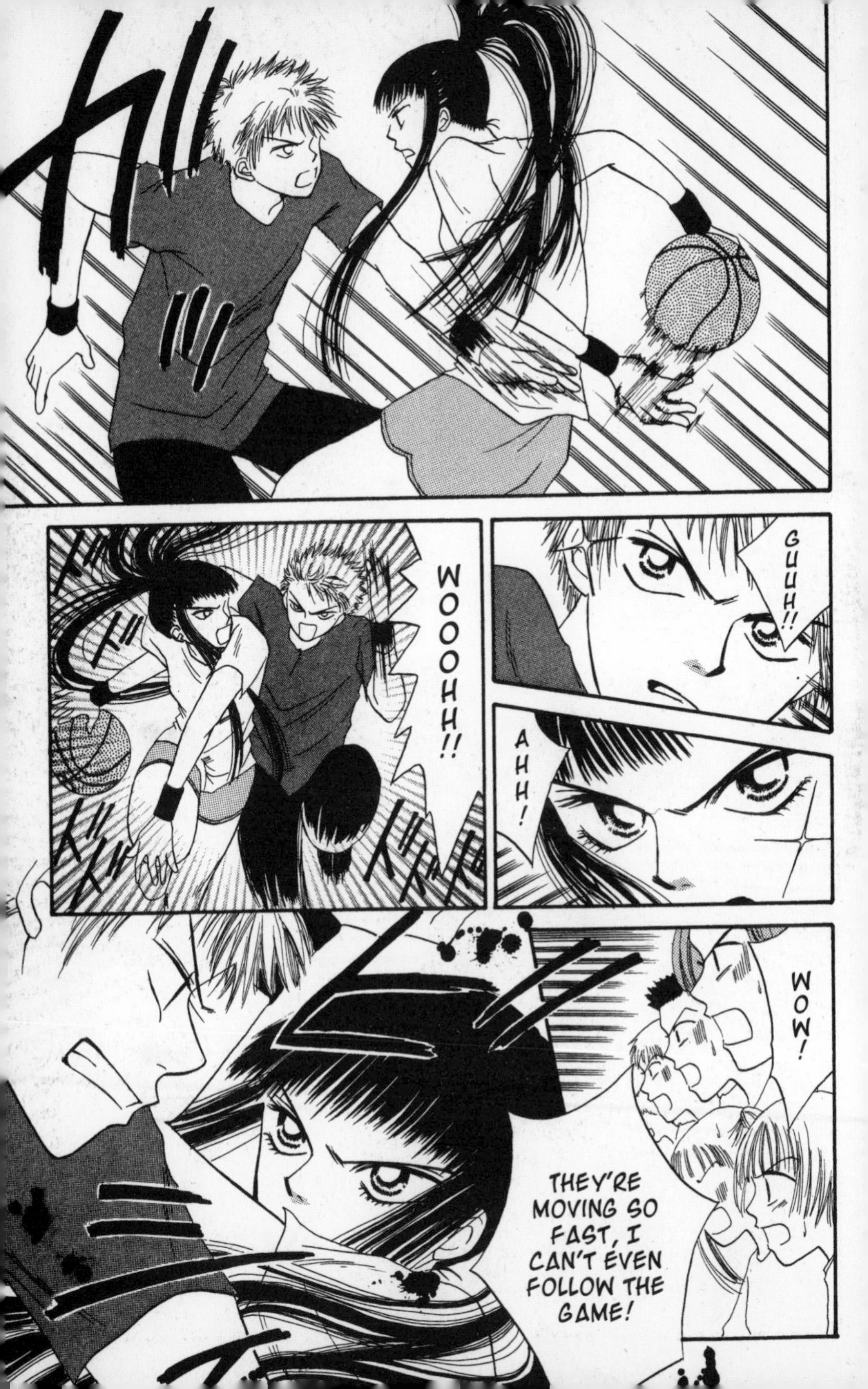
GUUH!!
AHH!
WOOOOHH!!
WOW!
THEY'RE MOVING SO FAST, I CAN'T EVEN FOLLOW THE GAME!

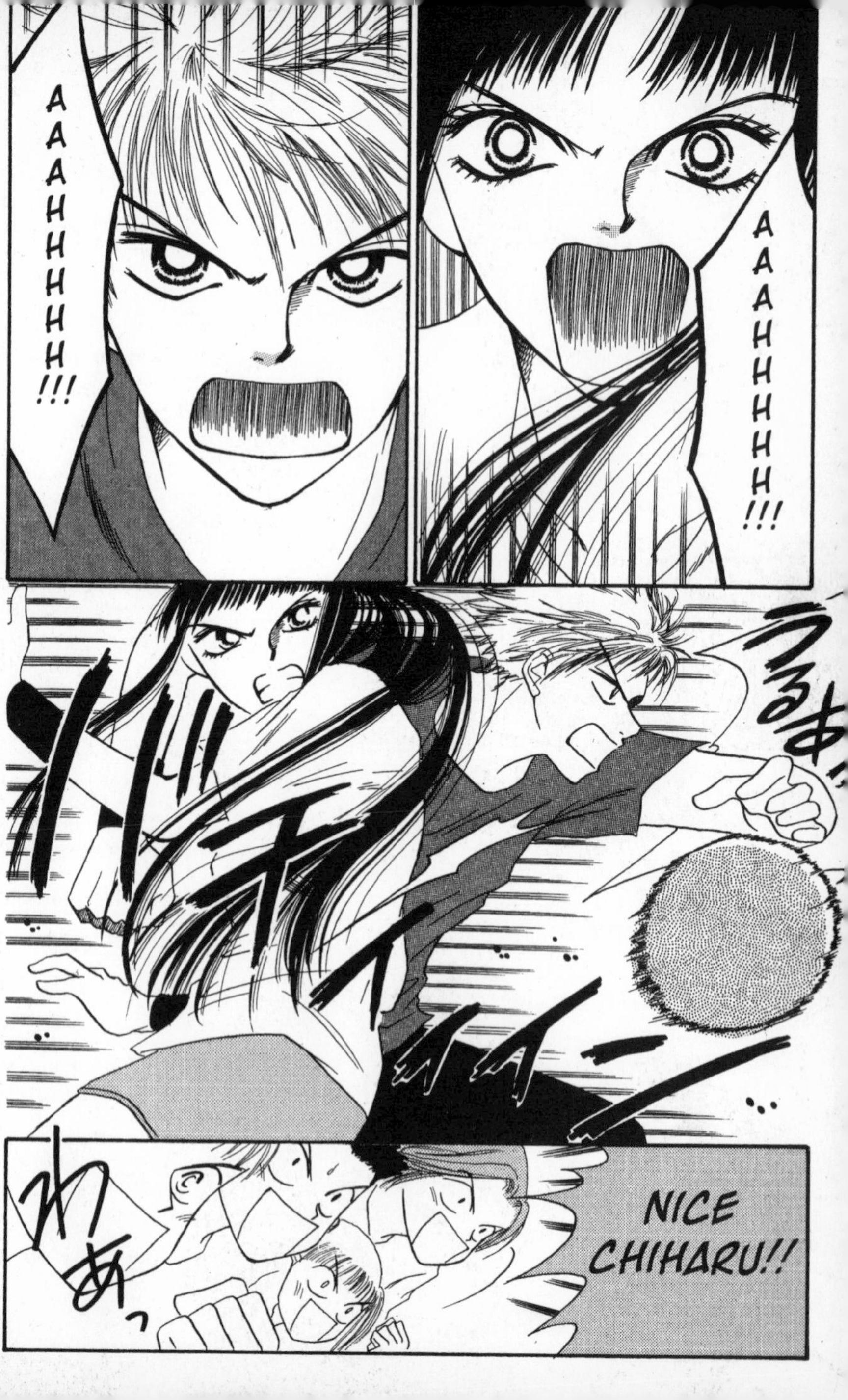
AAAHHHHH!!!
AAAHHHHH!!!
うるぁ!!
NICE CHIHARU!!
わあっ

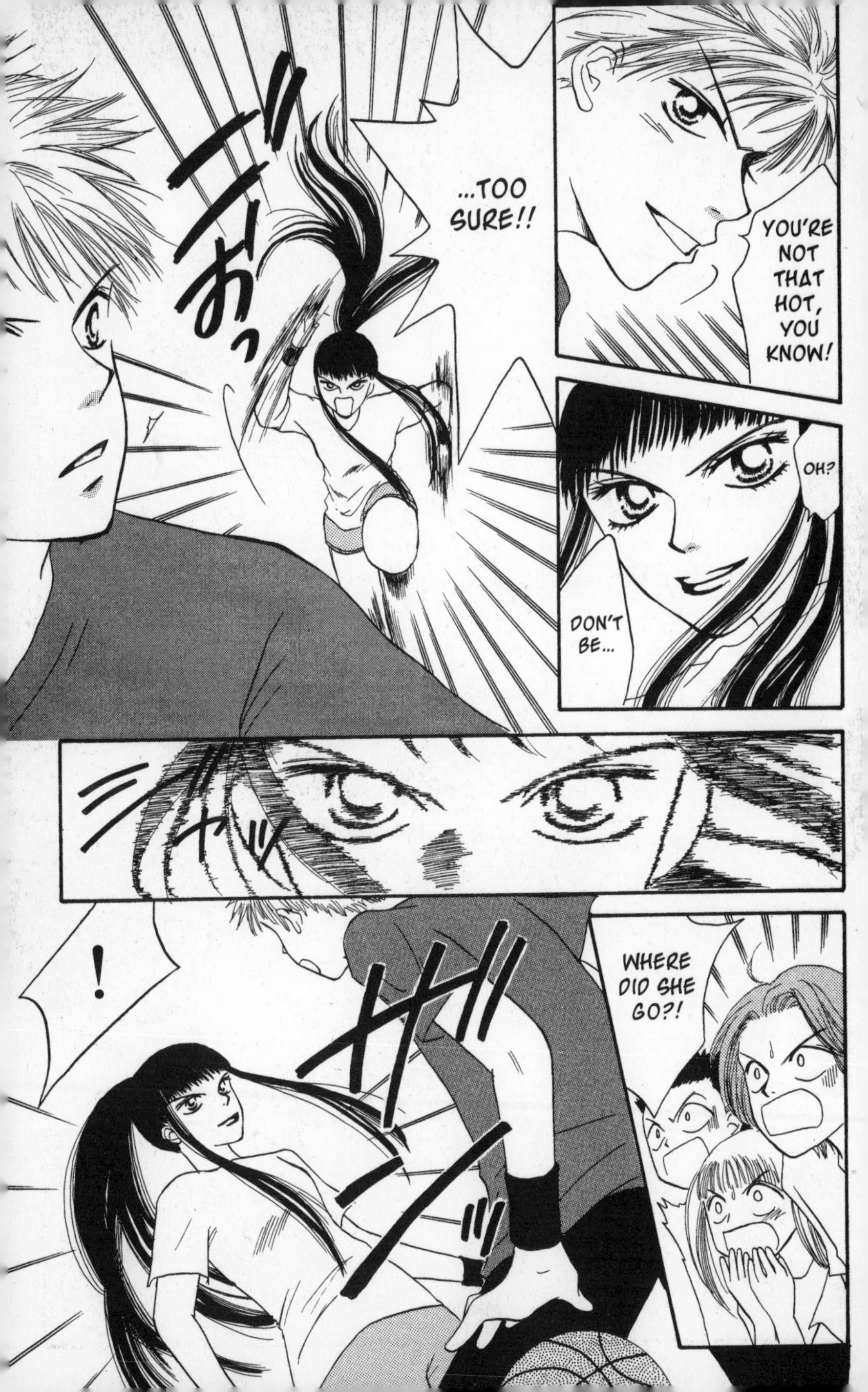
YOU'RE NOT THAT HOT, YOU KNOW!
OH?
DON'T BE...
...TOO SURE!!
WHERE DID SHE GO?!
!

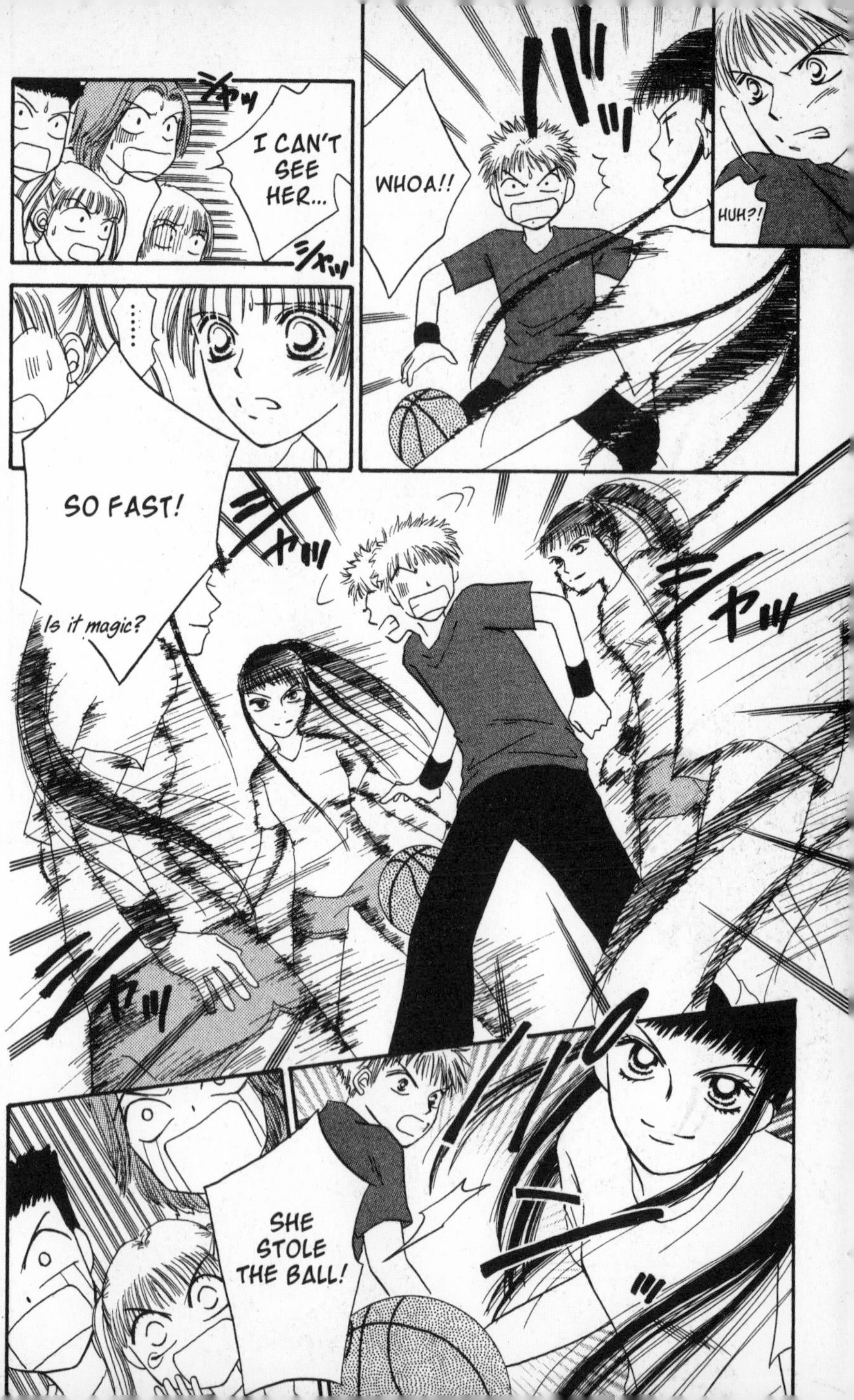
HUH?!
WHOA!!
シャッ
I CAN'T SEE HER...
シャッ
......
SO FAST!
Is it magic?
シャッ
シャッ
シャッ
SHE STOLE THE BALL!

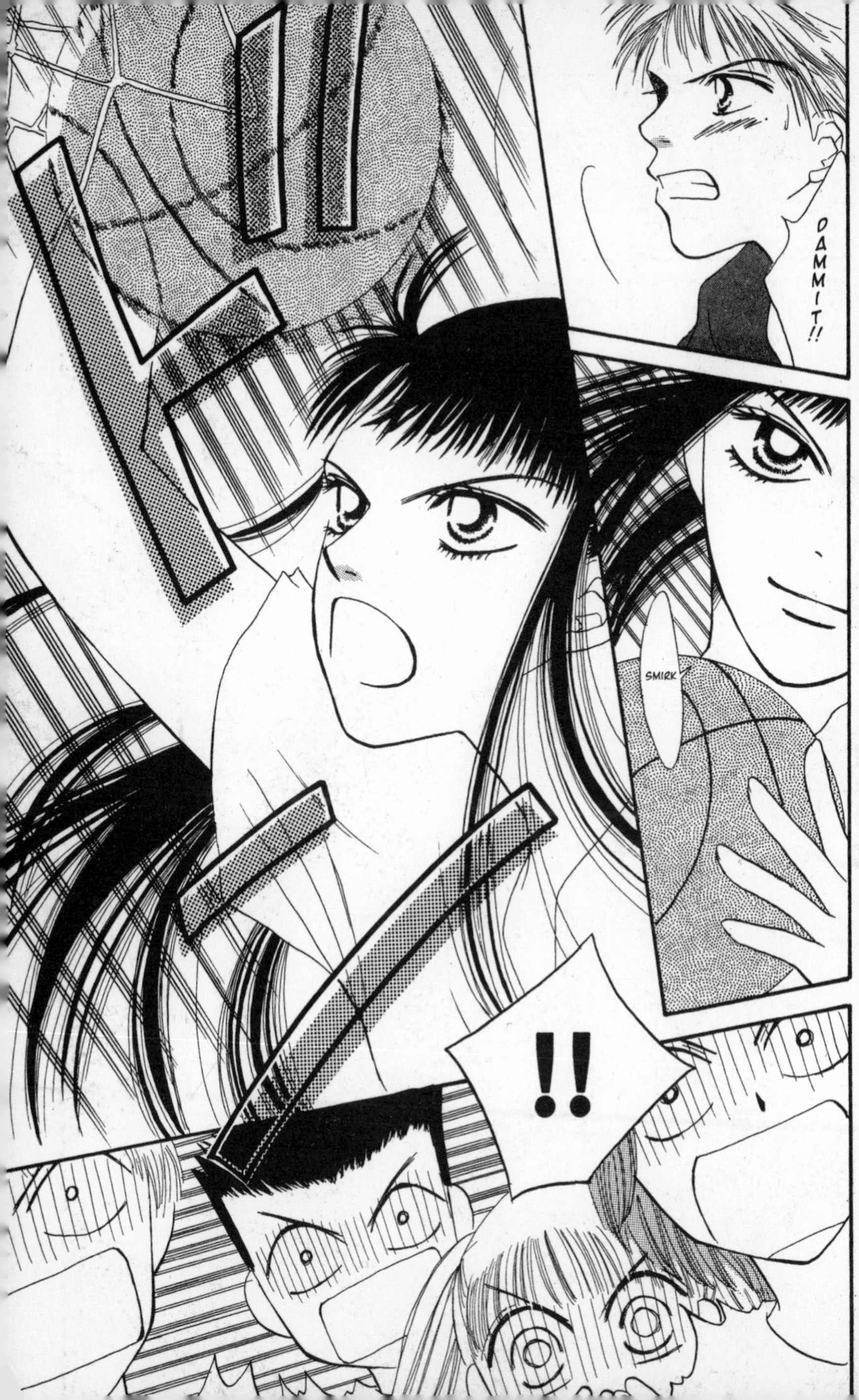
DAMMIT!!
SMIRK
!!

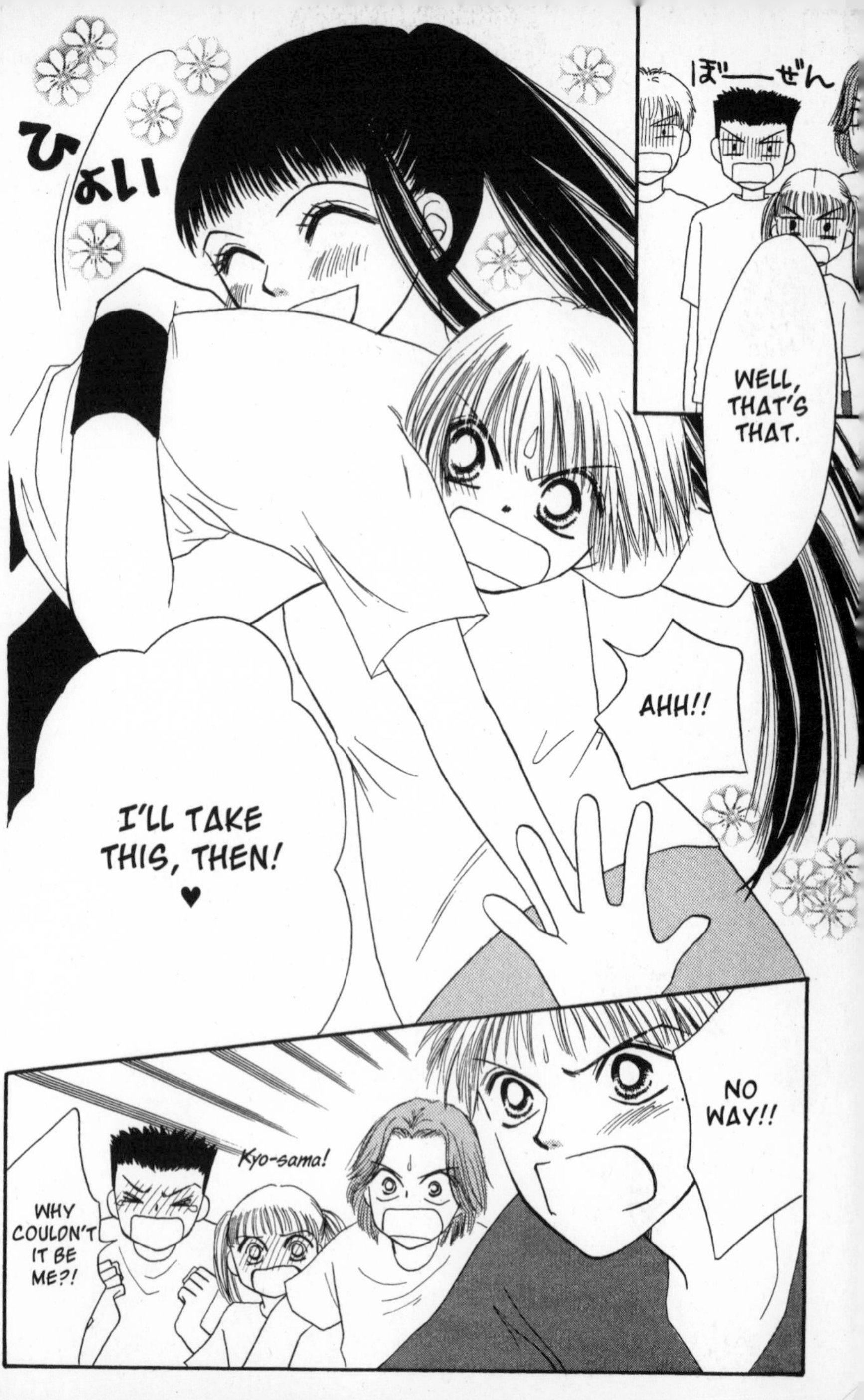
ぼーぜん
WELL, THAT'S THAT.
ひょい
AHH!!
I'LL TAKE THIS, THEN! ♥
NO WAY!!
Kyo-sama!
WHY COULDN'T IT BE ME?!

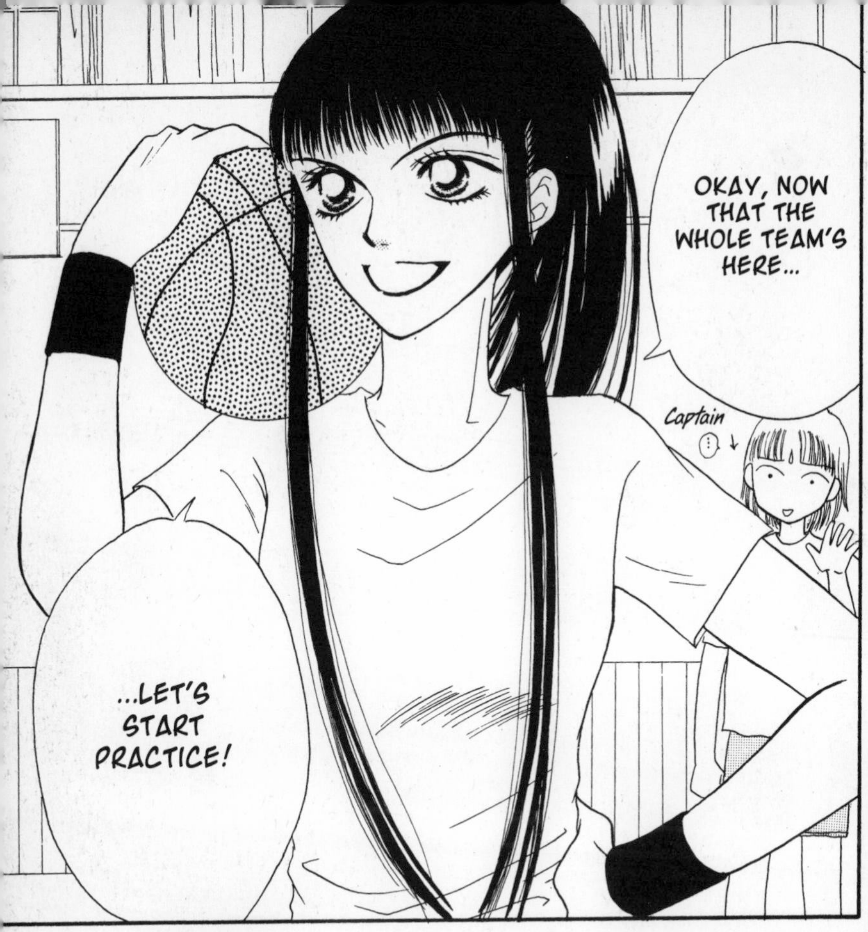
OKAY, NOW THAT THE WHOLE TEAM'S HERE...
Captain
...
...LET'S START PRACTICE!
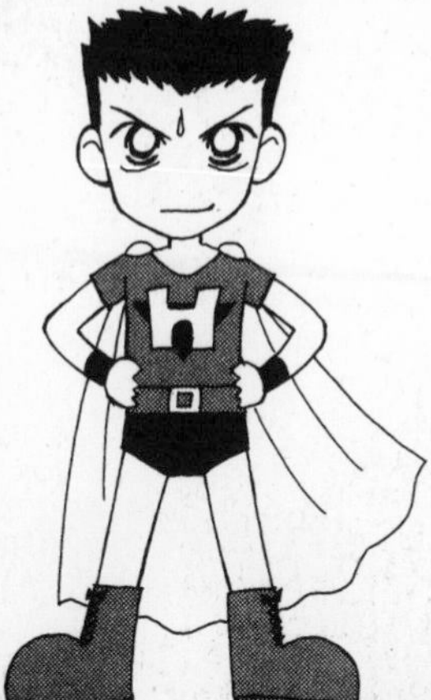

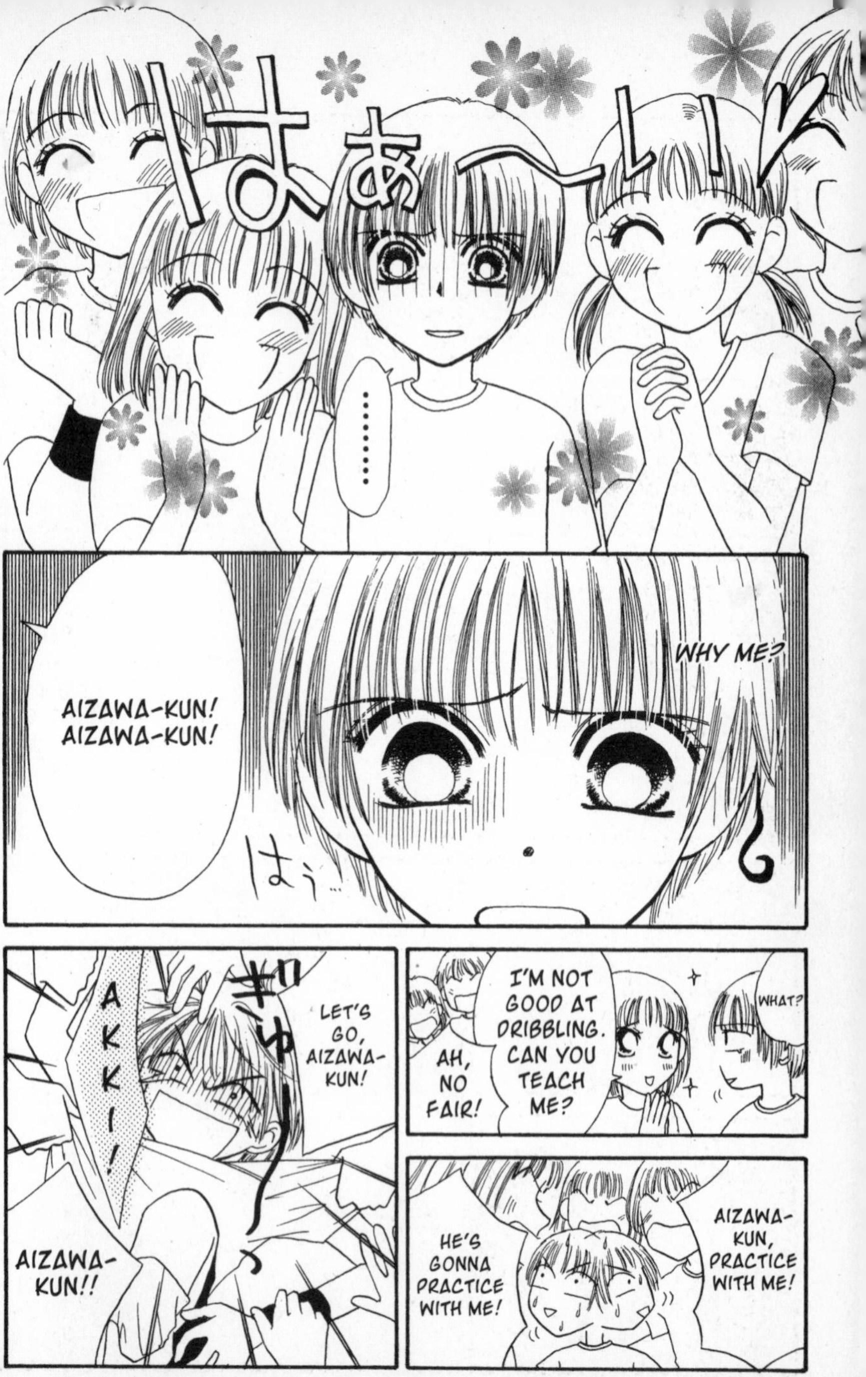
はあ～い!♡
......
WHY ME?
AIZAWA-KUN! AIZAWA-KUN!
はぅ...
WHAT?
I'M NOT GOOD AT DRIBBLING. CAN YOU TEACH ME?
AH, NO FAIR!
AIZAWA-KUN, PRACTICE WITH ME!
HE'S GONNA PRACTICE WITH ME!
ぎゅ～っ
LET'S GO, AIZAWA-KUN!
AKKI!
AIZAWA-KUN!!

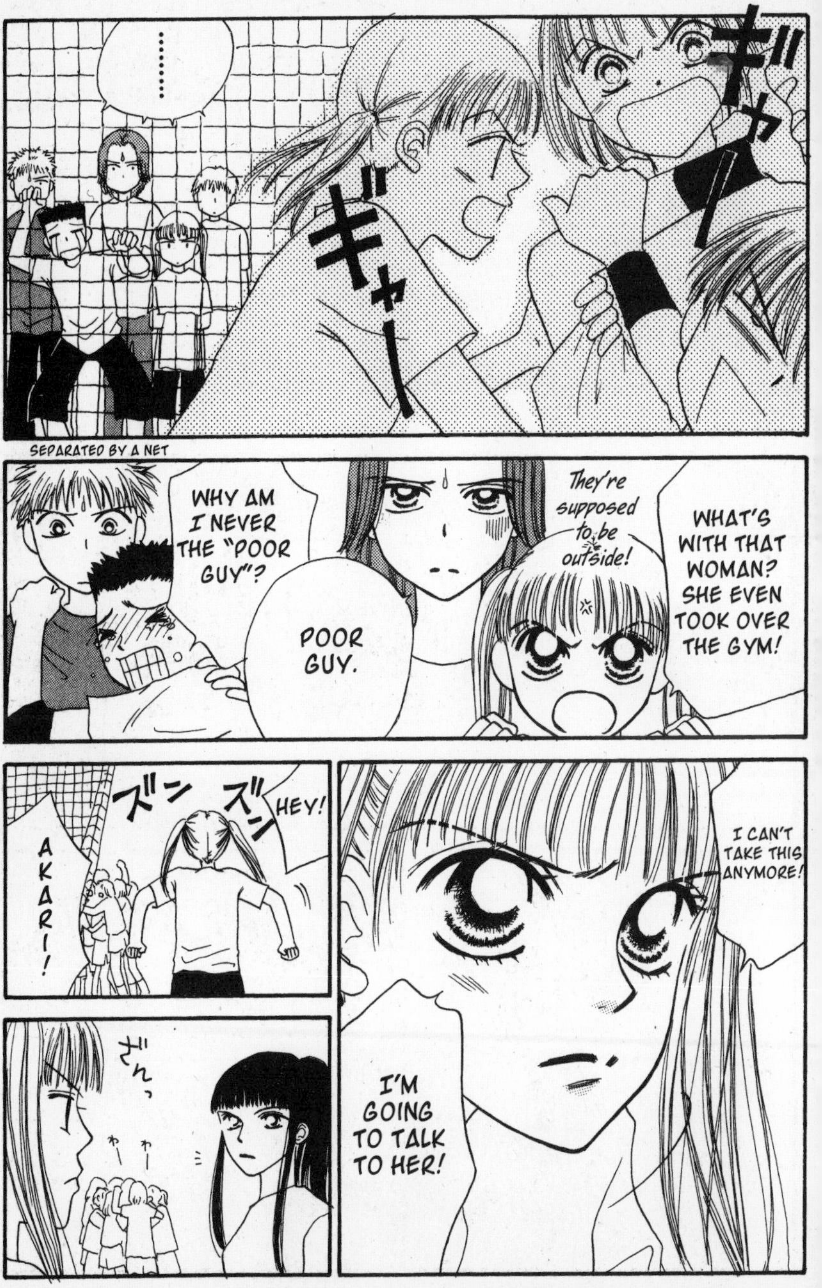
ギャー!
ギャー!
……
SEPARATED BY A NET
WHAT'S WITH THAT WOMAN? SHE EVEN TOOK OVER THE GYM!
They're supposed to be outside!
POOR GUY.
WHY AM I NEVER THE "POOR GUY"?
I CAN'T TAKE THIS ANYMORE!
I'M GOING TO TALK TO HER!
HEY!
ズン ズン
AKARI!
ざん
わー わー
ミ

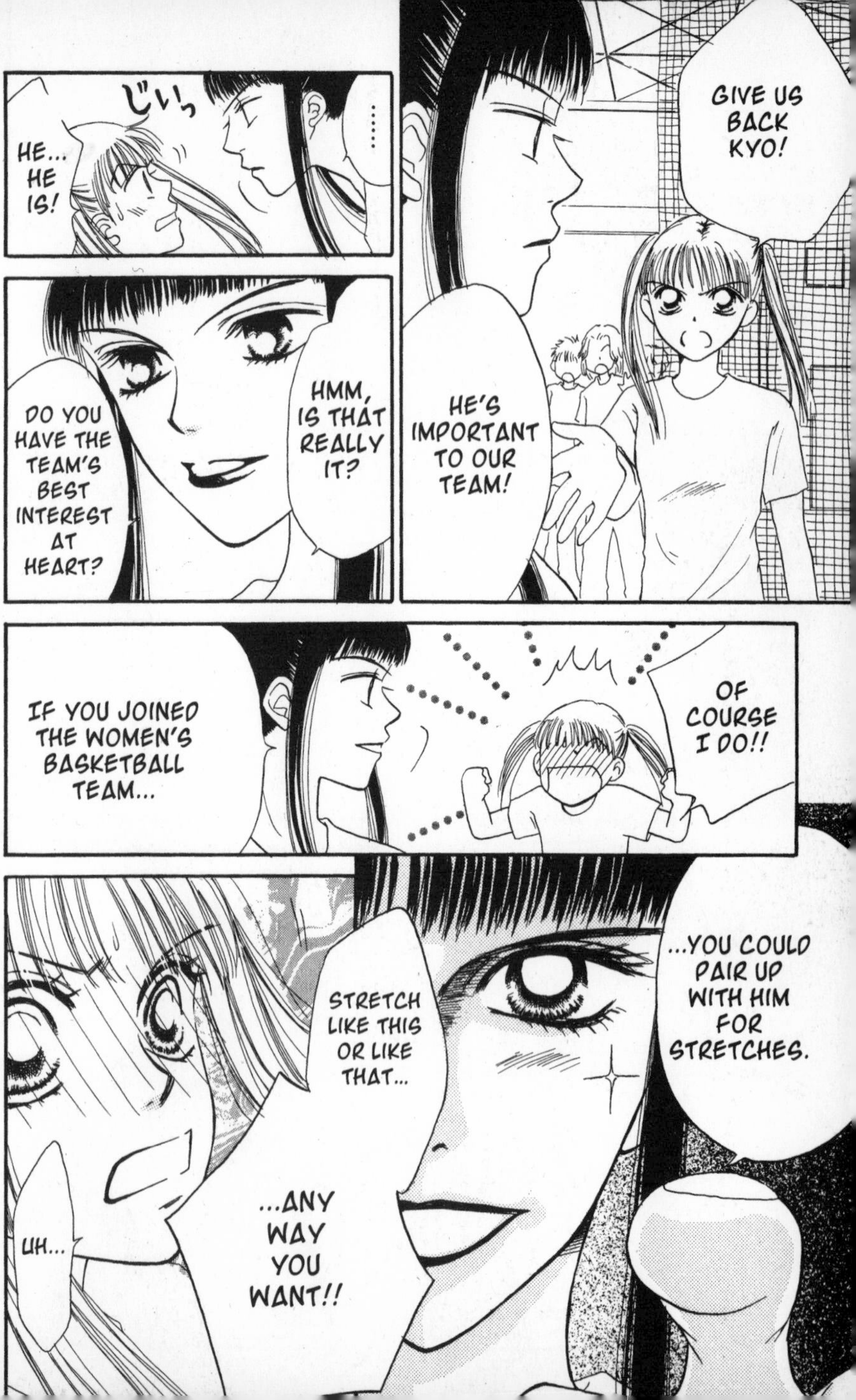
GIVE US BACK KYO!
HE'S IMPORTANT TO OUR TEAM!
......
じいっ
HE... HE IS!
HMM, IS THAT REALLY IT?
DO YOU HAVE THE TEAM'S BEST INTEREST AT HEART?
OF COURSE I DO!!
IF YOU JOINED THE WOMEN'S BASKETBALL TEAM...
...YOU COULD PAIR UP WITH HIM FOR STRETCHES.
STRETCH LIKE THIS OR LIKE THAT...
...ANY WAY YOU WANT!!
UH...

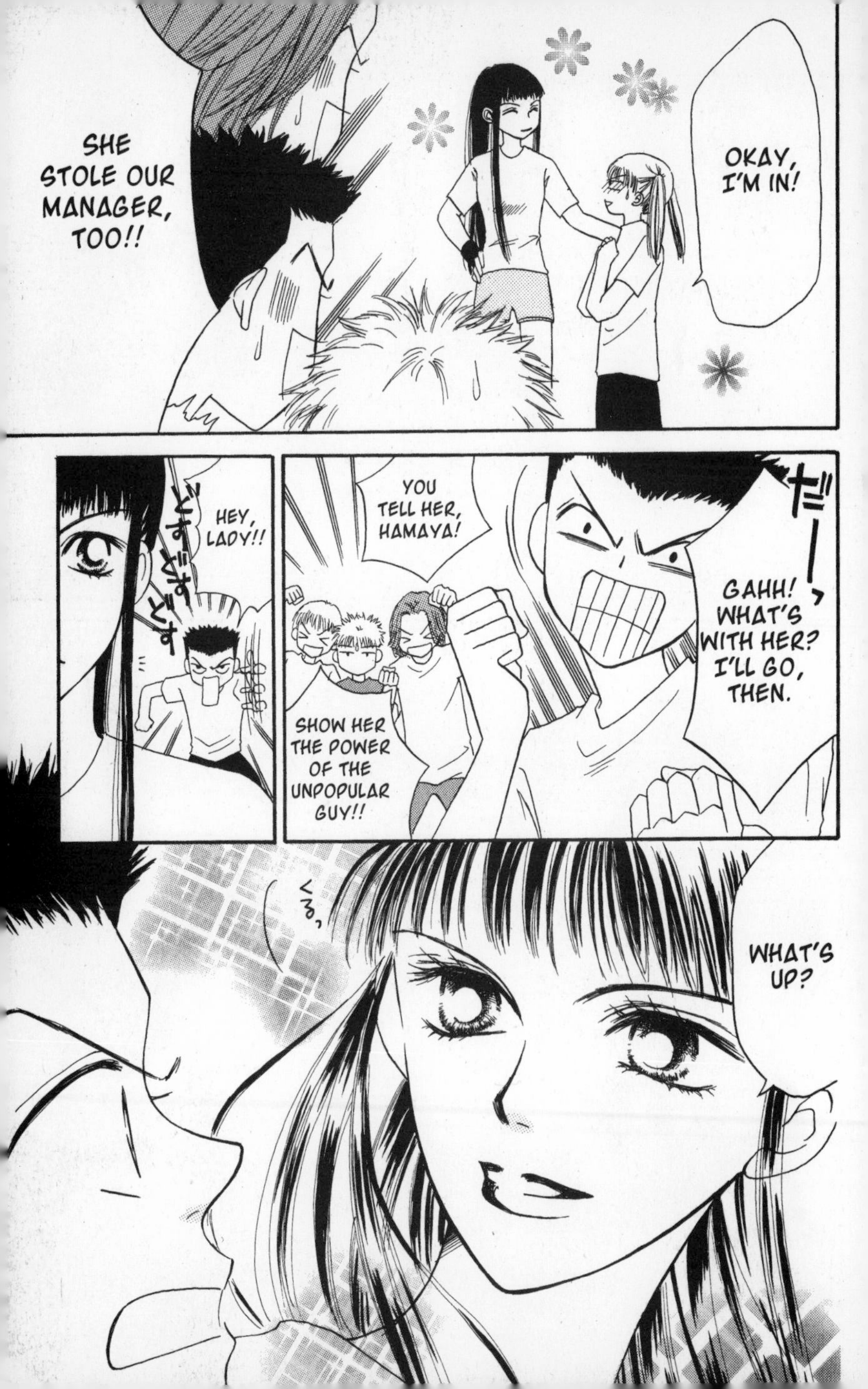
OKAY, I'M IN!
SHE STOLE OUR MANAGER, TOO!!
だー
GAHH! WHAT'S WITH HER? I'LL GO, THEN.
YOU TELL HER, HAMAYA!
SHOW HER THE POWER OF THE UNPOPULAR GUY!!
HEY, LADY!!
どすどすどす
WHAT'S UP?
くる

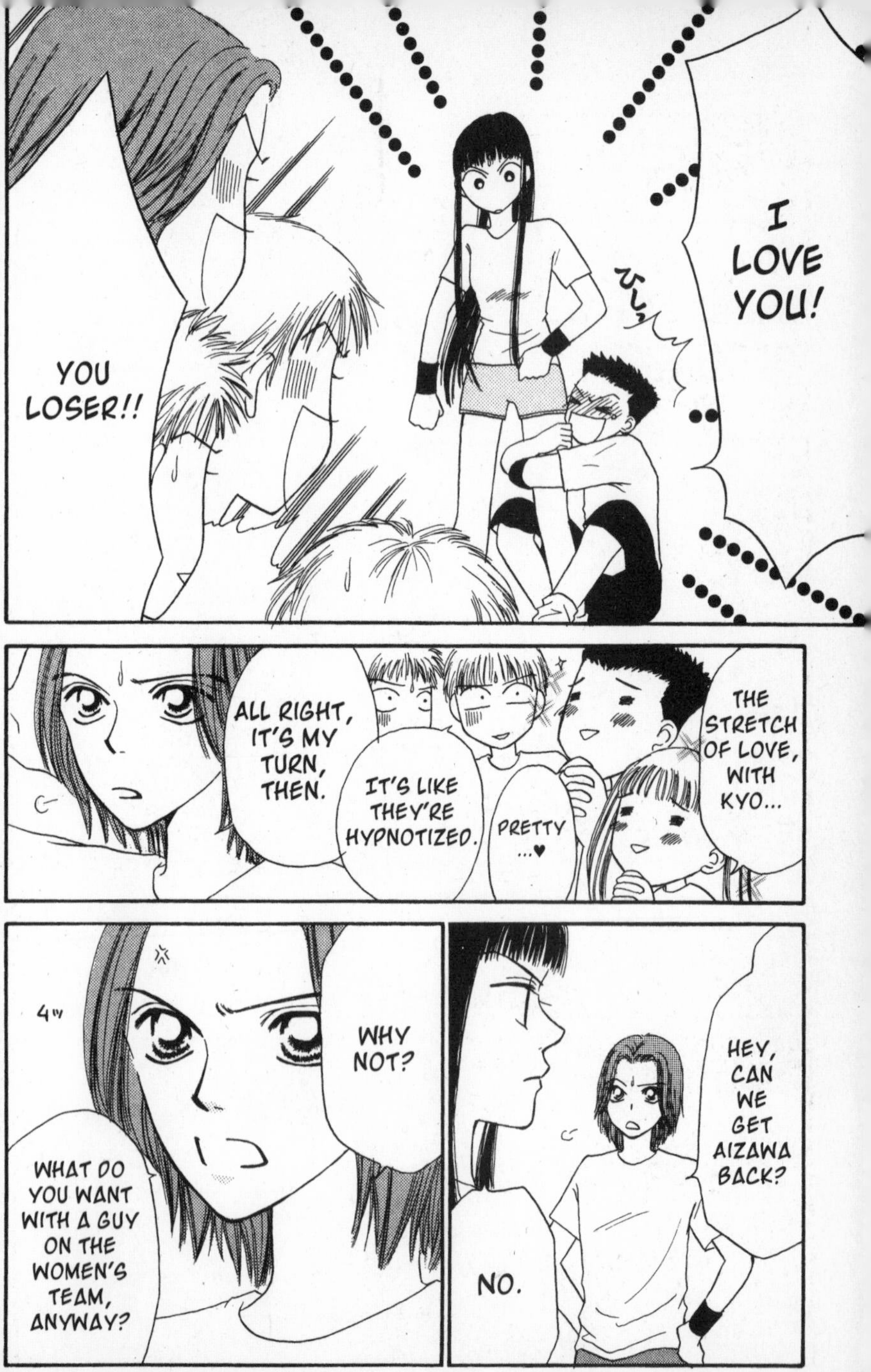
I LOVE YOU!
YOU LOSER!!
THE STRETCH OF LOVE, WITH KYO...
PRETTY ...♥
IT'S LIKE THEY'RE HYPNOTIZED.
ALL RIGHT, IT'S MY TURN, THEN.
HEY, CAN WE GET AIZAWA BACK?
NO.
WHY NOT?
WHAT DO YOU WANT WITH A GUY ON THE WOMEN'S TEAM, ANYWAY?

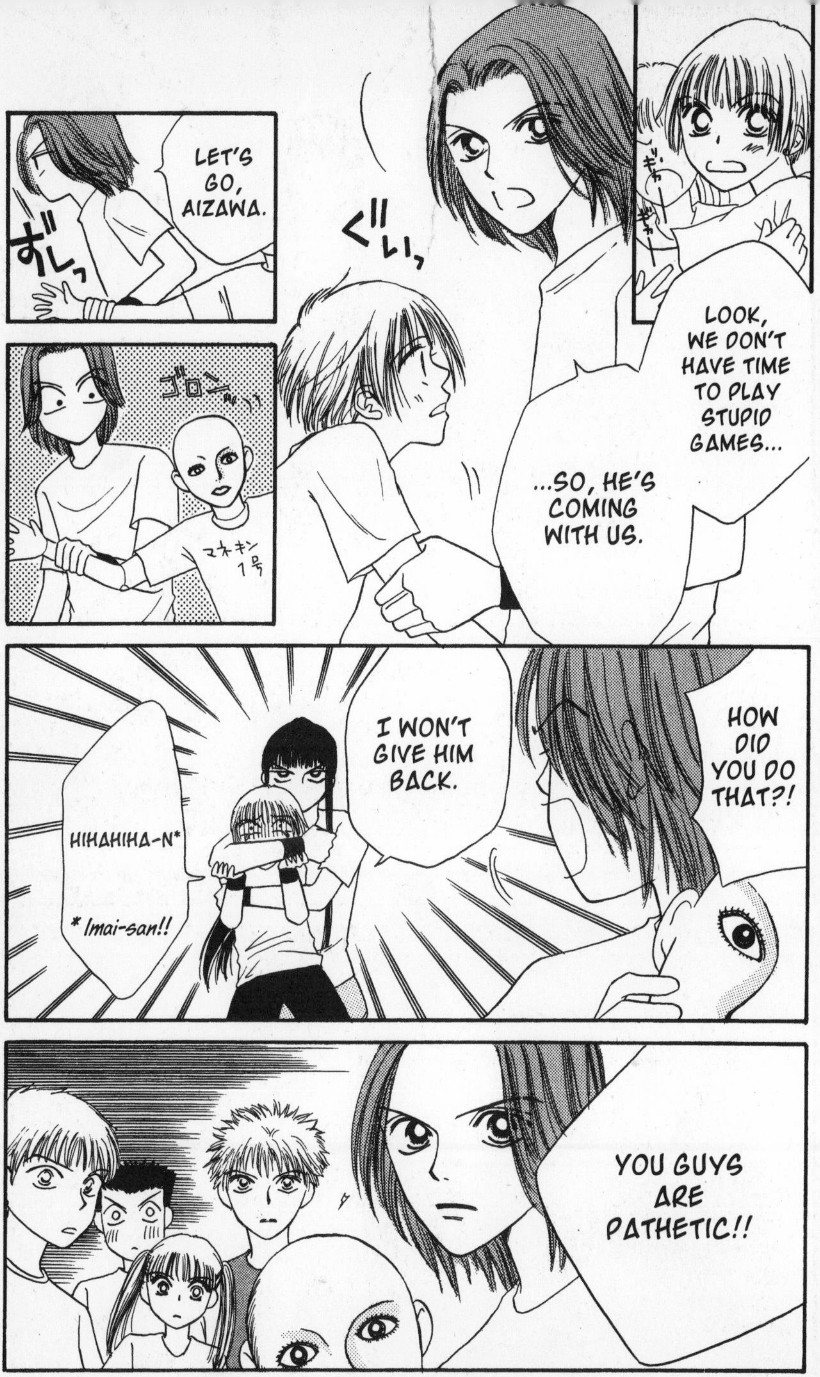
LOOK, WE DON'T HAVE TIME TO PLAY STUPID GAMES...
...SO, HE'S COMING WITH US.
ぐいっ
LET'S GO, AIZAWA.
ずしっ
マネキン1号
HOW DID YOU DO THAT?!
I WON'T GIVE HIM BACK.
HIHAHIHA-N*
* Imai-san!!
YOU GUYS ARE PATHETIC!!

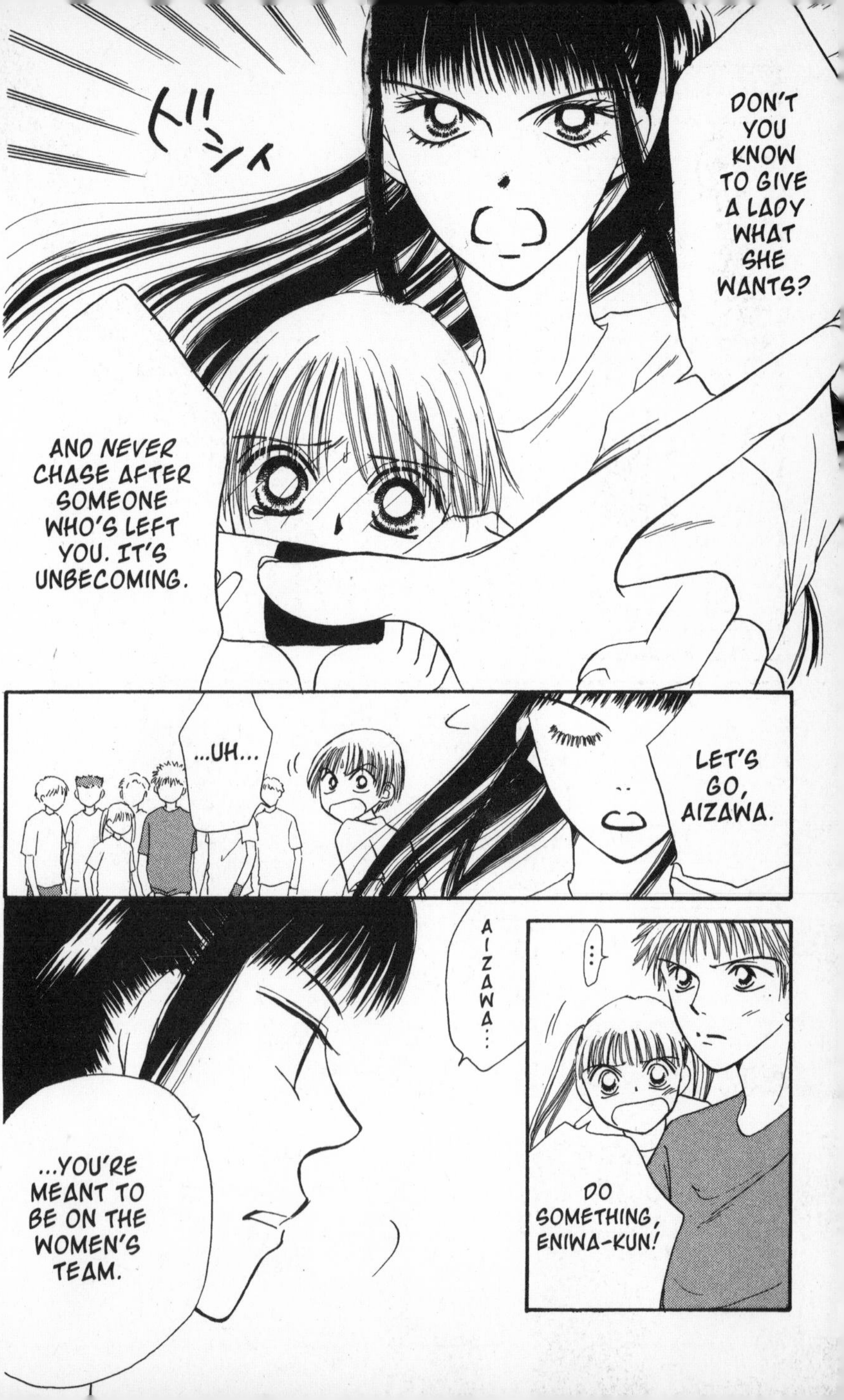
DON'T YOU KNOW TO GIVE A LADY WHAT SHE WANTS?
AND NEVER CHASE AFTER SOMEONE WHO'S LEFT YOU. IT'S UNBECOMING.
LET'S GO, AIZAWA.
...UH...
...
DO SOMETHING, ENIWA-KUN!
AIZAWA...
...YOU'RE MEANT TO BE ON THE WOMEN'S TEAM.

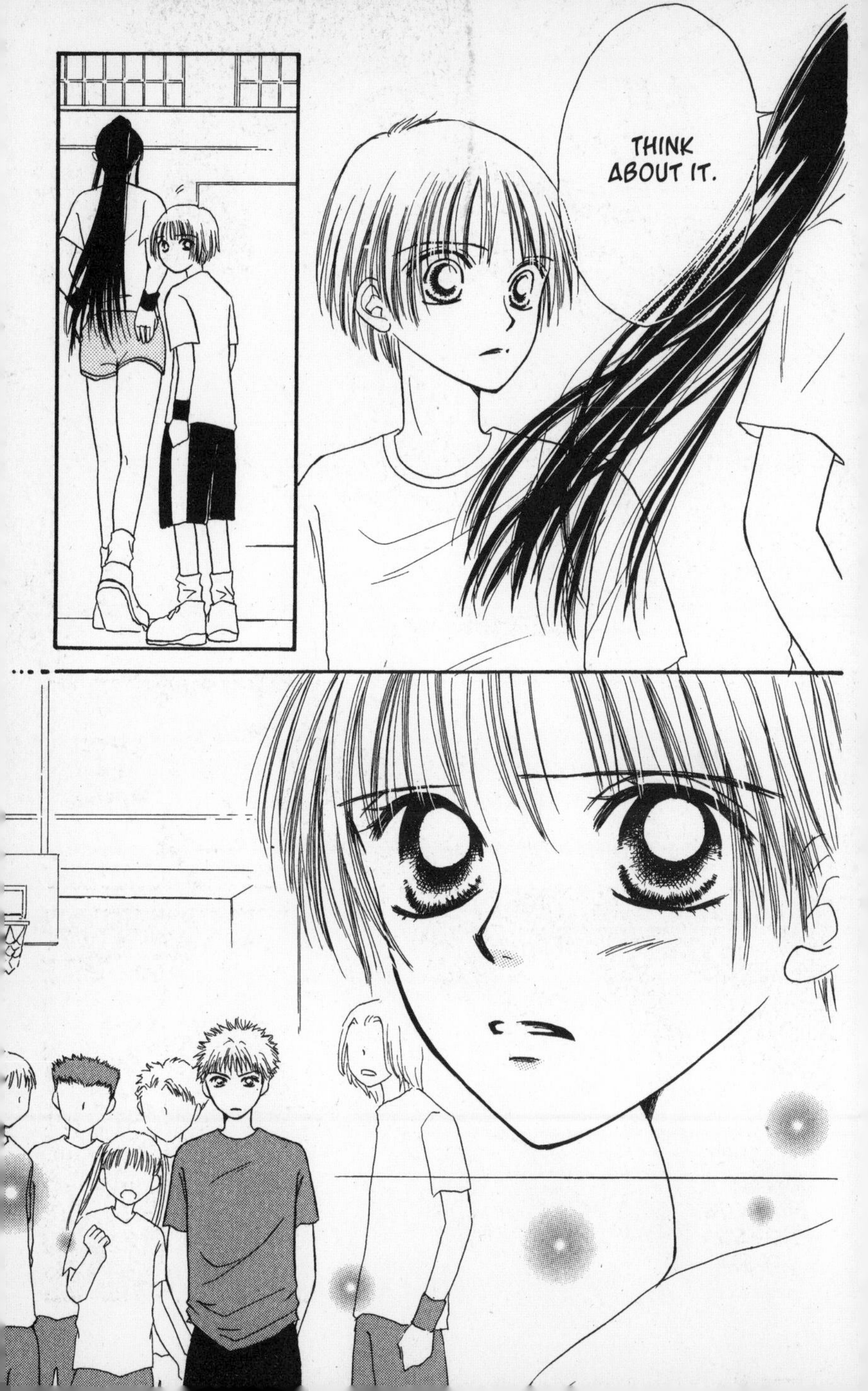
THINK ABOUT IT.

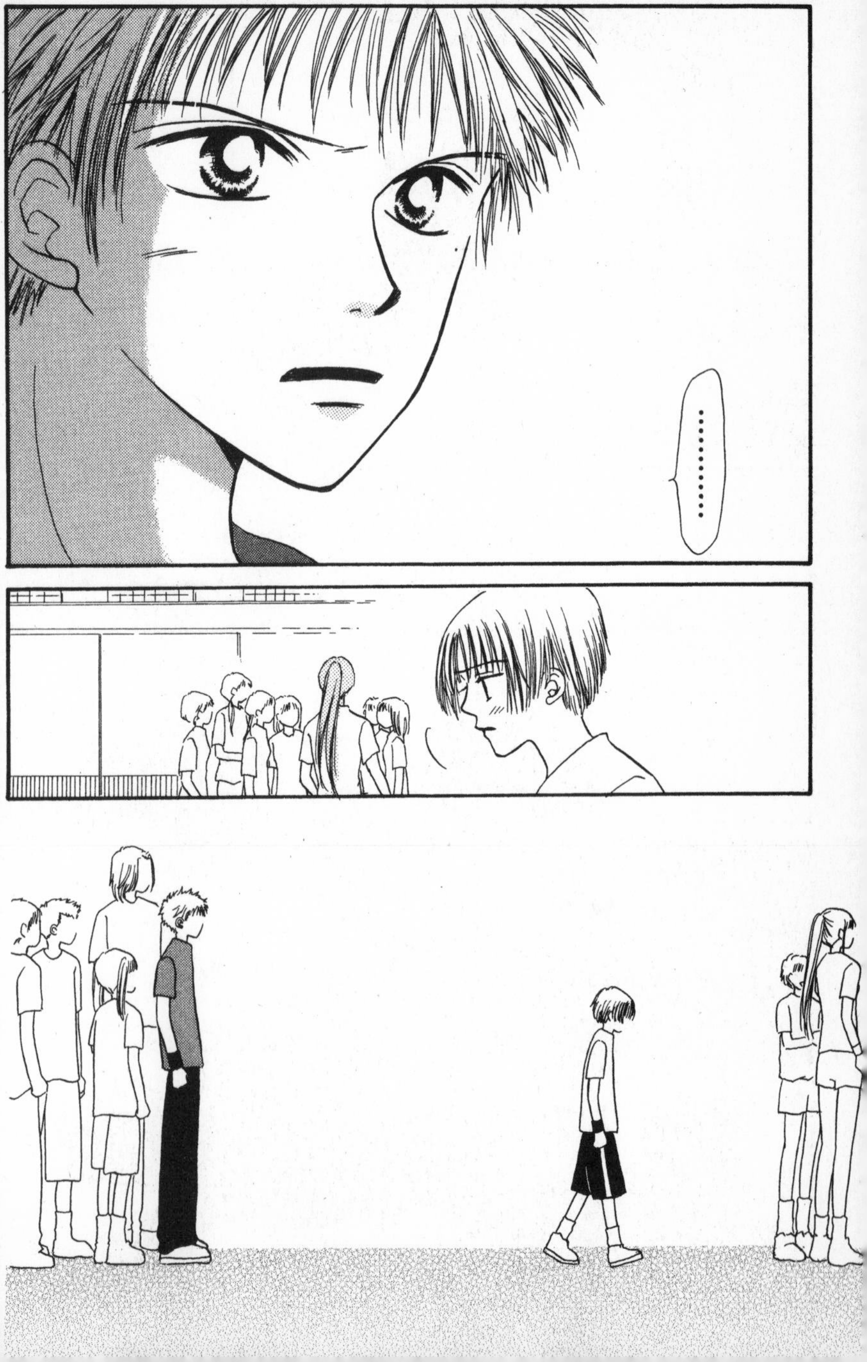
....

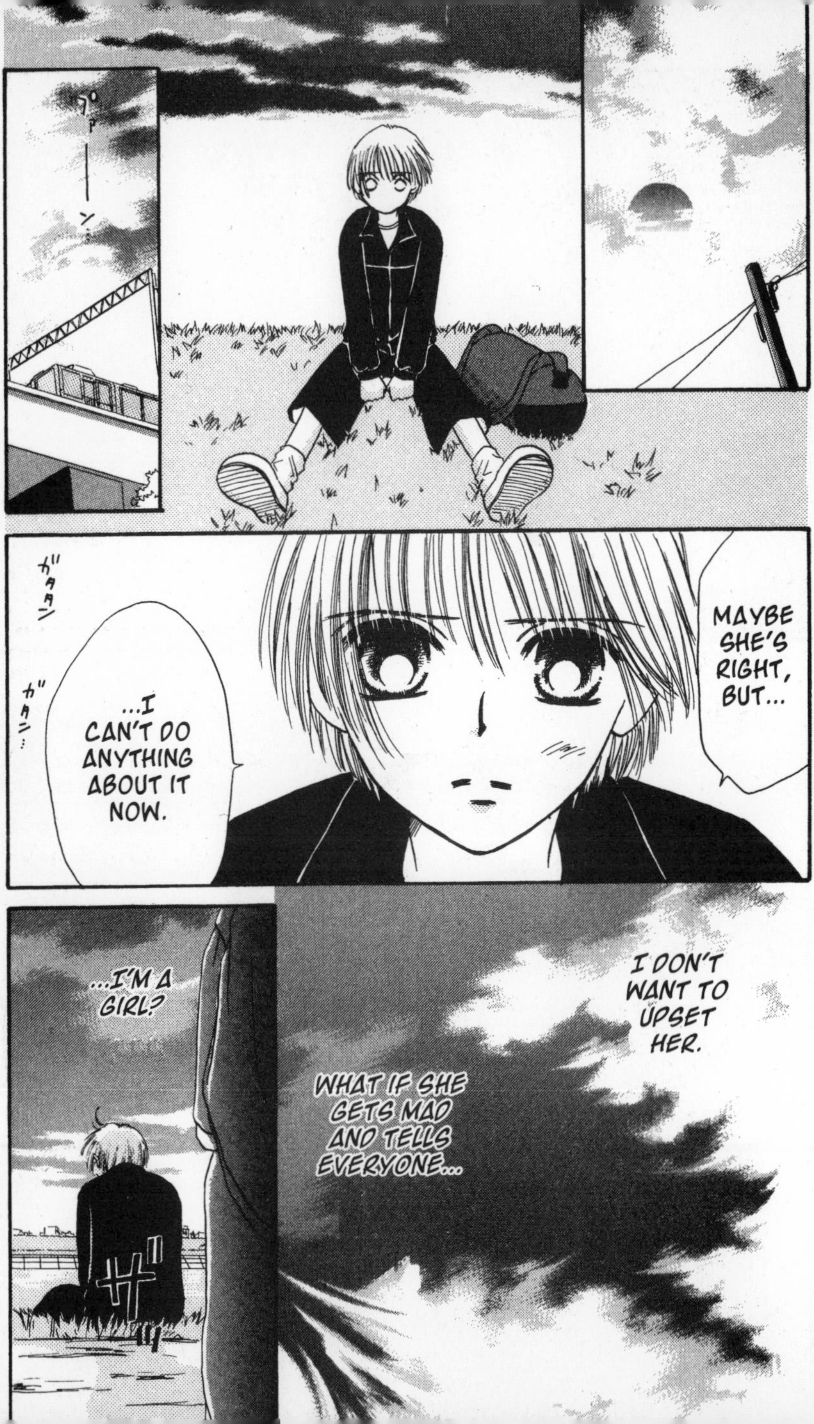
プァーーーン…
MAYBE SHE'S RIGHT, BUT...
...I CAN'T DO ANYTHING ABOUT IT NOW.
ガタタン
ガタン…
I DON'T WANT TO UPSET HER.
WHAT IF SHE GETS MAD AND TELLS EVERYONE...
...I'M A GIRL?
ザ

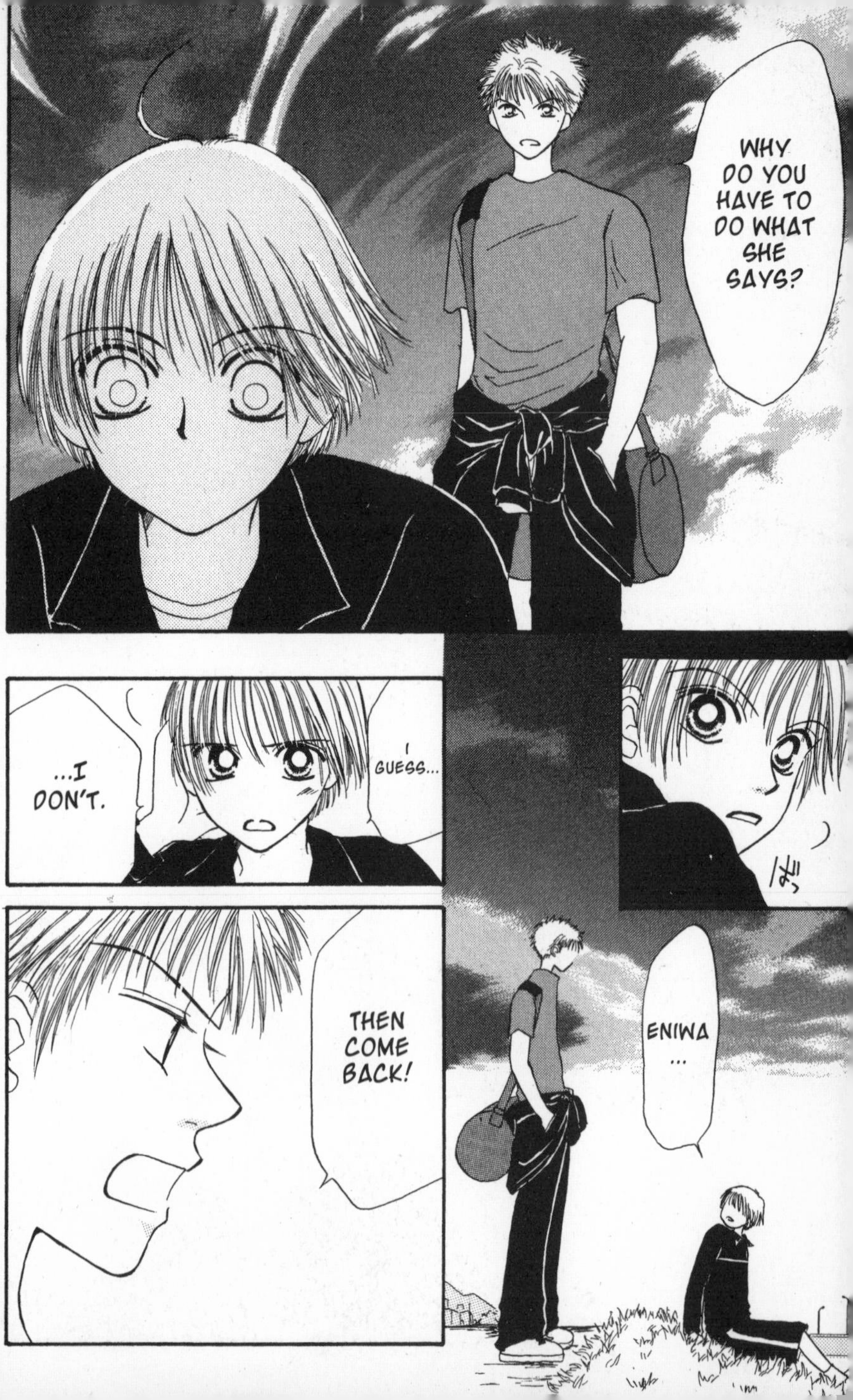
WHY DO YOU HAVE TO DO WHAT SHE SAYS?
I GUESS...
...I DON'T.
ENIWA ...
THEN COME BACK!

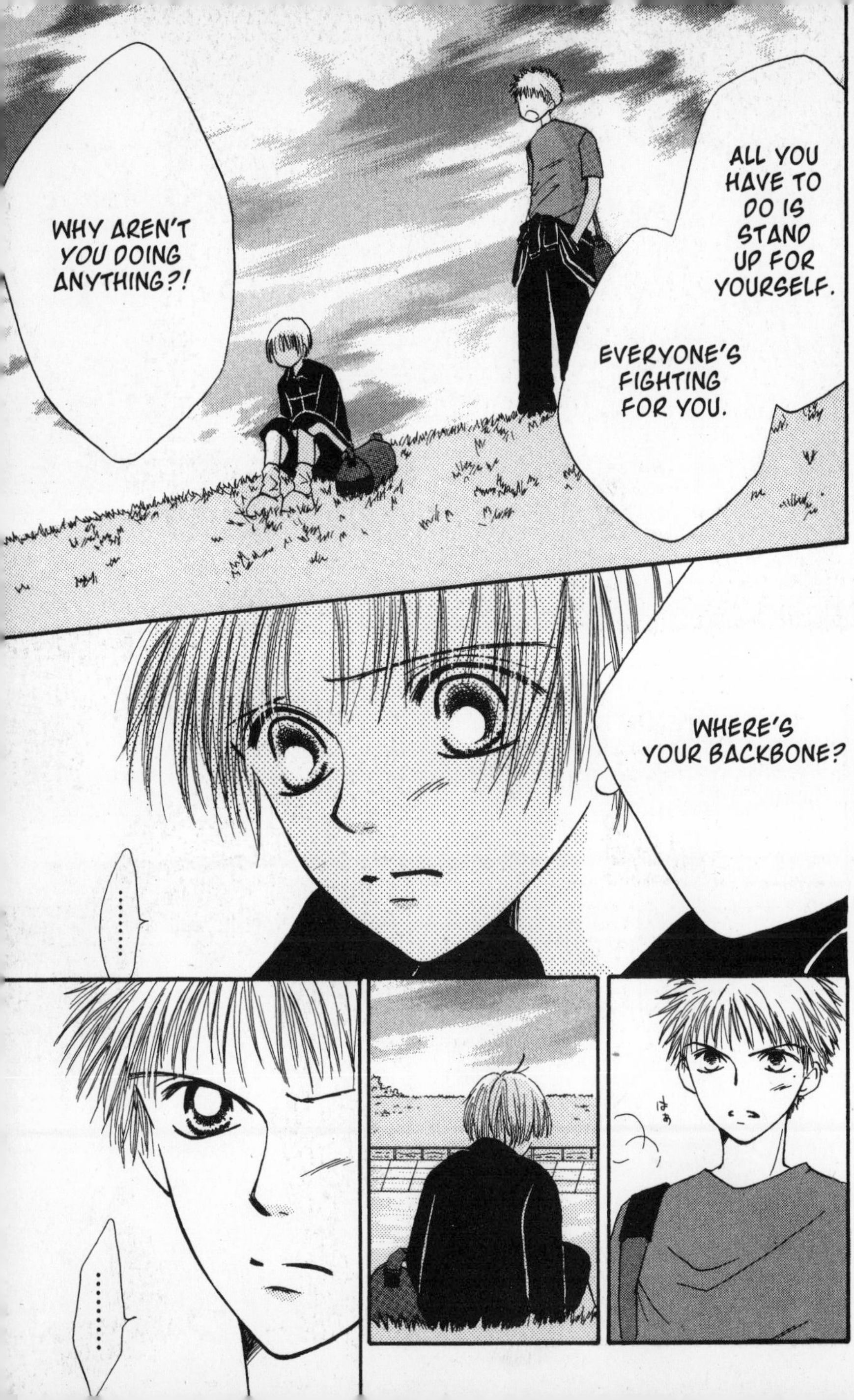
ALL YOU HAVE TO DO IS STAND UP FOR YOURSELF.
EVERYONE'S FIGHTING FOR YOU.
WHY AREN'T YOU DOING ANYTHING?!
WHERE'S YOUR BACKBONE?
......
はぁ
......

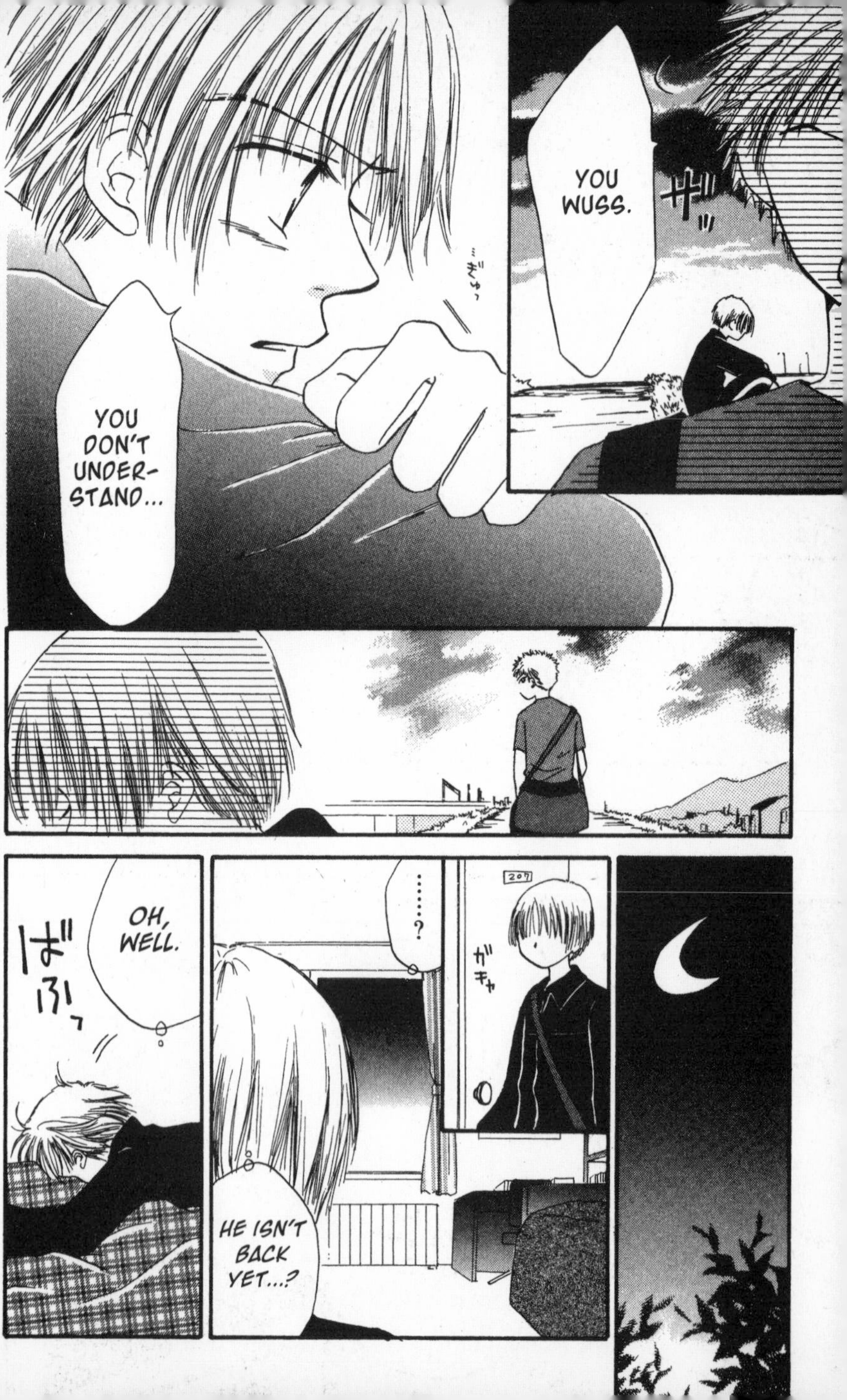
YOU WUSS.
ザッ
ぎゅっ
YOU DON'T UNDER-STAND...
ガチャ
......?
HE ISN'T BACK YET...?
OH, WELL.
ばふっ

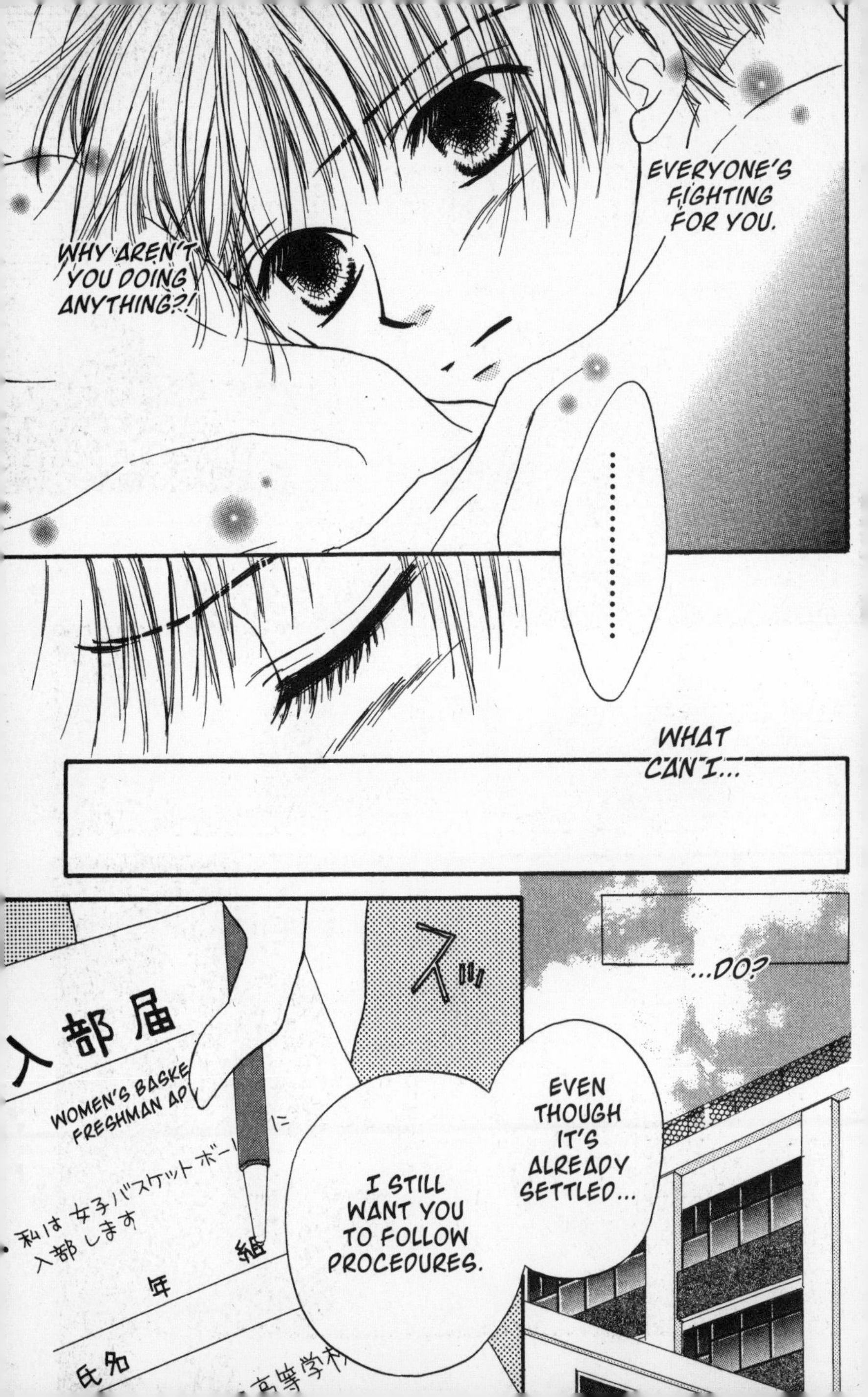
EVERYONE'S FIGHTING FOR YOU.
WHY AREN'T YOU DOING ANYTHING?!
......
WHAT CAN I...
...DO?
EVEN THOUGH IT'S ALREADY SETTLED...
I STILL WANT YOU TO FOLLOW PROCEDURES.
スッ
入部届
WOMEN'S BASKE
FRESHMAN AP
私は 女子バスケットボー に
入部 します
年 組
氏名

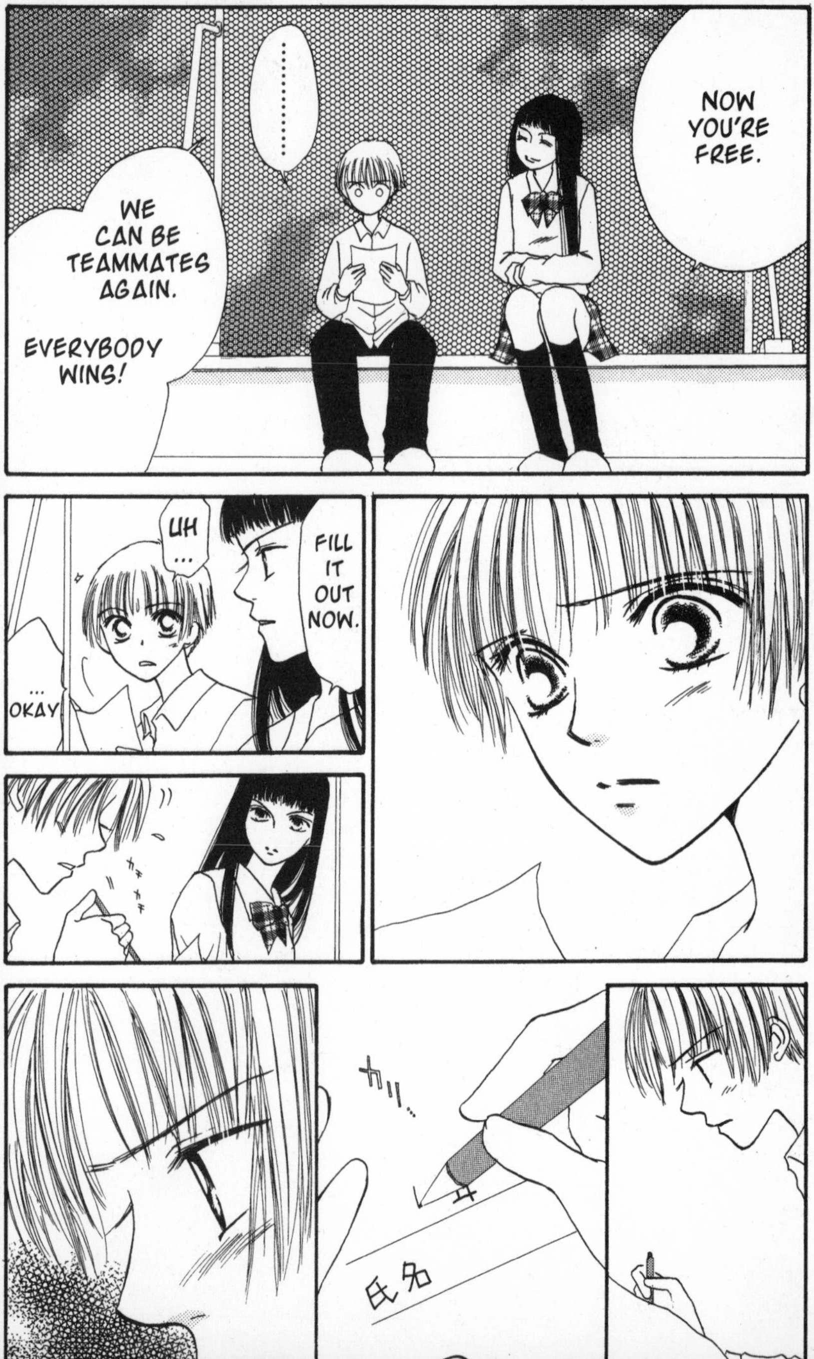
NOW YOU'RE FREE.
......
WE CAN BE TEAMMATES AGAIN.
EVERYBODY WINS!
FILL IT OUT NOW.
UH ...
... OKAY.
カリ...
氏名

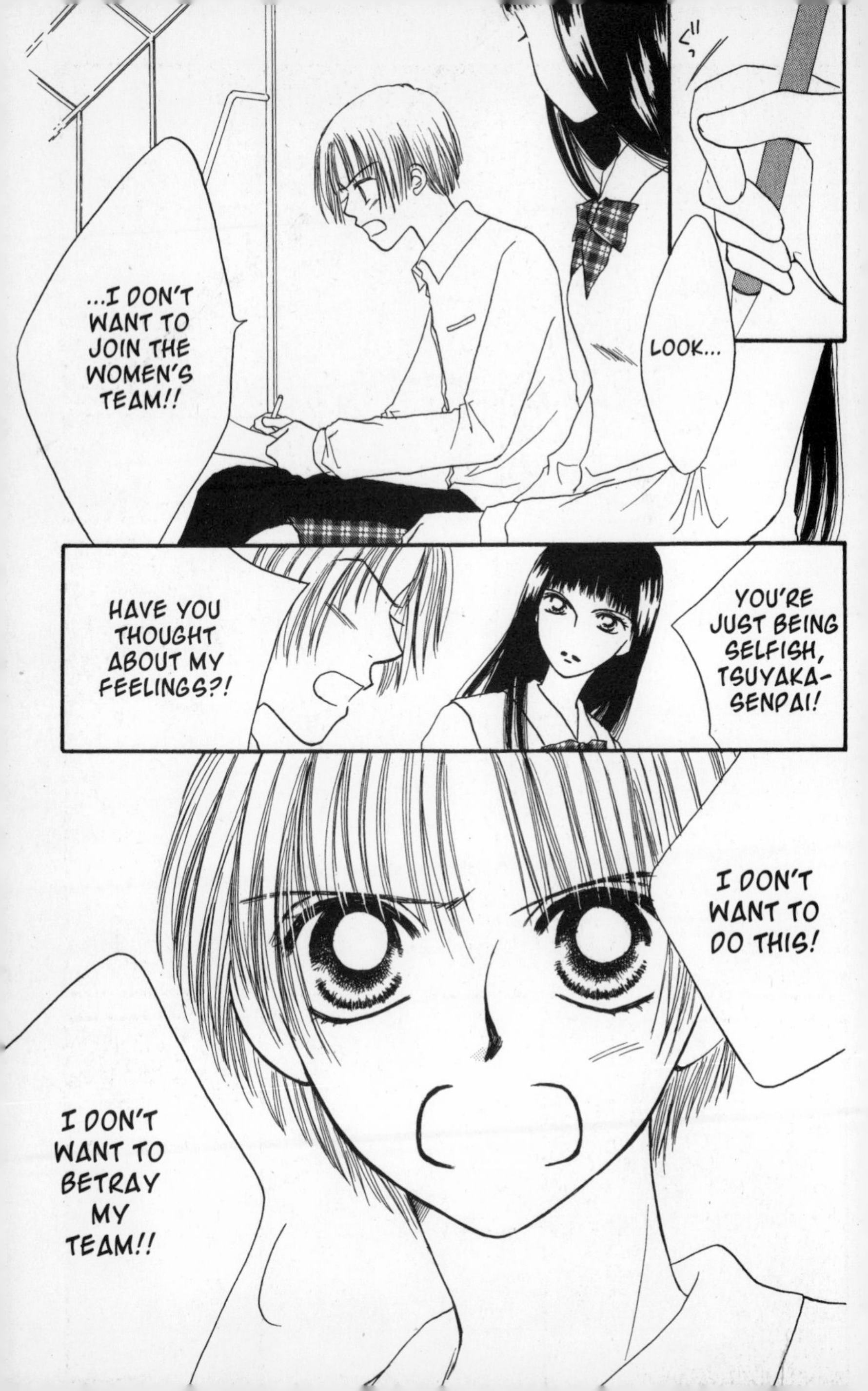

LOOK...
...I DON'T WANT TO JOIN THE WOMEN'S TEAM!!
YOU'RE JUST BEING SELFISH, TSUYAKA-SENPAI!
HAVE YOU THOUGHT ABOUT MY FEELINGS?!
I DON'T WANT TO DO THIS!
I DON'T WANT TO BETRAY MY TEAM!!

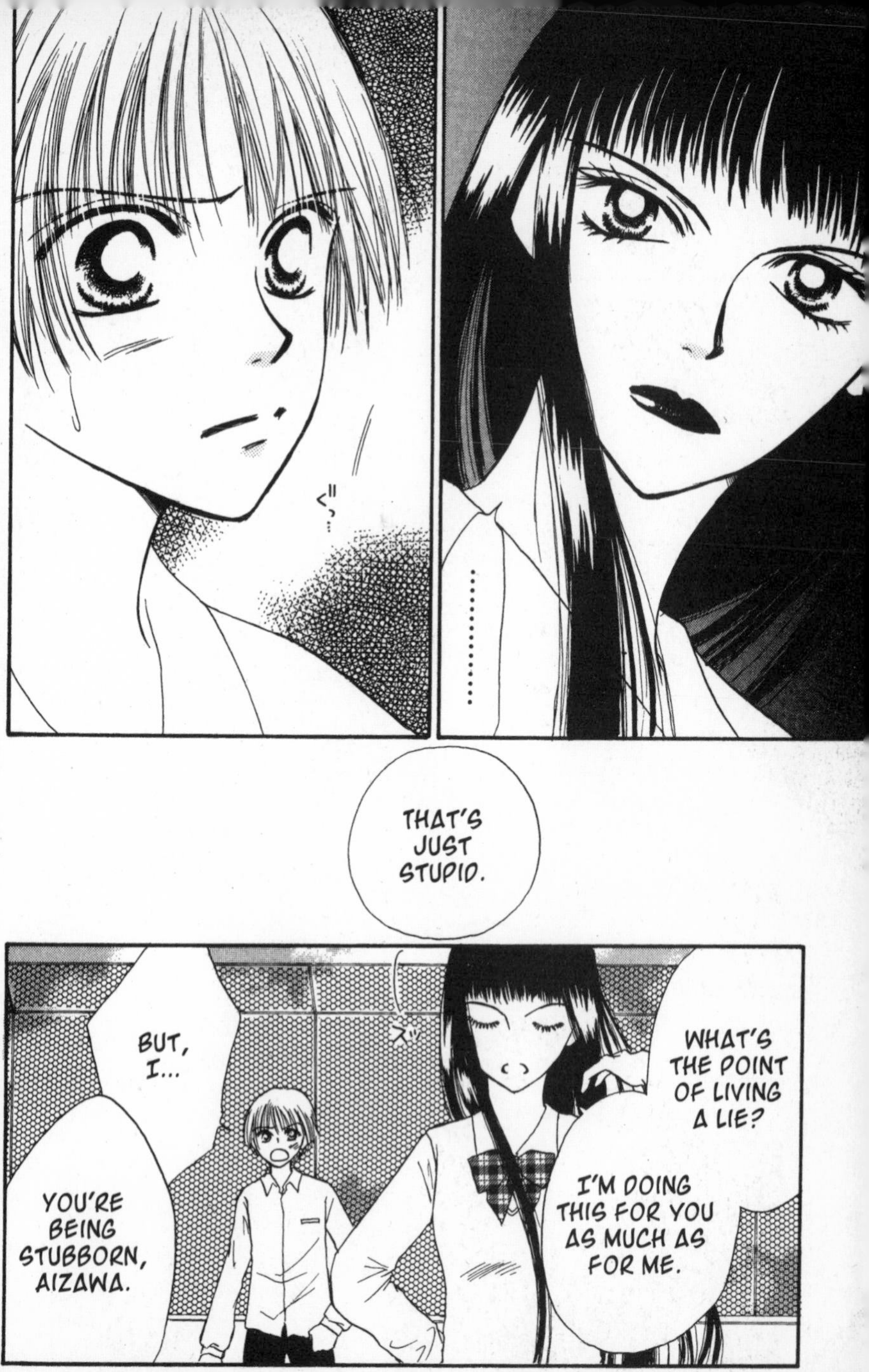

....
ぐっ
THAT'S JUST STUPID.
WHAT'S THE POINT OF LIVING A LIE?
I'M DOING THIS FOR YOU AS MUCH AS FOR ME.
スッ
BUT, I...
YOU'RE BEING STUBBORN, AIZAWA.

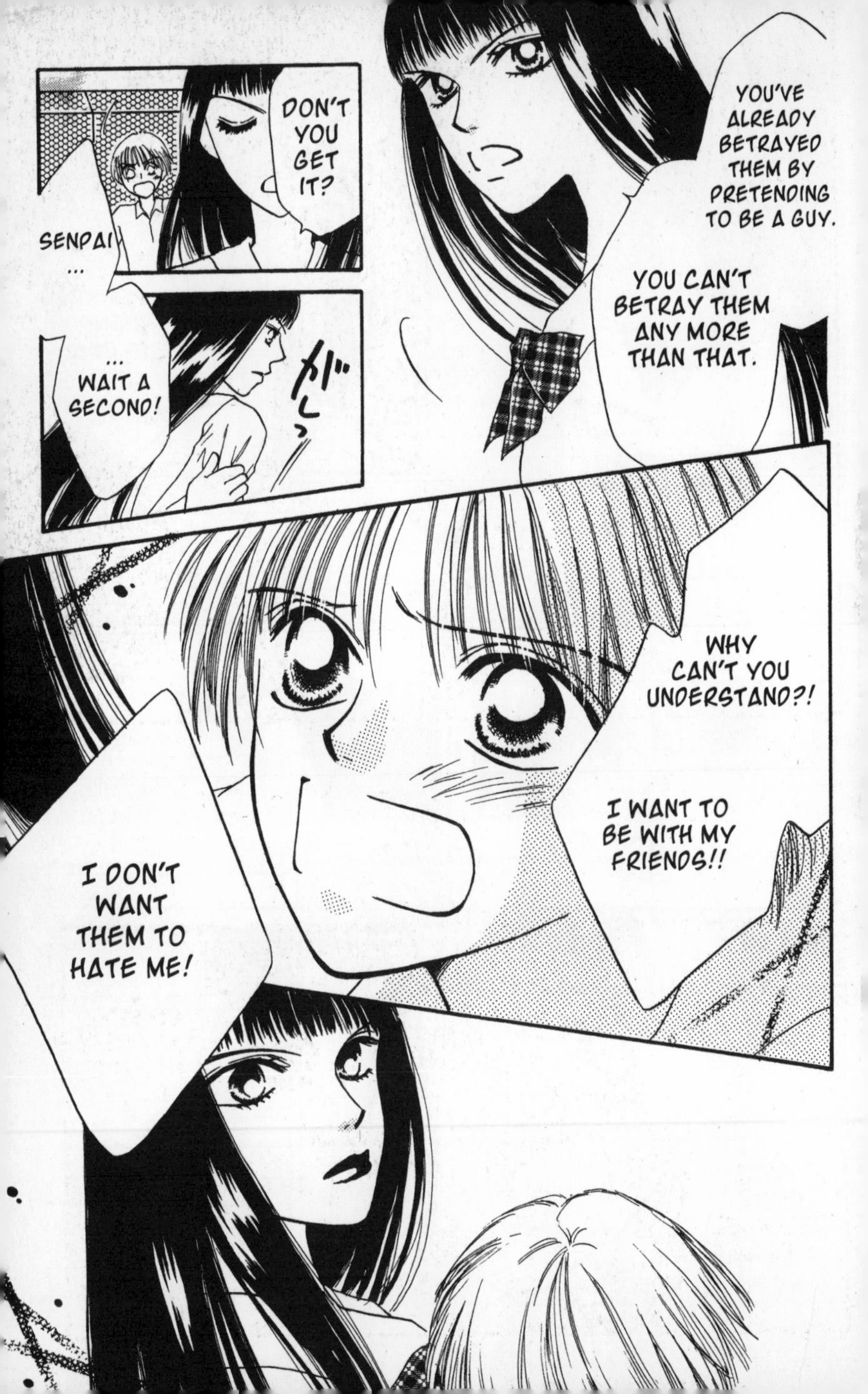
YOU'VE ALREADY BETRAYED THEM BY PRETENDING TO BE A GUY.
YOU CAN'T BETRAY THEM ANY MORE THAN THAT.
DON'T YOU GET IT?
SENPAI...
... WAIT A SECOND!
がしっ
WHY CAN'T YOU UNDERSTAND?!
I WANT TO BE WITH MY FRIENDS!!
I DON'T WANT THEM TO HATE ME!

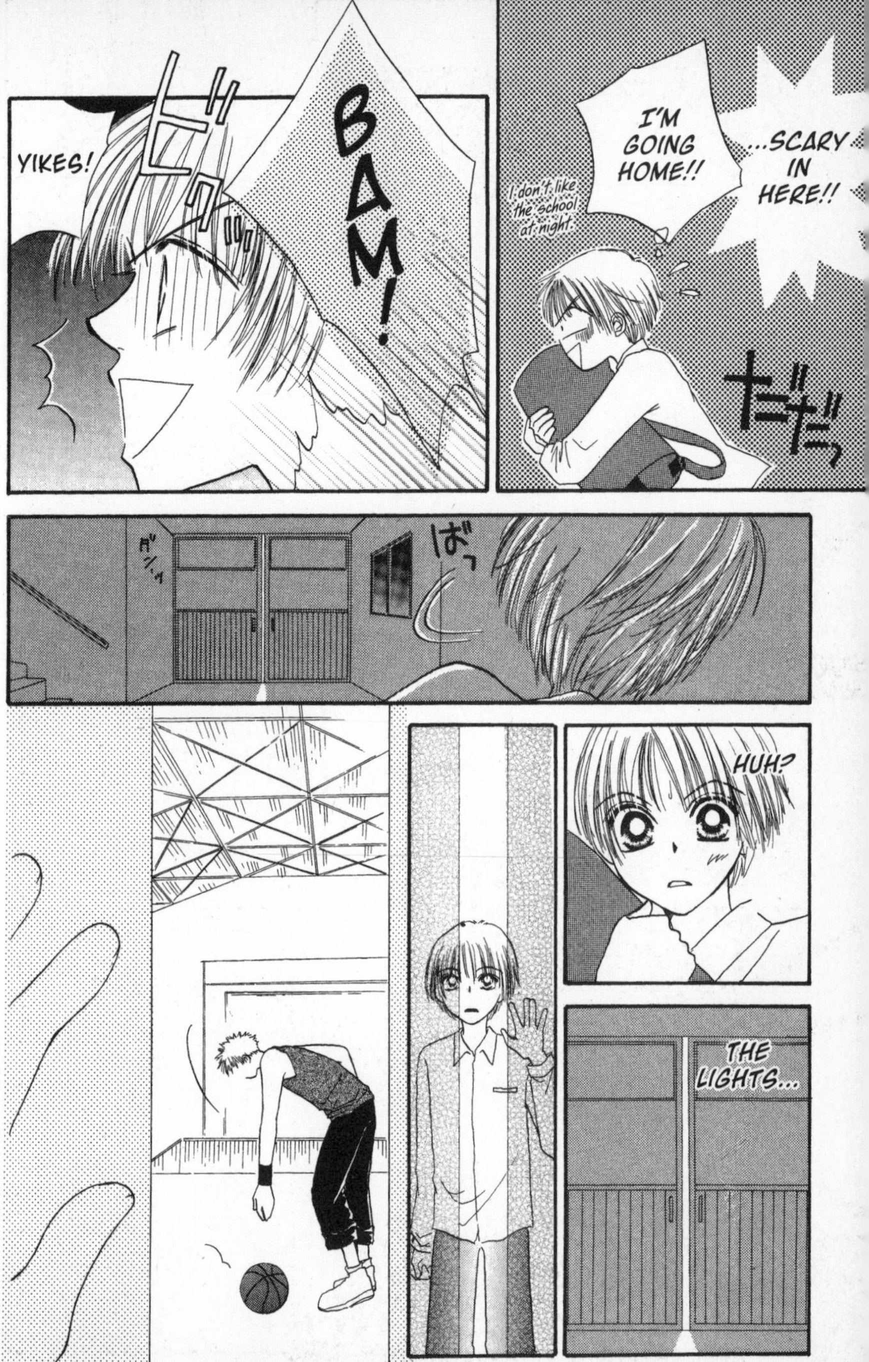
...SCARY IN HERE!!
I'M GOING HOME!!
I don't like the school at night.
BAM!
YIKES!
HUH?
THE LIGHTS...

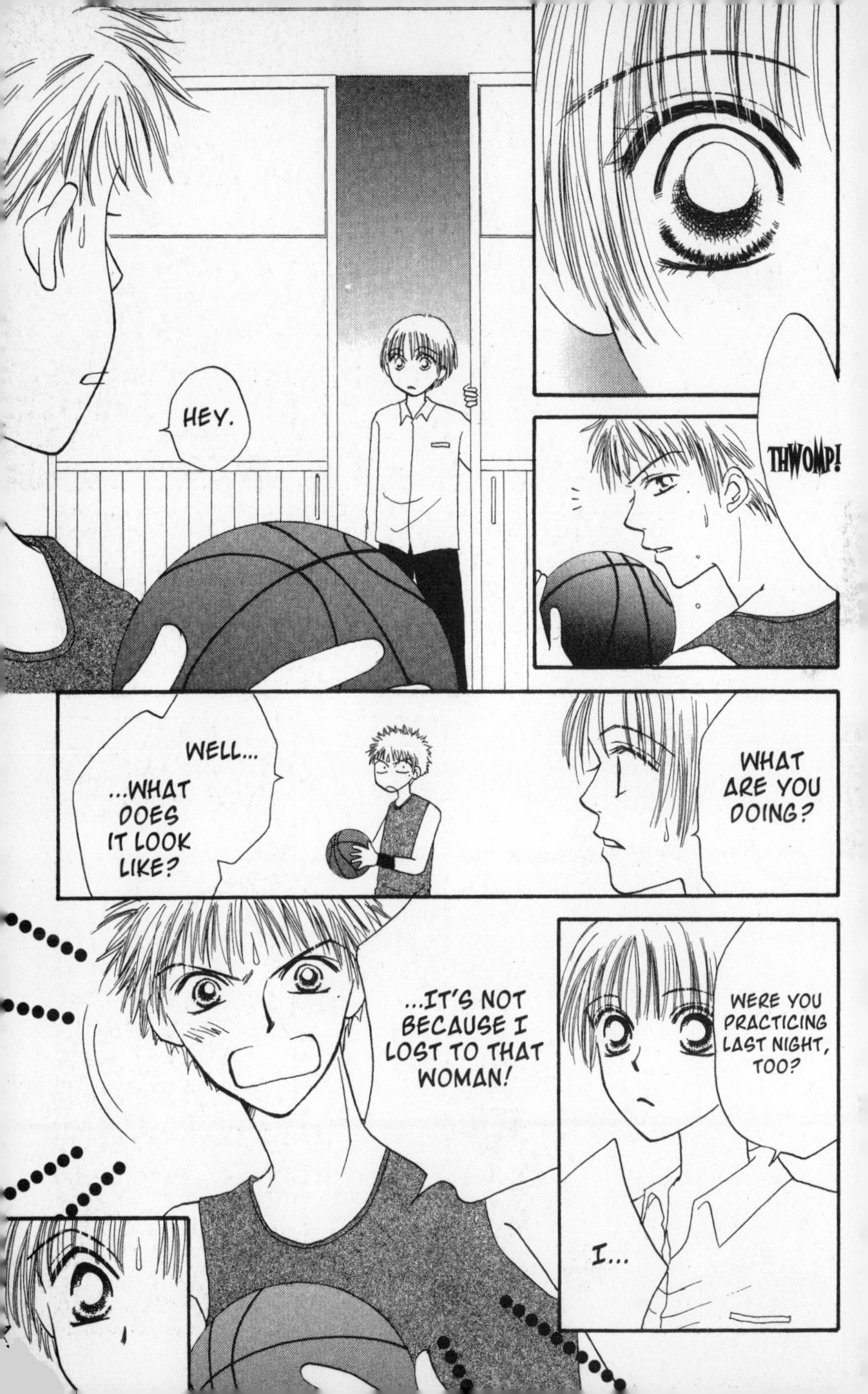
THWOMP!
HEY.
WHAT ARE YOU DOING?
WELL...
...WHAT DOES IT LOOK LIKE?
WERE YOU PRACTICING LAST NIGHT, TOO?
I...
...IT'S NOT BECAUSE I LOST TO THAT WOMAN!

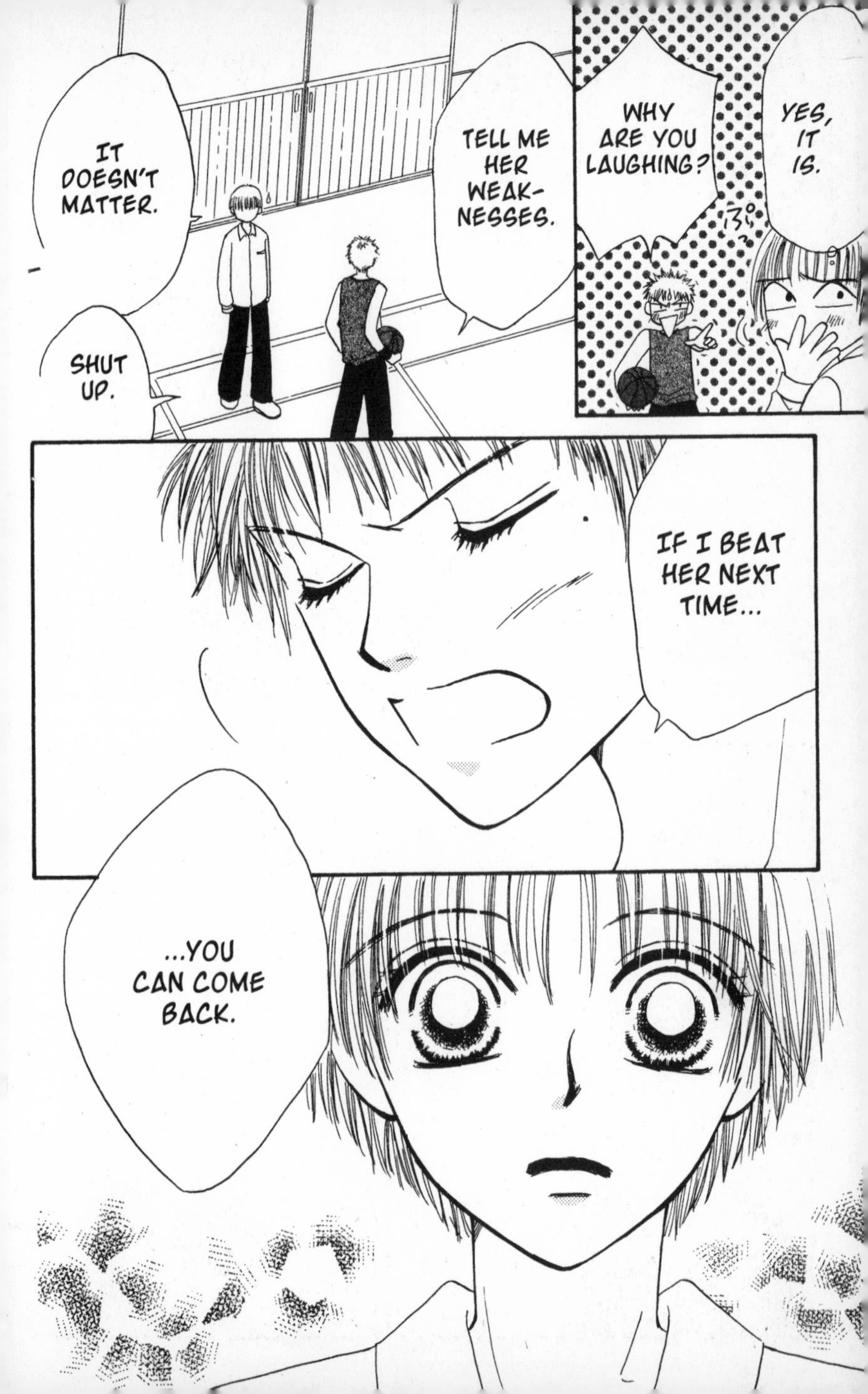
YES, IT IS.
WHY ARE YOU LAUGHING?
TELL ME HER WEAK-NESSES.
IT DOESN'T MATTER.
SHUT UP.
IF I BEAT HER NEXT TIME...
...YOU CAN COME BACK.

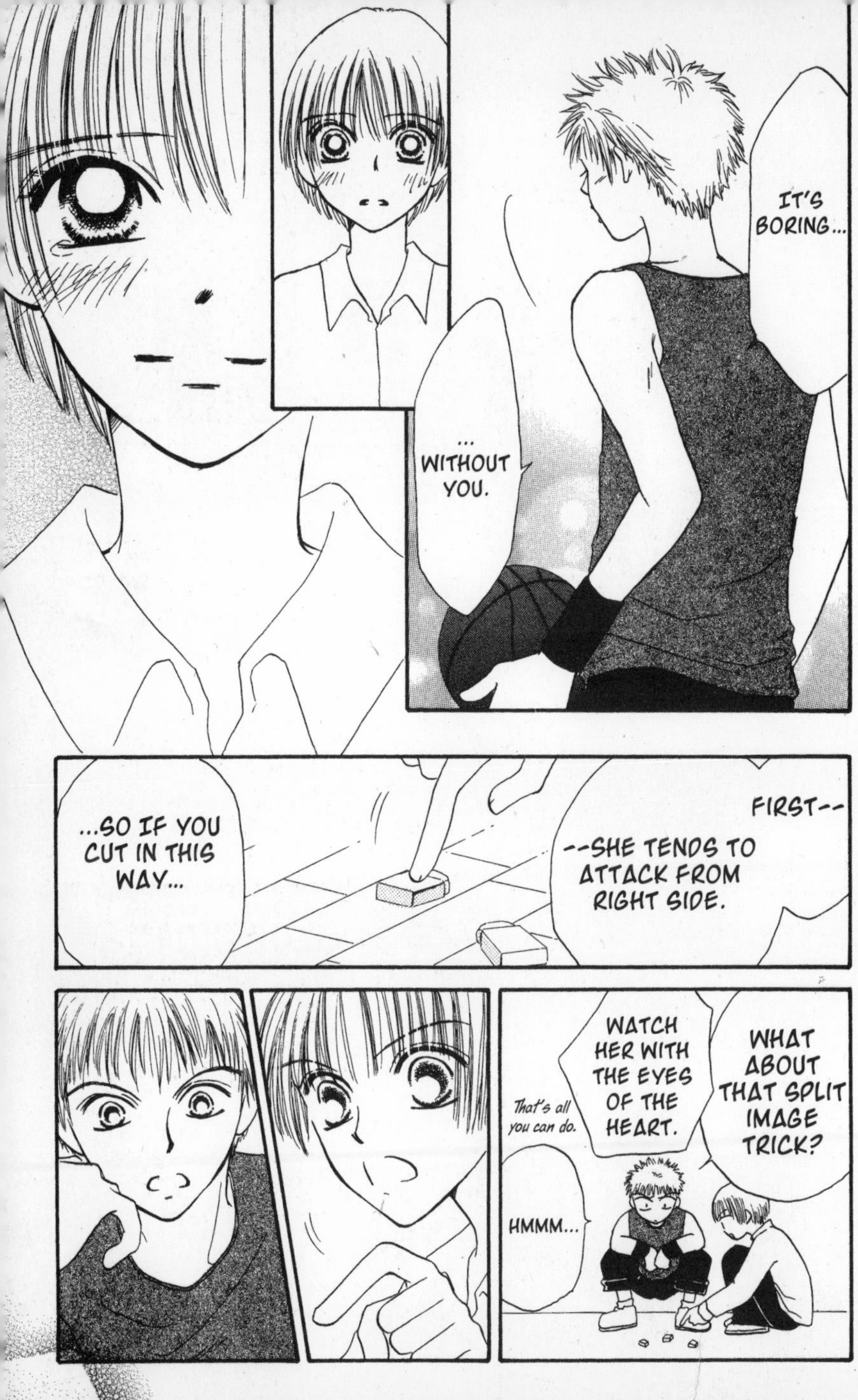
IT'S BORING...
...WITHOUT YOU.
FIRST--
--SHE TENDS TO ATTACK FROM RIGHT SIDE.
...SO IF YOU CUT IN THIS WAY...
WHAT ABOUT THAT SPLIT IMAGE TRICK?
WATCH HER WITH THE EYES OF THE HEART.
That's all you can do.
HMMM...

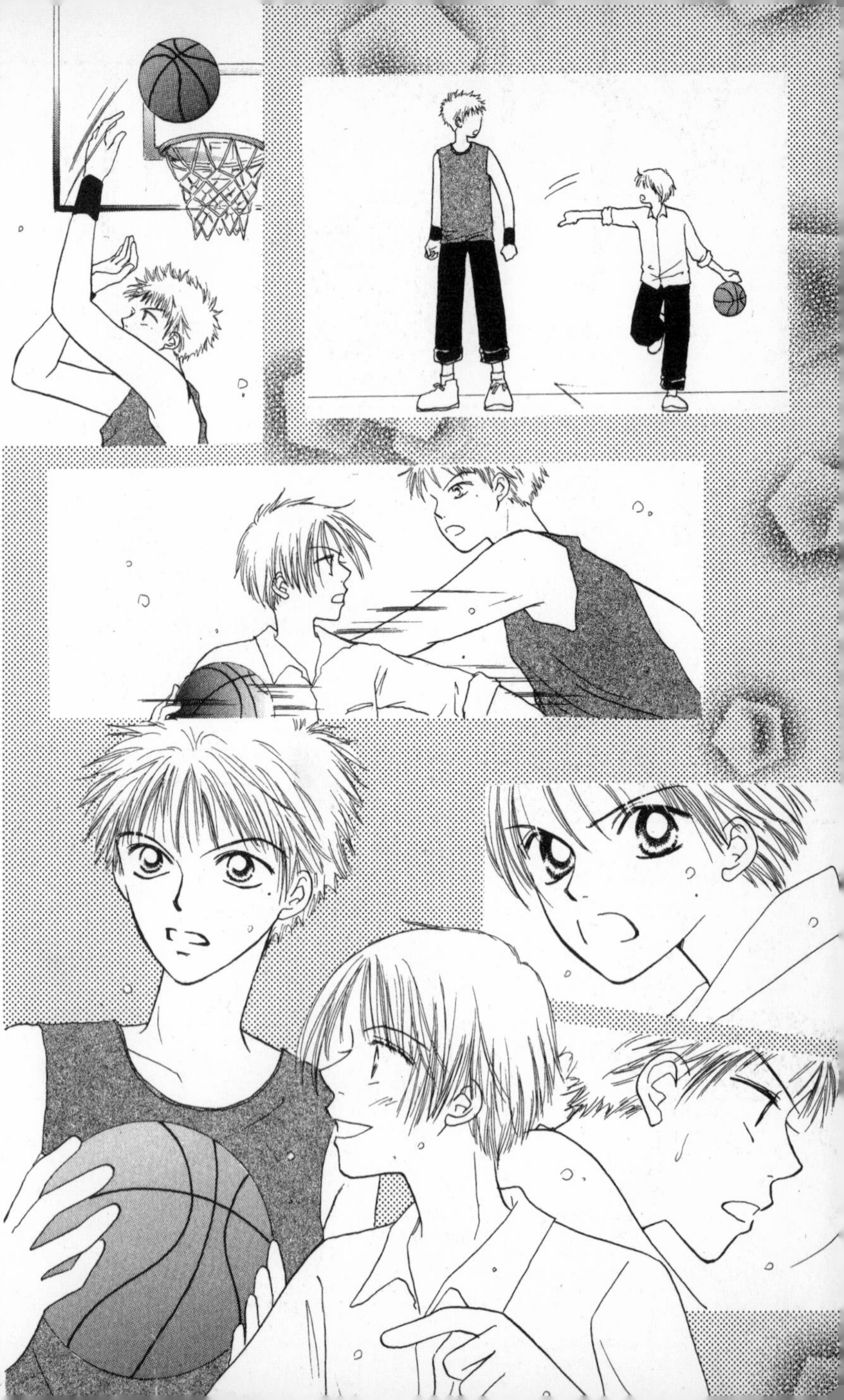

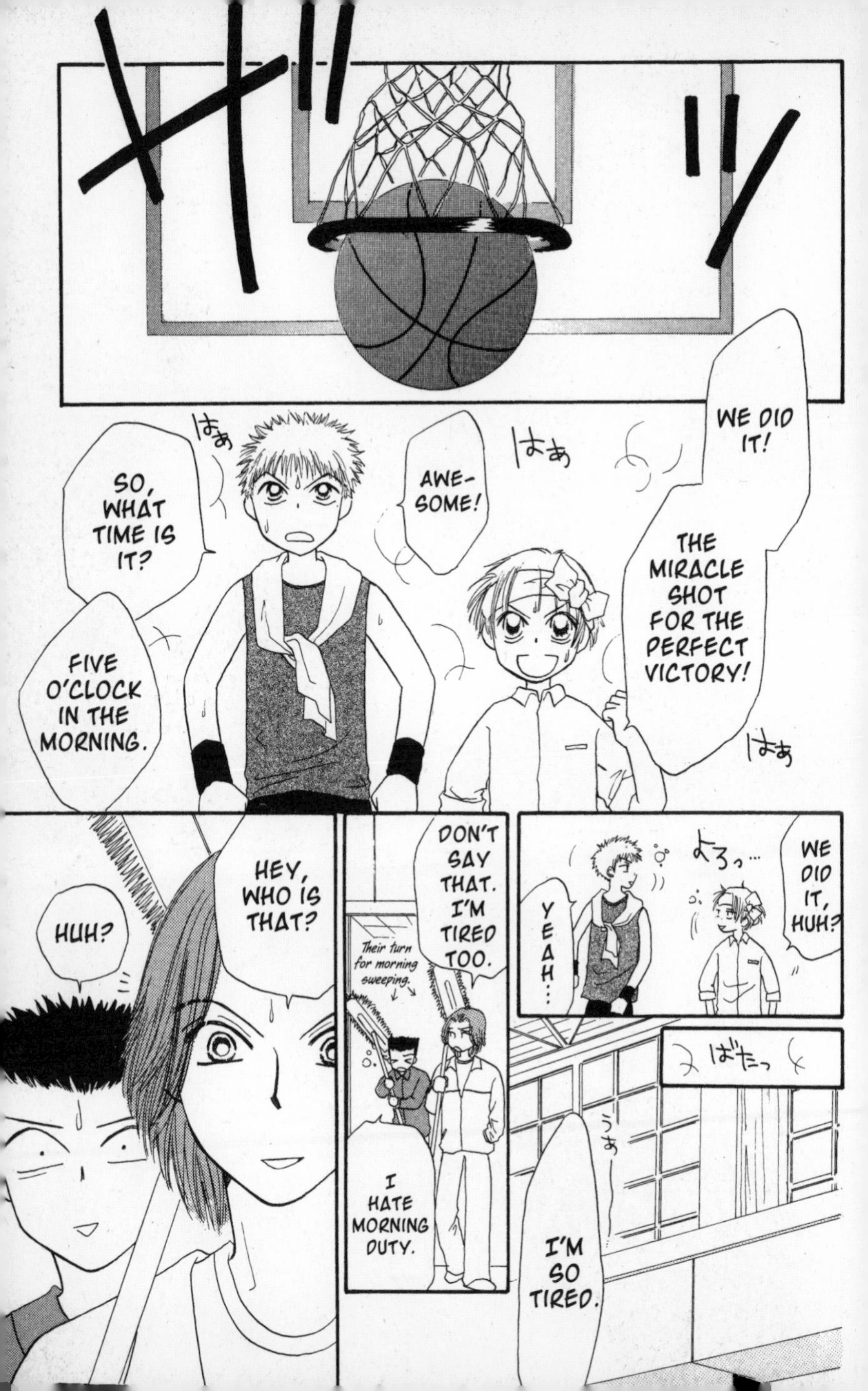
ザッ
WE DID IT!
THE MIRACLE SHOT FOR THE PERFECT VICTORY!
はぁ
AWE-SOME!
はぁ
はぁ
SO, WHAT TIME IS IT?
FIVE O'CLOCK IN THE MORNING.
WE DID IT, HUH?
よろっ…
YEAH…
ばたっ
うぁ〜
I'M SO TIRED.
DON'T SAY THAT. I'M TIRED TOO.
Their turn for morning sweeping.
I HATE MORNING DUTY.
HEY, WHO IS THAT?
HUH?

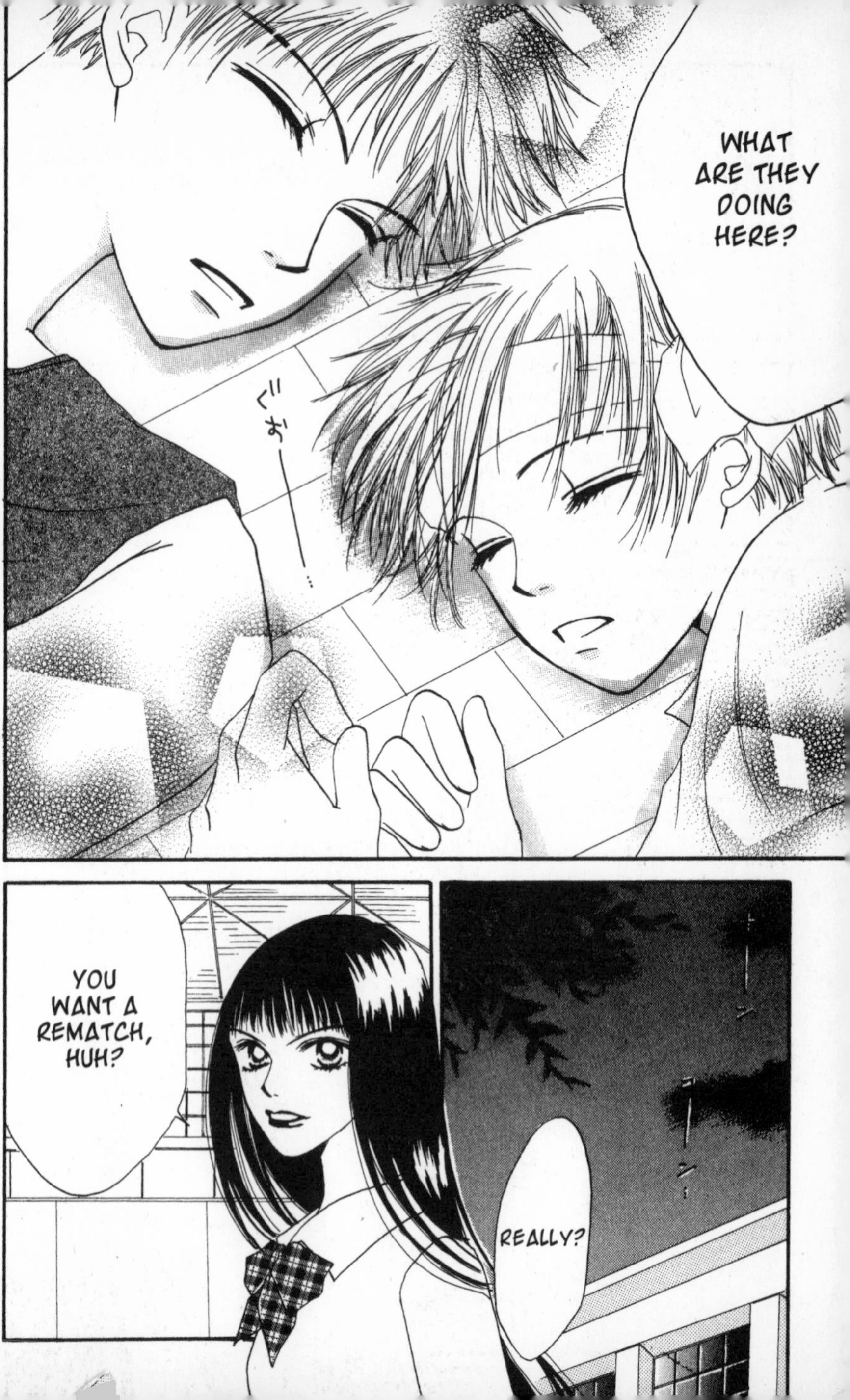
WHAT ARE THEY DOING HERE?
REALLY?
YOU WANT A REMATCH, HUH?

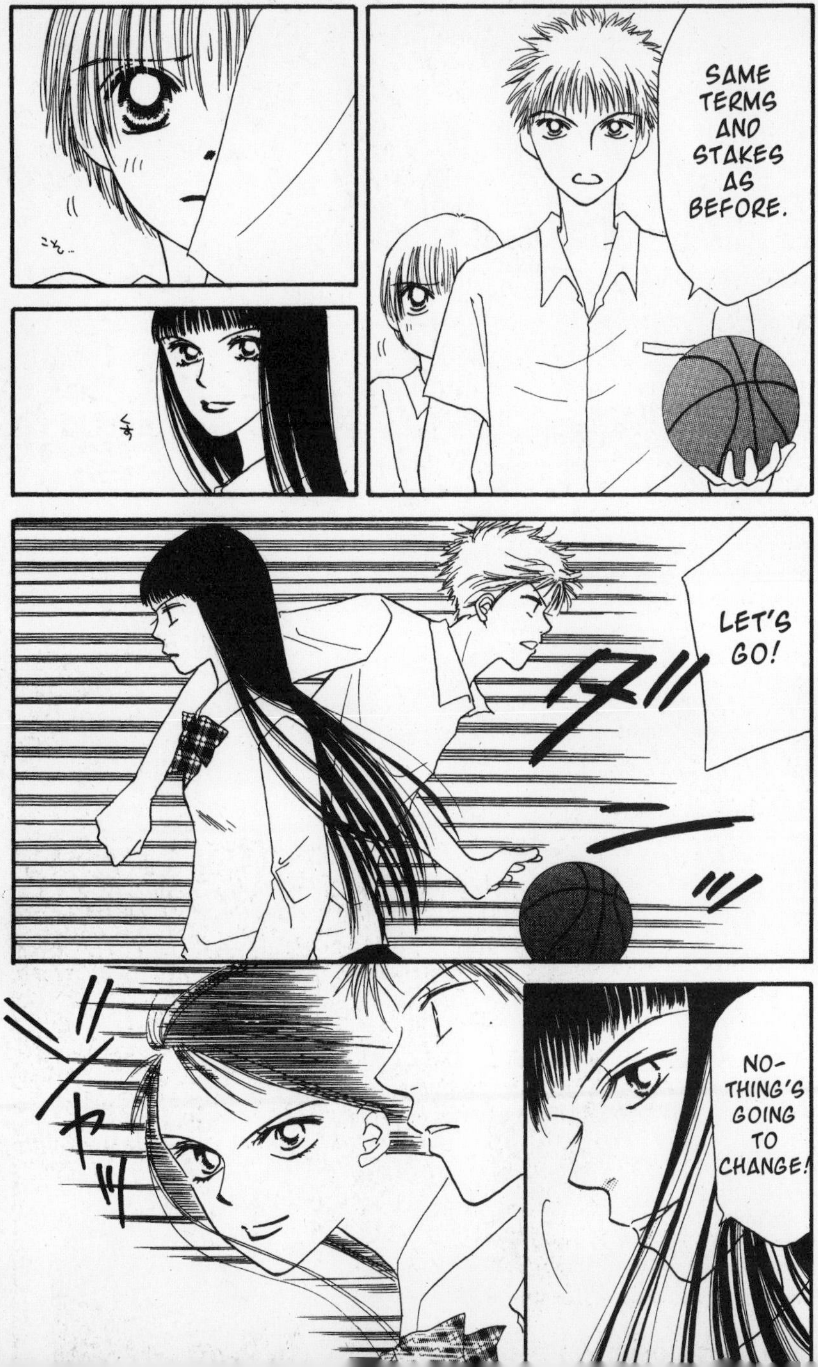
SAME TERMS AND STAKES AS BEFORE.
LET'S GO!
NO-THING'S GOING TO CHANGE!

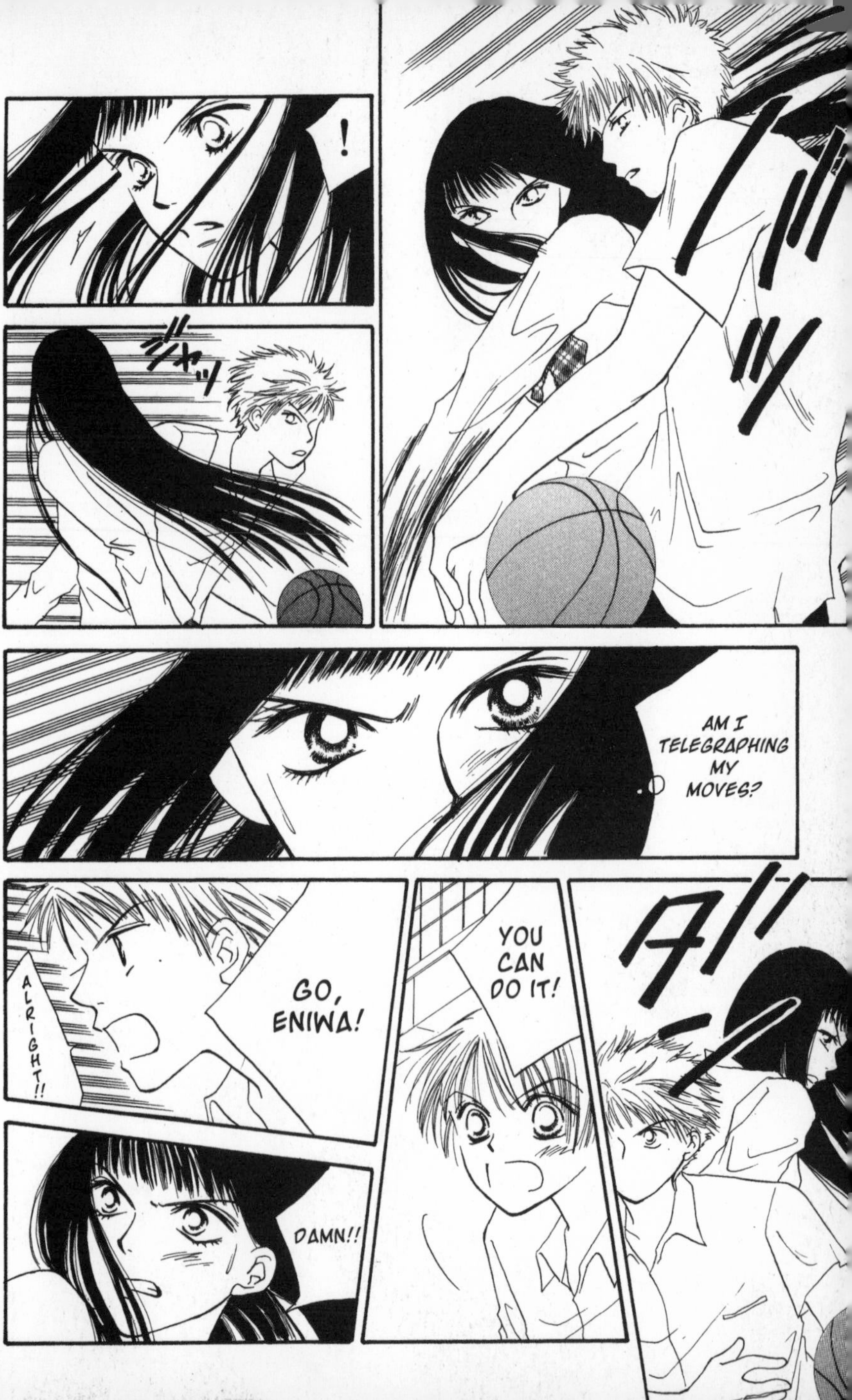
!
AM I TELEGRAPHING MY MOVES?
YOU CAN DO IT!
GO, ENIWA!
ALRIGHT!!
DAMN!!

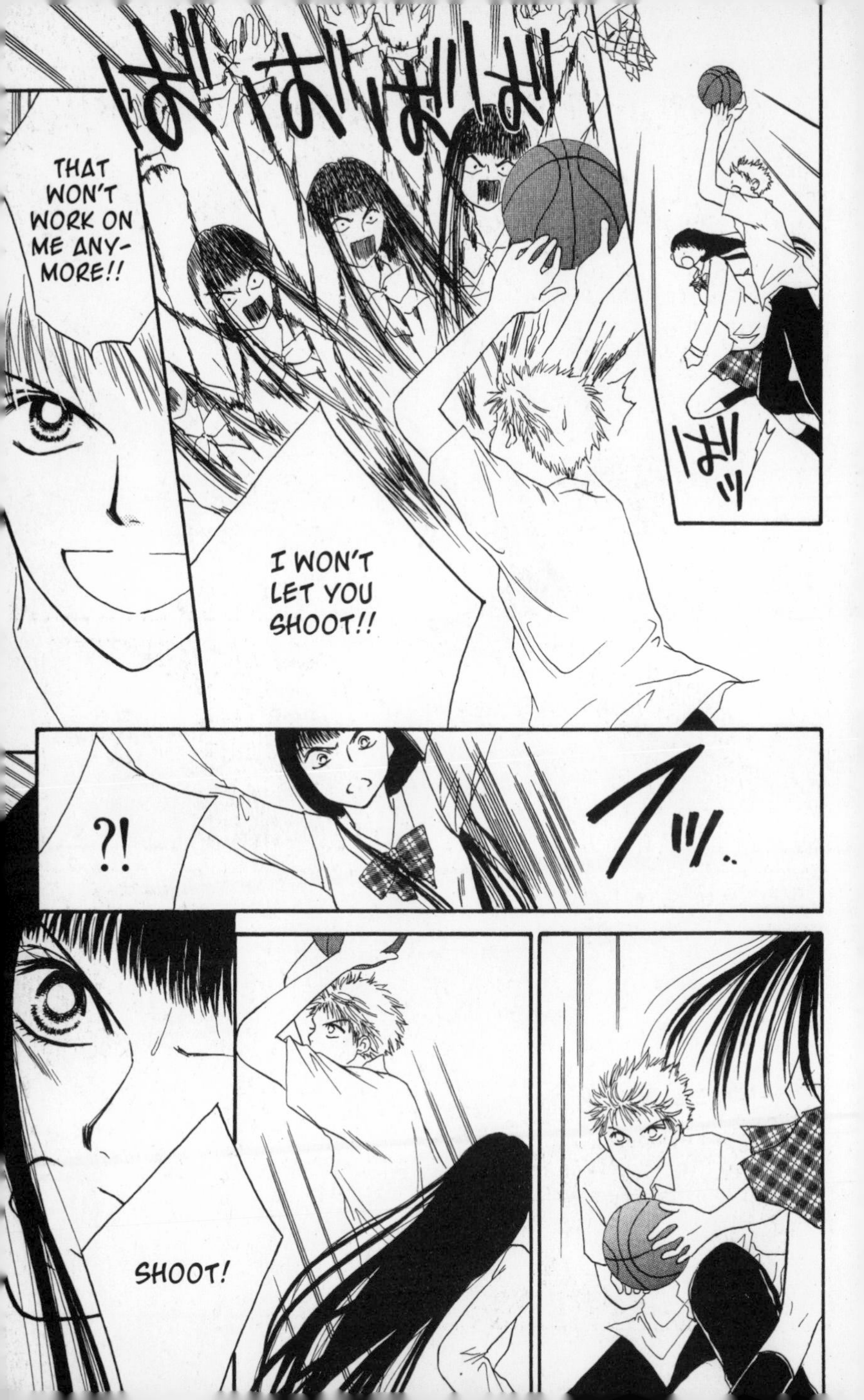
ばッ
I WON'T LET YOU SHOOT!!
THAT WON'T WORK ON ME ANYMORE!!
フッ..
?!
SHOOT!

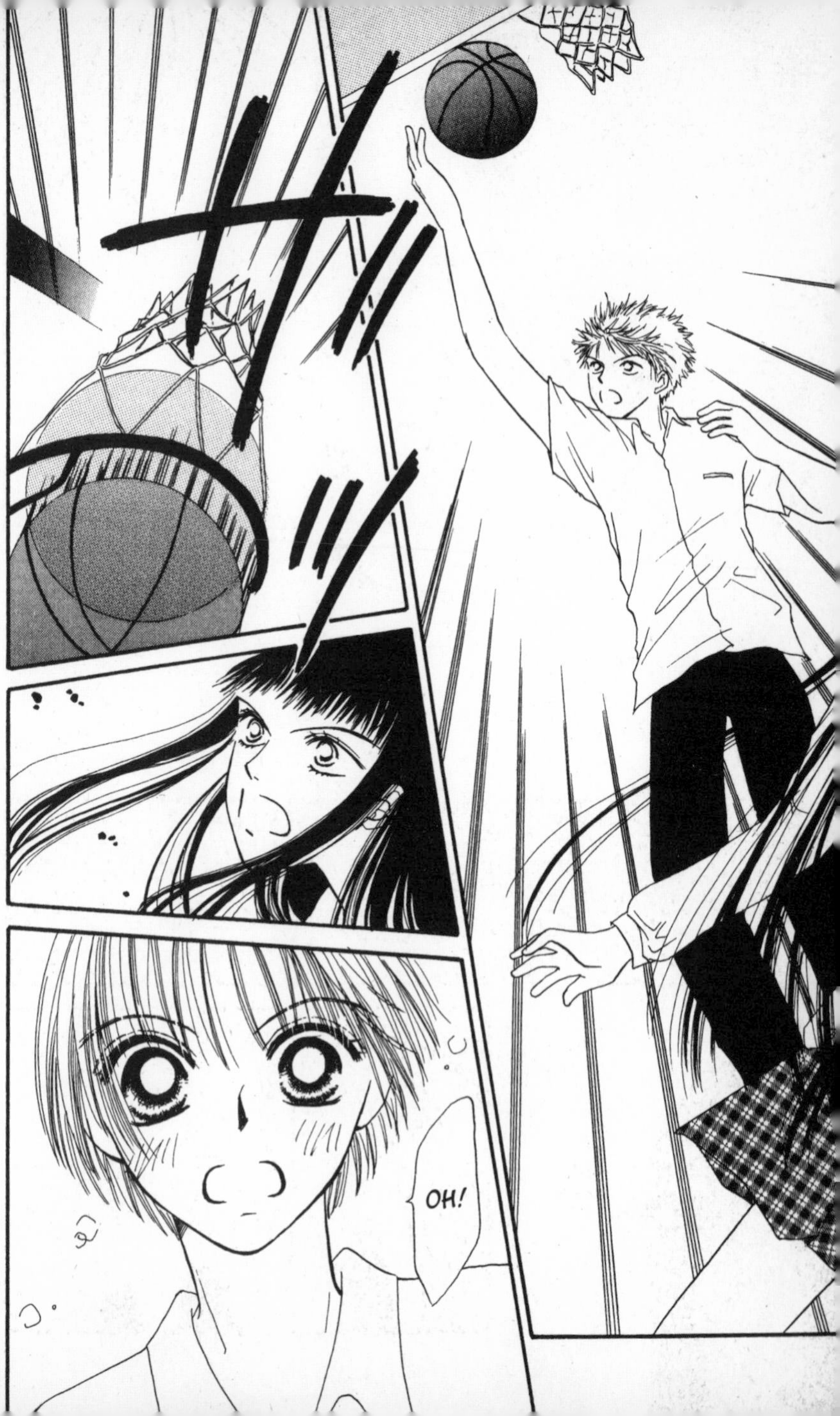
OH!

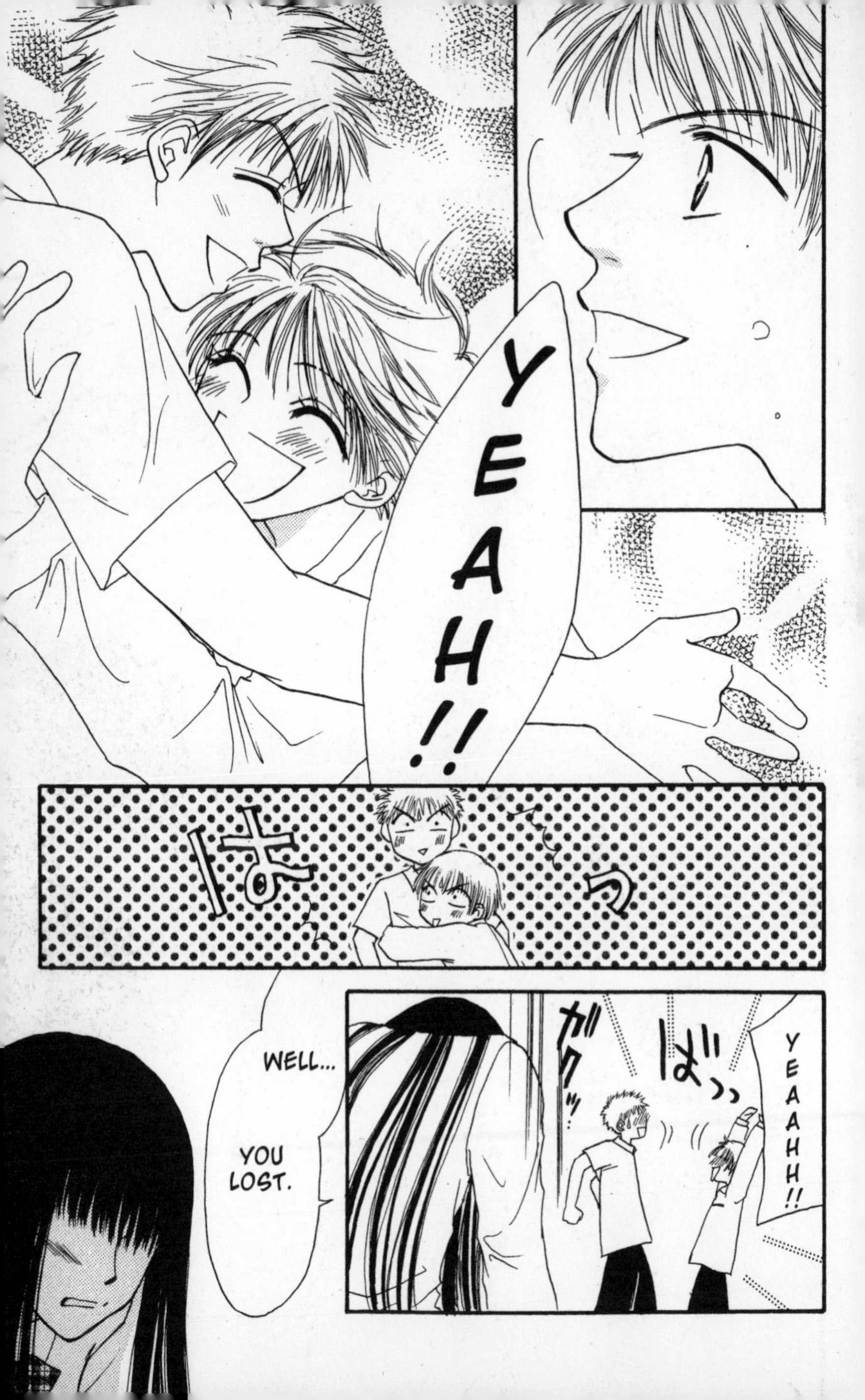
YEAH!!
はっ
YEAAAHH!!
ばっ
ガクッ
WELL...
YOU LOST.

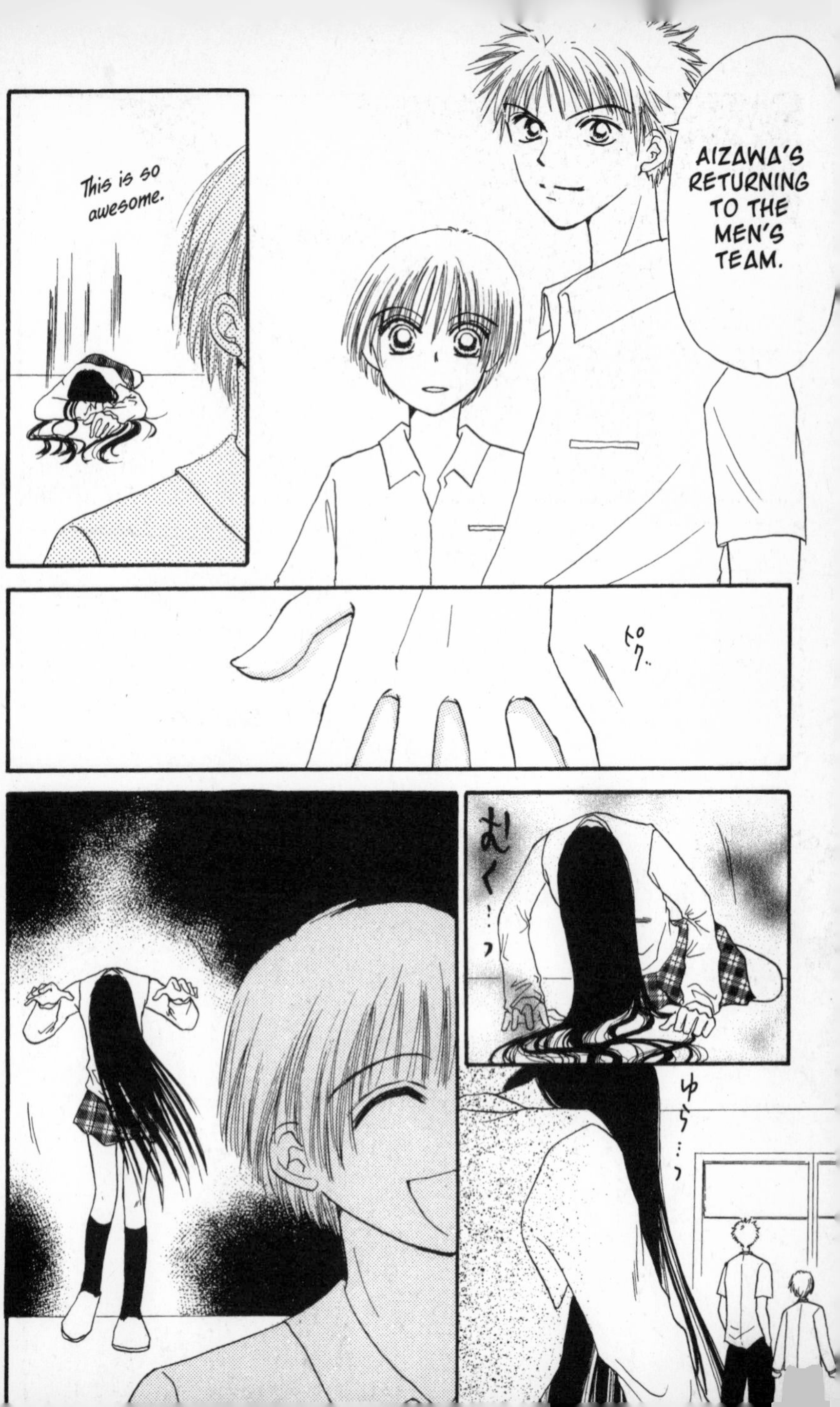
AIZAWA'S RETURNING TO THE MEN'S TEAM.
This is so awesome.
ピク゛
むく…っ
ゆら…っ

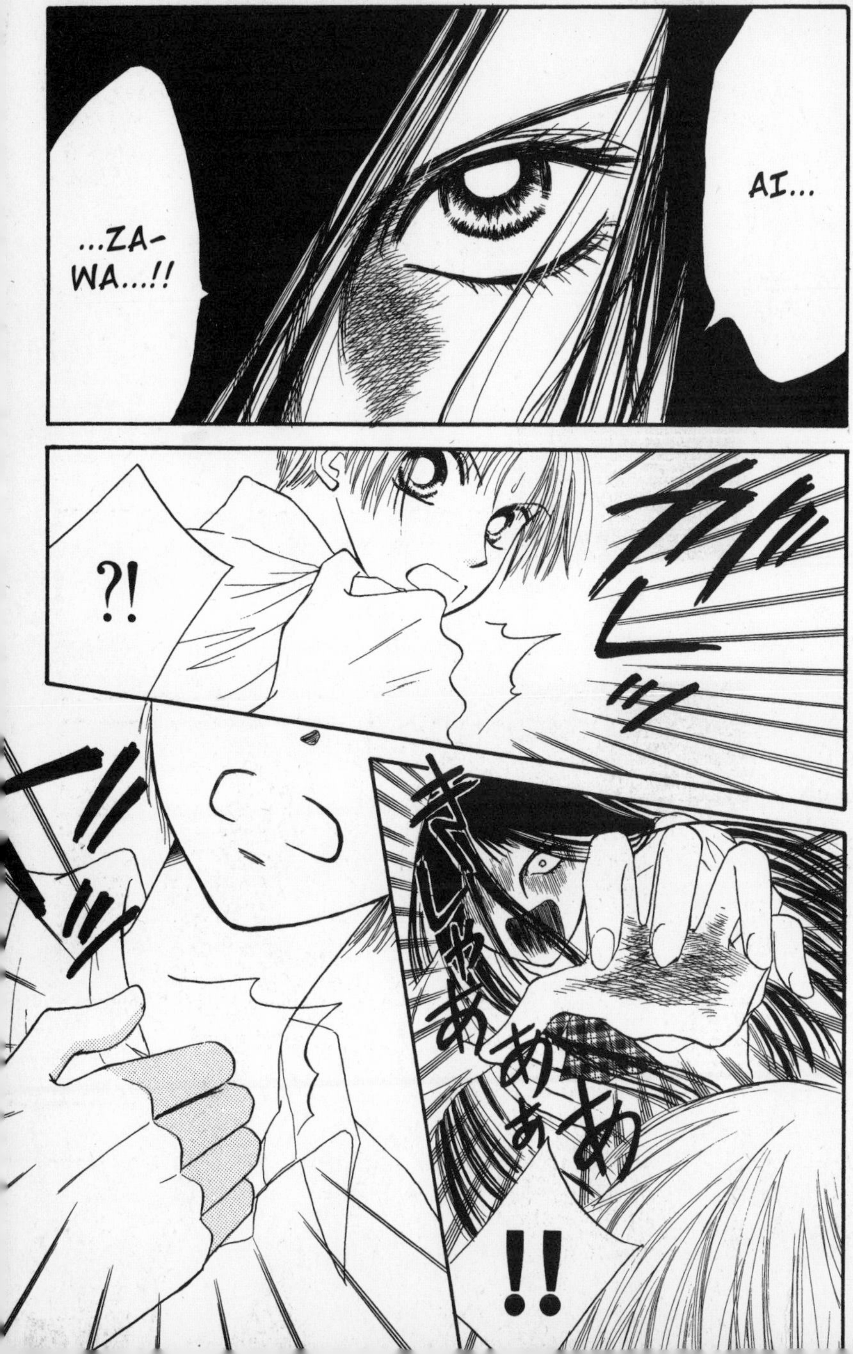
AI...
...ZA-
WA...!!
ガッ
?!
きしゃあああぁあ
!!

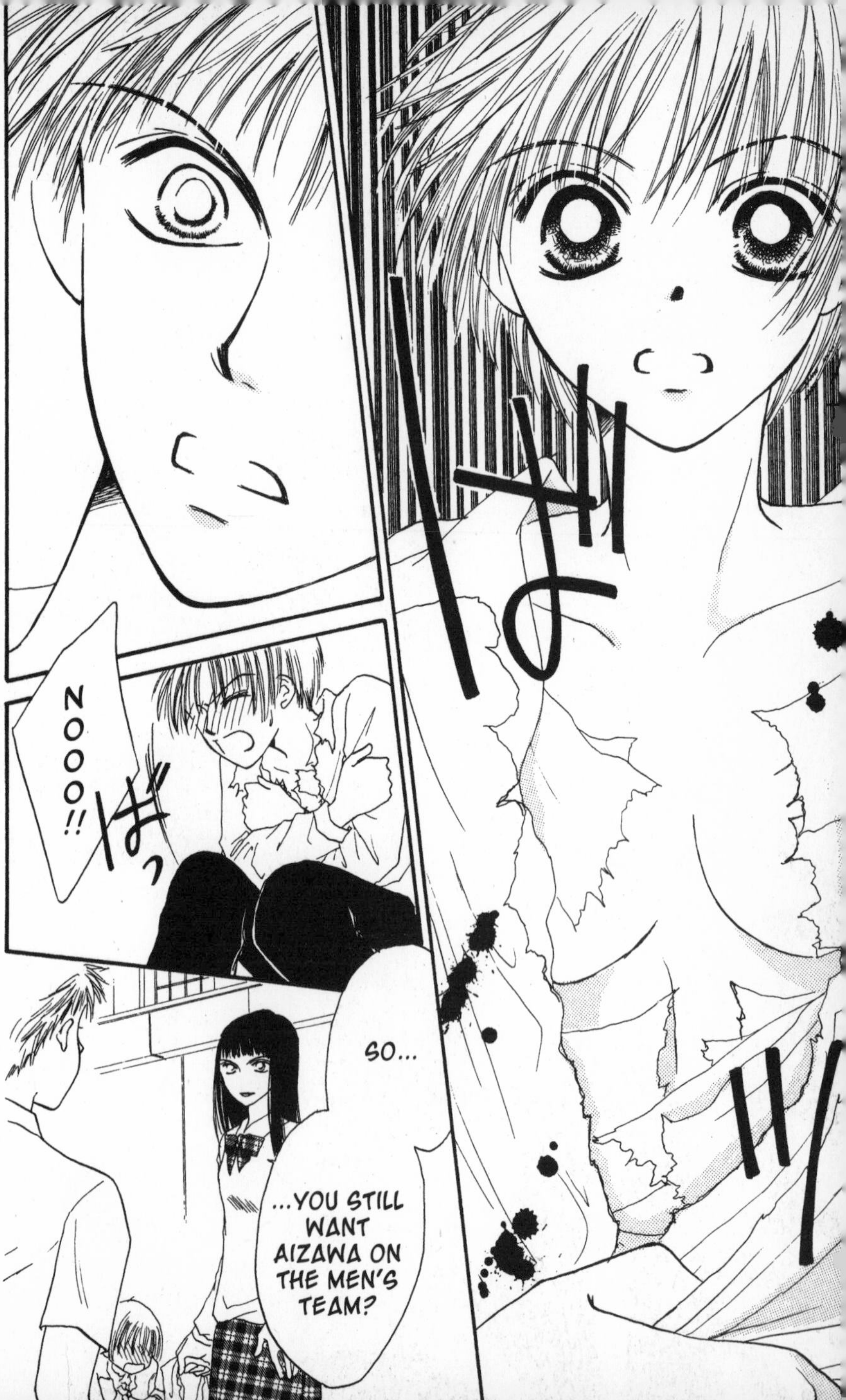
NOOOO!!
SO...
...YOU STILL WANT AIZAWA ON THE MEN'S TEAM?

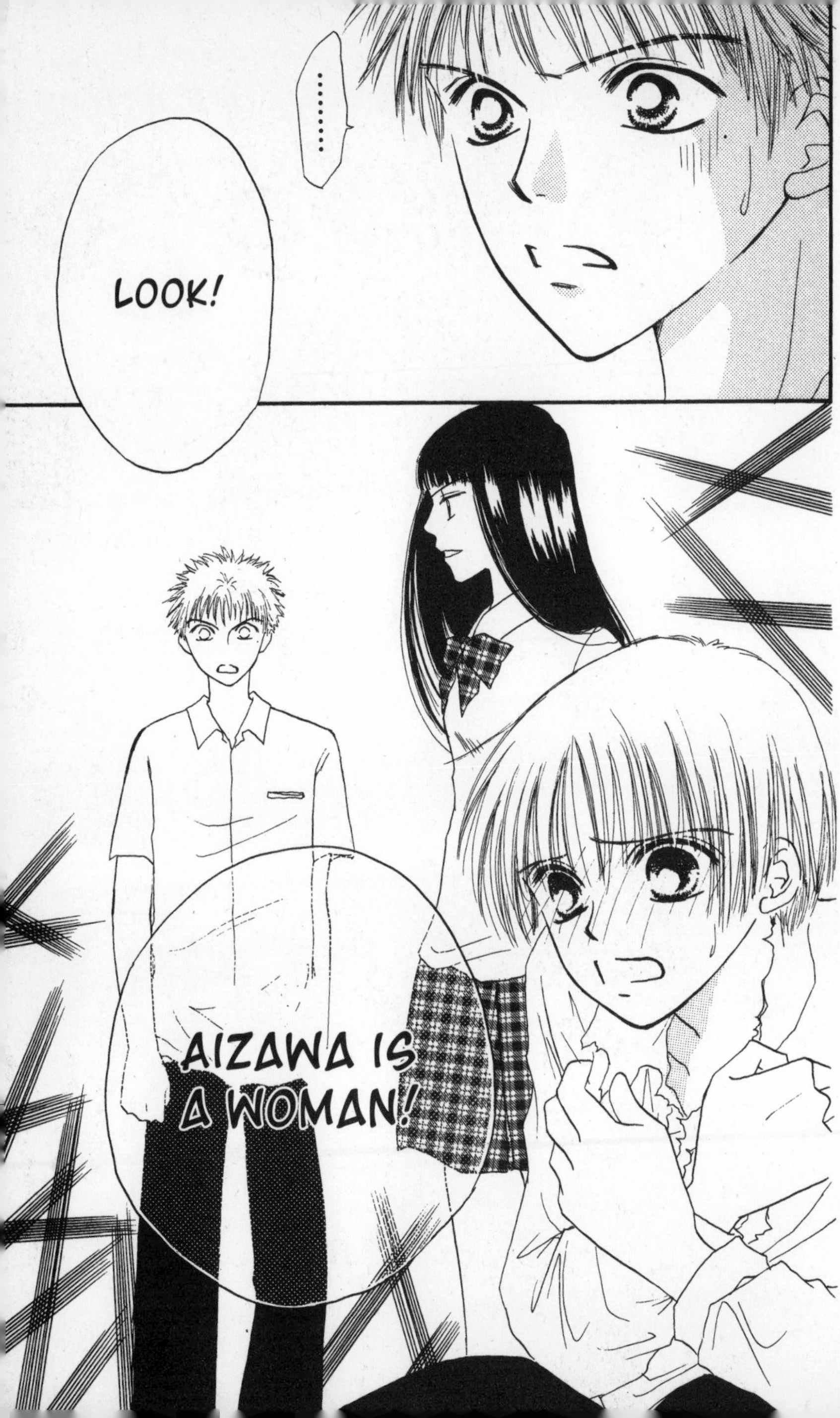
......
LOOK!
AIZAWA IS A WOMAN!

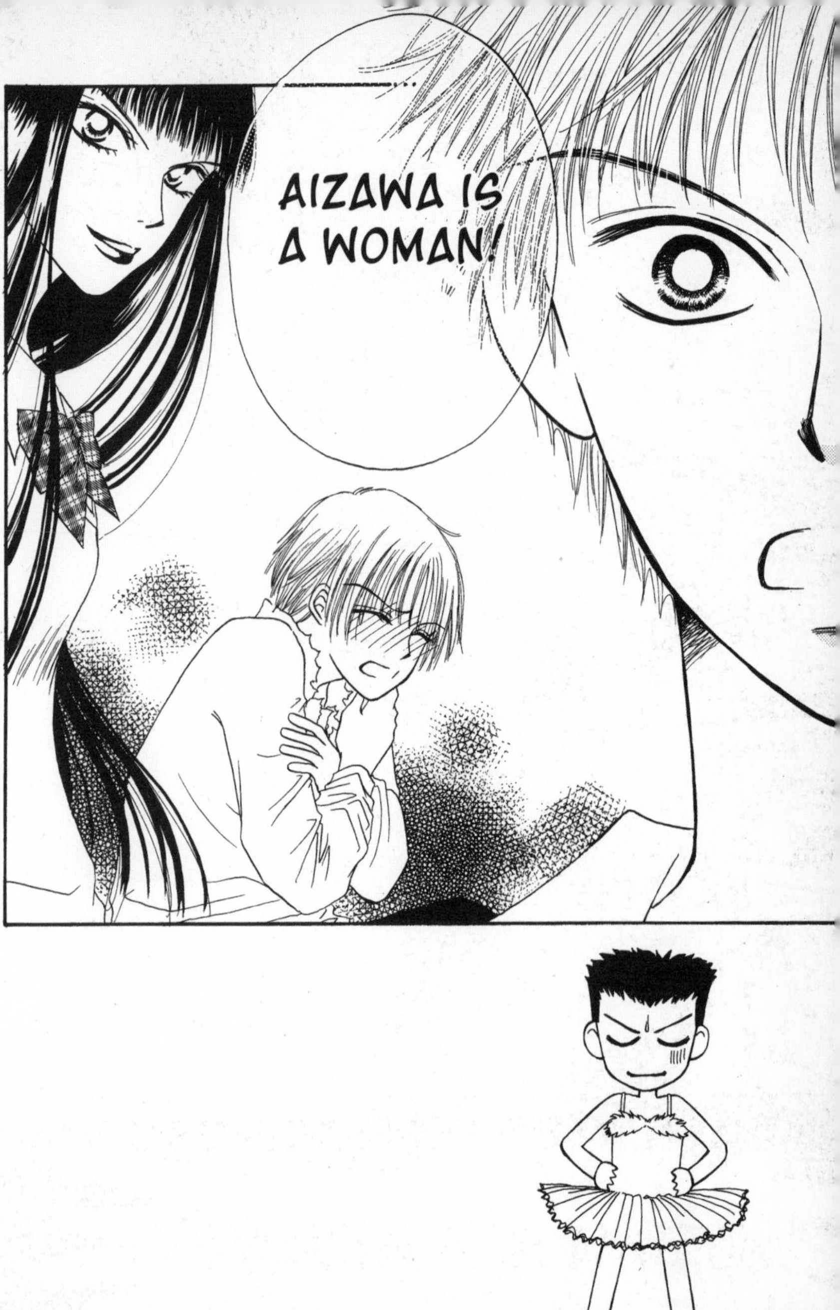
AIZAWA IS A WOMAN!

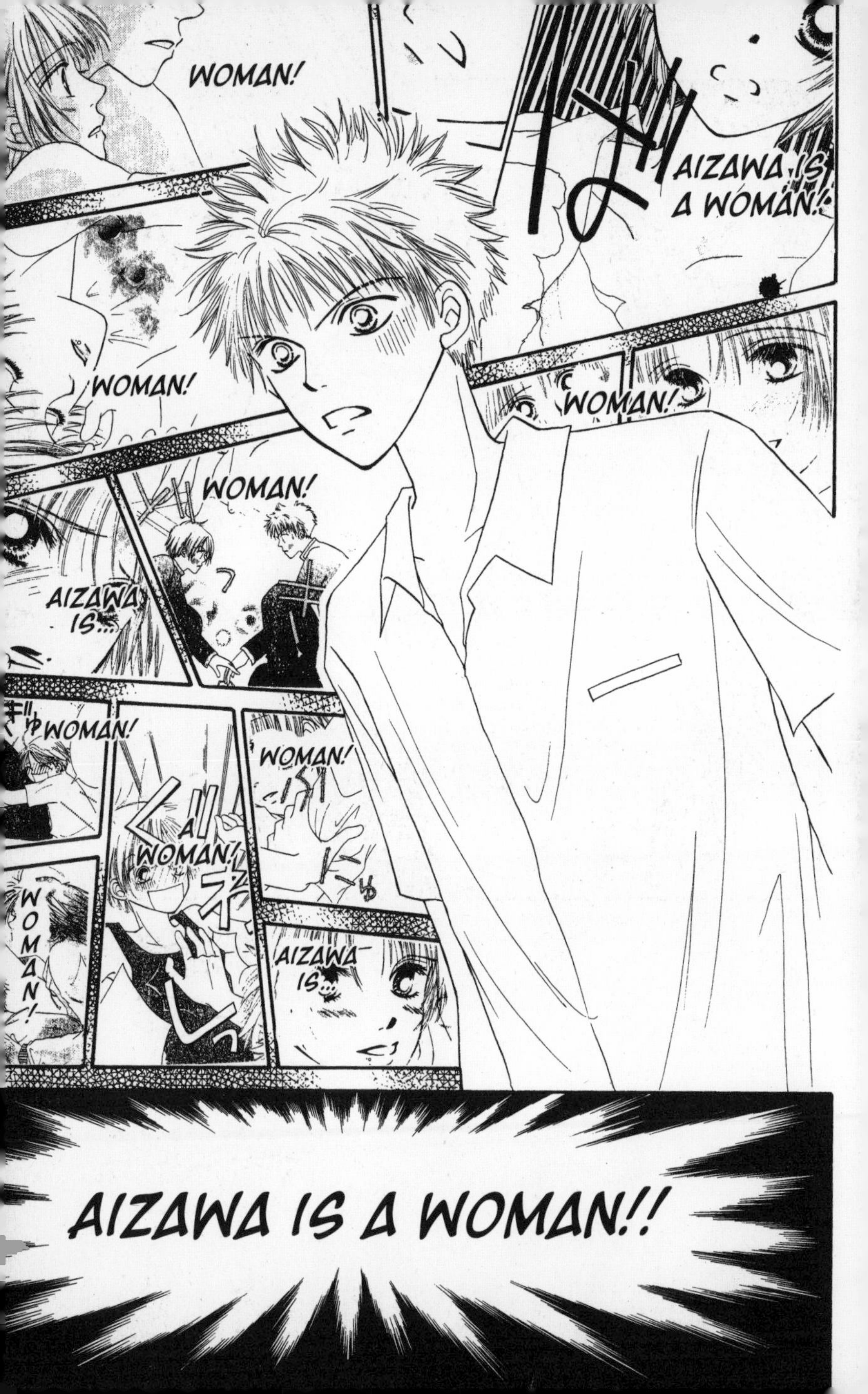
AIZAWA IS A WOMAN!
WOMAN!
WOMAN!
WOMAN!
WOMAN!
AIZAWA IS...
WOMAN!
A WOMAN!
WOMAN!
AIZAWA IS...
WOMAN!
AIZAWA IS A WOMAN!!

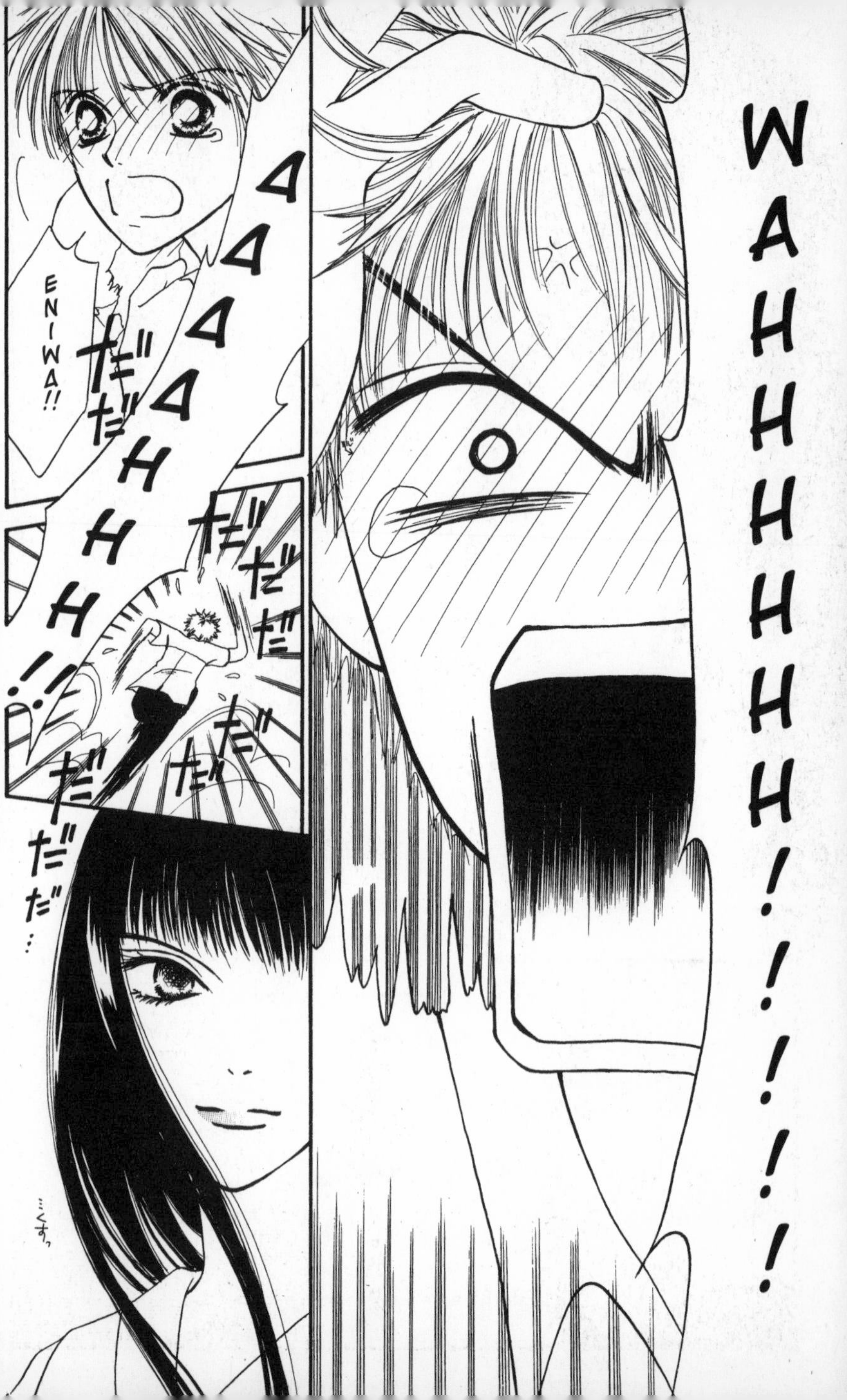
WAHHHHHH!!!!!
ENIWA!!
AAAAHHH!!...
だだ
だだだ
だだ
だだだ…
くすっ

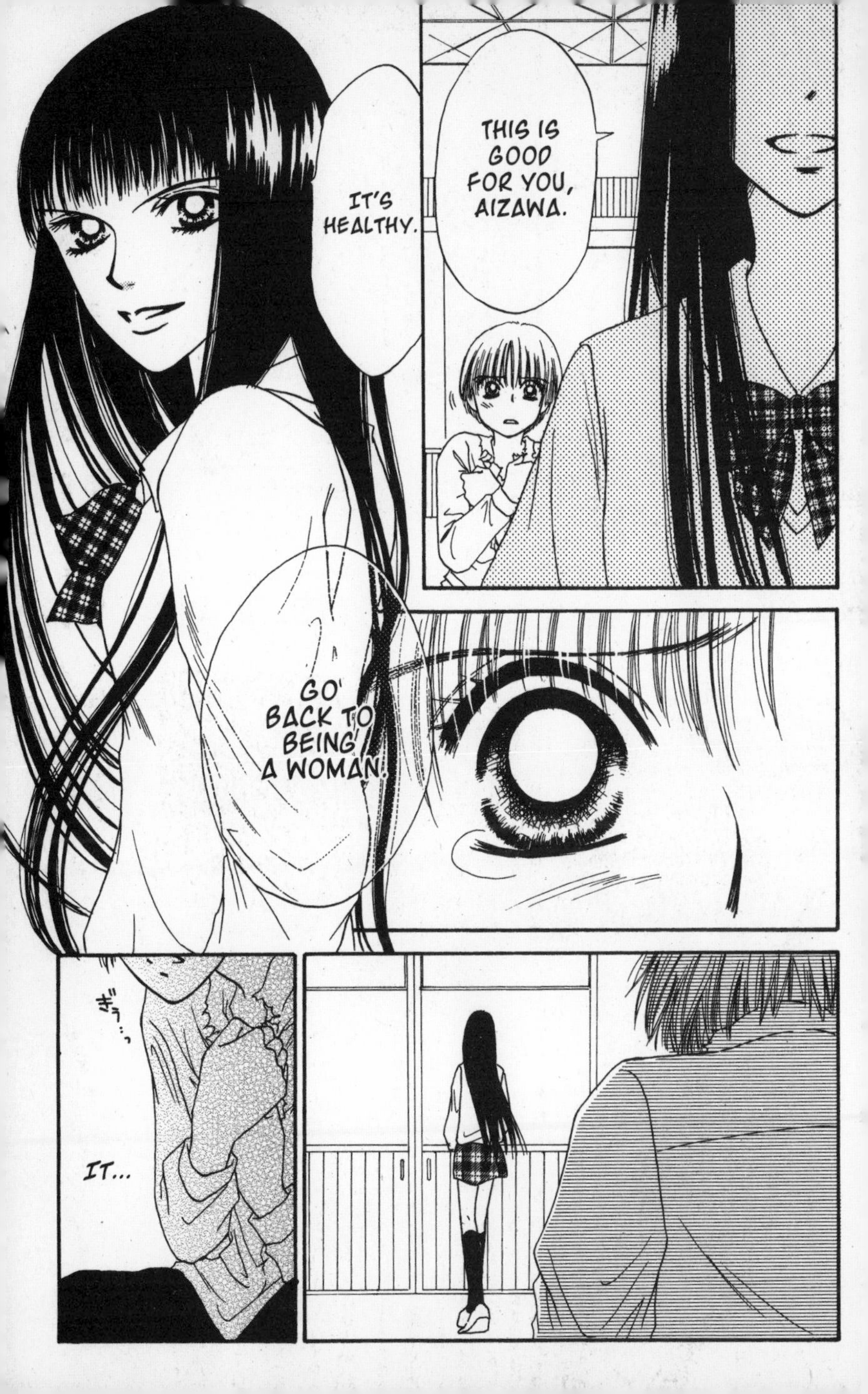
THIS IS GOOD FOR YOU, AIZAWA.
IT'S HEALTHY.
GO BACK TO BEING A WOMAN.
ぎゅっ…
IT...

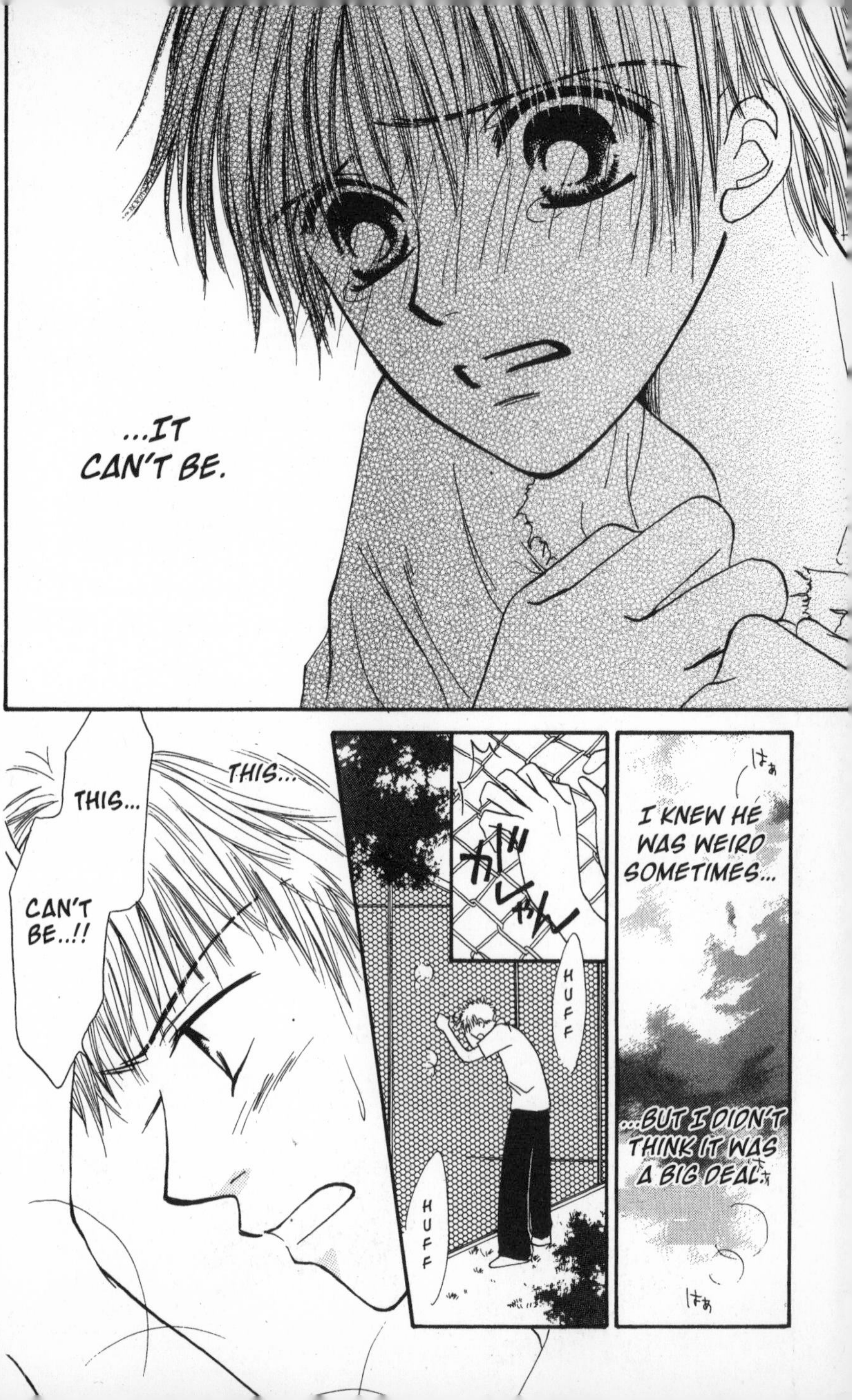
...IT CAN'T BE.
はぁ
I KNEW HE WAS WEIRD SOMETIMES...
...BUT I DIDN'T THINK IT WAS A BIG DEAL.
はぁ
はぁ
ガシャン
HUFF
HUFF
THIS...
THIS...
CAN'T BE...!!

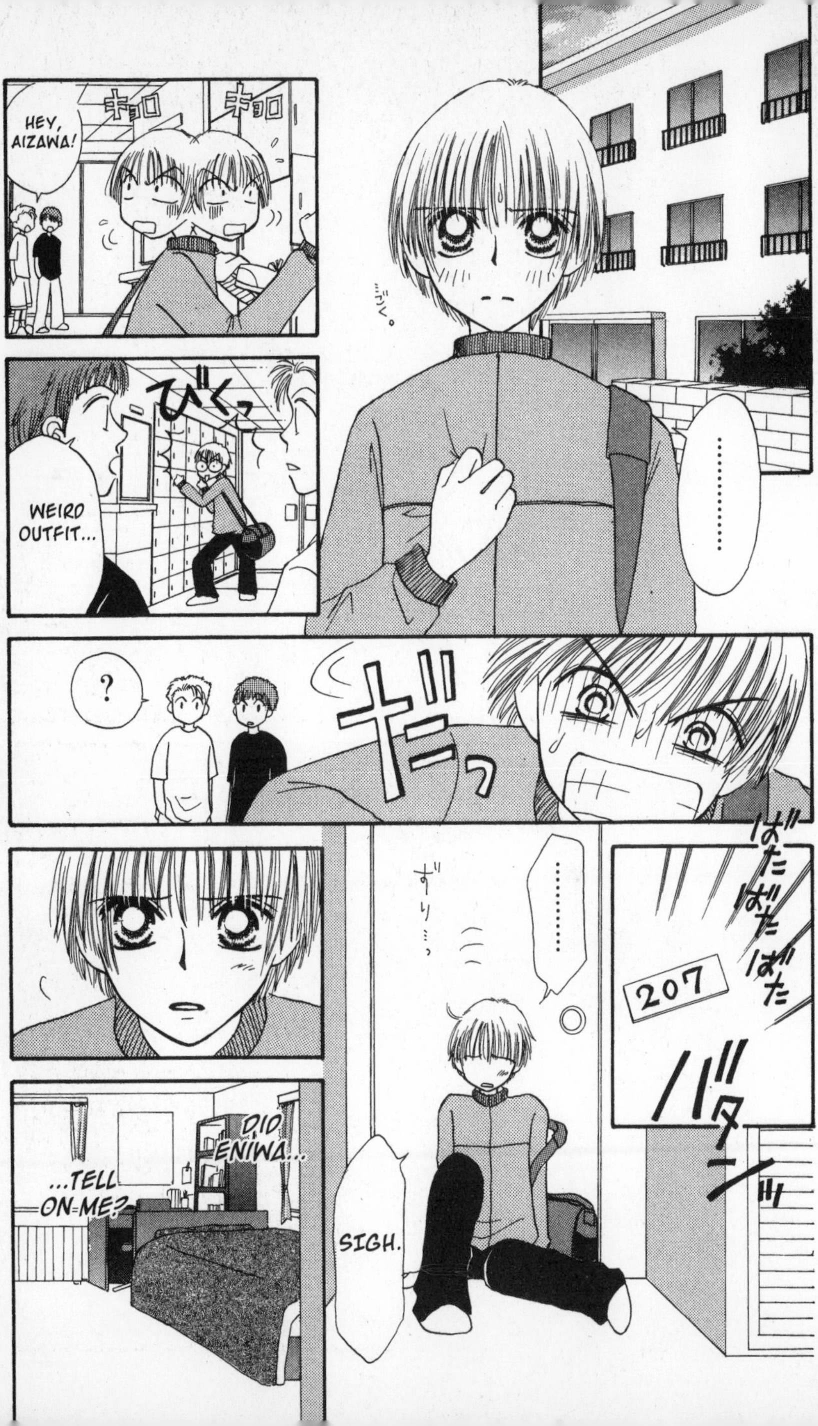
ぎく。
......
キョロ
キョロ
HEY, AIZAWA!
びくっ
WEIRD OUTFIT...
ダーっ
?
ばたばたばた
207
バターン
......
ずり…っ
SIGH.
DID ENIWA...
...TELL ON ME?

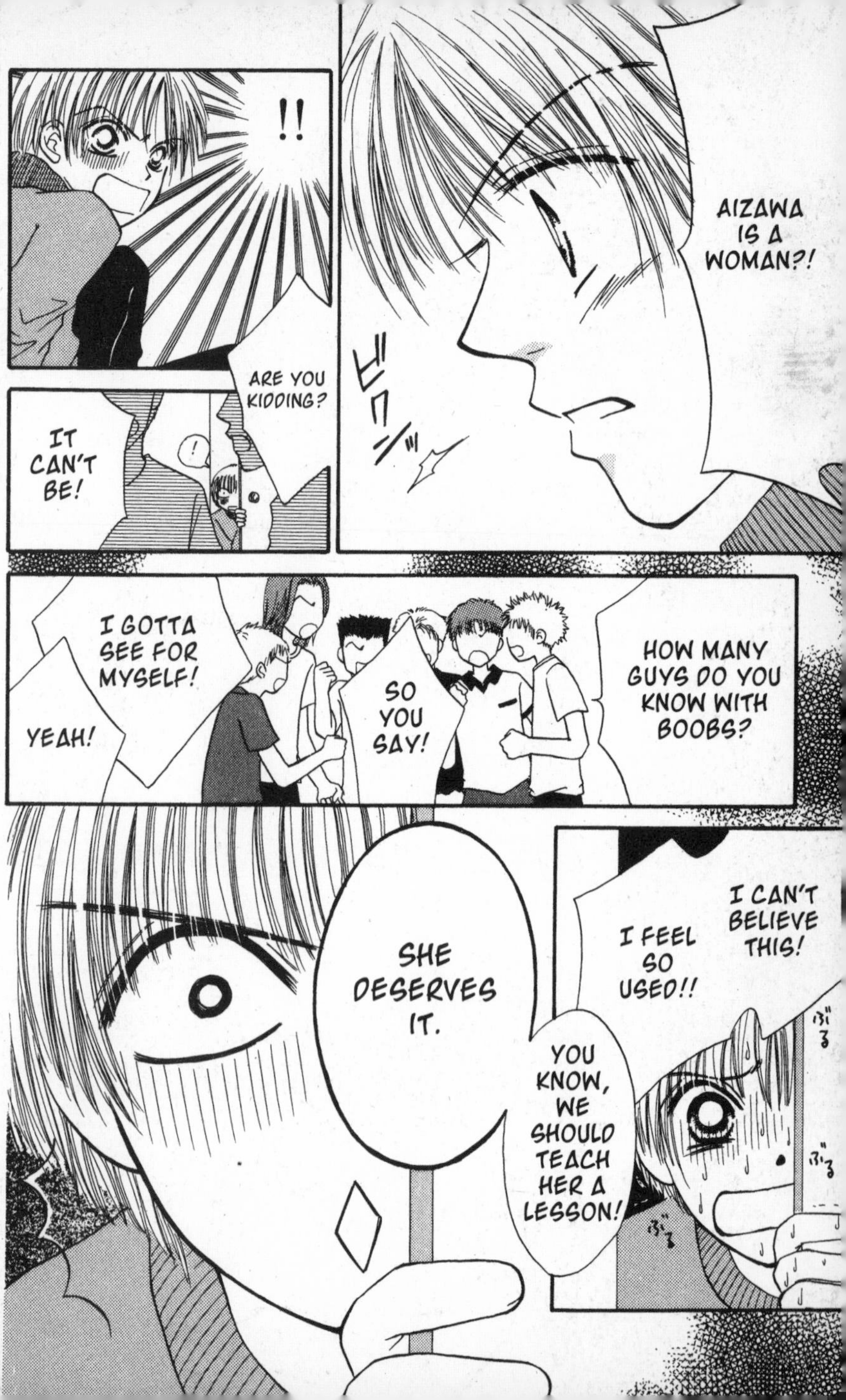
AIZAWA IS A WOMAN?!
ビクッ
!!
ARE YOU KIDDING?
IT CAN'T BE!
!
HOW MANY GUYS DO YOU KNOW WITH BOOBS?
SO YOU SAY!
I GOTTA SEE FOR MYSELF!
YEAH!
I CAN'T BELIEVE THIS!
I FEEL SO USED!!
ぶる
ぶる
YOU KNOW, WE SHOULD TEACH HER A LESSON!
ぶる
SHE DESERVES IT.

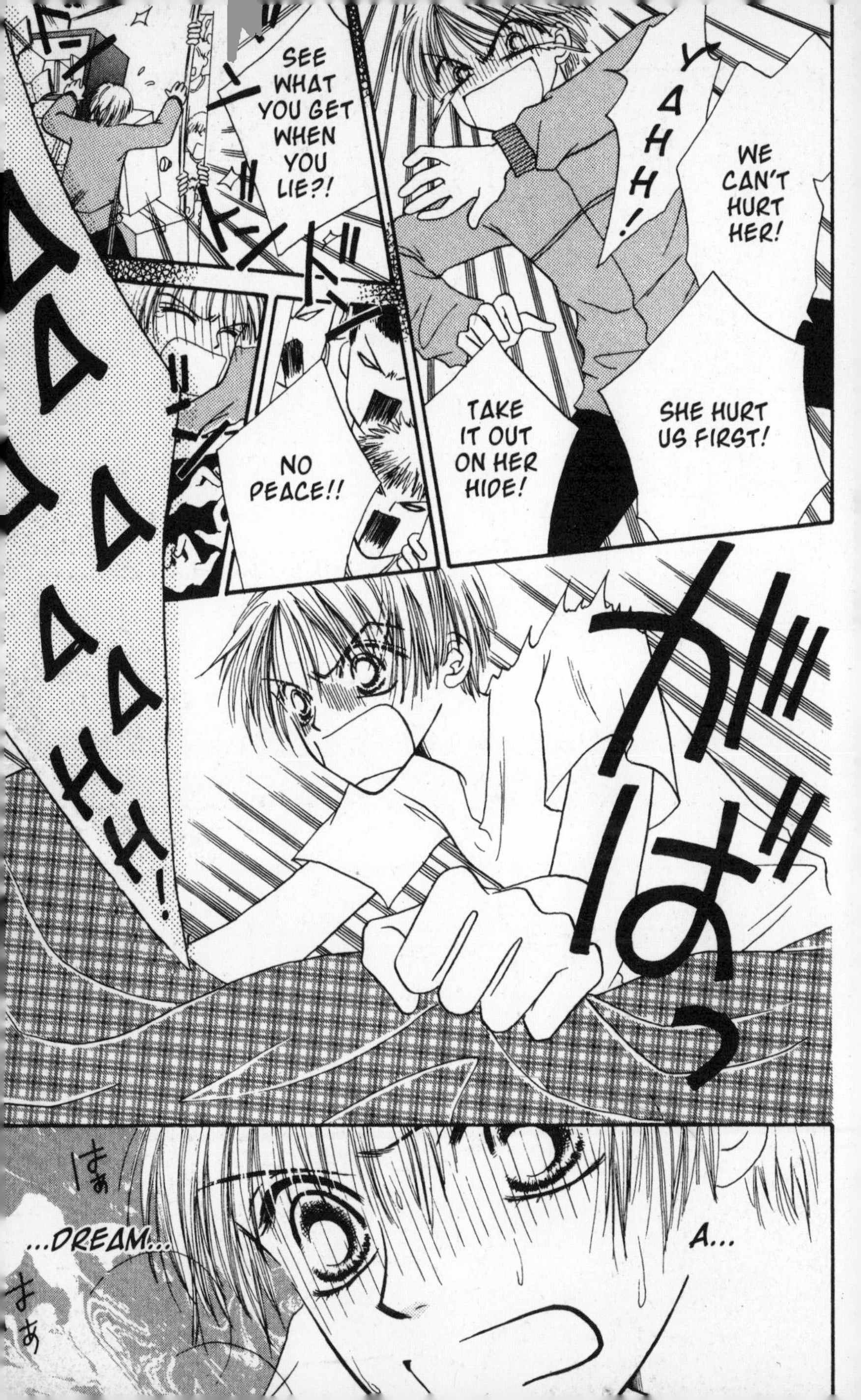
YAHHH!
WE CAN'T HURT HER!
SHE HURT US FIRST!
TAKE IT OUT ON HER HIDE!
NO PEACE!!
SEE WHAT YOU GET WHEN YOU LIE?!
AAAAAAHHH!
ばっ
A...
...DREAM...

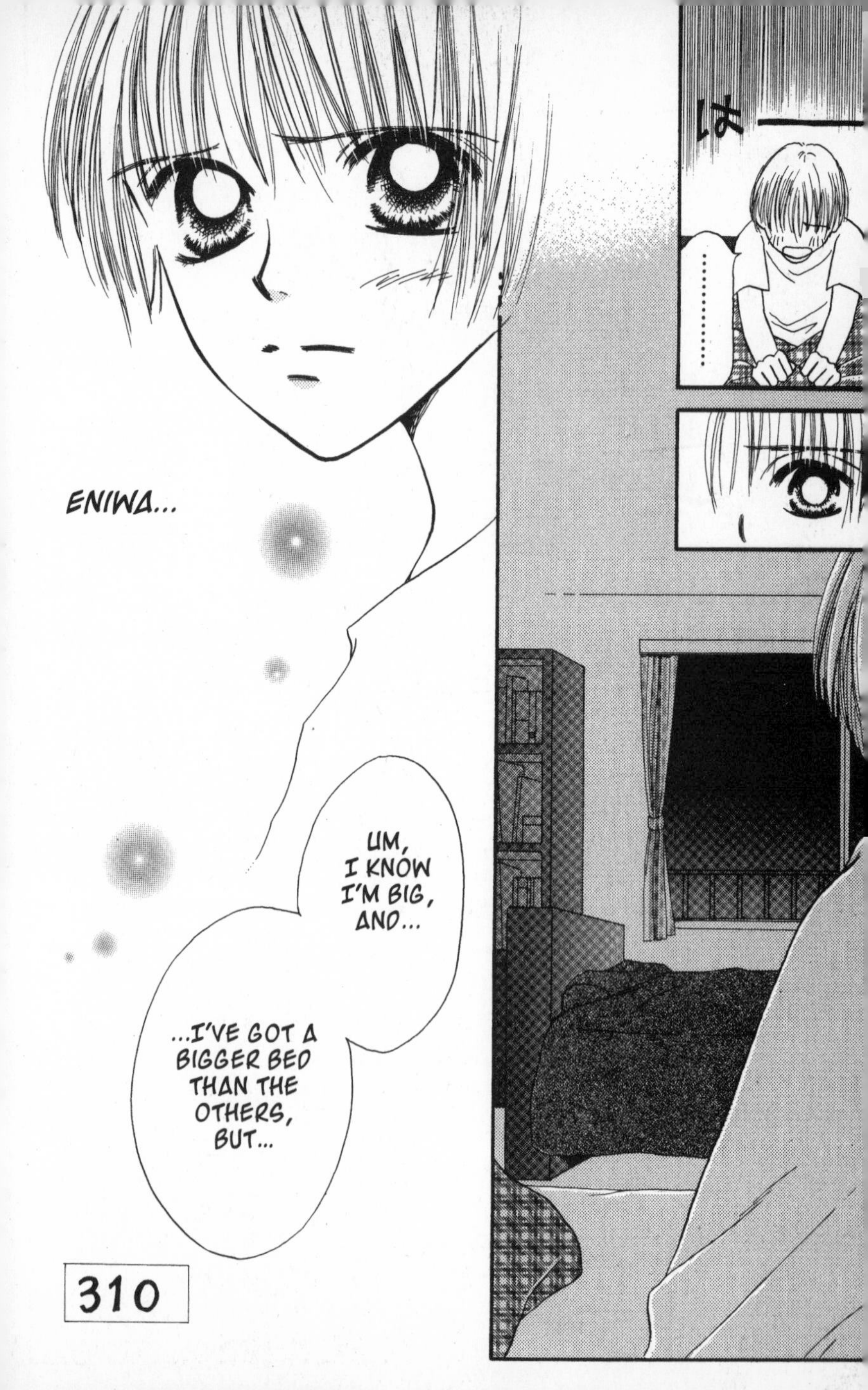
は——
……
ENIWA...
UM, I KNOW I'M BIG, AND...
...I'VE GOT A BIGGER BED THAN THE OTHERS, BUT...

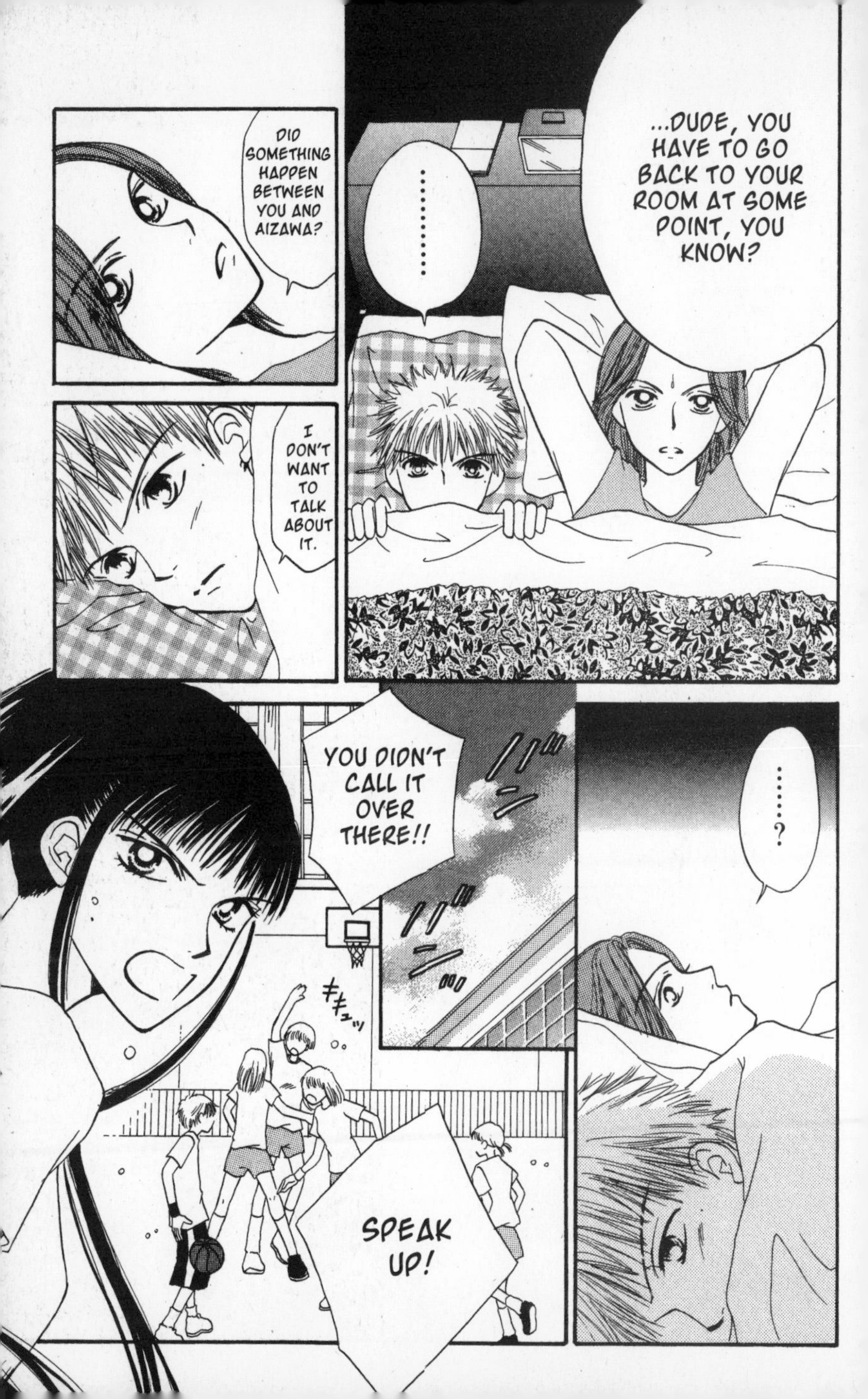
...DUDE, YOU HAVE TO GO BACK TO YOUR ROOM AT SOME POINT, YOU KNOW?
....
DID SOMETHING HAPPEN BETWEEN YOU AND AIZAWA?
I DON'T WANT TO TALK ABOUT IT.
......?
YOU DIDN'T CALL IT OVER THERE!!
SPEAK UP!

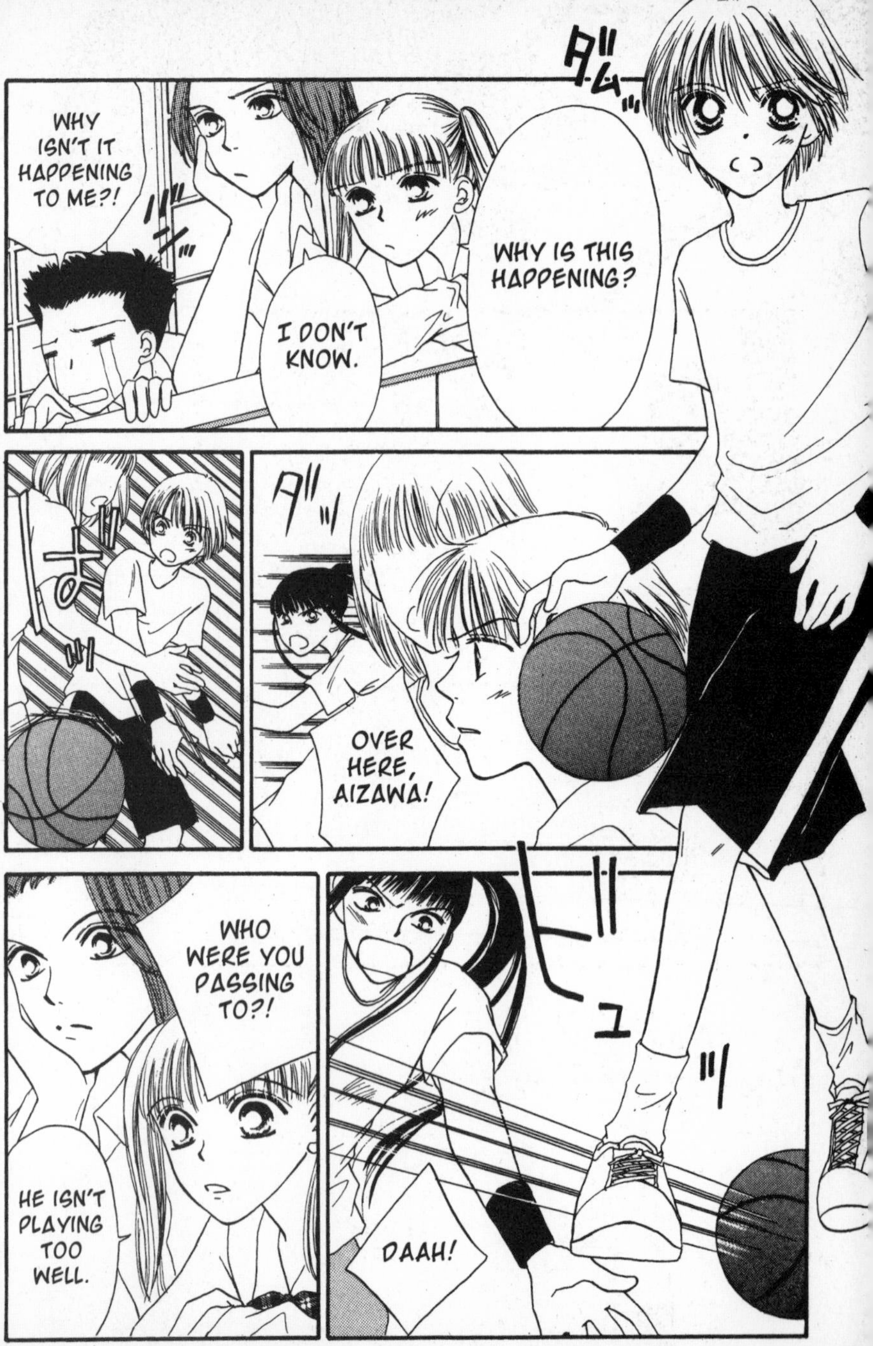
WHY IS THIS HAPPENING?
I DON'T KNOW.
WHY ISN'T IT HAPPENING TO ME?!
OVER HERE, AIZAWA!
DAAH!
WHO WERE YOU PASSING TO?!
HE ISN'T PLAYING TOO WELL.

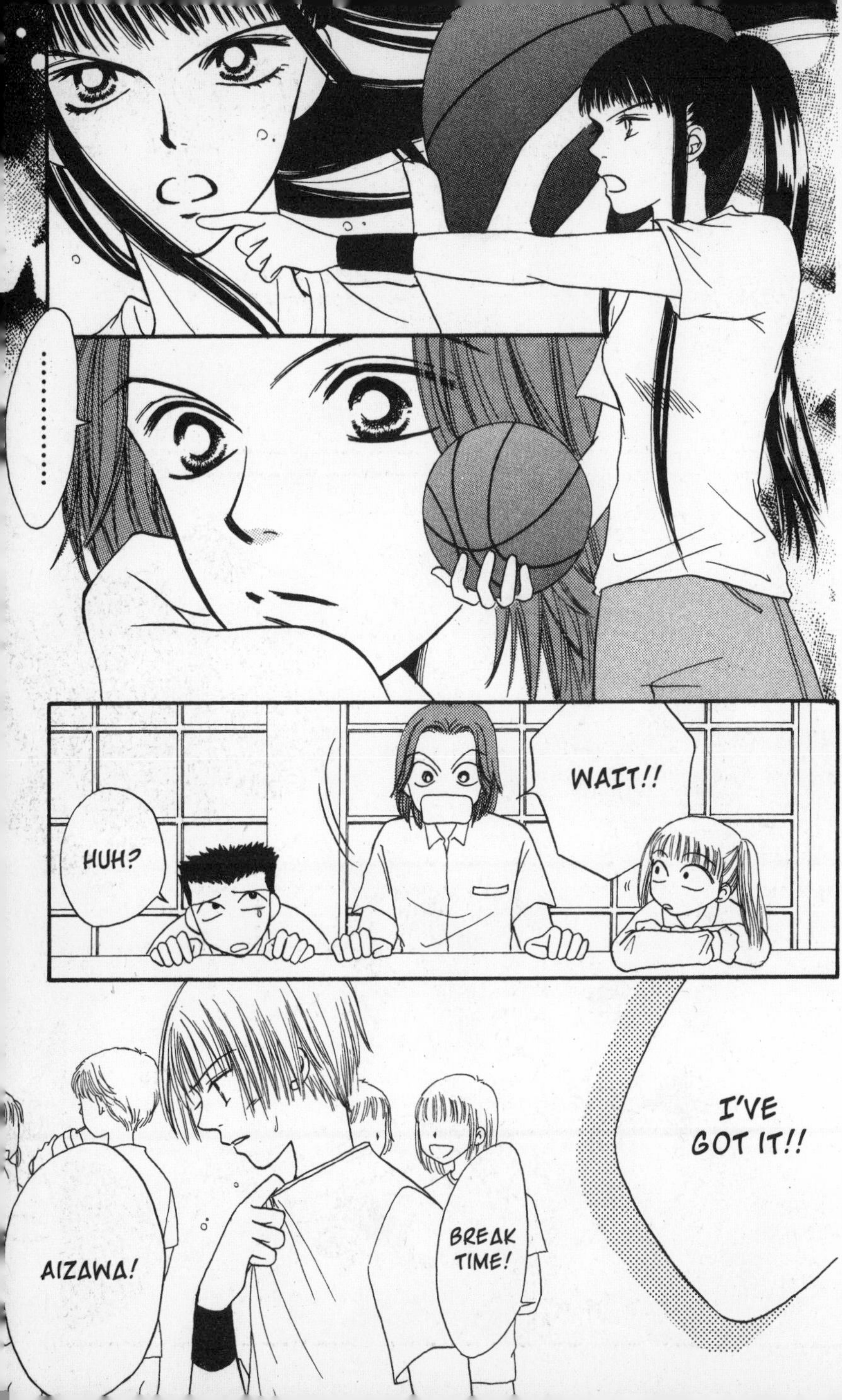
......
WAIT!!
HUH?
I'VE GOT IT!!
BREAK TIME!
AIZAWA!

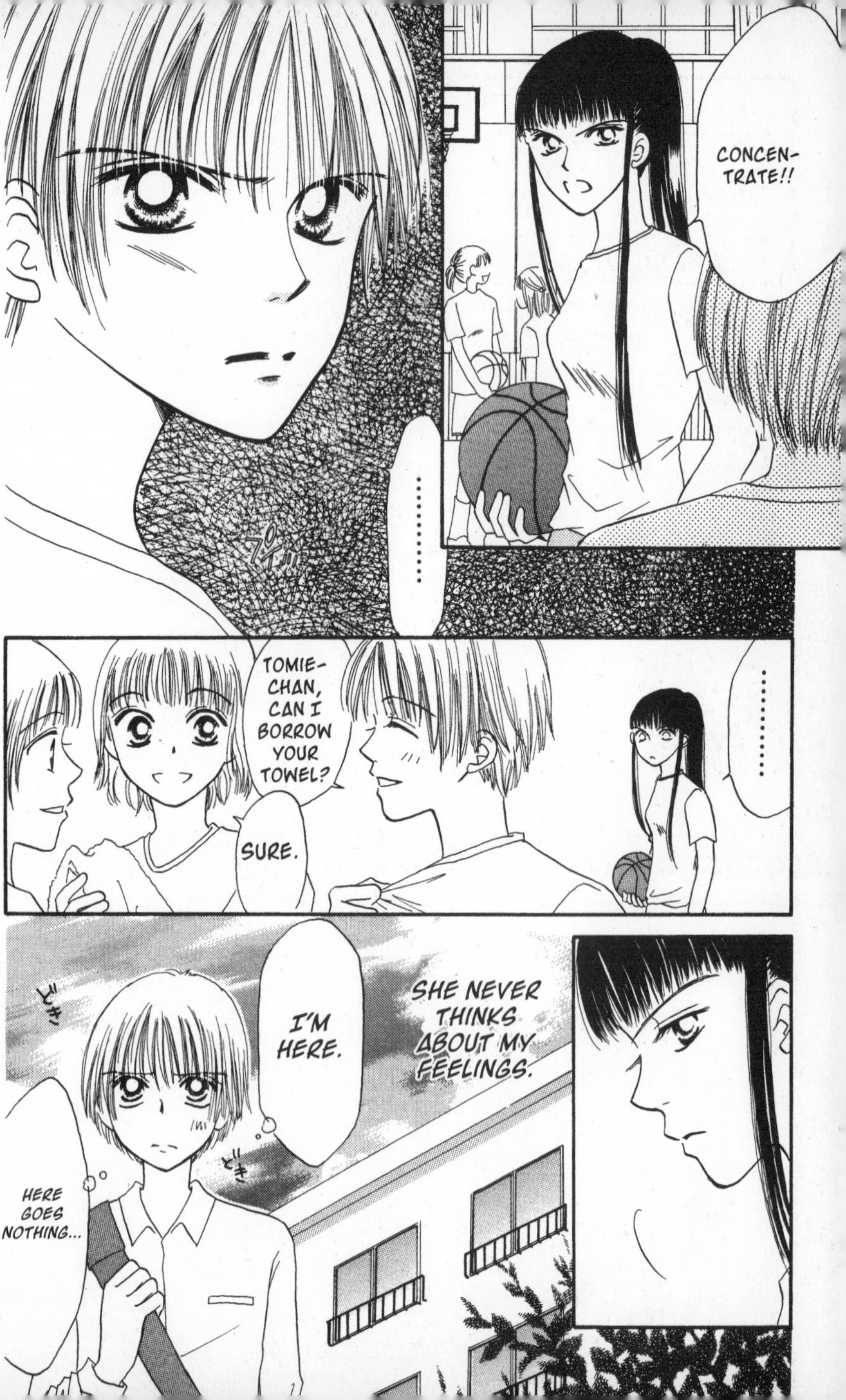
CONCENTRATE!!
......
......
TOMIE-CHAN, CAN I BORROW YOUR TOWEL?
SURE.
SHE NEVER THINKS ABOUT MY FEELINGS.
I'M HERE.
どき
どき
HERE GOES NOTHING...

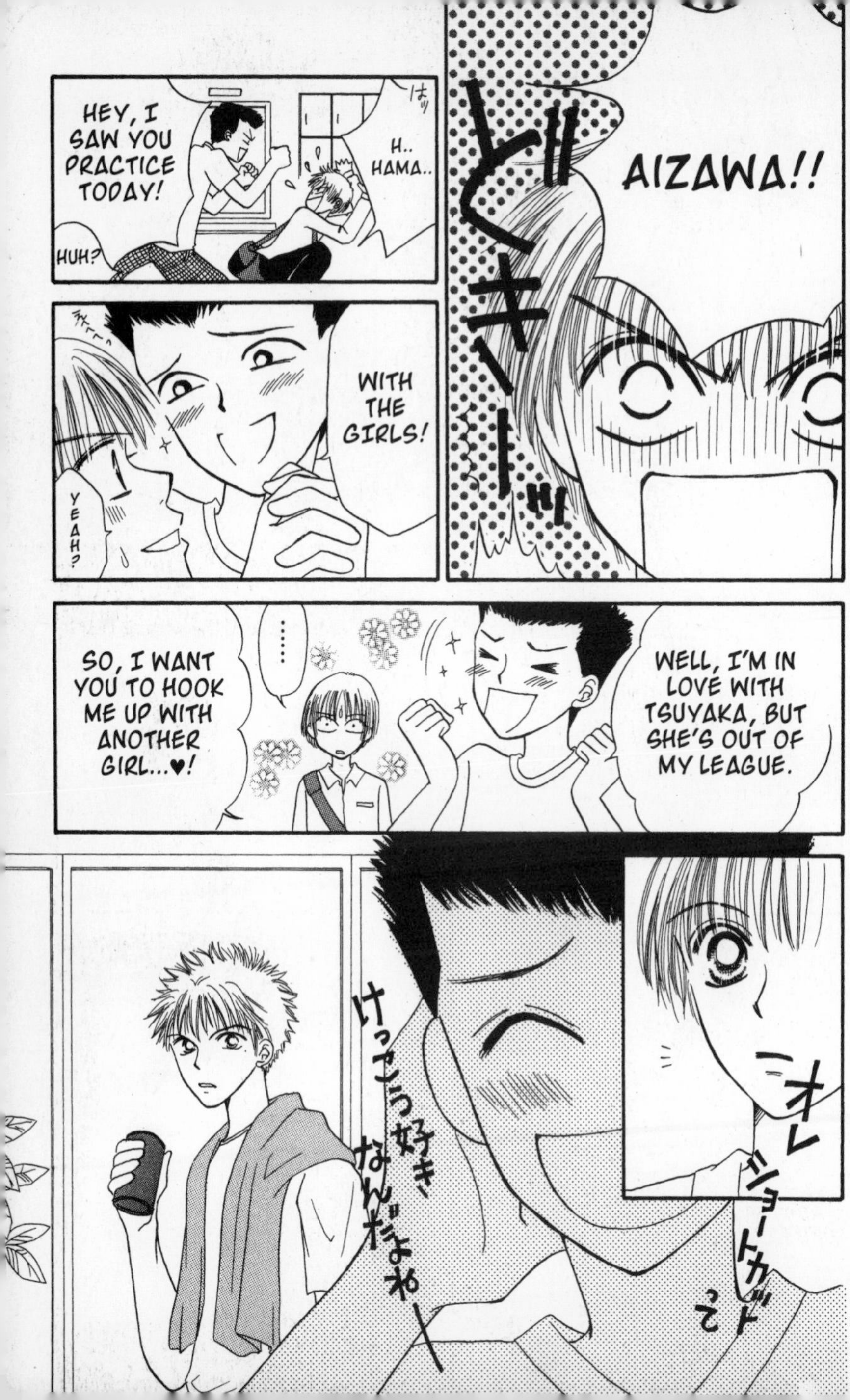
ドキーッ
AIZAWA!!
はッ
H.. HAMA..
HEY, I SAW YOU PRACTICE TODAY!
HUH?
WITH THE GIRLS!
YEAH?
WELL, I'M IN LOVE WITH TSUYAKA, BUT SHE'S OUT OF MY LEAGUE.
......
SO, I WANT YOU TO HOOK ME UP WITH ANOTHER GIRL...♥!
オレショートカットって
けっこう好きなんだよねー

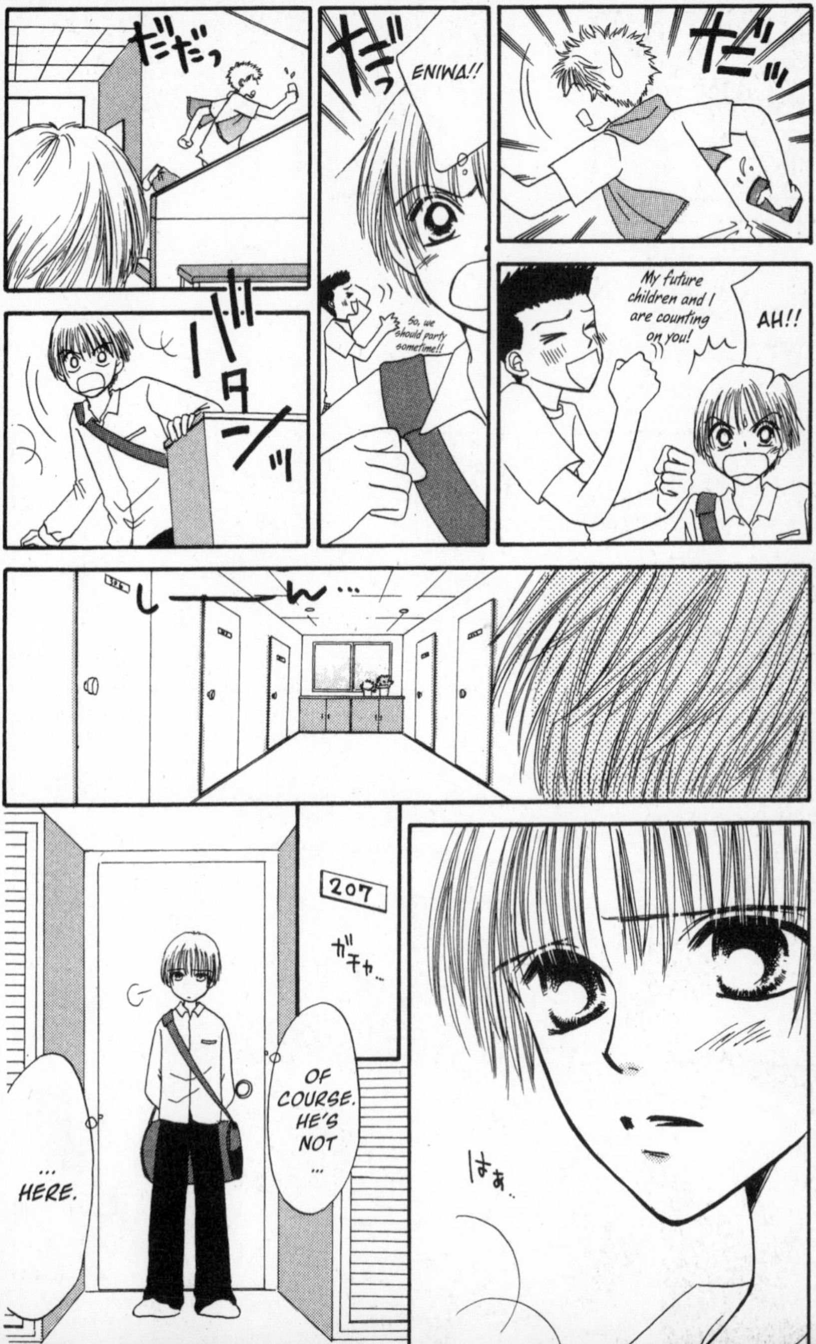
だッ
My future children and I are counting on you!
AH!!
だっ
ENIWA!!
So, we should party sometime!!
だだっ
バタンッ
しーーん…
はぁ..
207
ガチャ..
OF COURSE. HE'S NOT ...
... HERE.

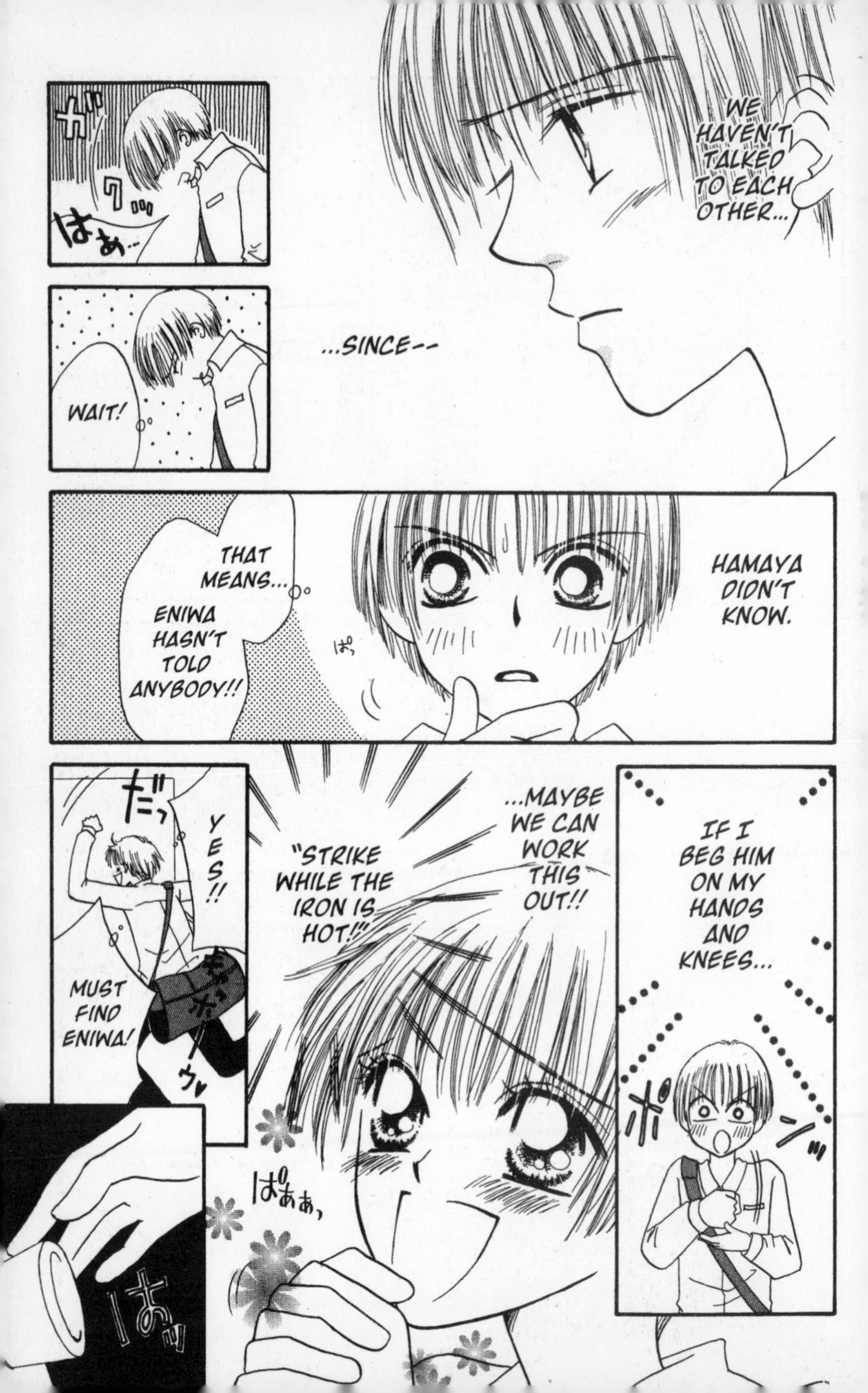

WE HAVEN'T TALKED TO EACH OTHER...
...SINCE--
はあ…
WAIT!
HAMAYA DIDN'T KNOW.
THAT MEANS...
ENIWA HASN'T TOLD ANYBODY!!
ぱっ
IF I BEG HIM ON MY HANDS AND KNEES...
...MAYBE WE CAN WORK THIS OUT!!
"STRIKE WHILE THE IRON IS HOT!!"
ぱあぁ
だっ
YES!!
MUST FIND ENIWA!
はっ

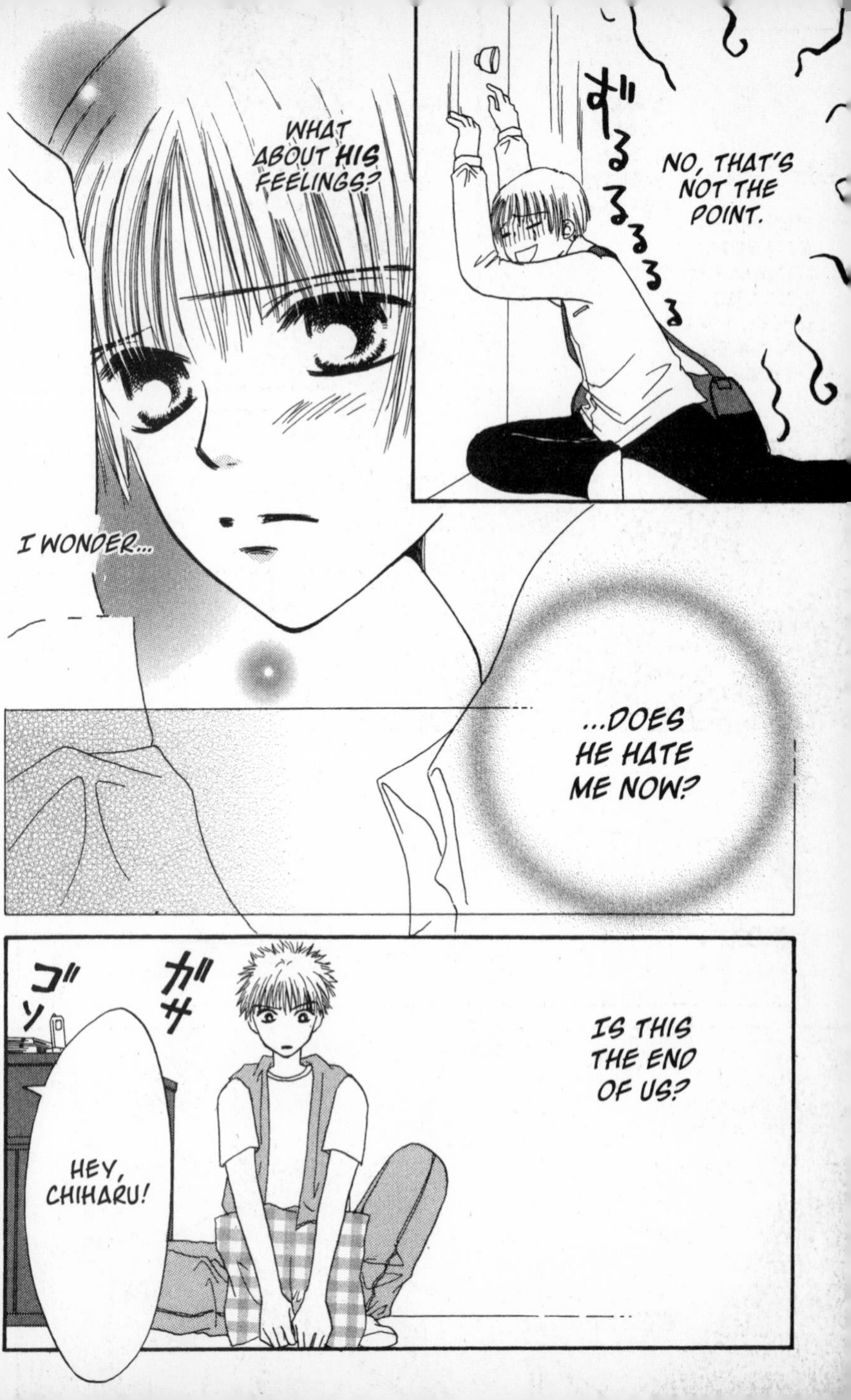
ずるるるる
NO, THAT'S NOT THE POINT.
WHAT ABOUT HIS FEELINGS?
I WONDER...
...DOES HE HATE ME NOW?
IS THIS THE END OF US?
ガサ
ゴソ
HEY, CHIHARU!

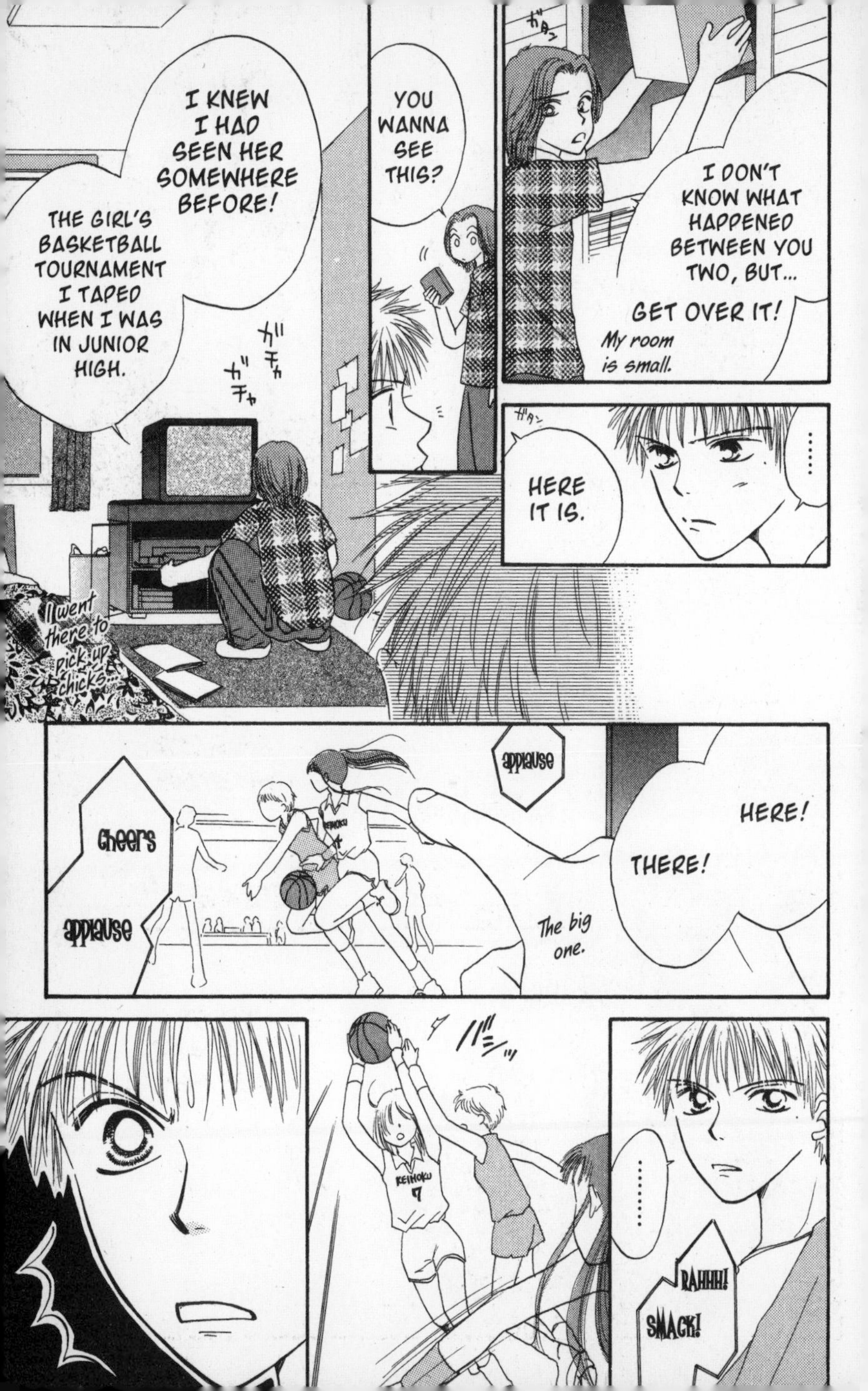
ガタン
I DON'T KNOW WHAT HAPPENED BETWEEN YOU TWO, BUT...
GET OVER IT!
My room is small.
YOU WANNA SEE THIS?
ガタン
......
HERE IT IS.
I KNEW I HAD SEEN HER SOMEWHERE BEFORE!
THE GIRL'S BASKETBALL TOURNAMENT I TAPED WHEN I WAS IN JUNIOR HIGH.
ガチャ
ガチャ
I went there to pick up chicks...
HERE!
THERE!
The big one.
applause
Cheers
applause
......
RAHHH!
SMACK!
バシッ

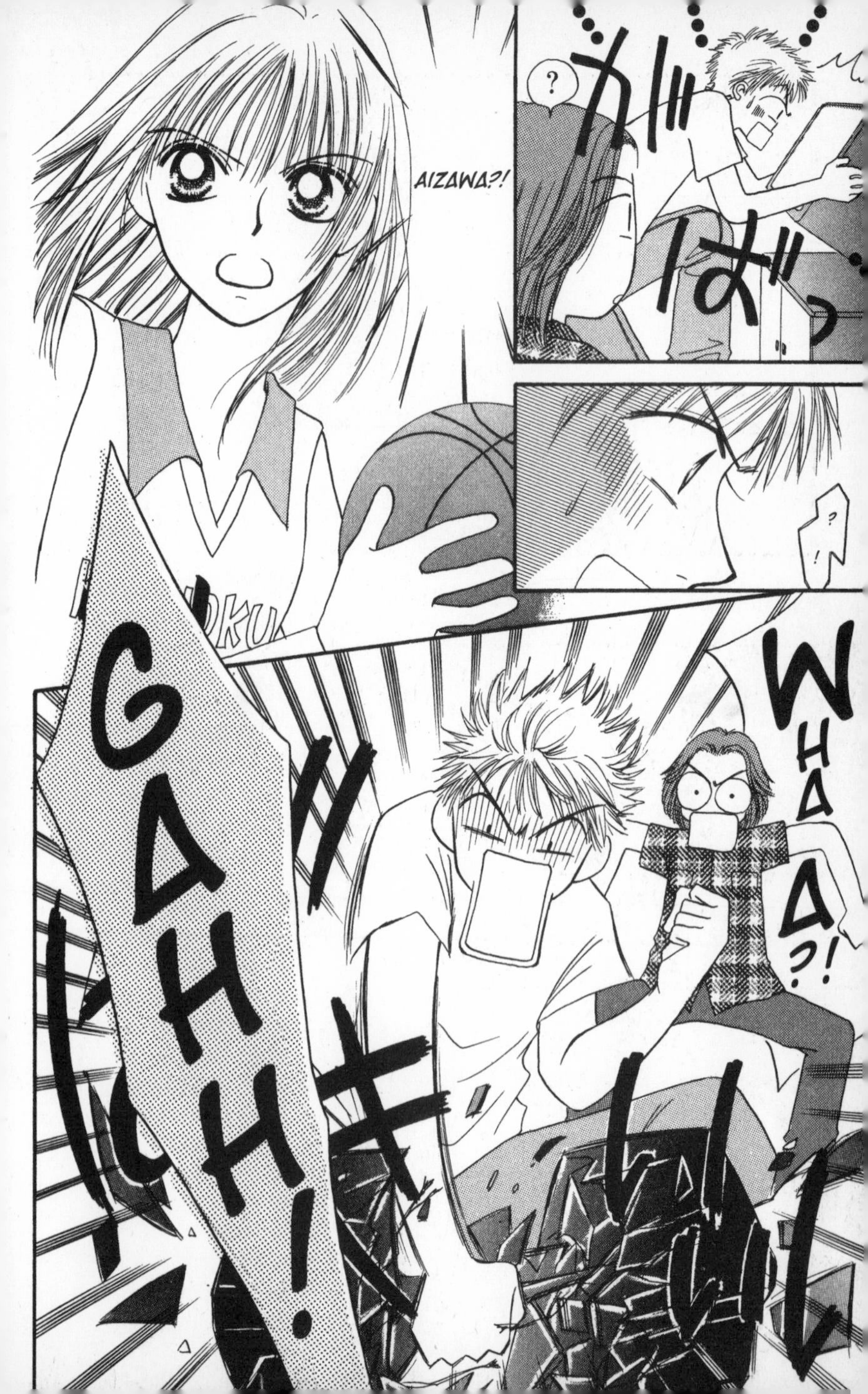
?
?!
AIZAWA?!
WHAA?!
GAHH!

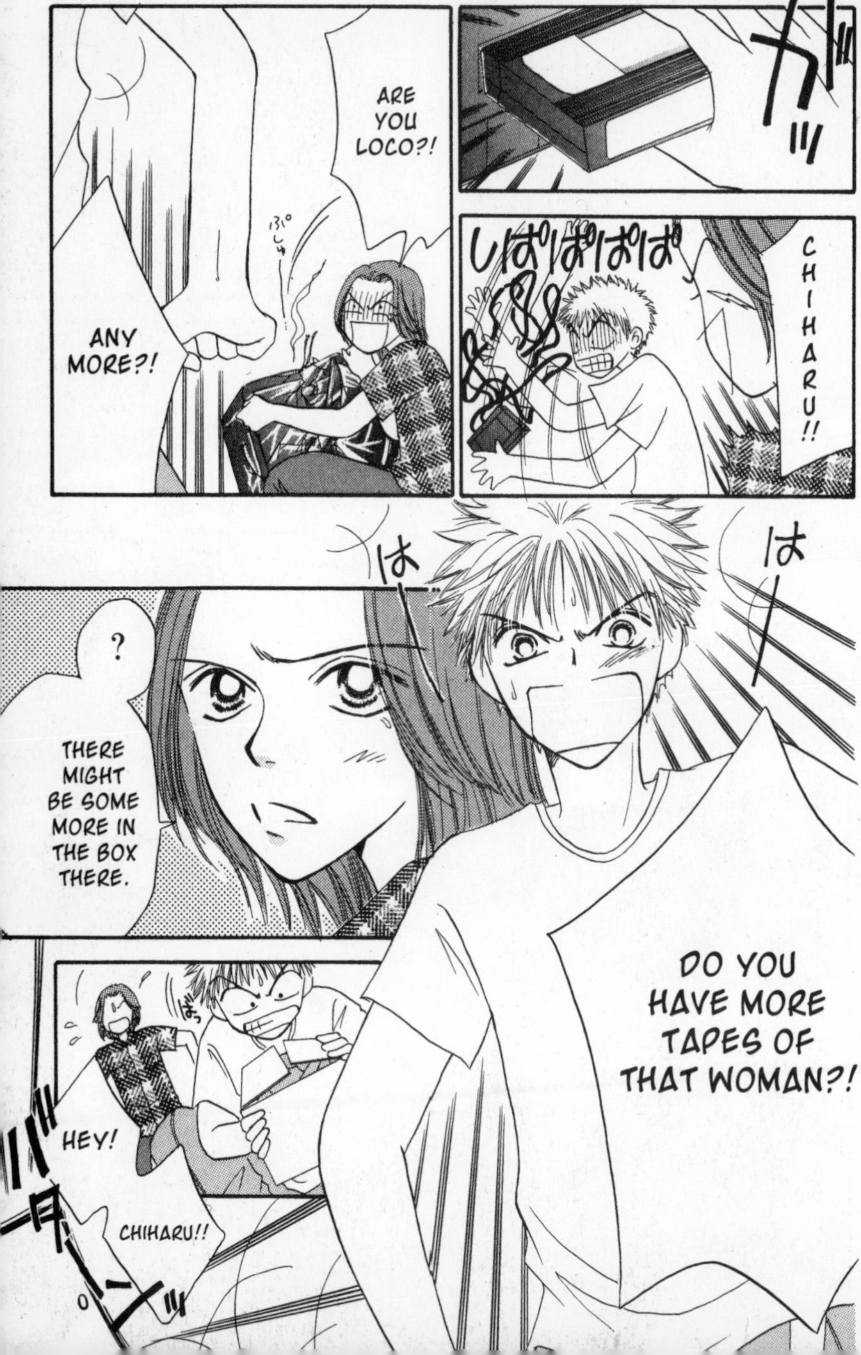
ガッ
しぱぱぱぱ
CHIHARU!!
ARE YOU LOCO?!
ぷしゅ…
ANY MORE?!
は
は
DO YOU HAVE MORE TAPES OF THAT WOMAN?!
?
THERE MIGHT BE SOME MORE IN THE BOX THERE.
ばっ
HEY!
CHIHARU!!
バターン

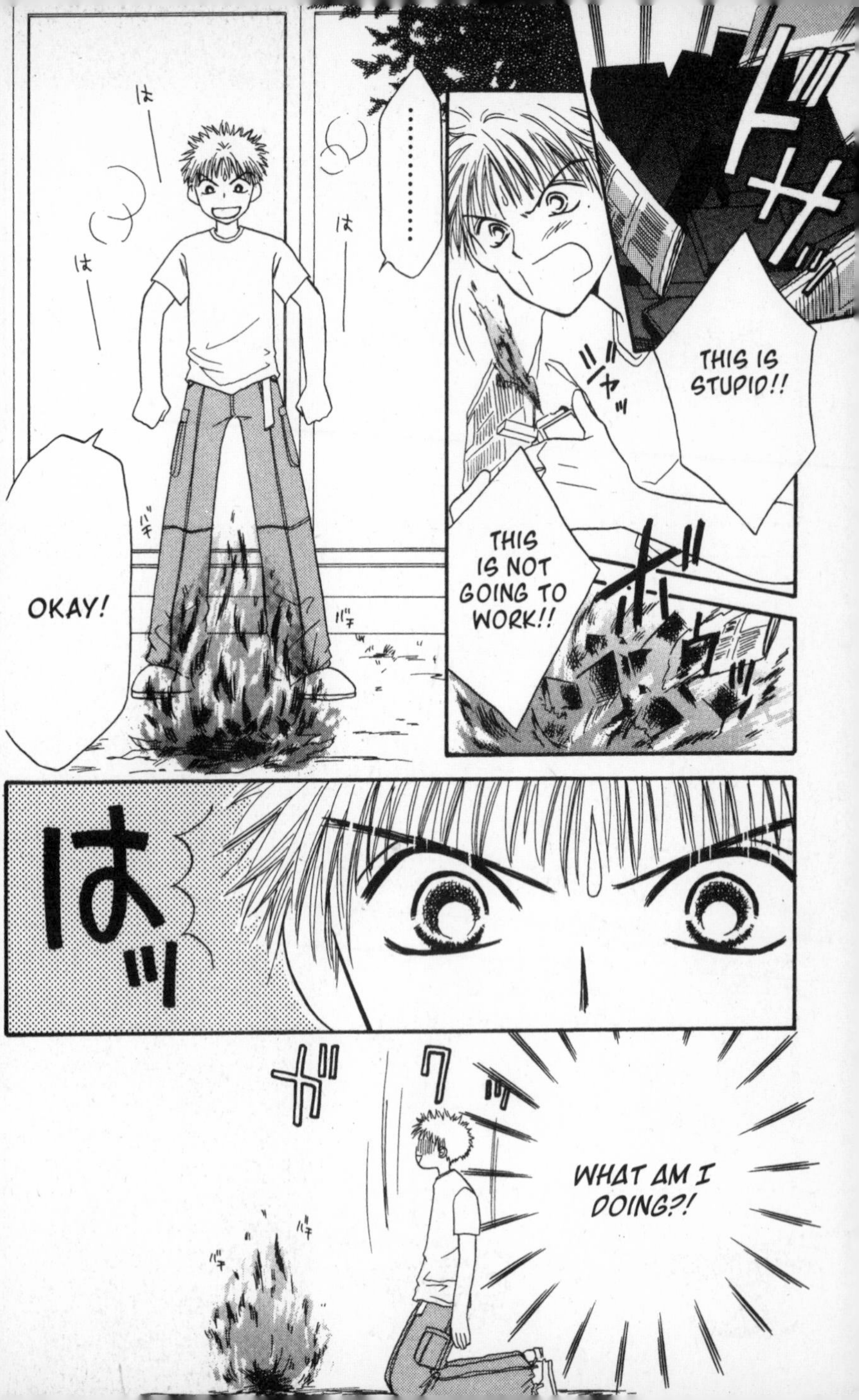

ドサッ
ジャッ
THIS IS STUPID!!
THIS IS NOT GOING TO WORK!!
は—
は—
は—
……
OKAY!
はッ
ガクッ
WHAT AM I DOING?!

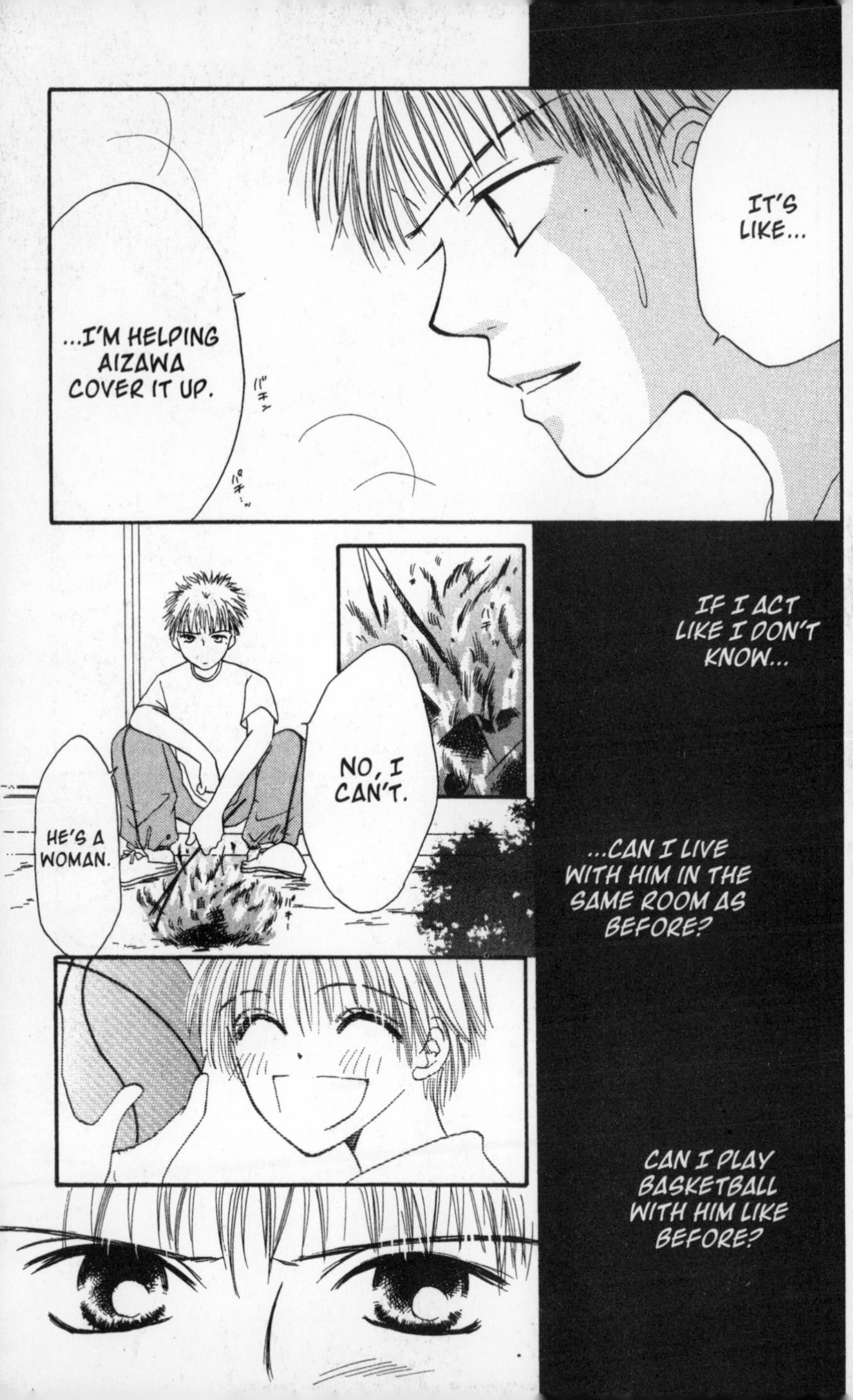
IT'S LIKE...
...I'M HELPING AIZAWA COVER IT UP.
IF I ACT LIKE I DON'T KNOW...
NO, I CAN'T.
HE'S A WOMAN.
...CAN I LIVE WITH HIM IN THE SAME ROOM AS BEFORE?
CAN I PLAY BASKETBALL WITH HIM LIKE BEFORE?

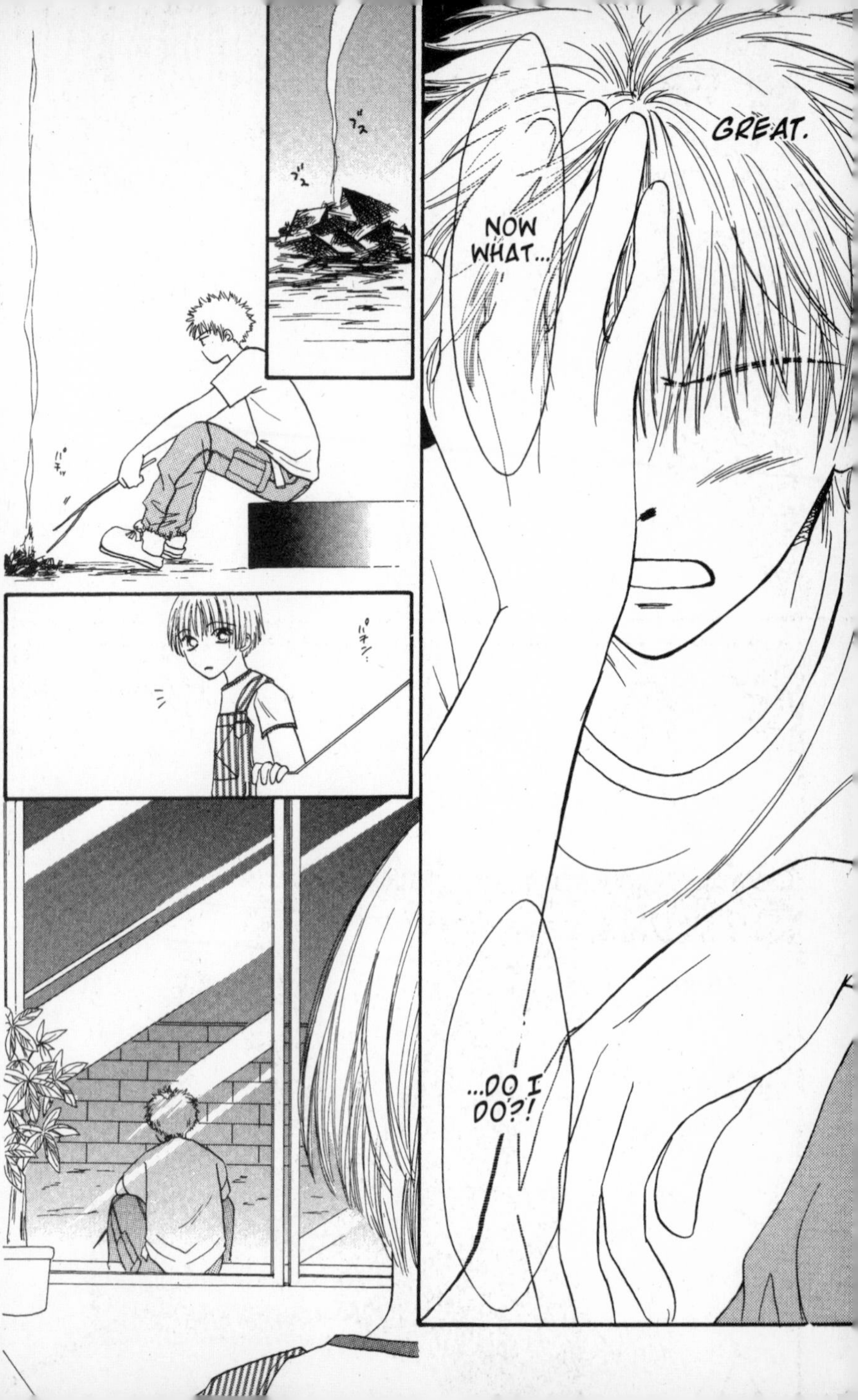
GREAT.
NOW WHAT...
...DO I DO?!

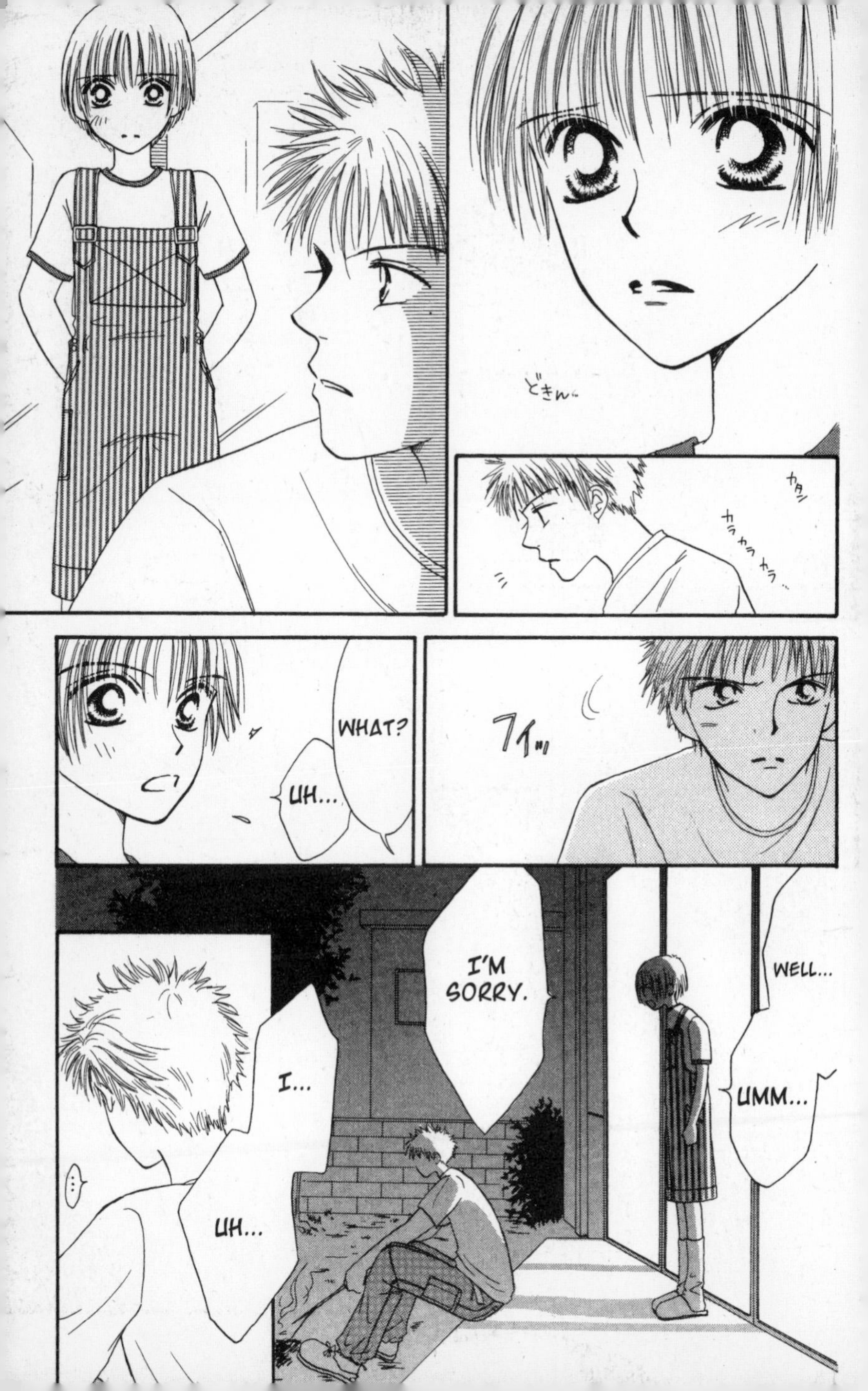
どきん
カタン
カラカラ カラ…
フイッ
WHAT?
UH...
WELL...
UMM...
I'M SORRY.
I...
UH...
...

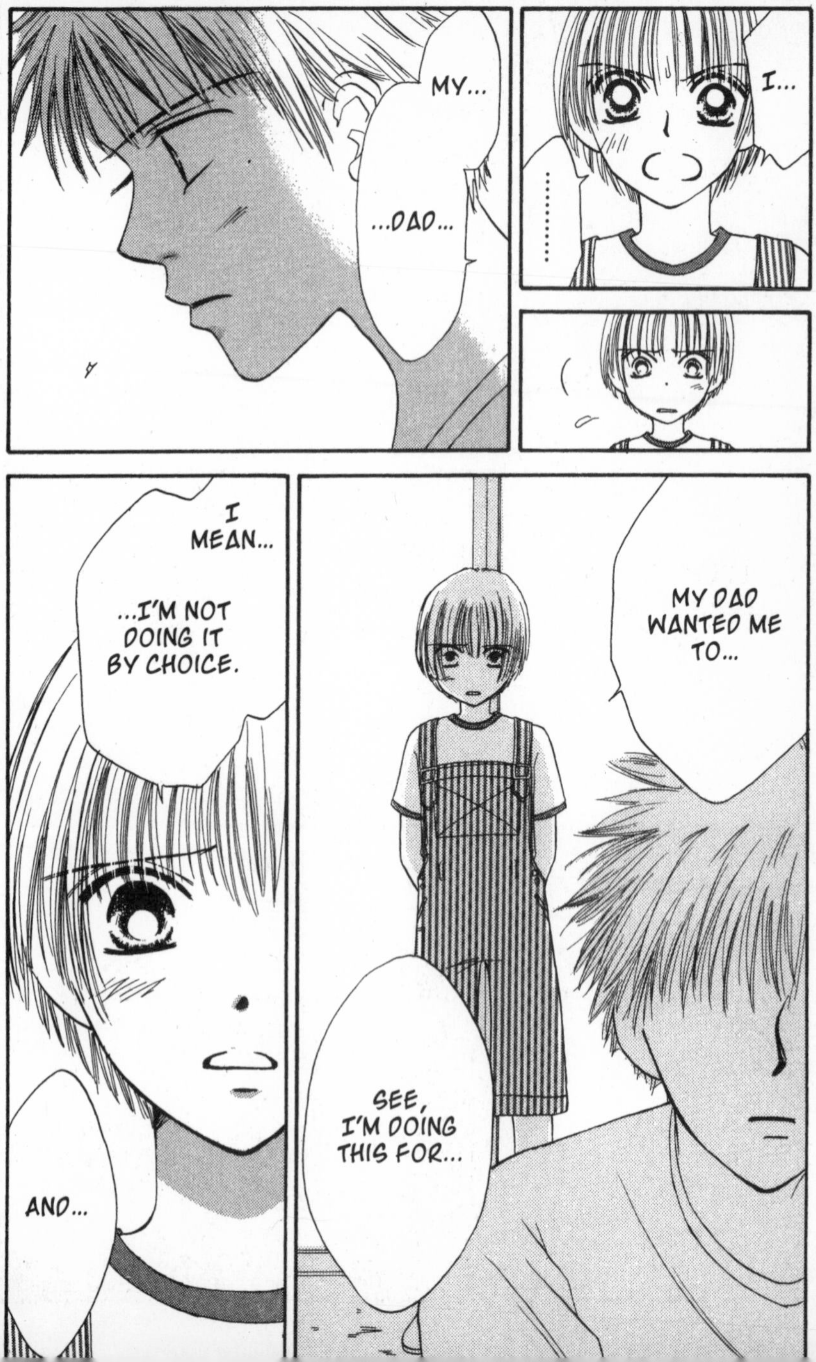
I...
......
MY...
...DAD...
MY DAD WANTED ME TO...
SEE, I'M DOING THIS FOR...
I MEAN...
...I'M NOT DOING IT BY CHOICE.
AND...

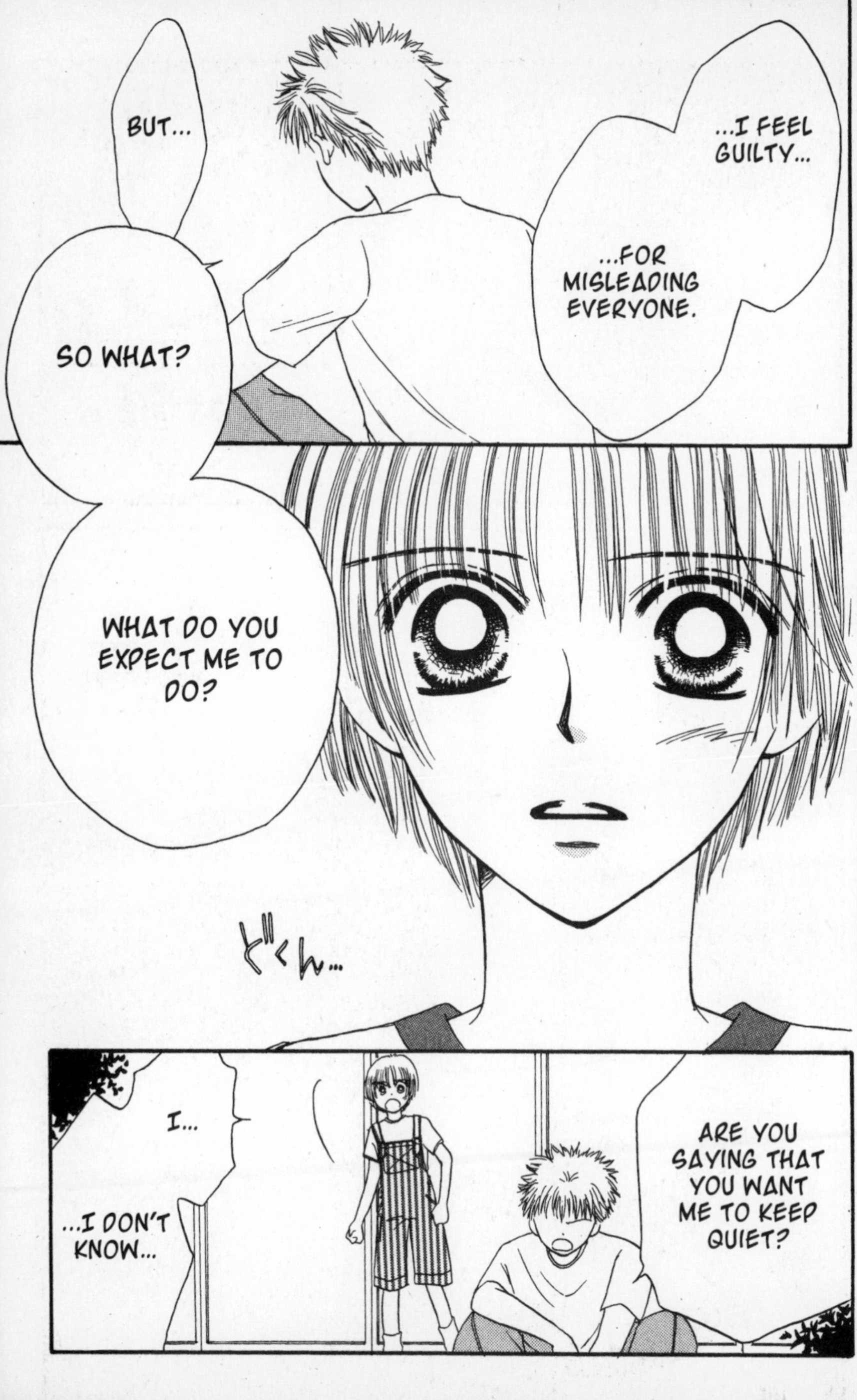
...I FEEL GUILTY...
...FOR MISLEADING EVERYONE.
BUT...
SO WHAT?
WHAT DO YOU EXPECT ME TO DO?
どくん...
ARE YOU SAYING THAT YOU WANT ME TO KEEP QUIET?
I...
...I DON'T KNOW...

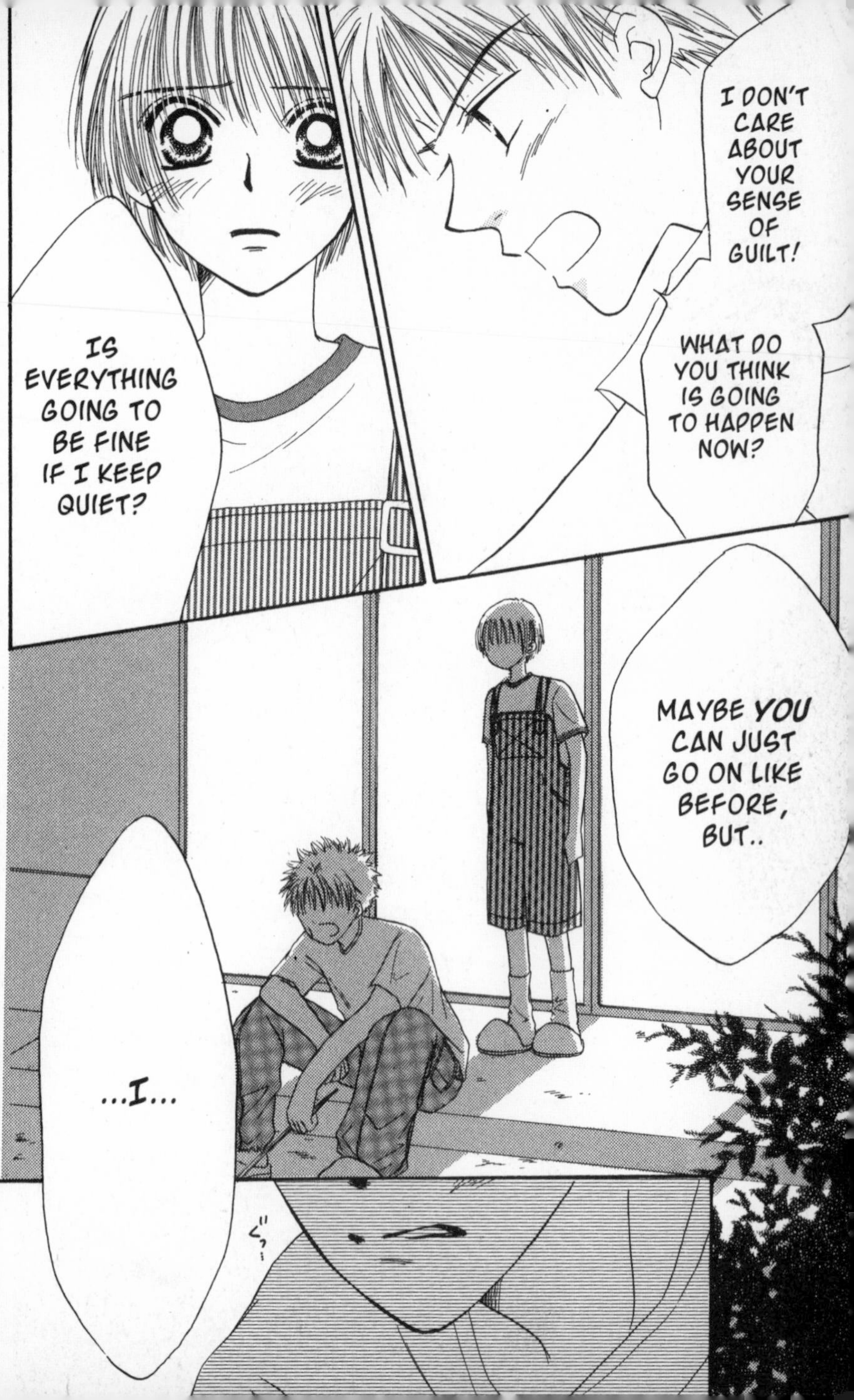
I DON'T CARE ABOUT YOUR SENSE OF GUILT!
WHAT DO YOU THINK IS GOING TO HAPPEN NOW?
IS EVERYTHING GOING TO BE FINE IF I KEEP QUIET?
MAYBE *YOU* CAN JUST GO ON LIKE BEFORE, BUT..
...I...
ぐっ

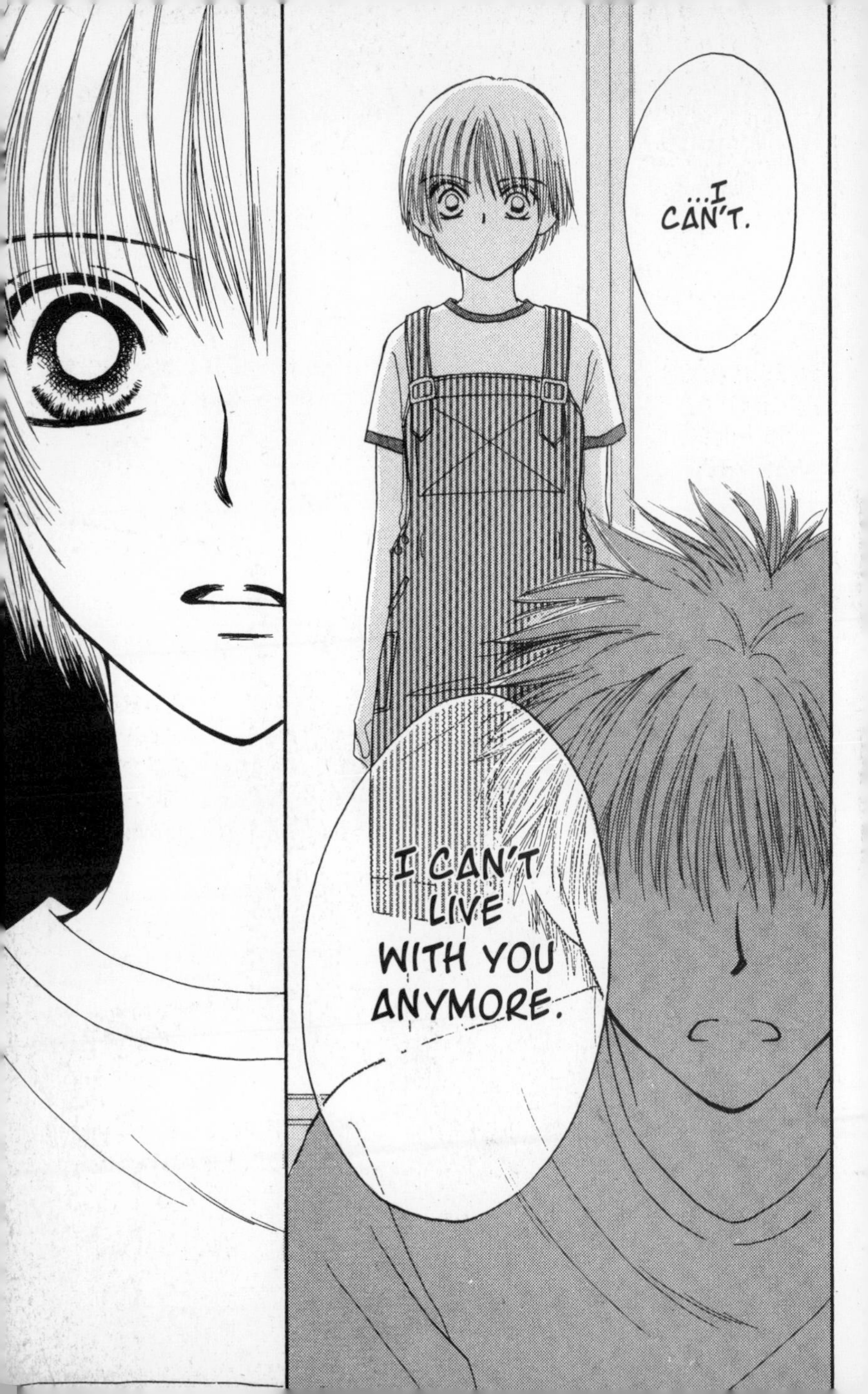
...I CAN'T.
I CAN'T LIVE WITH YOU ANYMORE.

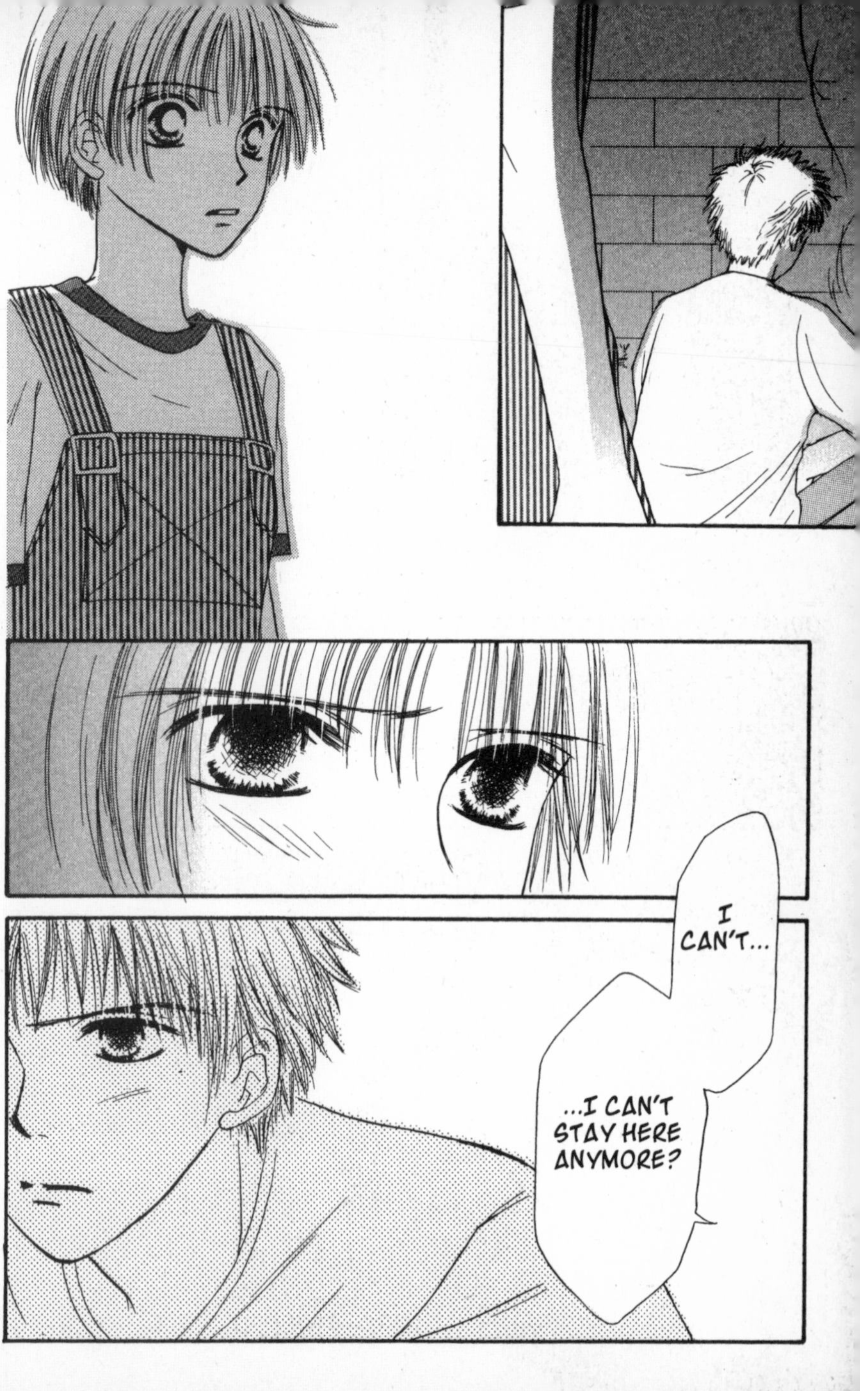
I CAN'T...
...I CAN'T STAY HERE ANYMORE?

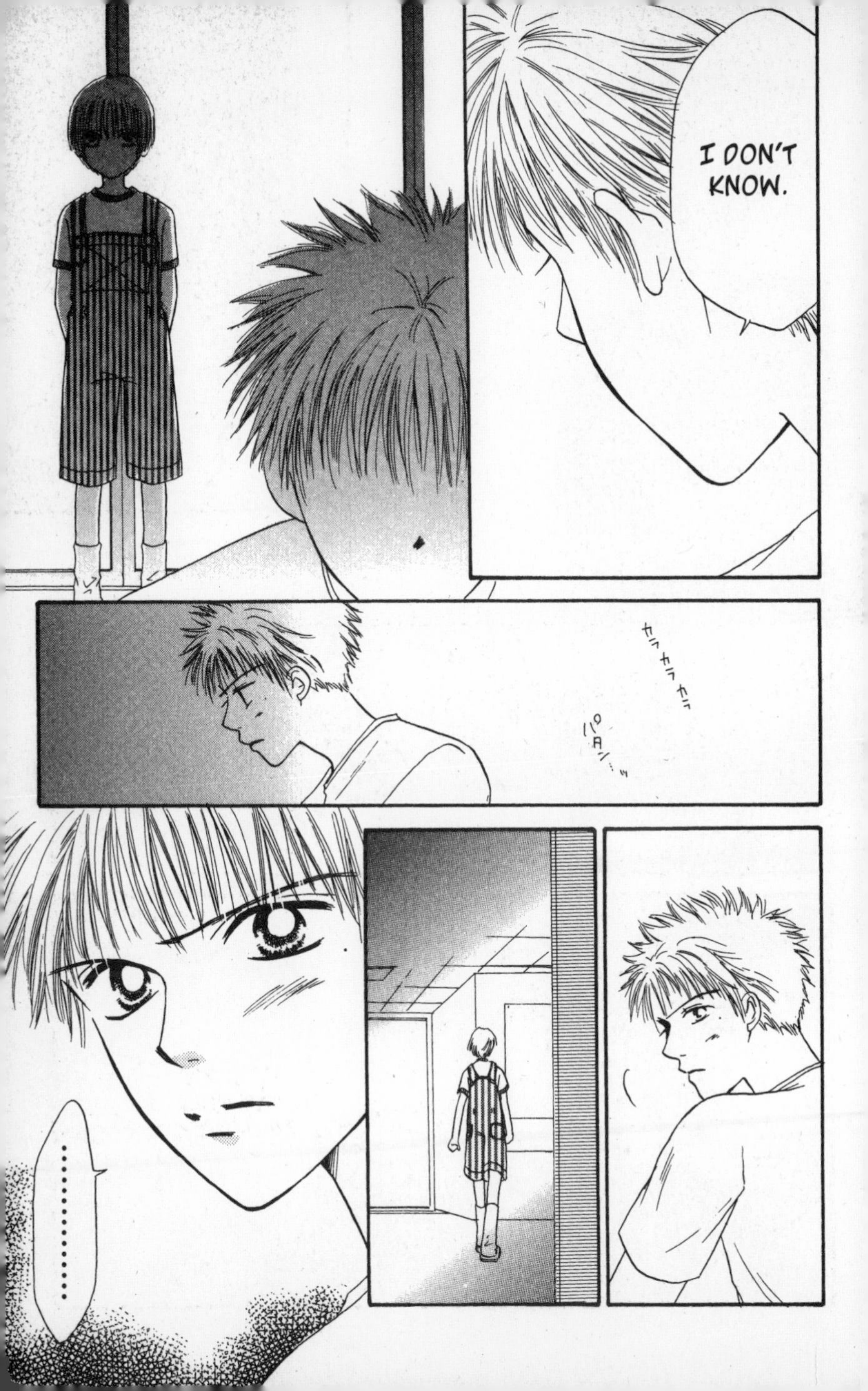
I DON'T KNOW.
カラカラカラ
パタン…
……

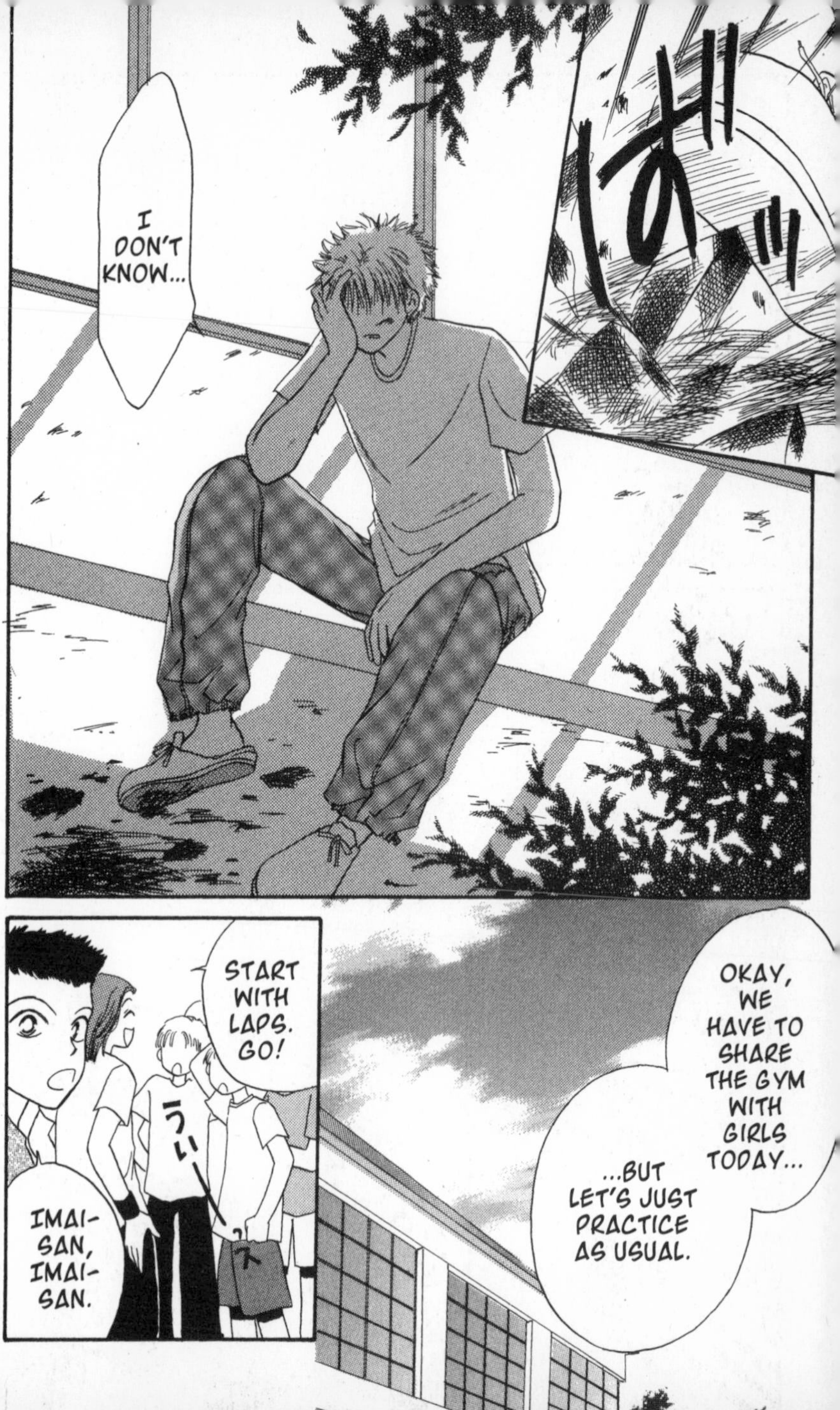
ばヅ
I DON'T KNOW...
OKAY, WE HAVE TO SHARE THE GYM WITH GIRLS TODAY...
...BUT LET'S JUST PRACTICE AS USUAL.
START WITH LAPS. GO!
うぃー
IMAI-SAN, IMAI-SAN.

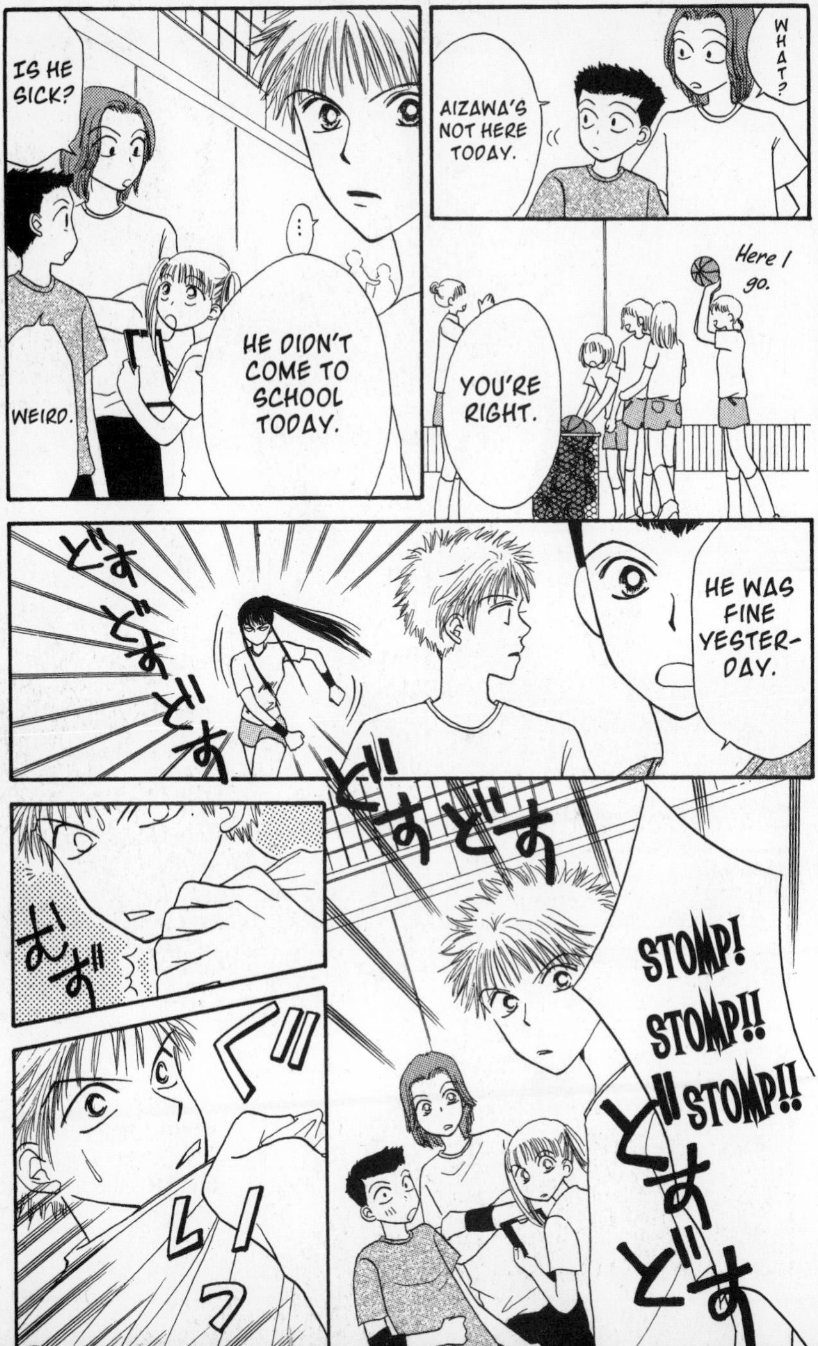

AIZAWA'S NOT HERE TODAY.
WHAT?
Here I go.
YOU'RE RIGHT.
HE DIDN'T COME TO SCHOOL TODAY.
...
IS HE SICK?
WEIRD.
HE WAS FINE YESTER-DAY.
どすどすどすどす
どすどす
STOMP! STOMP!! STOMP!!
どすどす
おず
ぐいーっ

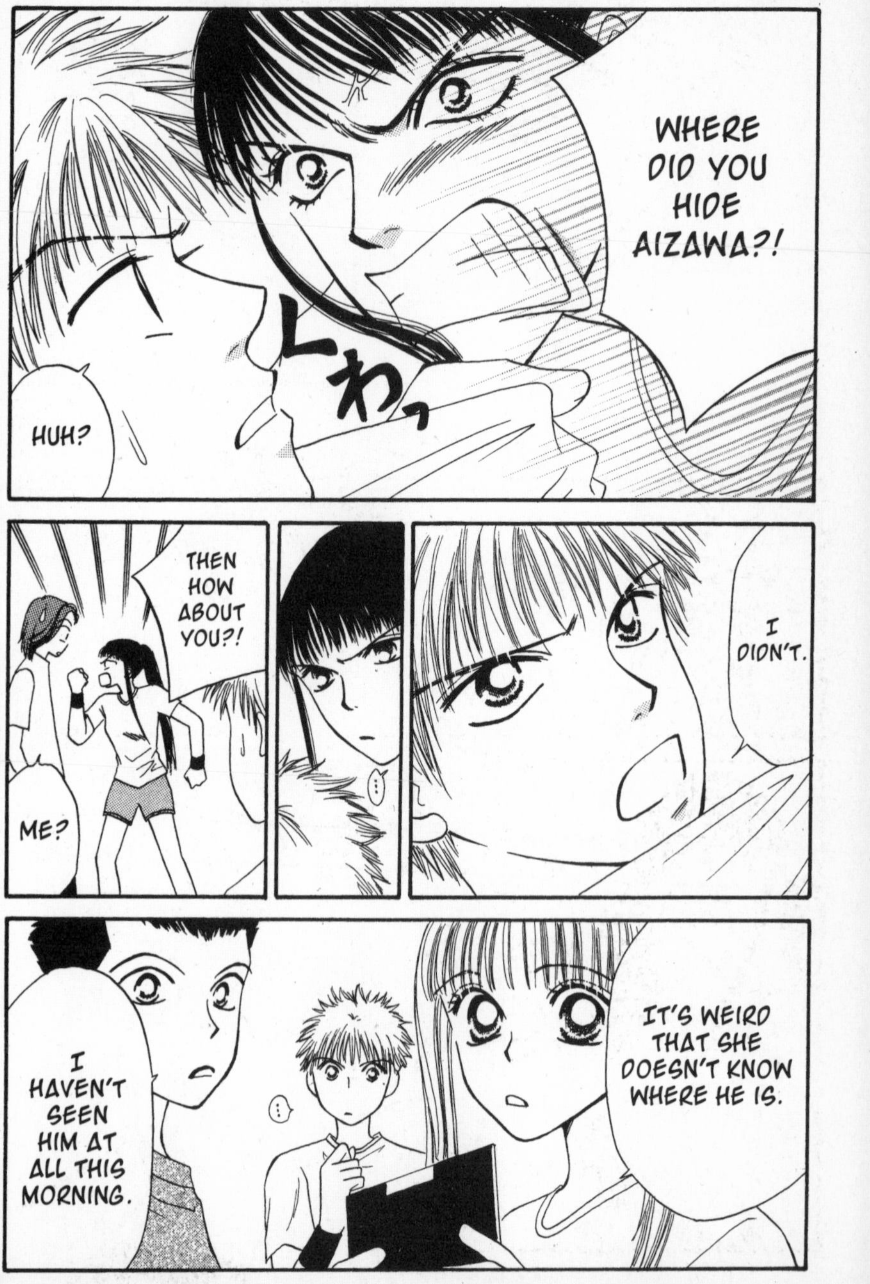

WHERE DID YOU HIDE AIZAWA?!
くわっ
HUH?
I DIDN'T.
…
THEN HOW ABOUT YOU?!
ME?
IT'S WEIRD THAT SHE DOESN'T KNOW WHERE HE IS.
…
I HAVEN'T SEEN HIM AT ALL THIS MORNING.

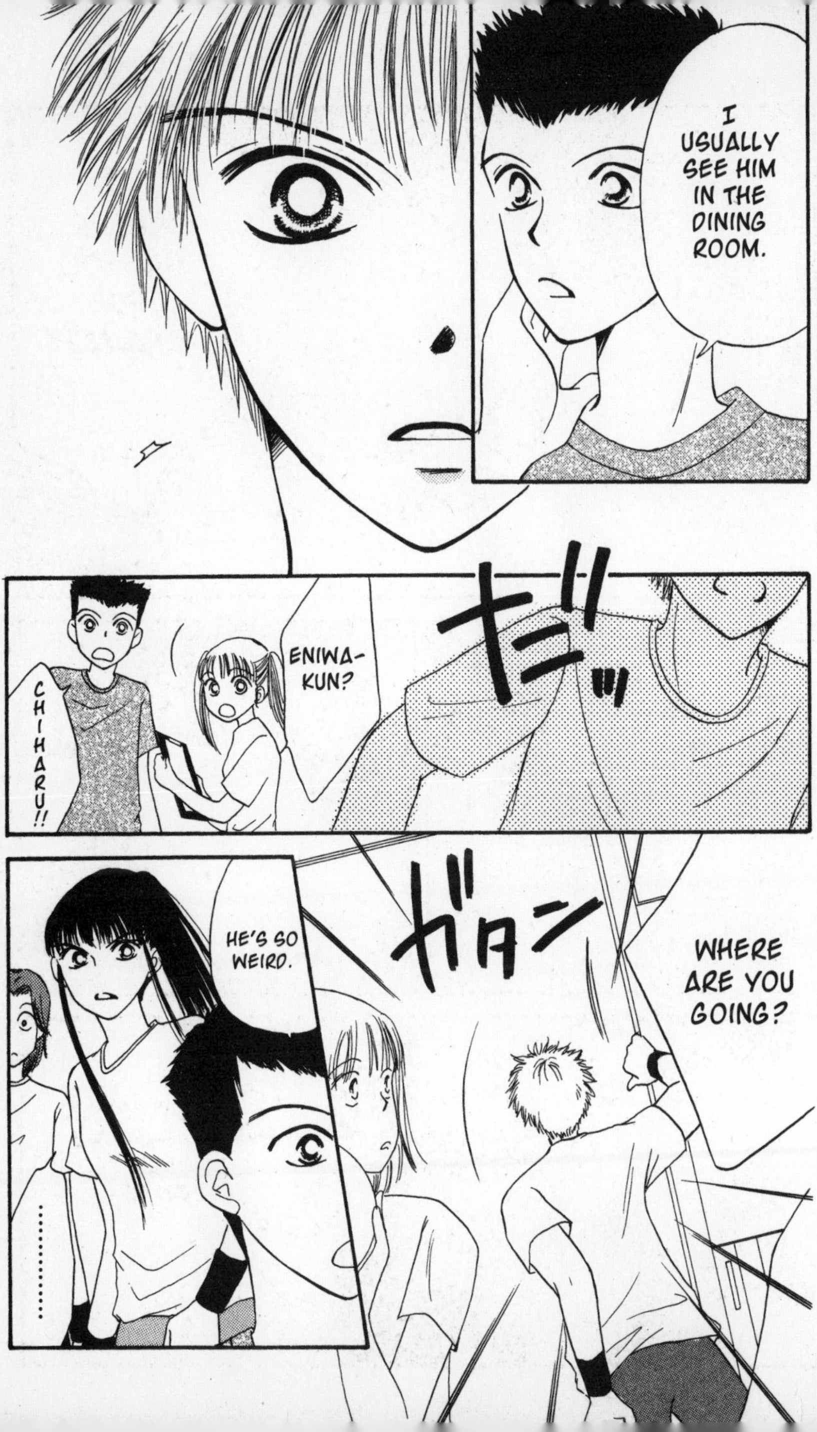
I USUALLY SEE HIM IN THE DINING ROOM.
ギッ
ENIWA-KUN?
CHIHARU!!
WHERE ARE YOU GOING?
ガタン
HE'S SO WEIRD.
……

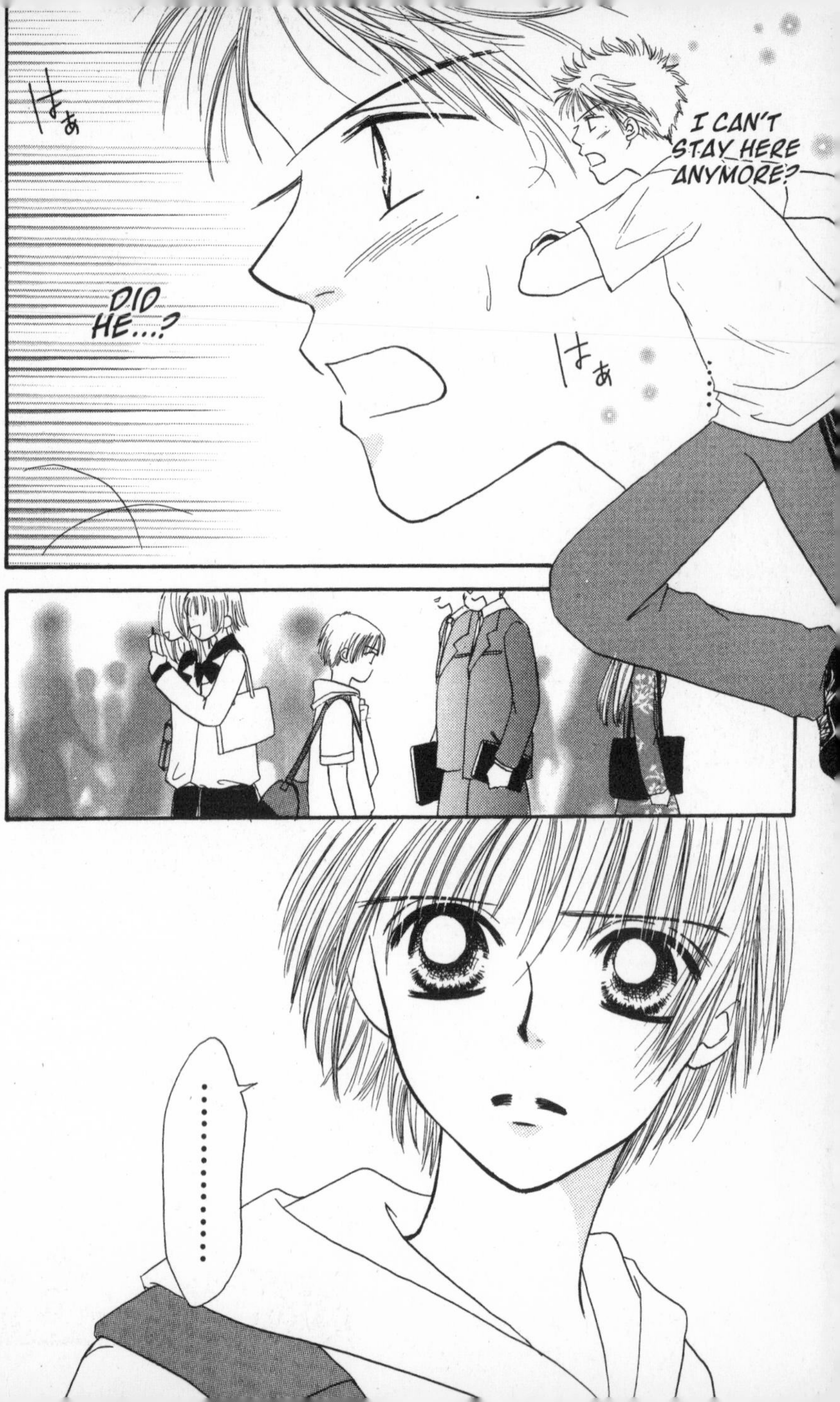
I CAN'T STAY HERE ANYMORE?
はぁ
DID HE...?
はぁ
......

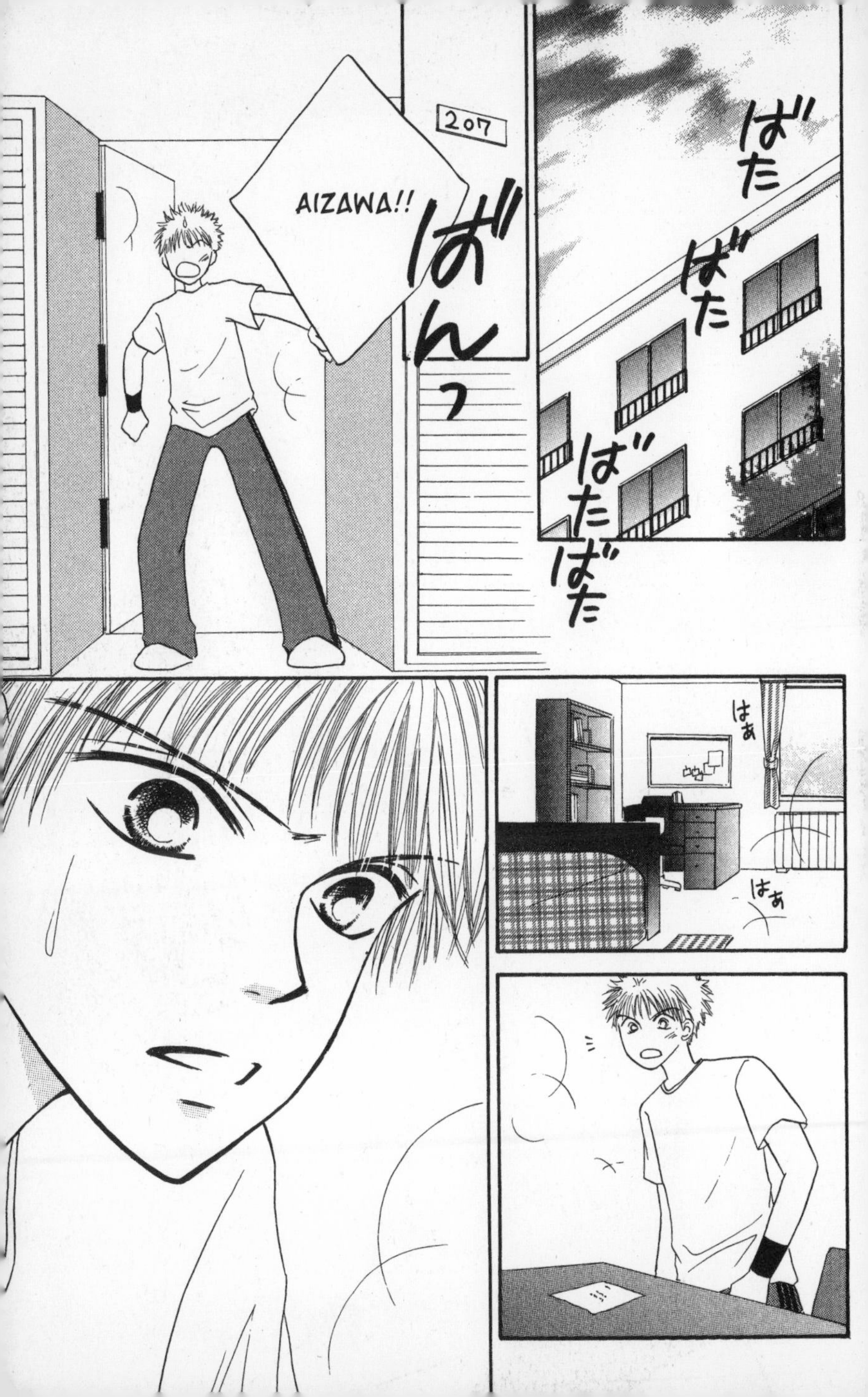

ばたばた
ばたばた
207
AIZAWA!!
ばんっ
はぁ
はぁ

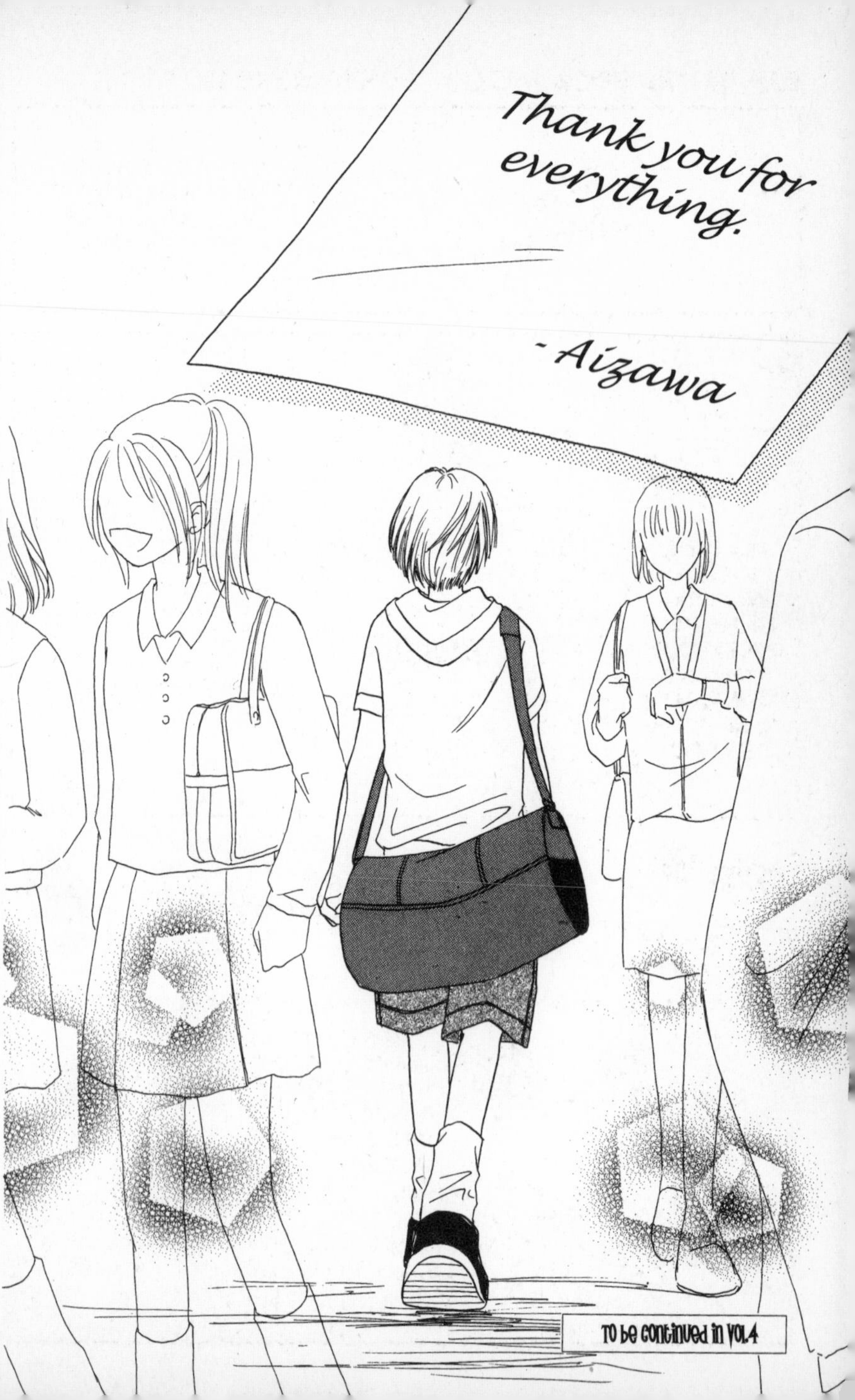
Thank you for everything.
- Aizawa
TO BE CONTINUED IN VOL.4

END OF THE BOOK SPECIAL BONUS MANGA!!

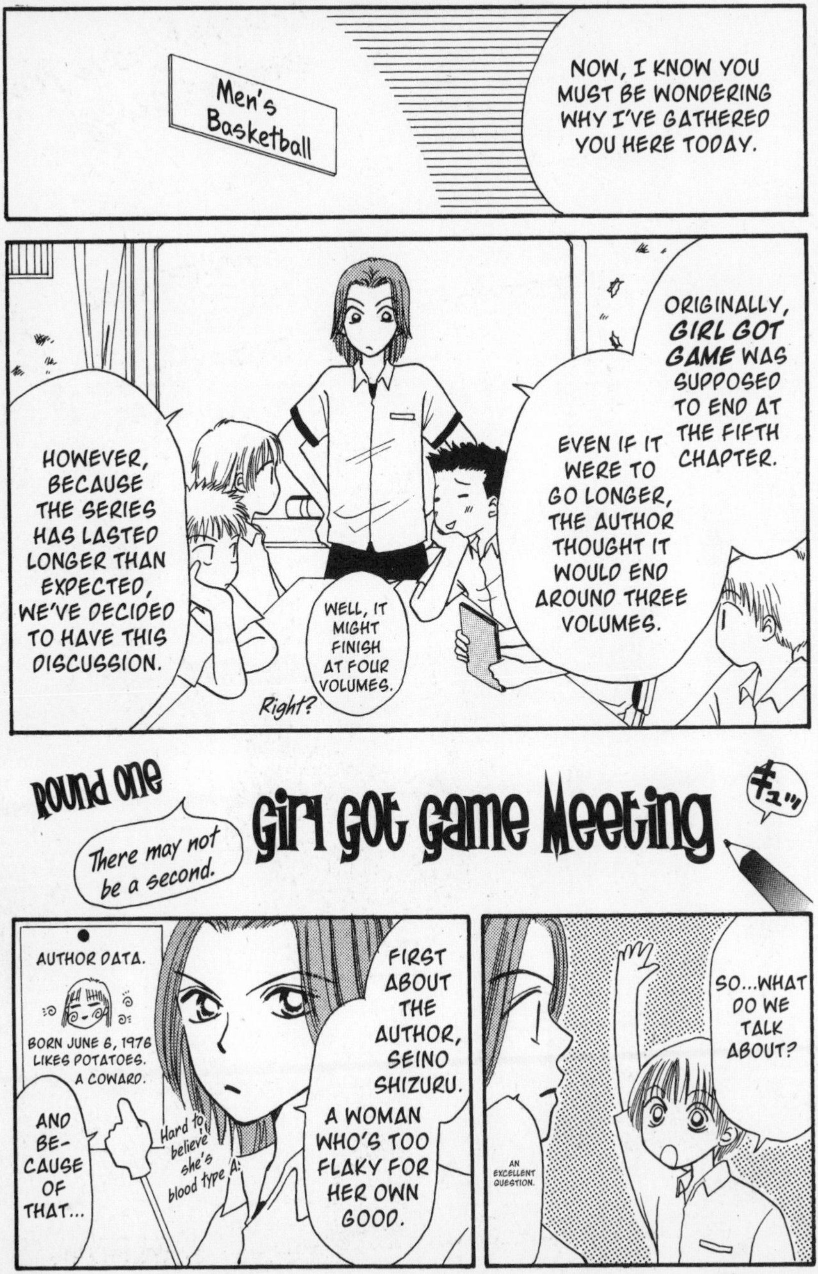
Men's Basketball
NOW, I KNOW YOU MUST BE WONDERING WHY I'VE GATHERED YOU HERE TODAY.
ORIGINALLY, GIRL GOT GAME WAS SUPPOSED TO END AT THE FIFTH CHAPTER.
EVEN IF IT WERE TO GO LONGER, THE AUTHOR THOUGHT IT WOULD END AROUND THREE VOLUMES.
WELL, IT MIGHT FINISH AT FOUR VOLUMES.
Right?
HOWEVER, BECAUSE THE SERIES HAS LASTED LONGER THAN EXPECTED, WE'VE DECIDED TO HAVE THIS DISCUSSION.
Round One
Girl Got Game Meeting
キュッ
There may not be a second.
SO...WHAT DO WE TALK ABOUT?
AN EXCELLENT QUESTION.
FIRST ABOUT THE AUTHOR, SEINO SHIZURU.
A WOMAN WHO'S TOO FLAKY FOR HER OWN GOOD.
AUTHOR DATA.
BORN JUNE 6, 1976
LIKES POTATOES.
A COWARD.
Hard to believe she's blood type A.
AND BE-CAUSE OF THAT...

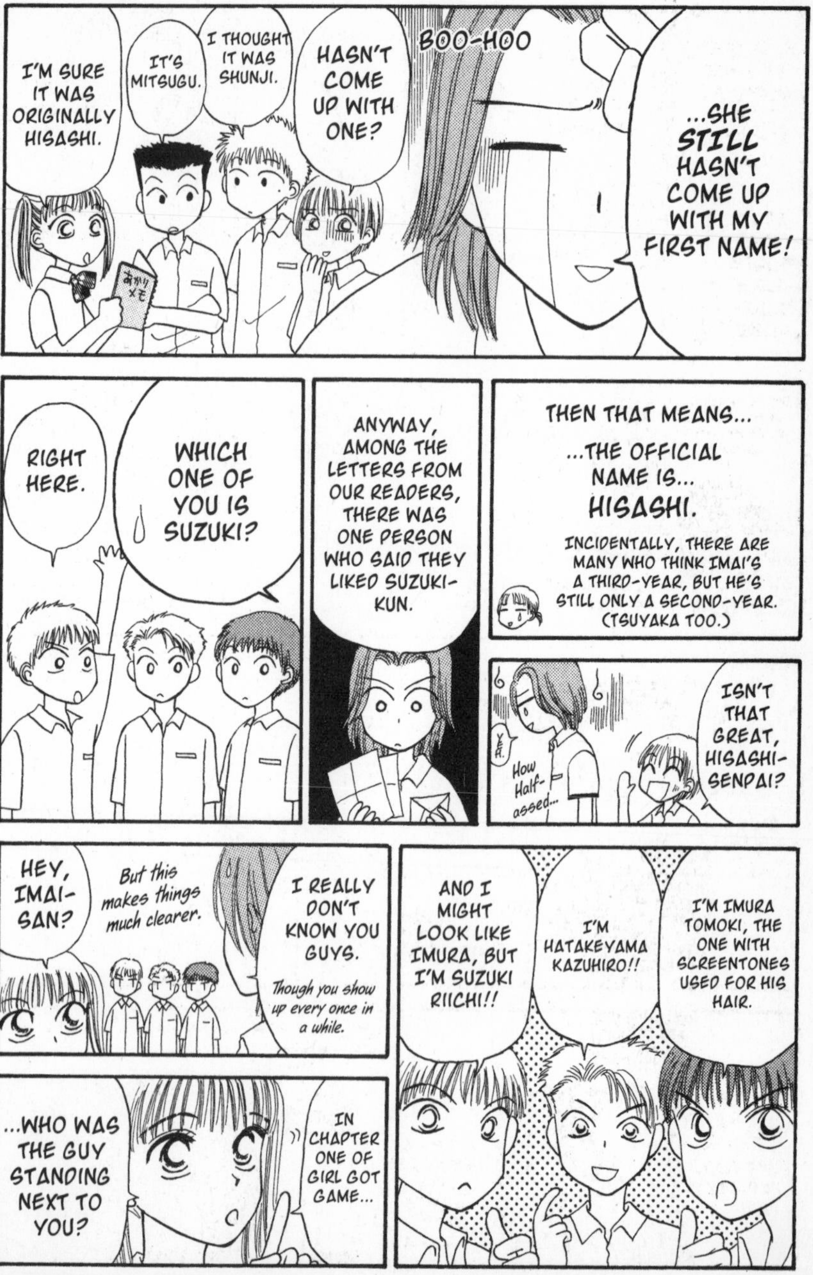
...SHE STILL HASN'T COME UP WITH MY FIRST NAME!
BOO-HOO
HASN'T COME UP WITH ONE?
I THOUGHT IT WAS SHUNJI.
IT'S MITSUGU.
I'M SURE IT WAS ORIGINALLY HISASHI.
THEN THAT MEANS...
...THE OFFICIAL NAME IS... HISASHI.
INCIDENTALLY, THERE ARE MANY WHO THINK IMAI'S A THIRD-YEAR, BUT HE'S STILL ONLY A SECOND-YEAR. (TSUYAKA TOO.)
ISN'T THAT GREAT, HISASHI-SENPAI?
YEAH.
How Half-assed...
ANYWAY, AMONG THE LETTERS FROM OUR READERS, THERE WAS ONE PERSON WHO SAID THEY LIKED SUZUKI-KUN.
WHICH ONE OF YOU IS SUZUKI?
RIGHT HERE.
I'M IMURA TOMOKI, THE ONE WITH SCREENTONES USED FOR HIS HAIR.
I'M HATAKEYAMA KAZUHIRO!!
AND I MIGHT LOOK LIKE IMURA, BUT I'M SUZUKI RIICHI!!
I REALLY DON'T KNOW YOU GUYS.
Though you show up every once in a while.
But this makes things much clearer.
HEY, IMAI-SAN?
IN CHAPTER ONE OF GIRL GOT GAME...
...WHO WAS THE GUY STANDING NEXT TO YOU?

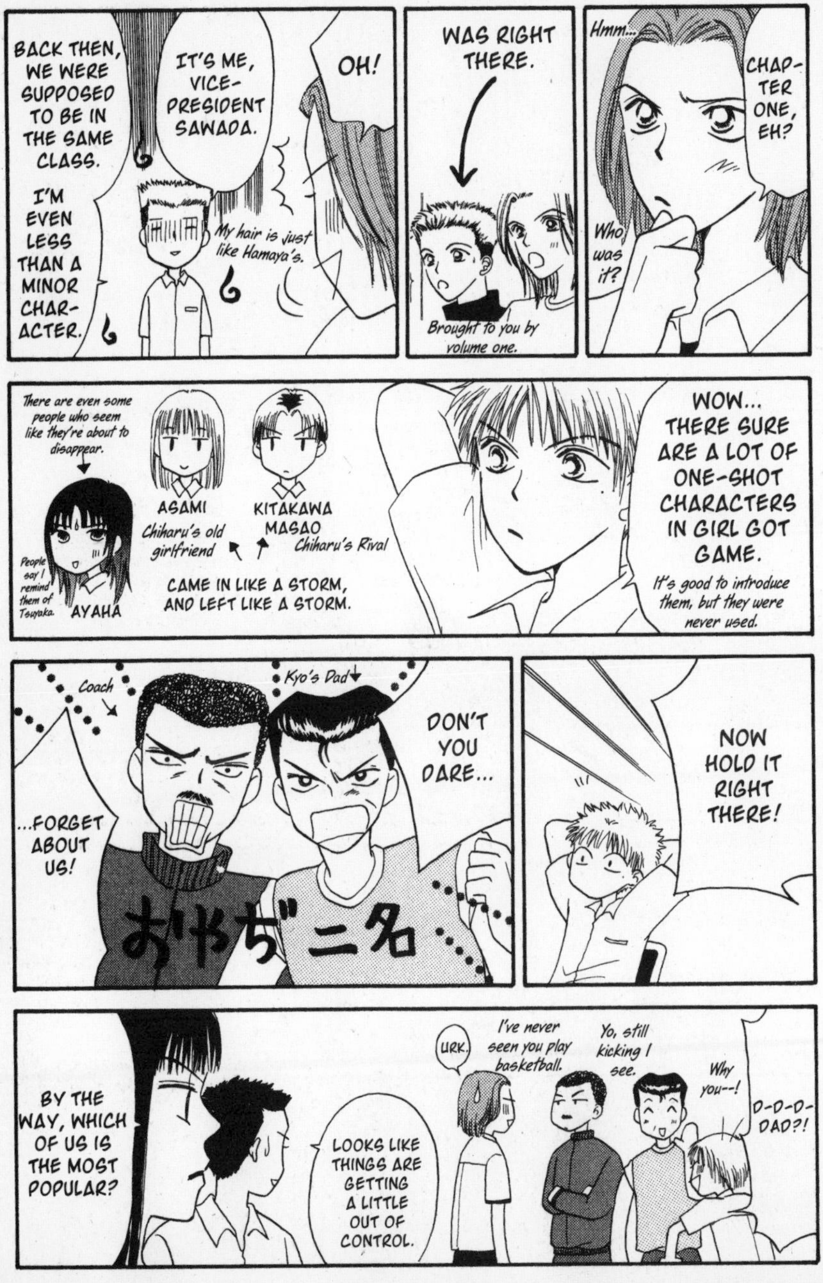
Hmm...
CHAPTER ONE, EH?
Who was it?
WAS RIGHT THERE.
Brought to you by volume one.
OH!
My hair is just like Hamaya's.
IT'S ME, VICE-PRESIDENT SAWADA.
BACK THEN, WE WERE SUPPOSED TO BE IN THE SAME CLASS.
I'M EVEN LESS THAN A MINOR CHARACTER.
WOW... THERE SURE ARE A LOT OF ONE-SHOT CHARACTERS IN GIRL GOT GAME.
It's good to introduce them, but they were never used.
KITAKAWA MASAO
Chiharu's Rival
ASAMI
Chiharu's old girlfriend
CAME IN LIKE A STORM, AND LEFT LIKE A STORM.
There are even some people who seem like they're about to disappear.
AYAHA
People say I remind them of Tsuyaka.
NOW HOLD IT RIGHT THERE!
DON'T YOU DARE...
Kyo's Dad
Coach
...FORGET ABOUT US!
おやぢ二名
D-D-D-DAD?!
Why you--!
Yo, still kicking I see.
I've never seen you play basketball.
URK.
LOOKS LIKE THINGS ARE GETTING A LITTLE OUT OF CONTROL.
BY THE WAY, WHICH OF US IS THE MOST POPULAR?

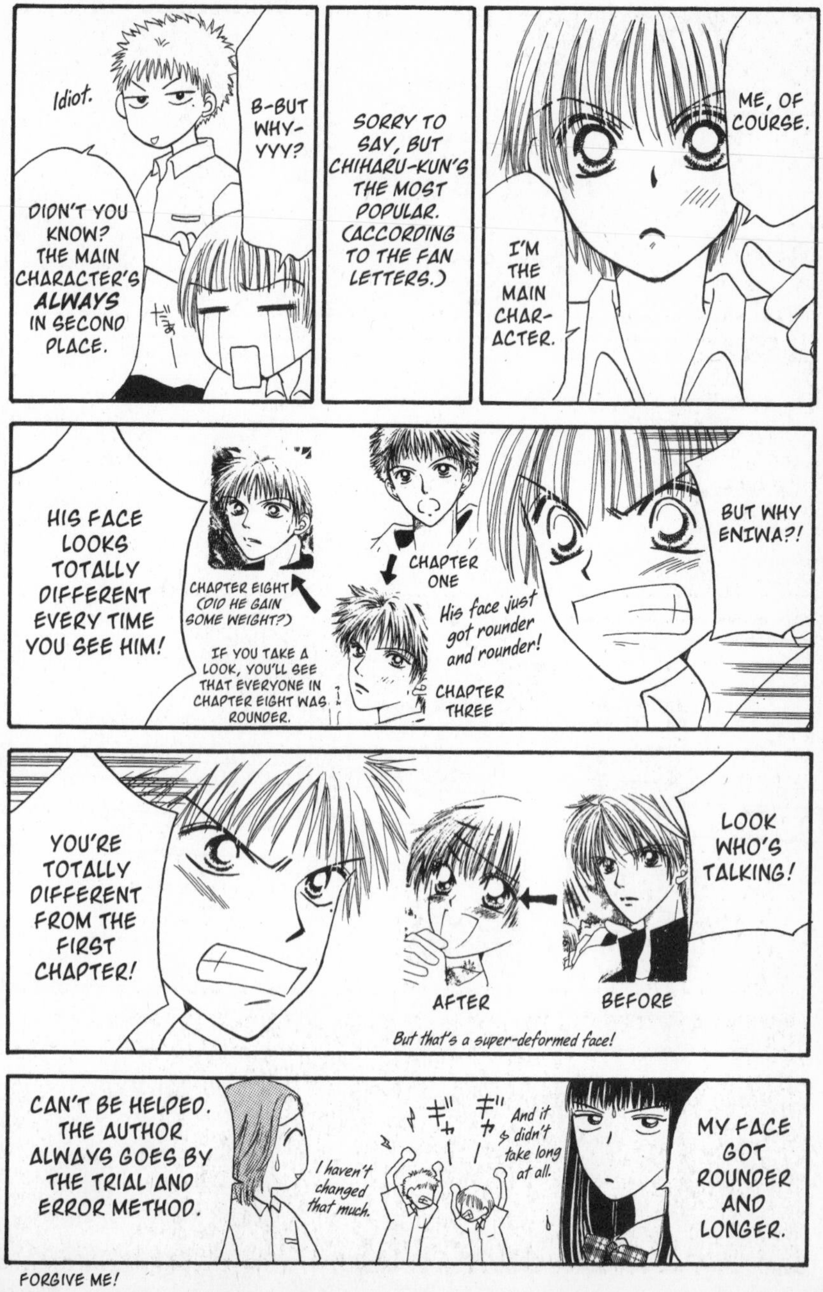
ME, OF COURSE.
I'M THE MAIN CHAR-ACTER.
SORRY TO SAY, BUT CHIHARU-KUN'S THE MOST POPULAR. (ACCORDING TO THE FAN LETTERS.)
B-BUT WHY-YYY?
Idiot.
DIDN'T YOU KNOW? THE MAIN CHARACTER'S **ALWAYS** IN SECOND PLACE.
BUT WHY ENIWA?!
CHAPTER ONE
His face just got rounder and rounder!
CHAPTER THREE
CHAPTER EIGHT (DID HE GAIN SOME WEIGHT?)
IF YOU TAKE A LOOK, YOU'LL SEE THAT EVERYONE IN CHAPTER EIGHT WAS ROUNDER.
HIS FACE LOOKS TOTALLY DIFFERENT EVERY TIME YOU SEE HIM!
LOOK WHO'S TALKING!
BEFORE
AFTER
YOU'RE TOTALLY DIFFERENT FROM THE FIRST CHAPTER!
But that's a super-deformed face!
MY FACE GOT ROUNDER AND LONGER.
And it didn't take long at all.
ギャー
ギャー
I haven't changed that much.
CAN'T BE HELPED. THE AUTHOR ALWAYS GOES BY THE TRIAL AND ERROR METHOD.

FORGIVE ME!

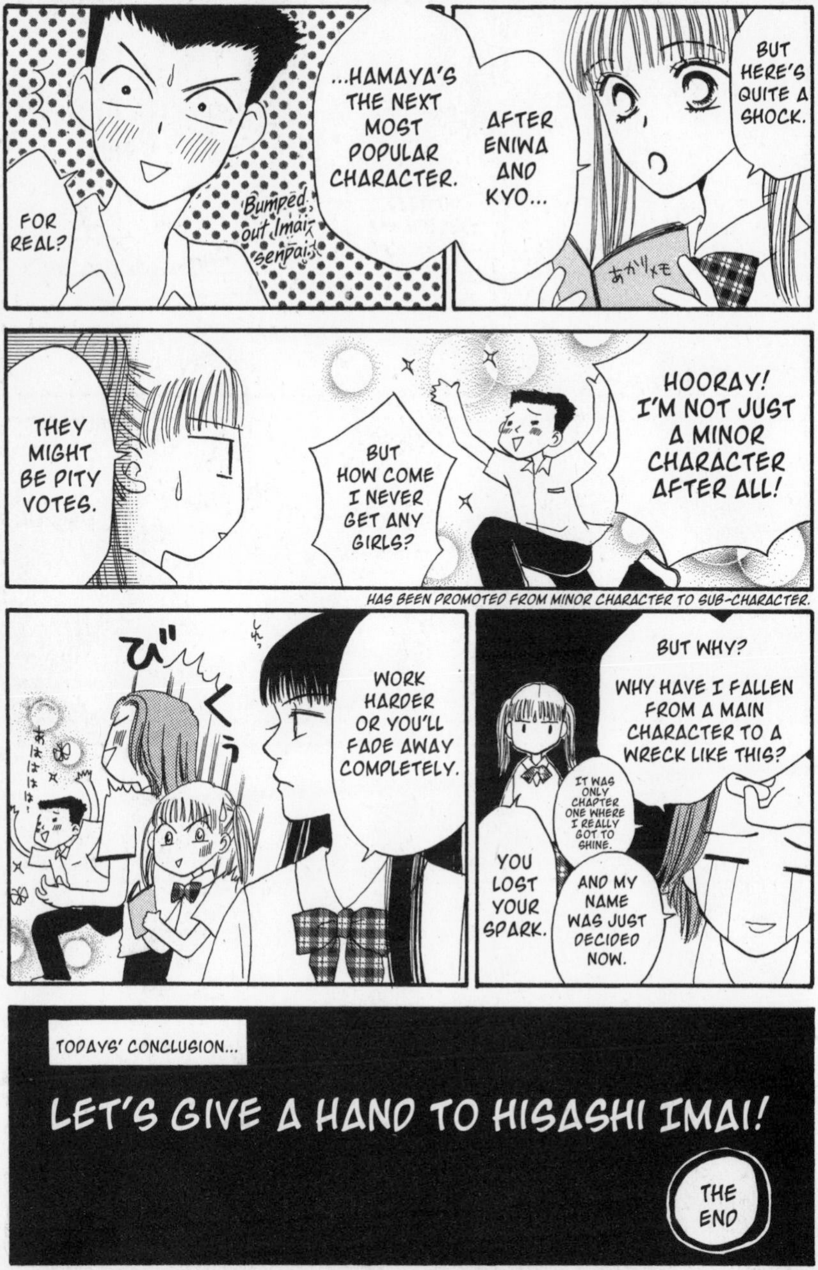
BUT HERE'S QUITE A SHOCK.
AFTER ENIWA AND KYO...
...HAMAYA'S THE NEXT MOST POPULAR CHARACTER.
あかりメモ
Bumped out Imai-senpai
FOR REAL?
HOORAY! I'M NOT JUST A MINOR CHARACTER AFTER ALL!
BUT HOW COME I NEVER GET ANY GIRLS?
THEY MIGHT BE PITY VOTES.
HAS BEEN PROMOTED FROM MINOR CHARACTER TO SUB-CHARACTER.
BUT WHY?
WHY HAVE I FALLEN FROM A MAIN CHARACTER TO A WRECK LIKE THIS?
IT WAS ONLY CHAPTER ONE WHERE I REALLY GOT TO SHINE.
AND MY NAME WAS JUST DECIDED NOW.
YOU LOST YOUR SPARK.
しれっ
WORK HARDER OR YOU'LL FADE AWAY COMPLETELY.
びくぅ
あははは!
TODAYS' CONCLUSION...
LET'S GIVE A HAND TO HISASHI IMAI!
THE END

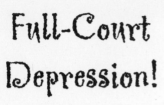

Full-Court Depression!

Kyo's secret is out and so is she...kicked out, that is. Now that Chiharu knows that Kyo's a girl, Kyo has to find somewhere else to live. Unfortunately, the only people she knows in town are the boys in the dorm! Can Kyo face her father-- the man behind her masquerade in the first place--or must she find her own way in the big, bad world?

All in the next...

And now, some comments
from Shizuru Seino,
creator of

★Girl Got Game★

THIS SERIES SURE IS A HASSLE. I ALWAYS
START RUSHING JUST BEFORE THE DEADLINE.
I JUST WANT TO RUN AWAY FROM MY DUTIES.
BUT THIS IS THE ROAD I CHOSE TO TAKE, SO
I'M JUST GOING TO KEEP WALKING IT WITH AS
LITTLE REGRET AS I CAN. I KNOW THERE ARE
PEOPLE WAITING FOR ME. I KNOW THERE ARE
THOSE WHO HAVE SUPPORTED ME. SO LET'S
ALL DO OUR BEST, AND I'LL DO MY BEST.

MY FATHER ALWAYS GAVE ME A CHANCE TO DRAW MANGA WHEN I WAS GROWING UP. HE SUPPORTED ME WHEN I FIRST DEBUTED AS A HIGH SCHOOL STUDENT, AND EVEN WHEN I JUST WANTED TO DRAW INSTEAD OF LOOK FOR A JOB. HE WOULD LAUGH AND SAY, "I WANTED TO BE A MANGAKA TOO, WHEN I WAS YOUR AGE." SIX YEARS AFTER MY DEBUT, MY FATHER DIED, AND I WOULD LIKE TO GIVE A HEARTFELT THANK YOU FOR EVERYTHING HE'S DONE FOR ME.

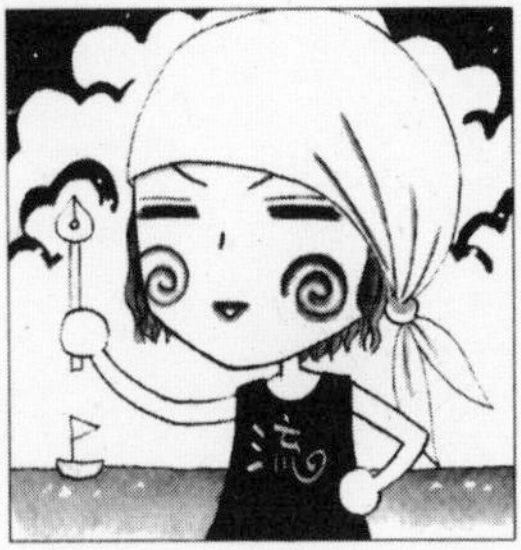

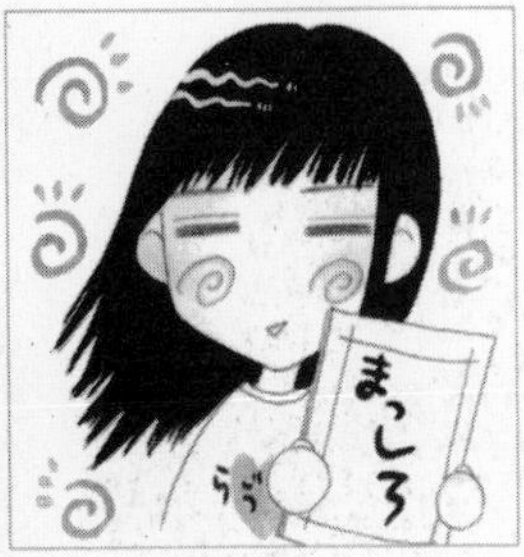
ましろ

I HARDLY EVER PLAY BASKETBALL, EVEN THOUGH I SEEM LIKE A FAN. I MEAN, I'VE ONLY DRAWN ONE COMPETITION SCENE. EVERY TIME I DRAW A BASKETBALL SCENE, I BEAT MYSELF UP OVER IT, THINKING, "HMM, THERE'S SOMETHING WRONG HERE." I STILL HAVE A LOT OF STUDYING TO DO, BUT I LOVE YOU GUYS FOR SAYING IT WAS A FUN READ, AND FORGIVING ME FOR MY MISTAKES!!

OTHER TITLES BY SHIZURU SEINO:

- *SUKI SUKI DAISUKI!* (I LOVE YOU, LOVE YOU, LOVE YOU!)
- *SUKI SUKI DAARIN* (LOVE LOVE DARLING)
- *USOTSUKINA KANOJO* (FALSE GIRLFRIEND)
- *POWER!!* (GIRL GOT GAME)

ALSO AVAILABLE FROM 🦎 TOKYOPOP®

**For more
information visit
www.TOKYOPOP.com**

03.03.04T

ALSO AVAILABLE FROM TOKYOPOP

MANGA

.HACK//LEGEND OF THE TWILIGHT
@LARGE
ABENOBASHI: MAGICAL SHOPPING ARCADE
A.I. LOVE YOU
AI YORI AOSHI
ANGELIC LAYER
ARM OF KANNON
BABY BIRTH
BATTLE ROYALE
BATTLE VIXENS
BRAIN POWERED
BRIGADOON
B'TX
CANDIDATE FOR GODDESS, THE
CARDCAPTOR SAKURA
CARDCAPTOR SAKURA - MASTER OF THE CLOW

CHOBITS
CHRONICLES OF THE CURSED SWORD
CLAMP SCHOOL DETECTIVES
CLOVER
COMIC PARTY
CONFIDENTIAL CONFESSIONS
CORRECTOR YUI
COWBOY BEBOP
COWBOY BEBOP: SHOOTING STAR
CRAZY LOVE STORY
CRESCENT MOON
CULDCEPT
CYBORG 009
D•N•ANGEL
DEMON DIARY
DEMON ORORON, THE
DEUS VITAE
DIGIMON
DIGIMON TAMERS
DIGIMON ZERO TWO
DOLL
DRAGON HUNTER
DRAGON KNIGHTS
DRAGON VOICE
DREAM SAGA
DUKLYON: CLAMP SCHOOL DEFENDERS
EERIE QUEERIE!
END, THE
ERICA SAKURAZAWA: COLLECTED WORKS
ET CETERA
ETERNITY
EVIL'S RETURN
FAERIES' LANDING
FAKE
FLCL
FORBIDDEN DANCE
FRUITS BASKET
G GUNDAM

GATEKEEPERS
GETBACKERS
GIRL GOT GAME
GRAVITATION
GTO
GUNDAM BLUE DESTINY
GUNDAM SEED ASTRAY
GUNDAM WING
GUNDAM WING: BATTLEFIELD OF PACIFISTS
GUNDAM WING: ENDLESS WALTZ
GUNDAM WING: THE LAST OUTPOST (G-UNIT)
GUYS' GUIDE TO GIRLS
HANDS OFF!
HAPPY MANIA
HARLEM BEAT
I.N.V.U.
IMMORTAL RAIN
INITIAL D
INSTANT TEEN: JUST ADD NUTS
ISLAND
JING: KING OF BANDITS
JING: KING OF BANDITS - TWILIGHT TALES
JULINE
KARE KANO
KILL ME, KISS ME
KINDAICHI CASE FILES, THE
KING OF HELL
KODOCHA: SANA'S STAGE
LAMENT OF THE LAMB
LEGAL DRUG
LEGEND OF CHUN HYANG, THE
LES BIJOUX
LOVE HINA
LUPIN III
LUPIN III: WORLD'S MOST WANTED
MAGIC KNIGHT RAYEARTH I
MAGIC KNIGHT RAYEARTH II
MAHOROMATIC: AUTOMATIC MAIDEN
MAN OF MANY FACES
MARMALADE BOY
MARS
MARS: HORSE WITH NO NAME
METROID
MINK
MIRACLE GIRLS
MIYUKI-CHAN IN WONDERLAND
MODEL
ONE
ONE I LOVE, THE
PARADISE KISS
PARASYTE
PASSION FRUIT
PEACH GIRL
PEACH GIRL: CHANGE OF HEART
PET SHOP OF HORRORS
PITA-TEN

03.03.04T

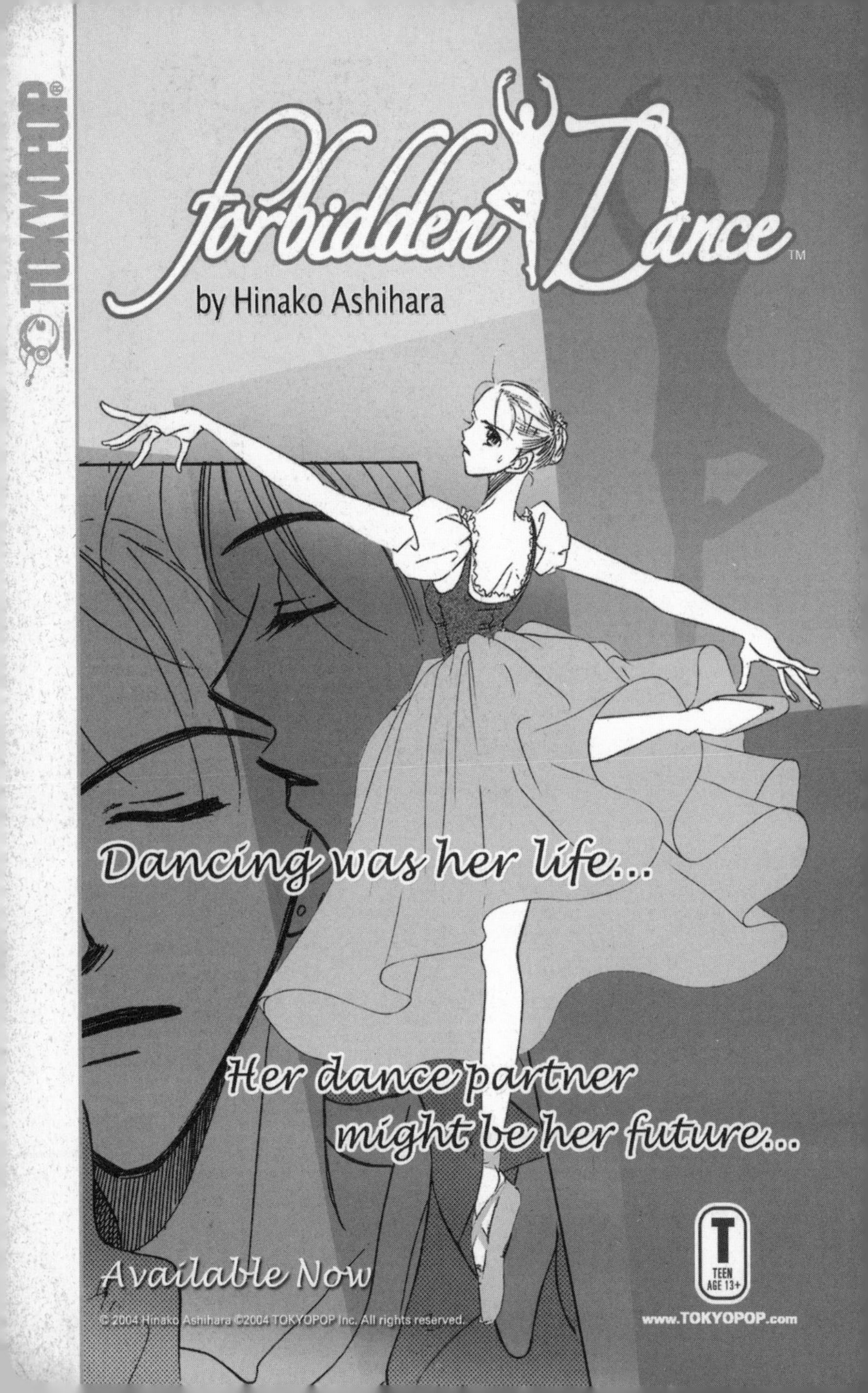
TOKYOPOP®
Forbidden Dance™
by Hinako Ashihara
Dancing was her life...
Her dance partner might be her future...
Available Now
T TEEN AGE 13+
© 2004 Hinako Ashihara ©2004 TOKYOPOP Inc. All rights reserved.
www.TOKYOPOP.com

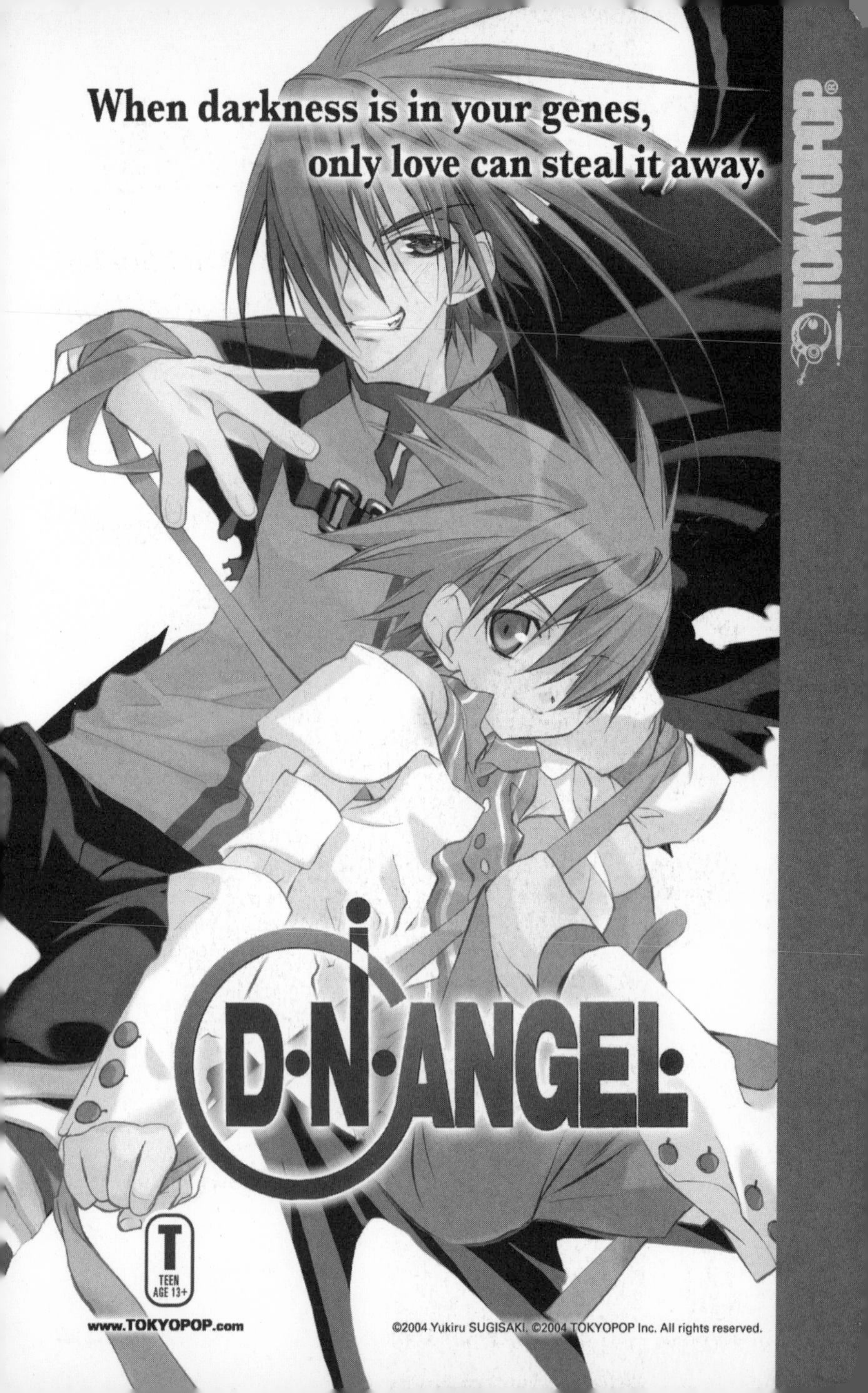
When darkness is in your genes,
only love can steal it away.
TOKYOPOP
D•N•ANGEL
T
TEEN
AGE 13+
www.TOKYOPOP.com
©2004 Yukiru SUGISAKI. ©2004 TOKYOPOP Inc. All rights reserved.

Fruits Basket™

Life in the Sohma household can be a real zoo!

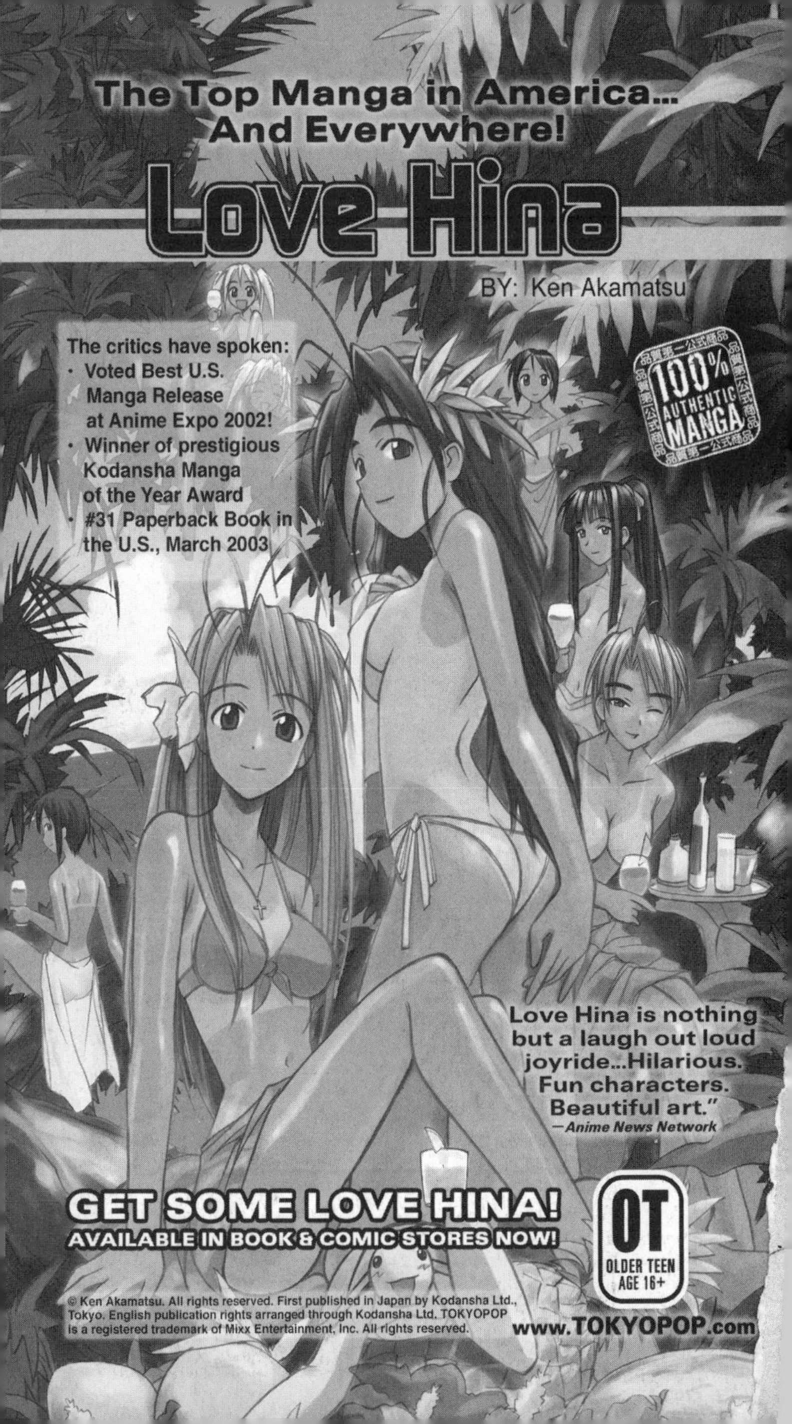

The Top Manga in America...
And Everywhere!
Love Hina
BY: Ken Akamatsu
The critics have spoken:
· Voted Best U.S. Manga Release at Anime Expo 2002!
· Winner of prestigious Kodansha Manga of the Year Award
· #31 Paperback Book in the U.S., March 2003
100% AUTHENTIC MANGA
Love Hina is nothing but a laugh out loud joyride...Hilarious. Fun characters. Beautiful art."
—Anime News Network
GET SOME LOVE HINA!
AVAILABLE IN BOOK & COMIC STORES NOW!
OT
OLDER TEEN AGE 16+
© Ken Akamatsu. All rights reserved. First published in Japan by Kodansha Ltd., Tokyo. English publication rights arranged through Kodansha Ltd. TOKYOPOP is a registered trademark of Mixx Entertainment, Inc. All rights reserved.
www.TOKYOPOP.com

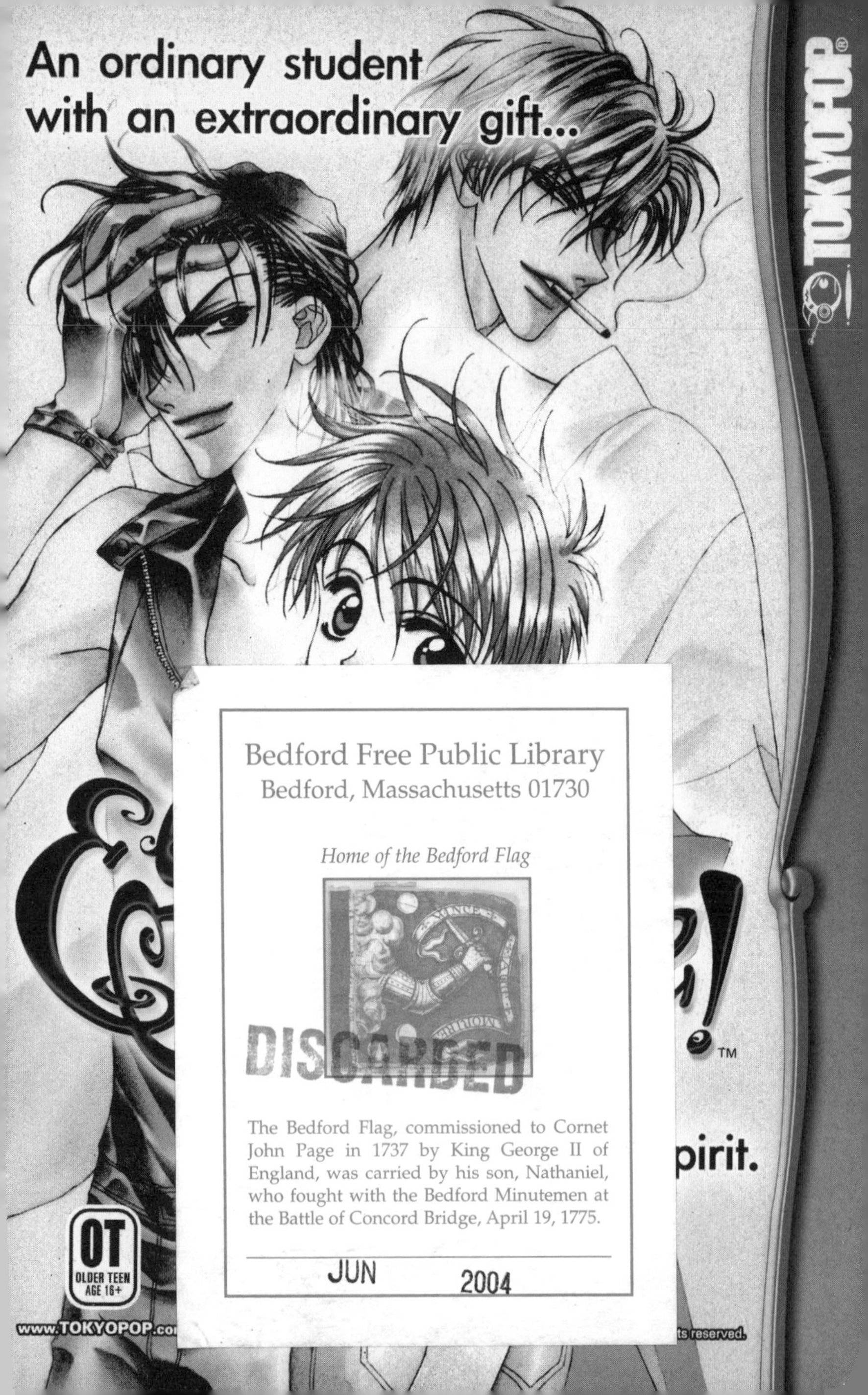

An ordinary student
with an extraordinary gift...
TOKYOPOP
pirit.
TM
OT
OLDER TEEN
AGE 16+
www.TOKYOPOP.co
ts reserved.